# THE
# BALLAD
## AND THE
# SOURCE

Rosamond Lehmann

# THE

# BALLAD

## AND THE

# SOURCE

REYNAL & HITCHCOCK, NEW YORK

To
C. D. I..

# THE
# BALLAD
## AND THE
# SOURCE

# PART ONE

## I

ONE day my mother told me that Mrs. Jardine had asked us to pick primroses on her hill, and then, when we had picked as many as we wanted, to come in and have tea with her.

"Mrs. Jardine?" we said. "Is that the lady the house at the top belongs to?"

"Yes," said my mother. "The Priory." She had the note in her hand: violet paper, a large, clear, square-looking spidery writing.

"The one who wrote to you before from France to say she was an old friend of our Grandma's and we were to pick primroses on the hill every year till she came back?"

"Yes. An old Mrs. Grant Dugdale lived there when I was first married. She was Major Jardine's aunt, I believe. She called, and I returned her call, but I haven't been there since. She became completely crippled with arthritis and she went away years ago to live in Bath. Then she died and Major Jardine inherited the place. But he never came there to live; he let it. I think his tenants only went there at week-ends—rich business people, I believe—I never came across them. Yes. . . . She wrote some years ago. . . . Yes. It was such a kind thought." My mother looked absent and dubious. She fingered the note and screwed her eyes up faintly to re-read it. " 'We are getting too old to wander all our days, and Harry's torn roots in England and his childhood home have ached more and more with the passage of the years. . . .' "

"Is that what she says?" I asked, startled. Immediately, I felt

*1*

attracted towards a lady who expressed herself with such picturesqueness.

"She means he was homesick," said my mother. " *'So we have come back; and are hoping that the climate will permit us to be well enough to enjoy these beauties for at least the major part of the year. Precarious health has prostrated me at intervals for the last twenty years: but who knows?—this may prove the right spot. I have liked to think of the children coming each year with primrose baskets to the hill. They have often appeared to me, like dreams, like images in poetry. . . .'* " My mother stopped, raised her eyebrows. Her expression was complex.

"Go on," I said.

"Hmm—hmm—*'like poetry—spirit-like, unreal, yet in another sense so real—coming, for me, from so far back in the past, linked to what is clearest and most cherished in my memory—promising me something still to come, as it were, out of the past, into the present and the future, in this spring primrose-picking. . . . Little Primaveras.'* . . . Primavera was the Goddess of Spring," said my mother, deprecating all this, but improving the occasion. "There's a very famous picture of her by—er—by a great Italian painter."

"Good gracious!" said Jess. "What on earth does she mean?"

I, personally, felt an extreme willingness to lend myself to the interpretation. My form appeared to me in an indistinct but pleasing diaphanous light, moving over the green hillside, spiritually and gracefully gathering blossoms.

"I believe Mrs. Jardine is a very unusual person," said my mother. "She reads a lot, and expresses herself in this—er—in this way. . . . *'But perhaps this will seem to you a tiresomely fanciful manner of speaking of your flesh and blood human three—or is it four?'* "

"Four," said Sylvia, bitter. "If she means us children."

" *'It is merely to show you how much it would mean to me to see my beloved Laura's grandchildren, how deeply I hope you and Edward will allow me this joy.'* . . . Laura was your grandmother's name," said my mother, "as you know."

We didn't. We had never thought of her as having a name.

2

"Was she a friend of Grandma's, then?"

"Yes. Yes, I believe a great friend a long time ago. Of course she was a good deal younger than Grandma. Still, she must be getting to be an elderly lady now. Your father knew her when he was a boy, but I have never met her. She says: '*The primroses will be at their best next week. May they come Thursday, the 12th—if fine? I know how busy you are and scarcely dare to hope that you will accompany them, and give me the happiness of meeting Edward's wife? If so—so much the greater the excitement for me. If not, I understand that you have a French lady in charge of your children*'—I wonder how she found that out—'*and hope to expect her with them. Please let them come early and pick their fill; and tell them to come in by the blue door in the garden wall at four o'clock.*' "

"Oh, good, good!" said Jess. "I've always wanted to see through that door. The wall's so high you can't see the house— only the chimneys. We may go, mayn't we? Will you take us, Mum?"

"Well, no," said my mother. "I couldn't take you."

"Oh *bother! Must* it be Mamselle? She'll spoil it all. Can't we go alone?"

"I haven't decided yet," said my mother, "whether I can let you go at all."

"Why not?"

"Well . . . I don't know Mrs. Jardine." Her voice was veiled, seeming, to our alarm, to conceal some serious motive for refusal.

"But Daddy does. And she was Grandma's great friend."

My mother mused.

"I don't suppose your father would object. . . ." She took up the letter again and looked at it doubtfully.

"Of course he won't. Why should he?"

We had never yet known him object to a treat for us. He was away on a visit to his constituency.

"It's all such a long time ago . . ." murmured my mother. "Very well. I'll write and accept for you, Jess and Rebecca. Sylvia, it's much too long a walk, dear, for your little legs."

3

"I don't want to go anyway," said Sylvia, "if it means Mamselle. I simply pity the girls."

"Don't talk like that, dear," said my mother cheerfully. "It's so foolish."

# I I

NEXT Thursday was fine. We wore our navy blue serge sailor blouses and skirts and jackets with brass buttons, and set off after lunch accompanied by Mademoiselle. She wore her best off-mustard flannel skirt, cream satin blouse with tucks, net yoke and whaleboned neck, hand-crocheted black bolero scalloped in violet, wide black waist-belt with clasp representing interlaced dragons in metalwork, and white felt tam-o'-shanter at a chic angle. We all wore brown laced boots.

This was our favourite walk at any season, leading as it did to Priory Copse, and the railings over which we turned somersaults. We left the last cottages behind us and went along the road that led up out of the valley until we came to the gate of the small park surrounding Major Jardine's property. A public road led through this, branching off left, to wind up into the copse, and right, round the shoulder of the hill, to fly up in a steep arc to the drive and the front door of the Priory. A footpath ran parallel to this road, close under the side of the hill, whose huge green eminence breasted up over us on our right; round, symmetrical, sudden as a hill in a child's drawing; green and smooth as a goose-girl in a fairy story. If one could only discover the right words, and say them, the side of the hill would open, and one would be able to go through, into the inside.

Soon we came to a kissing-gate in the iron-railed spiked fence. Once the other side of it, we were on the sheep-cropped grass,

4

staring up at what opposed us so formidably yet so enticingly—
the great slope, the primrose clumps splashed all over it, the
track that soared to the church, then on again, swerving to take
a milder angle, to the blue door in the brick wall that crowned
the summit. Up, up, we toiled, picking and filling our baskets.
Our fingers, when we smelt them, gave off that mysterious whis-
pering breath which seems half-animal, half-made of air and dew.

By the time we had reached the top and had decided we must
moderate the size of our bunches this year lest Mrs. Jardine think
us rude and greedy, there was still a quarter of an hour before we
were due to go through the gate. So we went into the churchyard to have a look at the graves. The church itself was tiny,
crooked, Norman, with a pretty, rosy, lichen-crusted roof of tiles.
Beside it grew a yew tree, said to be a thousand years old. Its
trunk was of gigantic girth, belted with a chain to hold it together, twisted and moulded into vast bosses, knots, inlays and
depressions, into sculptured reliefs of frenetic inspiration and
irresponsibility. Silvery, veined with iron black, its substance,
seen from close, gave a mineral impression: it had nothing of
the warmth and life of wood. From farther off, this stoniness
dissolved, became fluid, tender; became a column of water, pale
and dark, pouring down silently out of the core of the sombre
spread of branches, in snaky interlacing whorls and spirals.

In a corner of the churchyard grew a plantation of white violets, enormously plump and prosperous-looking. When I wondered why they should grow so exceptionally fat in that one spot,
Mademoiselle answered in a dry way that no doubt they had a
rich soil to nourish them; and I saw the dead stretched out under
me in the earth, feeding these flowers with a thin milk drawn
from their bones. One of the tombstones was engraved: *Sacred
to the memory of Silence, wife of John Strong of this parish, who
departed this life in the twenty-fifth year of her age.* The date
was of the seventeenth century. The word Silence, in deep, high
letters, in the midst of all the other names of dead women—the
Hannahs, Marys, Ediths, Louisas, Georginas—gave this one grave
a strange significance: as if among domestic griefs and protesta-
tions, something impersonal, cold, symbolic had been stated.

5

Once, when I mentioned the name disbelievingly to my father, he smiled, and said: "My gracious Silence!"—I did not understand why.

I put a small bunch of primroses on this neglected grave: then it was four o'clock, and we went through the blue door into Mrs. Jardine's garden.

As we crossed the lawn, a french window in the front of the long, low, creeper-covered house opened, and a woman's figure appeared. She waved. She gave the impression of arms outstretched, so welcomingly did she surge forward to meet us. She was dressed in a long gown of pale blue with wide sleeves embroidered thickly with blue, rose and violet flowers. She had a white fleecy wrap round her shoulders, and on her head, with its pile of fringed, puffed, curled white hair, a large Panama hat trimmed with a blue liberty scarf artistically knotted, the ends hanging down behind. She was small and rather stocky, with short legs and little feet shod in low-heeled black slippers with tongues and paste buckles.

When she came up to us, she said:

"I must kiss you, because I loved your grandmother."

We lifted our faces, and she gave us each a kiss. Her lips and cheeks were dry, warm, the skin so crinkled all over with faint lines it seemed a fine-meshed net. The most noticeable things about her were the whiteness of her face, the paleness of her large eyes, and the strong fullness and width of her mouth. Her teeth were regular, splendid, untouched by age.

We were deeply struck by her remark. It sounded strange to us that a person should so reveal her feelings: we did not say things like that in our family, though I dreamed of a life in which such pregnant statements should lead on to drama and revelation. I had at this time a sense that I might be a more romantic figure than my parents and other people realised.

She turned her full eye, that seemed to embrace more than it looked at, upon our primrose baskets, and said:

"Is that all you've picked?"

"We didn't like to pick too many," said Jess.

6

"Why not?" We were silent, and she continued: "My dears, are you very well-behaved?"

"We have to be," said Jess.

She gave a rough, chuckling laugh.

"Well, you can break out with our primroses another time. Anything so lavishly offered by Nature must be lavishly accepted. The real point of primroses is the amount—as with ice cream. Whoever heard of good manners over ice cream?"

"We have," said Jess.

Her laugh broke out again, and taking Jess's chin in her fingertips, she turned her face up and gazed at it.

"How came you by this unsoothed breast?" she said.

Her voice was rather harsh, yet warm, energetic, throaty, with a break in it.

I thought Jess would find it necessary to reply that she came by it through unfairness and Mademoiselle, but something in the look they exchanged loosened her obsession; and colouring with shy pleasure, she smiled.

"*C'est un esprit fier et intransigéant,*" remarked Mademoiselle in the benign and delicate manner she assumed for discussing our temperaments with people of social importance. "*Le fond est excel-lent.*"

"*Evidemment,*" agreed Mrs. Jardine, nodding, brooding over Jess. She looked sorry for her, amused and loving.

I was beginning to fear that the power of Jess's character would exclude me from the bonds being forged, and perhaps she guessed this, for she turned to me, raising her eyebrows in humorous questioning, as if to inquire: "What about *this* breast?"

"*Elle est douce, la cadette,*" murmured Mademoiselle, all honey. "*Douce—douce et serieuse.*"

"You have your grandmother's eyes," said Mrs. Jardine. She took up my hand and examined it. "When I was a young girl she gave me this ring." She showed me, on her little finger, a half-inch of small cut rubies set in thin gold. Her other fingers were covered with important-looking rings, diamonds and turquoises and emeralds, and this one looked girlish, incongruous among them. "My joints are swollen a little, and now I can only wear it on this finger—but I have worn it for forty years. Her own rings would only fit a child, her fingers were so slender. But they were very firm. They could touch the piano keys as no others could. Is there music in these fingers?"

I said I had begun music lessons; letting it be inferred that I showed promise. But Jess said:

"We can't any of us sing in tune—not a note. Daddy's tried us again and again, but it's no use. He says Mummy's influence is astonishing."

"I only saw your dear mother once," said Mrs. Jardine. "It was in Rome, soon after she married your father."

"Oh, then she must have forgotten," I said. "She said she didn't know you."

"No. We have never met. I was in Rome at the same time. I saw them—at the Opera. They did not see me. I watched her for a long time. I wanted so much to know what kind of girl your father had taken for his wife. Such a pretty, fresh, Puritan face, so much firmness. Yes. . . . I think she gave you these strong limbs and rosy cheeks. Your grandmother was rather an invalid, you know. Her chest was delicate; and none of her children was very robust. She used to get a dreadful cough in winter and had to leave England and follow the sun."

"I have bronchitis sometimes," I said.

"Do you?" she said gravely, observing me. "That must be watched. This damp foggy valley is so bad, if there is an inherited weakness—as well there may be."

"Oh, I cough all winter," I said recklessly; but Jess's mood was now so mellow that she let it pass.

We were in bliss: our hearts were bursting to give and to receive. Such reminiscent conversations are what children most delight in: they expand in the glow of an enhanced importance; their identity, to themselves so dubious, so cloudy, becomes clarified. The darkness they feel behind them, from which they are beginning to emerge, is suddenly, consolingly populated by familiar phantoms: shapes with eyes and hands from which theirs are copied, voices which have not altogether ceased to sound, but passed into their new throats. Brains, beauty are enhanced by establishment of their origin and continuity; a clue, a dignity is given to idiosyncrasy of temperament. Even disabilities—fatness, lack of inches, straight hair, tone deafness, failure to spell or do sums, distaste for mutton or greens— touched with the mystery of a recurrent phenomenon, receive a kind of consecration; also an absolution from total responsibility. Others before us compounded with these shames and handicaps: so why not ourselves?

Portraits, letters, albums in the library, family legends, all conspired to float these grandparents, dead before our birth, glamorously before us. Figures larger than life size surrounded them, mingled with them in a rich element of culture and prosperity. In that lost land it was always mid-summer; and the handsome, the talented, the bearded great moved with Olympian words and gestures against a background of marble-columned studios, hallowed giant writing-desks, du Maurier-like musical drawing-rooms, dinner tables prodigious with good fare, branched candlesticks and wit.

Without conscious awareness that our circumstances were a decline from all this, we did receive early intimations that our budding time was somehow both graced and weakened by echoes and reflections from the prestige of that heyday. When elderly relations came to stay, and the talk, punctuated with sighs and smiles, turned on the old days, we listened, drinking in wafts of air unknown, yet recognized, with rapt attention. When their eyes fell affectionately, speculatively on us, we felt them wondering what, if anything, was to be hoped for from this generation in the way of particular inherited promise. Although unmusical, and for that reason a disappointment, something, we felt, might be done with writing?—drawing?—acting? . . . We would be three brilliantly talented sisters, as in the generation before us, and the one before that. Yet sometimes a doubt blew across this simple optimistic programme. That mint was abandoned, the coins were passing out of currency. There seemed something that had once been generated in the family circle, and from thence radiated among friends and acquaintances—a life-wish so crackling with energy that it could overcome no matter what minatory fate, and electrify the whole human span from birth to death.

9

We had a great deal in our childhood, but we had not that. When our father in his middle years married a girl from New England, our cradles were swung at the meeting place of complex and opposing forces, and rocked rather bewilderingly in the process of their conjunction and redistribution. We did not quite know what we were, or from what quarters self-recognition would arise.

A curious figure formed part of our early lives. Her name was Tilly. For many years our grandmother's maid, she had been, subsequently to her death, distributed among various members of the family in the capacity of sewing maid, housekeeper or temporary nurse. She was a diminutive Cockney, just not a dwarf, cased always from head to foot in glossy black, with a little lace-bordered black silk apron, jet ornaments and a cornelian brooch. When she took the air, she wore a waist-length cape called a dolman, and a midget bonnet tied under the chin with broad black satin strings. Her reality belonged entirely to the Dickens world. She had a large pendulous face with caramel eyes on stalks, a long comedian's upper lip and chin, and on her bulging forehead a lump the size of a thrush's egg, which she concealed by arranging over it one circular varnished curl drawn down from her black "transformation." The effect of this was disturbing, as if a form of animal life—a snail or something—grew parasitically upon her brow. I could never take my eyes off it. Twice widowed before the age of thirty, she had married first one Mr. Pringle, to whom in the course of interminable reminiscences she never once referred; next a handsome and romantic Bohemian cabinet-maker, by whom she had had one son, known to us as the Little Feller. He had been all brains and no stamina, his little spine grew crooked, and she lost him at the age of six. She was now in her eightieth year, and had retired to lodgings in Camden Town, and from thence emerged twice yearly to pay us long sewing visits. She sat in a room at the top of the house, making loose covers, manipulating my mother's furs, exquisitely darning the linen and entertaining us with pink and mauve fondants and conversation.

She was a true Cockney, all sharpness, materialism, irony and repartee. She was also a consummate actress and mimic. In a trembling croak she sang us snatches of old music-hall airs; and she danced for us, holding her skirts with quirked fingers, sedately rotating on invisible feet, round and round and round, and dropping a low curtsey at the end. The remarks she threw off impressed us forcibly. She said: "I wouldn't marry a undertaker—not if 'is 'air was 'ung with diamonds." She told us that if a person looked a lady in her dressing-gown, then a lady she was. Our grandmother had been an outstanding example of this truth. I studied myself long before the mirror in my red woollen dressing-gown, considering whether the same could be said of me. She said I had her voice, and Jess her clever fingers with a needle, and Sylvia her joking ways. None of our more agreeable qualities could derive from anybody but Grandma. Not that she had ever been a beauty; we pressed her for this, but she was firm; no, never a beauty, not even pretty: it was the ways she had—the loving way, the quick way, that way of flying out; and she would drop her stitching and chuckle at some recollection of the wit, the stinging tongue. She was on her death bed, so weak they thought her gone past rousing, the nurse did something to displease her: up she sat, "as fierce as a maggot," to protest. Yes, our grandmother came all round us in the upstairs room, beside the cutting-out table and the sewing machine, through the smell of furs and camphor and new chintzes: passionate spirit, loving and loved; modest, self-confident; sheltered, sharply independent; despotic matriarch, young girl pliant and caressing; fragility, energy with a core like the crack and sting of a whip.

It was this, this last that had left our house, and perhaps most similar houses at that period. There were no words for it, of course, and the sense of it came only intermittently. Looking back now, one might express it by saying there seemed disillusionments lurking, unformulated doubts about overcoming difficulties; a defeat somewhere, a failure of the vital impulse.

Now here we were, emerged into this garden to confront this ageing lady who had loved our grandmother, stepping up out of the dead and gone to have our faces searched for clues. We knew we were linked back, as we were with Tilly, to the rich past. The fiery particle snapped in her eyes and in her voice, white, wrinkled, exhausted-looking as she was. Her lips were pale, bluish, but their outline was unblurred, sharply rising and dipping, meeting clear at the outer edges, neither slack, nor sour, nor frightened as many mouths of women grow. There was something about her lips and about her whole face—something dramatic, a sensuality so noble and generous it made her look austere, almost saint-like. Experience had signed her face with a secret, a promise whose meaning people would still watch, still desire to explore and to possess.

We followed her across the lawn into the house.

She showed us to the bathroom, shook rose geranium essence into the water for us, and left us to wash our hands. Then we hurried along the passage to join her in her bed-room. It was a long low spacious room, with white panelled walls and curtains of swathed and frilled white muslin, and a small four-poster bed with delicate columns of fluted mahogany and hangings of white Italian brocade embroidered in blue and gold. In front of the pretty fireplace stood a couch upholstered in mauve watered silk, with a rug of soft silvery fur folded at the foot of it; and over the mantelpiece hung the portrait of a little girl with long brown hair, very queerly dressed in a dark velvet jacket, and on her head a high fur cap. She sat half turned away, looking at us over her shoulder, hand on hip; her face was narrow, with big dark eyes.

"That is my daughter," said Mrs. Jardine.

"What's her name?"

"Ianthe." She gave the portrait a dwelling look. "Yes . . . I *bought* that picture some years ago. It was being sold at auction, I discovered. No doubt it would have been destroyed, but that it had a market value—being the work of a well-known painter."

Her eyes gave a flick. That was the first time I noticed this peculiarity of her eyes: as if they twitched far back, behind the pupil, then dilated in a long blank stare. There was something inhuman about the trick: it made her eyes look fierce and incandescent.

"I suppose she's probably grown up now?" I suggested, not knowing what to make of her last speech.

"Yes, quite grown up. She has children of her own."

"Your grandchildren, then! What are their names?"

"Maisie, Malcolm and Charity. Not names I should have chosen." She drummed with her fingers on the mantelpiece, still staring at the portrait, but not as if she saw it.

Jess, who was stroking the rug, said:

"Do you rest on this sofa?"

"Every afternoon."

"With the blinds down?"

"No, I do not pull down the blinds. I look out at the garden. I love it so much from here: it frames itself so beautifully in this big window."

Our eyes followed hers, and saw through the sash window that reached from floor to ceiling the stretch of lawn and two magnificent trees—a giant copper beech, now budding, and near it a silver birch, the tallest I have ever seen. They were as glorious, as different, as brother-and-sisterly as the sun and the moon. In the background rose the old brick wall that edged the garden, and spring flowers—primulas, daffodils, narcissi, crown imperials—massed in the herbaceous borders.

"And when you get tired of looking at the view you can look at the picture," I said.

She smiled.

"Yes, I look at them alternately. And so the time goes very pleasantly by."

"Why were they called those names, do you think?"

"I understand," said Mrs. Jardine, with marked brevity, "that they were named for various defunct members of their father's family."

"How old are they?"

"Malcolm is thirteen and Maisie is—let me see—she must be twelve. That makes them rather older than you two. The other little girl is a good deal younger." She looked at us attentively, and said in the brusque, electrifying way we were to know so well: "I have never seen my grandchildren."

We were dumb, shocked by the impact of what we recognised to be an important confidence. We waited, acutely aware of the trickiness involved in any attempt to follow on from this. What she had said, it was clear that she had said deliberately; we guessed it had been said to our grandmother's grandchildren. To crown all, we began to receive a curious impression: we were about to enter into some sort of conspiracy with Mrs. Jardine. We watched her, responsive as any instrument she had ever in her life fingered and drawn the heart from, to play the part she had appointed.

"Then you don't know if they're nice or not?" said Jess finally.

"I wonder very much," she said meditatively. "I often ask myself." She went over to the mirror, took out her turquoise hatpins and removed her hat, glancing at herself sidelong, as women do who think they have lost their beauty: repudiating a complete reflection. "I wonder what we should find to say to one another." She dusted her face all over with powder, took from a drawer a scarf of sky-blue gauze and wound it round her throat, pushed her hair up and added: "I think I shall see them soon. I *think* they are coming to stay with me. Then you must come to tea and make friends: at least, if they are nice, as I hope."

Mademoiselle now appeared with an air of modest good breeding from the bathroom, where we had been bidden to leave her, and told us not to fatigue Madame with our chatter.

"Come down now," said Mrs. Jardine, stretching a hand out to each of us and drawing us close. "Tea will be ready. You are going to meet Harry now. You will like Harry. Everybody loves him. But he is a little shy."

# III

A TALL man with a red face and thin grey hair was standing in front of the drawing-room fire, looking out of the window. "Oh, Harry," said Mrs. Jardine, "these are Edward's girls—my sweet Laura's grandchildren. Is not this a happy day for me?" His eyes turned from the window and came down upon us rapidly yet with reluctance. His lips which were long and thin gave a twitch, the travesty of a smile, but he did not say anything; and the rest of his face was quite unsmiling. Almost immediately his gaze returned to the long pane. .

He did not have a trace of any of the different kinds of manner —patronage, embarrassment, amusement, dislike, comradeliness— whereby grown-ups signalise their consciousness of meeting children; but we were prepared, and knew it was his shyness. Slender, upright, with military shoulders and a faultlessly-cut, new-looking tweed suit, he had, as he stood on his own hearth, the most curious look of having no connection with his surroundings. He seemed absolutely exposed. Under crooked bushy grey eyebrows, the whites of his sad butcher-blue eyes were bloodshot; they looked as if they might brim over with tears any moment. Children find a naturalness in eccentric social behaviour; and though his isolation gave him dignity, he did not disconcert us.

April sun struck brilliantly off many pale surfaces of chintz, wood and mirror, and when Mrs. Jardine with her puffy cloud of white hair and her blue gauze, sat down by the window to the tea-table, she looked half-spectral, dissolved in silvery spring light.

Tea was on the plain side, tasty but not lavish, with little home-baked scones and queen cakes and shortbread biscuits. It was memorable for a delicacy of intoxicating flavour, called guava jelly, which we had never before tasted. Mademoiselle bade us speak French, since so remarkable an opportunity had been offered to us of profiting by Madame's knowledge of the language; but Mrs. Jardine begged for us with such tact, praising our accents but explaining that the Major was not so proficient a linguist as herself, that Mademoiselle yielded gracefully, with apologies. We thought that possibly at this point the Major winked very slightly at us, but we were not sure. Little spasms and tremors, easy to mistake for winks, continually crossed his face. Certainly he took no other notice of us, and the meal passed without a word from his lips. Mrs. Jardine talked energetically, in French, to Mademoiselle, in English to us. She talked about the house they had somewhere in France, and said we must come and stay there one day. The word she used was château, which we understood to mean castle, and we asked how soon we could come. She did not put us off with a vagueness and an indulgent laugh, which would have proved to us that the invitation was a false one, but said with seriousness that she was sorry she could suggest no definite date at present. This was Harry's old home, where he had lived as a boy, and they had only just been able to come back to it after years, and Harry loved it very much and wanted to enjoy it for as long as possible before the English winter should force them abroad again. Nowadays, she said, she was like our grandmother: she could not be well in a damp foggy climate. Harry could, of course, he was very strong and healthy, but he never let her travel without him. We were glad to think he loved and cared for her so tenderly, but troubled because his enjoyment of his old home was not more manifest. She spoke for him, she spoke about him: he remained to all appearances unconscious. Their eyes never met. Another thing I noticed was that she filled his teacup scarcely half-way up and leaned across the table to set it down beside his plate. I realised why when I observed how his hand shook when he lifted and drank from it. The tea rocked wildly, but he did not spill it.

Presently the door began to rattle, then opened to let in an enormous cat, orange tabby. It posed in the doorway, glared with tawny eyes, then went streaking, tail up, stiff-legged, to his side. He lifted it on to his lap, folding it in his arms and bending his head to murmur inaudibly to it. Mrs. Jardine poured milk into a saucer, placed it before him on the table and continued her conversation. The cat sat on his lap and stooped its neck to drink. We left our seats and came round his knee, awestruck, to stroke the fabulous creature.

"What's its name?"

"Peregrine," we understood him to say. Then he did give us a rapid look, as if wondering whether he could trust us, and added: "He opens the door himself."

His voice startled us. It was so light and flat it seemed not to issue from his throat, but out of the air, out of nothing. Sometimes in dreams voices speak suddenly like this, empty ventriloquist voices making trivial statements whose tremendous meaning appals us.

"Will you make him do it again?"

"He won't do it again, there's no reason for it," he said rather snappishly. "He doesn't fool about—he plans his life. He opened the door because he wanted his milk. If I put him outside now and shut the door in his face, he'd sulk and I shouldn't see him again to-night."

This was the longest consecutive speech I ever heard Harry make. He got up, and as he did so the cat leaped up on to his shoulder; and thus in silence they left the table and went out, closing the door behind them.

In this room there were two portraits to look at. One was a large, full-length portrait of a fair girl of about seventeen, dressed in white muslin with a blue sash tied round her small waist, and roses in her low bodice. Her arms were round and bare, and she sat with her hands loosely clasped in her lap on what looked like a blue glazed earthenware barrel decorated with a pattern of dolphins. Behind were tall trees; and there were some doves on the grass round her blue-shod feet. White, serious, piercingly beautiful, blue, full eyes staring out with fanatical directness, she was recognisably Mrs. Jardine. As I gazed, the hopeless wish to grow up to look and dress exactly like that caused me a wave of almost nausea.

The other portrait hung in an oval frame over the mantelpiece, and showed the head and shoulders of a wonderful young man in full dress military uniform. He had poetic, delicate features, a fair moustache and a wistful expression.

"That is Harry when he was a young man," said Mrs. Jardine. "Harry was the handsomest man in London, and the best dressed. He was the handsomest man I ever saw, except perhaps your father."

"He's changed rather, hasn't he?" I said in a tactful way.

"People change as they get older. They get more firmness, more character in their faces—if they are good people. For instance," said Mrs. Jardine rapidly, in a matter-of-fact way, "Harry had an almost girlish beauty as a boy. As he grew older, and became such a brilliant soldier and led such a hard-working, responsible life, the quality of his looks changed. All the strength and manliness in him came out."

"I didn't know he was a soldier," I said.

"Of course," said Jess. "What d'you suppose Major means?"

"Well, he is a retired soldier," said Mrs. Jardine, stroking Jess's hair affectionately. "He had a terrible fall from his horse, and then his health broke down, and he had to give up the Army. It was a great grief to him."

I pondered, realising for the first time that it was the strength and manliness coming out in men that gave them purplish faces with broken veins. Yet my father was not red at all. Possibly it worked both ways: one could start highly coloured and grow paler, and the cause would be the same.

As if reading my thoughts, Mrs. Jardine said:

"I dare say your father has changed a great deal from when I knew him. But I am sure he must still be a very fine-looking man."

"Oh yes," I said; and preoccupied as I was at this time with the problem of marriage, I added: "If he was the *very* handsomest man you knew, do you wish you had married him instead?"

"*Mais voyons donc, Rébecca,*" interrupted Mademoiselle sharply. But Mrs. Jardine smiled and said:

"Well—it would have been delightful, of course. But the question never arose."

"I suppose he never asked you?"

"No, never. Apart from anything else, I was too old. As you know, men generally prefer to marry women younger than themselves. I am about half-way between him and your grandmother in age."

"So you could be friends with them both?"

"It was your grandmother who was my darling friend. Of course I was very fond of your father, but he was often away, at school, then at Cambridge, and I never saw him much." She paused, and added: "And then I lost sight of him altogether." She drummed with her fingers on the back of a chair, tapping out a brisk tune, then announced abruptly: "I was frightened of your father."

I felt myself colour violently with shock.

"Why?" said Jess, piercing her with an unblinking stare. But she was looking far away, over our heads and went on dreamily:

"Such charm he had! . . . Nobody could resist it."

"Everybody thinks he's very kind," said Jess.

"Perfectly true." She spoke with decision.

"Then why were you frightened of him?"

"He had a terrible temper," she said, still looking away, "when he was a young man."

"He still has," we assured her.

Mrs. Jardine seemed to come out of her dream and said in her most matter-of-fact way:

"Oh, he still has. What a pity."

"He shouts a bit sometimes," said Jess, dismissing his temper with a light shrug. "Mostly at Mossop. Not at us. There's nothing to be *frightened* of."

She glanced at me, irritable: I was frightened when he shouted. I said nothing.

Mrs. Jardine turned to the window, so that only her bleached stone profile was visible to us, and as if declaring herself, alone, before the judgment of the world, said:

"I have never been a person to be frightened. Physically, I am exceptionally brave. I may say that I have never known physical fear. I have known great pain in my life, and great danger. Each time I have thought: 'How interesting! A first class experience. Not to be missed on any account.' As for those ignoble anxieties which rule the lives of most human beings—they have never touched me. The world is full of unhappy men and women who have feared the opinion of others too much to do what they wanted to do. Consequently they have remained sterile, unfulfilled. Now myself—once I was convinced of what was right for *me,* that was enough! I might suffer, but *nobody* could damage or destroy me."

I could have listened all day to Mrs. Jardine, for the sheer fascination of her style. She enunciated with extraordinary clarity and precision, giving each syllable its due, and controlling a rich range of nervous modulations and inflexions. I wondered at first if she could be reciting from Shakespeare or someone. Then I thought: She's boasting: why? I had heard declarations somewhat similar in the nursery or the "hall" after a reprimand from authority. I thought also what an unsuitable way this was to talk in front of Mademoiselle; and hoped the latter's command of English was as inadequate as she sometimes for her own purposes asserted it to be. But Mrs. Jardine, true to her principles, was not bothering about Mademoiselle. She went on:

"But *violence!*—that I do fear. The lid blown off suddenly in your face—and oh! what comes out of the black cauldron . . .?" Her eyes dilated. *"Horrors!*—that don't shrivel up harmlessly in the air and light of day, and drop back into the stew they came from, but swell to *monsters* that nobody dreamed of and nobody can deal with. . . . Ravaging monsters that live for *ever!* . . ." She turned to us again and changing her manner suddenly, said in a light bantering way: "Bad temper, I'm talking about, my darlings. Never let it get the better of you. Being angry is the same as being mad, and mad people can be dangerous."

"Was he angry with *you?*" I said.

She looked at me, smiling secretively.

"I have made a number of people very angry in my life."

"Why?" said Jess.

"Because I myself am so very reasonable," declared Mrs. Jardine, touching her gauze scarf with light sharp flicks of her fingers. I noticed that her hands were shaking. "It is a knack I have never learned—to allow passion and prejudice to guide my behaviour. Better for me, I have sometimes thought, if I had." She drew in a loud hissing breath. "I could have fought with more equal weapons. However, there it is—I am ill-equipped in some respects. Confronted with anger, I cannot get angry. This is sometimes a disadvantage; because the unreasonable cannot be met with reason—they are impervious to it. They understand only their own barbaric language."

We were by now completely out of our depth. We could only concentrate upon her the whole of our attention, and wait. She was—yes, she was actually trembling all over, as if an electric storm were passing through her body.

"I never lose my temper either," I observed.

"But you sulk," said Jess. "That's worse. Some people say it's a good thing to lose your temper. It all comes out quick, and then it's over, and you feel all right."

"Our baby brother has a ghastly temper," I said. "He holds his breath and goes black in the face. Once Nurse had to dash him under the cold tap with all his clothes on."

"Let us hope he will outgrow that," said Mrs. Jardine gravely. She looked up in a brooding way at the Major's portrait and said: "Ianthe was a very equable child. And Harry has the temper of an angel."

I was relieved; and wishing to be rid of the impression that Mrs. Jardine had trodden a path unremittingly beset by furious fiends, said eagerly:

"Then you are glad you married him?"

"Very glad," she said briskly. "Oh yes. Yes, certainly."

"And that Ianthe has such a kind father?" I relentlessly suggested.

Her reply came readily.

"Oh, Harry is not Ianthe's father. She had another man for her father. You see, I was married to somebody else before I married Harry. No. . . . Harry never had a child of his own. A great pity. He is devoted to children, and so unusually good with them."

21

Our further questions died upon our lips. It was the final piece of information, the definite statement that the Major had a particular weakness for and way with children, that silenced us completely.

Mademoiselle flutingly announced that it was time for us to make our adieux. She asked our hostess to excuse our indiscretions, adding that with us the zeal for accuracy was a veritable malady.

"*C'est très bien,*" said Mrs. Jardine, with an incisive nod. "*Il n'y a rien au monde de plus important.*"

She had stopped trembling, and seemed now all affection and serenity. She went on to say, in French, that she had conducted her life on the sole principle of discovering and speaking the truth in all circumstances, and that this principle must naturally apply in dealing with the young—with the very youngest. Mademoiselle replied with a gesture of indescribable delicacy—something between a bow, a shrug and a deferential *moue*.

"Au revoir, my dear *dears*. You must come and see me again soon," said Mrs. Jardine, stooping to print on our cheeks a soft dry perfumed kiss. Then she said low, with great tenderness: "One more kiss, because I love you."

Jess put her arms up, round her neck, and said:

"Please, can I speak to you alone?"

They left the room together, and almost immediately returned. Mrs. Jardine came back with exactly the same expression on her face: a hostess's cordial solicitude. Jess looked stubborn and triumphant.

We picked up our primrose baskets and went through the garden in the April dusk; out by the blue door, down the grassy hill at a jog-trot.

Mademoiselle inquired disagreeably what Jess had had to say that could not be said aloud to all, in a spirit of straightforwardness and good manners. Jess replied:

"Nothing."

For this she received a punishment: immediate bed without supper on arrival home. She curled her lip in scorn, and marched with her head high. She muttered for my ear: "Off with their heads!"—a code phrase, arising out of our governess's marked physical resemblance to Tenniel's Queen in *Alice in Wonderland*, employed by us to convey warning and signalise defiance.

My mother heard us open the front door, and called us into the drawing-room, so the punishment lapsed. Later Jess told me what had passed between her and Mrs. Jardine.

"Next time we come, may we come without Mademoiselle? We should enjoy it more."

"Certainly," said Mrs. Jardine. She took Jess's hand, gripped it, and added: "When my grandchildren arrive, I shall send for you to come *alone*, you and Rebecca, to play with them in the garden."

"Do you promise?"

"I promise. I want you to be friends. Remember that."

# I V

I DO not know whether it was a long time or not long before we went again to tea with Mrs. Jardine. Looking back into childhood is like looking into a semi-transparent globe within which people and places lie embedded. A shake—and they stir, rise up, circle in inter-weaving groups, then settle down again. There are no dates. Time is not movement forward or backward through them, but simply that colourless globe in which they are all contained. Adolescence coalesces in a separate globe; heavier, more violent and confused in its agitations when shaken.

I think it was a few months later: I know it was summer, because Mademoiselle had vanished unlamented to Belgium for her long annual holiday, and there was no difficulty about going to tea without her. We were invited to come and play with Mrs. Jardine's grandchildren; and when the note came we overheard

23

my father say low and with annoyance to my mother: "There's not got to be too much of this, you know." And she murmured back: "Well, shall I make an excuse?"

A moment of ghastly suspense and anxiety followed; but it was not in him to deprive us of a pleasure, and he shrugged his shoulders and made some cryptic reference to claws being pulled after all these years. My mother reminded him of the charming letter about us she had received after our first visit. "Oh yes," he said. "She'd charm the birds off the trees." My mother said something about people like that always ending up the most respectable and orthodox of all. He uttered a light amused snort. "Let them go," he said. "So long as it isn't the thin edge of the wedge. . . . It won't hurt them to get a last-hour impression of her classical dimensions. . . . Her days of action must be done." He paused, sighed and added: "Poor old Harry Jardine. . . ." And then: "I wonder if she's kept anything of her looks. . . ."

There must have been a long spell of drought that summer, for I remember the brownish-green canvas-like look and feel of the expanse of lawn stretching out parched and dazed in the sun as we came through the blue gate. We saw basket chairs and a table beneath the copper beech, and a figure in white lying on a garden couch. A hand waved. It was Mrs. Jardine. When we came up and stood beside her, we saw that she was propped on cushions, and that she drew loud and labouring breaths.

"Dears, dears," she said, not smiling. "The virtue has gone out of me. I have not had a bad attack for five years, and now it has its talons in me again. It is my heart. I have, in an acute form, a nervous instability of the heart. Extremes of heat and cold affect it—among other things. But I shall not die of it." She did smile then, and fanned herself with a large Japanese paper fan. "Oh, dear me, this is so very tiresome!" she exclaimed irritably. "The very *day* they arrive, I collapse. Four days ago. I wanted to have so much to give them. They find a sick old woman. So disastrously unfortunate. They come from a house of sickness. Nothing is more detrimental to the young." Closing her eyes, she wiped a dew of sweat from her forehead with a filmy handkerchief. "Suffocating heat," she gasped. "I have been indoors. It

24

seems I am better indoors. But I wanted to see you coming across the lawn. Pretty pets. You look so fresh. I wanted to be present when you meet——" She picked up a little handbell from the table beside her, and swung it with a will. "They will come," she murmured. "I told them to appear as soon as I rang. They *lurk.*" Her eyes flicked, dilated. "They lurk all day in those tunnels. Emerging at meal times. *I* don't know what they do."

"What tunnels?" asked Jess.

"Have not you noticed the lime alleys?" she asked in that rather harsh didactic voice she always used, I was to realise later, for speaking of the particular beauties of her house. There was apparent pride, almost arrogance, in the tone; yet in my ears it rang hollow from the first, as if her insistence sprang from the necessity of remaining set in some blind alley of circumstance, some course she knew to be sterile. It was an angular voice of the will, a parrot voice. "No other country house in England," she went on, "has anything to compare with them. They were planted by Harry's grandfather, and Harry used to love to play in them when he was a little boy."

Feeling reproved for lack of æsthetic observation, we looked about us and saw, running down the length of the garden, starting near the outer edges of the house's rose brick façade and flanking the lawn, two high broad square-clipped tunnels of compact foliage. At the end, each of these was developed into a formal square like a leafy temple with arches cut in it, and beneath the arches we caught a glimpse of stone figures, erect, in pliant dreaming attitudes.

"The fragrance in spring . . ." said Mrs. Jardine, meltingly now. "Enough to die of, in aromatic pain. And the bees hum and hum in the green daze. It is like drowning." Then she said sharply: "Where can they be?" and rang her bell again, with violence.

After a few moments, three figures emerged from beneath one of the arches and came slowly across the lawn towards us: a boy in a cricket shirt and grey flannel trousers, a girl in a brown holland frock leading by the hand a much smaller child in a navy blue overall. They came and stood at the foot of Mrs. Jardine's couch.

"Malcolm and Maisie," said she, "here are your guests. This is Jess. This is Rebecca. I rang the bell twice."

"Sorry, Grannie," said the boy awkwardly.

"We heard you the first time," said the girl.

"Oh, you did," said Mrs. Jardine in her matter-of-fact voice. "It seems rather a pity then that you did not come. Since that was our arrangement."

"Cherry didn't want to come," said the girl. "I had to persuade her. I wasn't going to have any more tears."

"I see," said Mrs. Jardine.

She closed her eyes and fanned herself rapidly. Yes, she lay there with her eyes sunk and her nostrils looking pinched, as if beaten down by the rudeness of her granddaughter. An overwhelming sense of outrage and struggle oppressed the air.

"Well, perhaps you would not object to shaking hands with your guests," said Mrs. Jardine in the same dry, equable way, her eyes open again, but not looking at any of us.

We shook hands formally all round, and said how do you do. The three stared at us, and we at them, absorbing one another warily through all our senses.

"How are you feeling, Grannie? Shall I fan you a bit?" said the boy politely. He seemed anxious to show good will.

She turned her face to him.

"Thank you, dear boy."

Voice, eyes, smile bathed him in streams of tender love. He waved the fan clumsily at her, and she took up his disengaged hand, rough, red, with bitten nails, and held it against her papery cheek. The small girl disengaged herself from Maisie and came and leaned on the arm of the couch, watching the movements of the bright red and blue flowery fan. She was a very pretty child, with long dark wavy hair in profusion, a pale transparent skin and deep blue eyes rayed round with dark curling lashes: dazed-looking eyes with abnormally large pupils.

"Would you like a fan of your own, little one?" said Mrs. Jardine.

26

"Yes."

"I will find you one."

"When will you?"

"When I go in."

"Cherry will have a fan and fan herself."

"Don't talk in that babyish way, Cherry," said Maisie sharply. "It's silly. When you talk about yourself you say me, not Cherry, you know perfectly well. I'm not going to have you getting into these idiotic habits. Anyway you don't want a fan now. You're coming for a picnic with Malcolm and me."

"Cherry will—I will stay with Grannie."

"My pretty," murmured Mrs. Jardine, caressing her hair.

Maisie went black, heavy, swollen; and Mrs. Jardine continued briskly, between labouring breaths: "Well, you are going to take your tea out, and eat it in the trees, or under them somewhere. I told Mary to pack the basket and put it in the hall. Jess and Rebecca, my darlings, I hope you won't hurt your pretty frocks. I see you did not change out of that brown overall after all, Maisie. Perhaps you were right? Cherry's also looks extremely soiled.. It cannot be helped."

"I wasn't going to let her get another cotton dirty," said Maisie, "just for a picnic. What does it matter what we look like? It's all so stupid, this fuss."

She gave our clean pink and white striped ginghams a look of disgust and contempt.

"What fuss can you be referring to?" asked Mrs. Jardine, with marked lightness. "It always matters what we look like. Harry likes to see people cleanly and neatly dressed. He is very particular. His feelings matter, because he is your host. You have worn an unprepossessing brown holland garment for three days now. He is tired of it. I will not speak of myself." Her eyes snapped, staring ahead of her. She was powerful and cruel; and Maisie set her lips, flushing sullenly. "Malcolm will care, later on, to have attractive sisters, girls he can be proud of, to take about. Perhaps he does already."

Malcolm laughed awkwardly, amiably.

"Oh, Maisie!—she'll never care what she looks like. She'd really

27

prefer to shove herself into a sack and tie it up at the neck, wouldn't you, Mais?"

"I'd rather wear a sack and black my face than be taken about like a prize poodle just to be shown off," she said, with raging scorn.

"Keep your hair on," he said good-naturedly. "Nobody's likely to burst themselves in the effort to show you off."

"Cherry has the bud of beauty in her," remarked Mrs. Jardine. "Why should she be disguised? Is it deliberately done?"

"How do you mean disguised, Grannie?" said the boy, still embarrassed.

"Cherry has her mother's eyes," said Mrs. Jardine, her voice vibrating. "Even when she was a baby I dressed her in brilliant, definite colours—blues and reds. For her sixth birthday I sent her, from America, a black velvet frock, long, to her ankles, with a fitted bodice and a sash of watered silk, the colour of a dark red rose."

"Cherry would like that," said Cherry, looking hypnotized.

Maisie began in a choked voice:

"Father doesn't——"

"Oh yes, yes, yes," interrupted Mrs. Jardine quickly, coldly. "Your father does not approve of beauty. He would like it to be wiped off the face of the earth. The fatal gift of beauty: the unpardonable. . . ." Once again, she was trembling all over. "You tire me rather, Maisie. I must go in. Where is Harry? One of you go and find him, please, to carry me in."

"He's just coming out of the house, Grannie," said Malcolm. "He's coming."

"Ah, I knew he would! He said he would come for me at four, and four it is exactly. Look." She held up to Cherry the tiny watch she wore, like a pendant, on a long pearl-studded chain. Its back was a pansy, enamelled in rich blues and purples, outlined in minute diamonds. "This is the watch he gave me when I married him. I wear it always. It has never lost or gained a minute." Her eyes swept the whole silent group of us, and she said triumphantly: "Harry has never broken his word—never. To me, or to any one. Malcolm, do you know what a gentleman

28

is? One who never, by act or word, wounds a fellow creature. One who is incapable of unkindness. This may sound trite—perhaps you do not yet know how rare a quality kindness is. The world is choked with cruel people and their victims. I have met very, very few gentlemen and gentlewomen in my life: none like Harry."

Again she wiped the dew of sweat from her forehead, and then lay perfectly still, as if making a strong effort to compose herself. The Major came towards us, stalking lightly, in a suit of biscuit-coloured shantung, a Panama hat bound with Leander ribbon upon his head. Presently she remarked in a weak voice, the suppressed excitability and bitterness all gone out of it:

"Myself I hate ugliness. Particularly ugly manners."

When Harry reached her side, she gave him, as if to a stranger whom she designed to fascinate, her long mysterious upward-pointing smile, and said softly:

"I am ready to go in, Harry."

His eyes which looked always so unfocused on any visible object did, I suppose, take in her exhausted appearance, for he said rapidly:

"I told you you weren't fit to come out."

He took no notice of any of us.

"Oh," she exclaimed gaily, "but I had to see Laura's darlings. I had to be there when they met these. That was understood. You promised me. Now there they all are together, just off for their picnic. And so I will come in and rest; as I promised *you*."

Thus declaring to him, to us, that the whole thing had gone off successfully, delightfully, just as she had planned it, she raised her arms to put them round his neck and be lifted.

"Is he going to carry you?" said Cherry.

"Yes. He carried me out and now he is going to carry me in."

"Cherry would like to be carried." She yearned up at him. "A ride on your shoulders. Like Dadda used to, only now he doesn't."

"Harry will give you a ride on his shoulders later."

"When will he?"

"Ask him."

She clasped his wrist with both hands, and swung on it, twisting and sidling.

"When will you? Now?"

"Not now."

He looked down at her, not smiling, but with the faintest shade of inquiry and watchfulness, as if wondering whether a kitten could possibly be playing with his hand. She went on squirming, perfectly at ease, feline, sure of herself and of him.

"When I come back from my picnic? Before I go to bed?"

"Perhaps."

"Oh! I shall be so high up! As high—as high as the trees," she cried wildly, throwing herself back from his arm. "You'll run with me, gallop and run, gallop and run till I call out stop *Stop!*"

"Indeed," said the Major. The ghost of a laugh came out of his throat. Then he shook her off gently and stooped, his small, neat, sparsely covered head brushing his wife's white curls, the blood suffusing neck, face, scalp as he gathered her up and straightened himself again. He puffed a bit as he held her.

"No featherweight," she said, smiling down at us. "Au revoir, my loves and doves. Enjoy yourselves. Mary has packed peaches in a separate basket."

He started off with her across the lawn, and we looked after them; and as the distance between us widened they grew more and more strange and romantic. His figure was so slight, graceful and upright, he looked from the back like a tall young man carrying his white bride into his house. As I watched, a queer feeling came over me, hard to describe, though unforgotten: one of those intimations, or premonitions, which visit children, of a whole range of complex personal emotions, far ahead of their present capacity, alien to their experience, yet recognised in a prophetic flash as theirs to come. What love would be like. . . . Was that it? It rose up and vanished, a featureless phantom, infinitely unfamiliar, irreconcilable with the homely shapes of love I knew.

Mrs. Jardine had been carried off the field, but the day was hers: no doubt of that. We were all disconcerted and unhappy— all but Cherry, who was obviously impervious to moral conflicts;

concealing beneath a cool elastic surface an agate core of ego-centric desires, and intent on the consolidation of her gains. I was aware without being told that the commotion in the lime alley had been a round—doubtless not the first—in the fight of Maisie for Cherry's soul. Cherry had been threatened, coaxed, exhorted to remember something or other. . . . No use. However ferociously, perseveringly, she was hauled away out of the enemy's sphere of influence, she would flip back into it like an eel, over and over again. Mrs. Jardine had got her, and Maisie had lost her.

Since the last outburst, Maisie had remained silent, as if non-plussed, hanging her head. She must be telling herself she would never give in, never; but at the same time she looked so lonely, I guessed an enormous dismay behind her resolution. That solitary defiant look of the about-to-be-defeated I knew well: both Jess in conflict with Mademoiselle and Sylvia in conflict with Nurse were not infrequently lit by its sombre halo. It set them apart from me, and across the gulf I yearned to them with mingled shame, distress and admiration. I could never stand up to anger, and must compound with the oppressor and be smiled at, rather than bear the flaming placard: *I am a naughty girl.* I had never been naughty in my life.

Now that Mrs. Jardine had gone, the electrifying meanings with which her presence always charged the air began to dissolve. The arrows of her words fell harmlessly out of the copper beech on to the grass around us, and we kicked them aside and drew together, an ordinary group of children going for a picnic. The job in hand was to make friends. It was always done as soon as the grown-ups went away, and we had no more than the usual qualms about doing it. We looked at one another with tentative smiles. Maisie nibbled her thumb.

She was a rough-surfaced, vivid, broad girl with a long back and short legs with bulging hairy calves. Her skin was dark and freckled, the colour was brilliant in her lips and over her prominent cheek bones. She had short hair, immensely thick, springy and coarse; it looked as if no hairbrush had ever been through it. She had an altogether uncared-for plebeian appearance, as of a girl scrubbed perfunctorily with inferior soap and put into cast-off charity clothes. Her features were too bold and bony, but her eyes were magnificent—large, wide open, in colour that clear green which is found sometimes with very dark hair. I thought her extremely attractive.

Malcolm was a plain boy with a weak, untidy, amiable face, large teeth that needed both cleaning and straightening, and the same rough skin as his sister, only his was fairish and pinkish. His hair jagged down over his forehead and stuck up in spikes in the crown.

"You are an ass, Mais," he said.

"Well, I won't be bossed by her," she said gruffly. "Other people can be if they like."

"Oh, go and boil your head. Who wants to boss anybody? They've got to do *something* with us, haven't they? Perhaps they don't like it any more than you do."

"They may not like it, but they want it. At least, she does. She wants to keep us here. Besides, you know what Father said."

"What?"

"*I* was to look after Cherry."

"Oh, well . . ."

"And you know what else he said."

"Oh well. . . . No, I don't as a matter of fact." He took a couple of marbles from his pocket and juggled with them aimlessly. "All I can say is, I simply fail to see the point of spoiling everything for everybody. This is a ripping place, and they're being jolly decent to us. She's getting fed up with you, though, and we'll probably be packed off. Then where'll we go?"

She jerked her head and looked away, flushing and blinking hard. I thought she was blinking back tears. There was a silence; then Jess said:

"Don't you like staying here?"

Instead of answering, Maisie made a pounce on Cherry who had seated herself in one of the basket chairs and was rocking herself monotonously to and fro, and sucking two fingers. She whisked her to her feet by one arm and shook her.

"For goodness' sake," she cried furiously, "stop sucking your fingers! Since you've been here you've started all your ghastly babyish tricks again. *I* don't know what to do with you."

Cherry set up a wail, and Malcolm told her to shut up; and Maisie, after standing a moment with the same non-plussed look, turned her back on her and said to Jess:

"We have to be here because Father had to send us away. He's in hospital. He's got cancer of the throat."

Malcolm shuffled his feet and looked away, as if something acutely embarrassing had been said.

"We would have gone away with Auntie Mack," continued Maisie, "but she couldn't have us. So we've to stay here till he's better. Then we shall go home."

I said:

"How soon will he be better?"

"We don't know for certain. We've got to wait for the treatment to work. He's having treatment."

"Does his throat hurt?"

Maisie paused, then said stiffly:

"He doesn't have any more pain, because when it starts they give him something to stop it."

"Oh, come on," said Malcolm. "Let's go if we're going." He flung a pebble with all his might and watched it spin up and away out of sight. "Over the roof," he said. "Cheers for M. B. Thomson."

"Rot," said Maisie. "Nowhere near. Here, give us one. Bet I chuck farther than you."

"Bet you sixpence you don't. You'll slam it straight into her bedroom window and knock her out cold."

She giggled.

"I wouldn't. Still, over the wall if you funk the roof. Go on, you first."

He threw; then she threw. This time he muffed it, and his pebble hit the wall and fell in the herbaceous border. Hers went sailing over, still on the upward arc as it crested the wall. She threw like a boy, powerfully, free from the shoulder. Grinning, she held out her hand.

He turned to us and said politely:

33

"Have a shot?"

We said we couldn't. He smacked Maisie's hand down and said:

"Haven't got it on me."

"Skunk, you haven't got it at all. What happened to that tip from Harry?"

"Spent it, my good woman. Whose stomach benefited, may I inquire?"

"Yours."

"*And* yours."

"One tuppenny nut milk bar. Greedy hog."

"I wonder if he's good for another small donation." He looked meditatively towards the house; then, as if a doubt about gratitude and good taste had come over him, added: "It was jolly decent of him really. I wonder why we have to call him Harry. Seems all wrong to call a rum, dignified old bird like him by his Christian name."

"I don't think he'd notice if we called him Wee MacGregor," said Maisie. "I don't think he notices anything. She goes on all day: Harry likes this, Harry does that, Harry thinks the other——"

"And he never opens his trap."

Planted feet wide apart on her muscular legs, she directed towards the house a prolonged intent stare; and under fringes of jasmine and climbing roses, the house stared back with all its eyes. All houses, even suburban brick and stucco villas, fade on such an afternoon as this into the outermost veils of the sun's antiquity; and the long gabled time-burnished house of Major and Mrs. Jardine, lapped in that violently dreaming light, its blood-orange roof scattered with white somnolent pigeons, looked inexpressibly old, mysterious, burdened with human lives and deaths. We might have been standing in the heart of the old gardens of the sun.

"It's not a bad house," said Maisie; and then: "Anyway, she can't go on about what *she* did here when she was a little girl."

"Who can go on about who?" said Malcolm.

"Her . . . about Mother. Because she didn't ever come here."

"Of course not," said Malcolm abruptly.

34

"I bet she'd kid us she did if she could."

"Come on," said Malcolm, "for the Lord's sake, if we're going. I'm famished."

Maisie turned to Cherry, then flung out her arms and enveloped her in them with tender roughness.

"There's a ducky old Cherry Pie," she said. "Come to Mais. We're not cross-patches to each other, are we?"

They hugged.

"Is her real name Cherry?" asked Jess.

"I'm Charity Mary Thomson."

"After our other grannie," said Maisie. "Our proper one, but she's dead now. She called herself Cherry when she was little, so we all got into the habit. It's a silly sort of name, really."

"For a prize silly," said Malcolm. "I call her raspberry pip."

Cherry rushed at him head down and butted him. He swung her up and she pummelled at his chest, and he turned her head over heels on to the grass where she lay kicking, squealing and giggling. Her curly hair tumbled back all round her head and she looked wildly pretty and wanton.

We witnessed all this with fascination, delighting in the evidences of family feeling. The way brother and sisters treated one another reminded me of E. Nesbit's books: astringent chaff, home truths, sterling loyalty.

I wondered if one of the upper windows hid Mrs. Jardine lying on her mauve couch, watching us.

We started for the picnic.

# V

S O our friendship with the Thomsons began. Summer wore away
and they still stayed on, and we saw each other almost every day.
Our time was chiefly devoted to strenuous physical recreation—
climbing, somersaulting, jumping, turning cartwheels, riding bicycles. My passion for tree-climbing was equalled if not surpassed
by Maisie's; it was the basis of what burst rapidly into a close and
emotional relationship. I never knew a girl exercise herself as
she did: when she was not ranging over walls and among
branches, or pedalling furiously round the paths, she would fall
upon and wrestle with me. She was several years my senior, and
much heavier, and she generally got me down, but I could climb
higher and with more agility.

The garden was given over to physical displays. Sometimes
Harry would emerge from the study where he spent hours alone
with his cat, and watch us all competing in the long and the
high jump. He seemed to enjoy doing this: he seemed to concentrate on it, and sometimes raised the rope himself with an
unsteady hand. He, or rather Mrs. Jardine in his name, had presented all three of them with magnificent bicycles, and we
brought our rather inferior ones and played follow my leader for
hours on end, whirling in and out of the alleys, toiling, nose on
handle bars, up banks and steps, tottering and colliding among
the intricacies of the shrubbery. Maisie liked best to lead, but
Malcolm was the best leader. He had an offhand slick virtuosity
on the wheel which none of us could approach; his balancing
feats would not have shamed a music-hall trick cyclist. Maisie
took a world of pains, but she was clumsy. Beetroot-coloured, her
hair soaked with perspiration, she laboured grimly in his wake.
Jess and I had more style but less stamina and frailer nerves: this
made the standard of our performances capricious. Cherry began
by tagging along with us, and we were patient with her, though
she spoilt the games because she had not yet learnt to dismount

unaided; but soon she dropped out of her own accord, and sought the more appreciative society of the domestic staff. She had pretty ways, old-fashioned ways, and became the pet of the kitchen, where she made little jam tarts and showed off and prattled about herself in the third person to her heart's content. She formed the habit, too, of trotting into Harry's study and climbing on to his lap. There she would lie against his shoulder, sucking her fingers, her dopey eyes staring, unfocused, unblinking, through half-lowered lids. Obviously she was building him up into a powerful and comforting father-figure, and she clung rapaciously to his male touch. Once during a game of hide and seek, while I was in concealment in the rosemary bush under his window, I overheard her say—in the manner of one sending up coyly, dubiously, a trial balloon—that she was going to call him Daddy. I heard him murmur a word or two of dissent. "Then Grandpa . . .?" "No. Harry." She uttered a formal deprecating little laugh, and exclaimed: "Fancy me saying Grandpa! Oh dear, what a silly I am! You're not nearly old enough for that, are you? You're a young, *young* Harry. . . . You're more like a sort of Uncle Harry really, aren't you, I suppose?" He uttered a brief chuckle. "Miss," he said. "Miss Puss." It was very odd to hear him laugh: it was as if he didn't know how to do it, and was practising. But she did make him laugh. He began to love her tenderly. When she was playing with the rest of us in the garden, he would appear suddenly in our midst, just to see that she was getting on all right—not being left out or left behind. Sometimes one discerned his figure haunting one long window after another, as if watching her from different angles. He had always been so freakish, so apparently aimless in his comings and goings, it was at first difficult to realise that he was now guided by one definite motive—to watch over her.

This was in the beginning: afterwards—quite soon, I think— her presence became a simple necessity to him. Though a caressing she was not an affectionate child; perhaps because of this, because she was all intuition, calculation, without heart, she knew exactly how to meet him three-quarters of the way and draw from him the sustenance she needed. She soon had the father-daughter ritual established—the romp before bedtime, the good-night visit after she was in bed. They talked fantasies about the cat, and read aloud to each other from the Beatrix Potter books Mrs. Jardine had given her. He read slowly, in a rather quavering solemn monotone; she very loudly and rapidly—(she knew them by heart) pausing now and then to fling out such warnings and encouragements as: "This bit is rather frightening"; or "It's a little sad here, but it gets all right in the end." She had a shrill sing-song voice with a plaintive break in it; it always sounded as if tears were behind it. She sang to him too, long droning compositions in mournful *récitatif*. Obsessed as she was with age and death, her themes were always very morbid, and her renderings caused her face to assume a comic look of strain and anguish. He would listen without a quiver, and thank her politely at the end.

All this time, while the relationship between Harry, the Thomsons and ourselves was being established, Mrs. Jardine seemed to retire into the background, or to be somehow muffled. Like a constitutional sovereign, without administrative political powers, she presided, she dispensed bounty, graciousness and tact, receiving us as it were in audience on our arrivals and departures. She ceased to confide in us, and never attempted to draw us apart and question us about the grandchildren. We neither spied for her, nor were spied upon.

She got on very agreeably with Malcolm: he admired her and trusted her, and she showed him an easy straightforward affection, and encouraged him, and was patient with his uncouthness. His incipient puberty was particularly raw, grubby and graceless, and she who so loved order and distinction, so valued charm, never allowed his unattractiveness to irritate her. "He can't help it, Lucy," I once heard her say to her maid after some large-scale breakage. "He is not inside his skin yet, he is all over the place. How can he tell what his legs and arms will do?" She would stroke his dust-coloured scrubbing-brush hair, and call him her fellow. She must have settled that her job was to help him—by making him feel loved, not a disappointment—to fit more satisfactorily into his skin. I thought it was sad that she had never had a son: she would have been so nice to him. I thought it must be difficult for her to believe that Malcolm, so common, so non-descript in his flesh, could possibly be descended from her flesh and blood. I did not realise then what poisons from what far-back brews went on corroding her; but not a drop fell on these children—fruit though they were of everybody's misconceptions and misfortunes. Mrs. Jardine had so fine a respect for human life that she was able to bestow an entire, an objective, uncorrupted value upon every individual, even where her passions and prejudices might have made for most distortion. That was her grandeur.

Malcolm had unpleasing traits in his character. He was deferential, almost obsequious, to any form of authority, as if he wished—awkwardly enough, poor Malcolm!—to ingratiate himself as a precaution against detection. He cheated just a little in all the games, and did not share his sweets all round, but kept them secretively among the hairy, clogged grey debris of his jacket pocket and consumed them rapidly, on the sly; though sometimes he did offer the bag to Jess, whom he was keen on. He liked to swing with her, standing face to face, on the swing the gardener put up in the walnut tree. Owing to the violence of his exertions, they swooped to dizzy heights. Also he used to wind her up tight in the swing and then let her go. Eyes tight shut, squealing, she would spin round with a whirl of legs and skirts to a bucketing conclusion. He would never be bothered to wind up Maisie or me. Then he would place a cushion for her on the bar of his bicycle and invite her to mount, which she did demurely, side-saddle. Gruffly bidding her to lean against him, he would wobble away with her for secluded rides in the lime alleys.

In those odorous, subaqueously-lit tunnels, he would share his sweets with her; and once suddenly kissed her cheek. She was flattered by his preference for her, but not reciprocally attracted; and I think his strangled brooding sensuality, the furtiveness of his advances and withdrawals, caused her a bored uneasiness.

Maisie could not be won, so Mrs. Jardine behaved towards her as a sovereign might towards a Communist M.P. at a royal garden party: she extended hospitality to her, avoided any field of controversy, serenely ignored all treasonable insinuations. Never, in my presence, after that one time, did she permit the battle to be between equals and in the open. Their strategies ran on contradictory lines and never engaged one another for the show-down; but all the same Mrs. Jardine gained the advantage. Maisie's integrity quickly took on the appearance of mere pig-headedness and ill-breeding.

Maisie was always falling off objects and falling down, and Mrs. Jardine tended her injuries with exquisite skill and kindness. A relationship might have developed from this,—though it never did—for the sight of blood was Maisie's heel of Achilles and reduced her to green-faced shuddering sickness and paralysis. It was curious in one so bent upon physical hazards, and so particularly tough to outward view. I got a fearful shock the first time I saw her sitting on the ground, staring with gasps and whimpers at her flowing knee. Mrs. Jardine attempted neither to sympathise nor to stiffen her morale by a bracing attitude. She simply bathed, bandaged with her strong light certain hands, and sent her to lie down for an hour with a hot drink and a book. Each time Maisie fell down the process was repeated. Her surrender was total, abject, but no advantage was taken of it.

Cherry she treated with indulgent yet somehow remote tenderness. She watched her a good deal, but as it were from the other side of a glass shutter, which she only opened to call her to her side for practical reasons: for instance, when Cherry looked too flushed or too white. She was a delicate creature; what colour she had ebbed and flowed between one hour and the next. Sometimes she had a bluish unearthly pallor. She had constant colds and stomach upsets, and Mrs. Jardine made her rest a lot, and, sick or well, kept her in bed one whole day each week. Maisie fought hard at first against this decree, muttering that there was nothing wrong with her, it was only because she was having too much rich food, and now on top of that she was being made into a mollycoddle; but Mrs. Jardine summoned Dr. Gibson to examine Cherry; and then, during the course of a long private conversation, bewitched him; and then he had a tactful jolly confidential chat alone with Maisie; and after that Maisie threw up the sponge. Sick or well, Cherry greatly enjoyed her days in bed. She cut out dolls' clothes and chalked and sang. Mrs. Jardine showed her how to cut chains and patterns from delectable sheets of coloured paper. Harry spent hours by her bedside. I observed that it was part of Mrs. Jardine's policy to leave them together. Listening from a distance to their uninhibited conversations, an expression at once tranquil and expectant would come into her face.

Once she was in bed with a cold and I had come in to have a grazed hand dressed by Mrs. Jardine. We were in the bathroom, which was opposite to the bedroom she shared with Maisie. Both doors were open, and I could see Harry sitting by her bed. I heard her say:

"The next one will be still more sad. Lily and Willy both get stolen away. But I'll put some gladness in. Their mother comes for them. Their mother is a guardian angel, you see, but they don't know it. Nor do you yet, do you?" He nodded, and leaned his cheek on his hand to listen. When the song was over, she said: "Did you like that? It was beautiful, wasn't it? Now can I light your cigarette? Your hands smell nice, you have nice smelling soap. What shaky hands you've got, haven't you? Why do they shake so?"

"Well, I don't know. It's just a bad habit they've got into."

She said in an anxiously casual way:

"Is it because you're old?"

"That might have something to do with it."

She was silent, then she said with false, loving simplicity:

"You are a shaky man, aren't you? Shaky, shaky old Harry.
. . . Do ill people have shaky hands?"

"Sometimes."

"I know they do, because—I know."

"But I'm not at all ill."

"No!" she cried triumphantly. "You're *very well!* And you're

41

not old either—not to me. You won't die—oh, for fifty years I shouldn't think, should you?"

"I shouldn't think so."

"Not ever . . .?" Her voice was cunning.

"Some time. Everybody does."

"Yes, that's what Maisie says. It does seem a shame really. I don't want to. I don't want anybody to. Do you want to?"

"I don't think I shall mind much. People don't, you know, when they've had a lot of life."

"Perhaps something will be invented to stop it. If I was God, I should say——" She sat up straight in her dressing-gown and called out in a tone of imperious proclamation: "I have made up my mind! Nobody is to die any more!"

A sound came out of his throat, stifled, sudden, as if his heart turned over with tenderness and pity. He took the small hand she had raised in the act of decree and held it to his chest.

"I say, look here, old girl," he said, even more huskily than usual. "Look here. Listen. We'll stick together. See? I'll be here as long as you want me. You'll be all right. I promise. See?"

Mrs. Jardine, who had been listening intently while she washed and dressed my hand, dropped the bandage she was rolling and leaned back against the basin. Her hands sank to her sides, she looked far away out of the window, and said, very low:

"Now she is his child. He will live for her."

The tears started to pour down her cheeks, but without blurring or staining her contours. Her eyes remained wide and more than ever brilliant, and the tears went on slipping down as if over the face of a statue. She looked at me, smiling; her smile lit by tears had a wild and tragic glitter. She whispered: "I knew it would be so"; and kissed me. She put her fingers to her lips, and we went out, tiptoeing past the open door, downstairs again.

The stronger Maisie's feelings for me grew, the weaker became her grasp on Cherry. I satisfied her violent and jealous sense of ownership. She began to relax. Her scrubbed, harsh, mongrel look disappeared, her face filled out and glowed like a poppy.

At rarer and rarer intervals did she pounce on her sister and try to snatch her from the bonfire. For one thing it was into Harry's hands rather than into Mrs. Jardine's that Cherry had fallen; and Harry presented no sort of target for desperate acts of will and duty. Assuming no authority, exercising none by word or deed, he took away her weapons. If she shared nothing else with her mother's mother, she had in common with her an outstanding positiveness of nature. Their feet rang on concrete, their fare was solid. But Harry was a world extinct. Appearing and vanishing in room and garden, haunting the window, he seemed to be proclaiming: "I am nothing"; and this sole assertion, made with singular delicacy and weight, made a cloak, vaporous but impenetrably enshrouding, to throw over Cherry.

One day, instead of locking herself into the bathroom with Cherry to supervise her evening bath, Maisie simply stayed out in the garden with me. "Ask Lucy to bath you," she said.

That was the end.

# V I

MAISIE was the first woman friend I ever had. There were plenty of girls, then, and afterwards, with whom I played games and exchanged confidences, but my relationship with Maisie was so far removed from the waist-entwined, I've got a secret, giggle and whisper it, cross your heart you won't tell level that I think of it now as adult. It was she whose steadfast passion and disillusionment, laid bare so firmly, so without obliquity or reserve, first planted deep within the feathery shifting webs and folds of my consciousness that seed which grows a shape too huge, too complex ever to see in outline, clear and whole: the monster, human experience.

We sat in the fork of the walnut tree, and she said:

"You know, I loathed you when I first saw you. I thought you were going to be the most ghastly beast."

"Oh . . . why?" I felt hurt.

"She would go on and on about you . . ."

"What did she say?"

"Well, saying your Grannie had been godmother to my mother and how she hoped this what d'you call it—generation—would be friends again, and all that sort of muck."

I reflected. It seemed a venal offence, but to Maisie it had appeared a sinister plot. She added:

"And now you're my best friend." She picked up my hand and gripped it in hers, which was tanned, freckled, bony, and said: "Promise something."

"I promise. What?"

"You'll be my best friend."

I considered one or two others among my circle who had qualifications for this title, but decided to grade them down, and replied without hesitation:

"Yes. All right."

We sat silent for a few moments, holding hands. I was conscious of the flattery, from a girl older than myself. I see now that her life had split her, so that part of her was unusually childish and part had taken the rigid form of premature maturity. After a while she said:

"She's given up talking about my mother—I wasn't going to have any of that. Malcolm can let her feed him up with it if he likes, but I won't. Besides, I promised Father . . ."

"What did you promise him?"

"That I'd *never* . . . that I'd never, never listen to her."

The words burst forth with explosive violence. She stared out into the garden. The leafy, sun-saturated shade we sat in brought out a burning green light in her eyes.

"He told me she's a liar. And she made my mother a liar. He said if ever he caught any of us lying he'd whip us within an inch of our lives. Once he found out Malcolm had told a lie. He was quite young—only eight—it was soon after Mother went

44

away. He said he hadn't gone to the Park to sail his boat when he had. . . ."

"What did your father do?"

"He thrashed him."

I wanted to ask: "Within an inch of his life?"—but I could not muster the question. I was silent.

"Malcolm's afraid of Father," said Maisie. "I despise cowards, but it's not all his fault. Father's awfully down on him. They're not quite fair to each other really. After that time—when he told a lie—Auntie Mack went in to Father, and I heard them arguing in very loud voices. I don't know what they said. When I went to say good-night to Father he was crying."

"Are you sure?"

"Certain. Sobbing."

"What did you do?"

"Nothing. There was nothing I could do. He was missing Mother. I couldn't say: 'Cheer up, she'll be back soon,' or, 'Cheer up, we'll manage all right without her.' He'd forbidden us ever to mention her name again. He pulled me on his lap and said he was a very cruel, unkind father to us, so of course I said no, he was the nicest one in the world. I suppose Auntie Mack had been saying things."

"Is she your real aunt?"

"Oh no. She's an old spinster cousin of father's, or something. She came to look after us after Mother went away."

"Do you like her?"

"No, not much. She's a fussy old ass, always talking about her stomach or her liver. Her name's Miss Flora Mackenzie. Still, she not too bad. She's quite fair." She paused to put a toffee in her mouth and to give me one, and then added: "She did one thing that was decent. After Mother went, she used to send us postcards, masses of them, from all over the place—abroad. Of course we loved getting them. It showed she hadn't forgotten us anyway. But Father had made Auntie Mack swear if any letters did come she wouldn't let us have them. So what she used to do was—when these postcards came she gave them to us secretly and let us keep them a whole day, and then we were on our

45

honour to give them back to her, and she burnt them. We steamed the stamps off and kept them in a box—locked. It's a Spanish box mother gave Malcolm once. Father never knew. He'd have turned her straight out of the house if he had."

"For doing something behind his back . . .?"

"Mm. It was awful for her, I do see. First she'd sworn and then she'd broken her sworn word. She explained to us. She said it was a burden she'd have to bear to her dying day, but she'd thought it over and over and taken it to God, and she'd decided we ought to have Mother's postcards and she could never, never tell him so; so there was nothing to do but trust us not to betray her. So we promised. It was a pity deceiving Father, but we had to because we couldn't have made him understand. . . . She always chose lovely postcards. There was never anything on them except: Love. No address. Of course we couldn't let Cherry have hers. She was only a baby. She'd have blabbed."

She lay back full length along the bough, and gazed up into the tree's great branch-plaited lucent crown of foliage.

"But after about a year," she said, "the postcards stopped coming."

"I wonder why . . .?"

"I suppose she thought it wasn't any use going on. I thought perhaps she'd died, but Auntie Mack said no, they'd have heard for certain. She said mothers didn't ever forget their children, so . . ." I stole a nervous glance at her, but there was no need to be nervous: she spoke and gazed upwards with reflective calm. "I wonder if I shall ever see her again," she said. "It would be queer . . . she's been gone about five years now."

After a silence, during which I indulged in fantasies of bringing about a reunion, I asked:

"Why did she go away?"

"Because she didn't like living with Father."

"Why did she marry him then?"

"I suppose she liked him at first and then she didn't." She continued with a touch of irritation: "People can change their minds, can't they? Haven't you ever liked a person to begin with and then gone off them?"

"Oh, yes."

But as applied to married couples, this came to me as a new conception. Till this moment, in my view, men and women got married, had children, lived in the same house until they died. They did quarrel, that I realised; but I had never imagined their relations governed by feelings susceptible of total revolution.

"Did she tell you she didn't like living with him?"

"No. But you could tell she didn't. Afterwards I asked Auntie Mack, and she said that was the reason. She said it was the fatal mating of two warring natures: like putting a delicate Arab thoroughbred and a plain working sort of English cob into one team."

"Is that what she said?"

"Yes."

"Did you know she was going away?"

"No. She went to pay a visit to a friend in London. And she never came back."

"Of course," she went on judicially, "Father's got an awful temper. Living in the East gives people bad tempers. Malcolm and I were both born in India. Once when I was a baby, Father came in one night and found a huge, deadly poisonous snake curled up on my cot, ready to strike."

I nearly fell out of the tree.

"What did he do?" I asked in a cold faint.

"He got a gun and shot it in the head. Shot it dead. Mother was out at a party and our Ayah had dozed off on the veranda. There was an awful row. He sent away our Ayah. They say I was much too young to remember anything about it, but it's funny, I always think I do remember it." She sat up again, astride of the bough, swinging her bare legs. We had another toffee. "I only *really* remember a few things. I left when I was four. Mother brought me and Malcolm back. We lived in a hotel in London. It was very nice, because we saw much more of Mother. Oh!—there was such a funny old lady. . . ." Her eyes went suddenly fixed, illumined with reminiscence. "She used to come and take us in the Park, and to the Zoo. I do remember her. She'd known Mother when she was a little girl. She had a little

*47*

cape of curly black fur, like black lamb, and a wee bonnet with jet things in it, and jet earrings. We liked her very much. She *was* small. Almost a dwarf, I should think."

An electric shock whizzed through me.

"It sounds exactly like Tilly!" I cried.

"It *was* Tilly. That was her name. Tilly."

We stared at one another, choking with agitation. I tumbled out an explanation of Tilly—that she was ours, and had been our grandmother's; and promised to present her in the flesh to Maisie when she came on her next visit. I had a confused but powerful notion that thus I should be instrumental in reforging some mysterious vital missing link in Maisie's family history. We discussed how it could have come about that our Tilly should, for a brief space, have been their Tilly.

"I bet," said Maisie, "*she* had something to do with it."

"Who?"

She jerked her head towards the house.

"Mrs. Jardine?"

Maisie had already told me that never, never would she be persuaded to call Mrs. Jardine Grannie. When speaking to her she stubbornly avoided any form of address. For the rest, she was a personal pronoun, emphatically enunciated; or else she was Mrs. Jardine.

"Because that's when *she* turned up." Maisie looked deeply, darkly, into my face, as if to interpret there the sinister meaning of that visit. "Yes. That's another thing I sort of remember and don't remember. She came to the hotel. . . ." She paused, struggling with the blank, stiff shutter of memory. "I know she did. Somebody in white, with a white parasol, sitting on the sofa, and we came in—and she turned round and looked at us— and Mother told us in a sharp sort of voice to go up to our room at once. . . . That's all I can think of. But it's funny: the first moment I saw her here, I thought: She's exactly like I thought she'd be." She sighed and lay back again. "Then we left London and went to Paris. I remember *easily* the lift man there. Then a man with a dark sort of face, called Marcel, began to come. I've often wondered if she went to live with him when she went away. He called her *mignonne* or *chèrie,* things like that, and he was always teasing her. I hated him because when he first saw Malcolm and me he said something that meant——" She stopped a moment. "We were ugly."

"What did he say?"

"I couldn't understand, but I know he meant we weren't like her to look at. He laughed; and she gave a kind of laugh too. It's true, of course, we're not—not a bit. Cherry is more."

"What sort of face did she have?"

"Wait here," said Maisie. "Don't move till I come back. I'm going to fetch something."

She swung down from the tree, ran full gallop across the lawn and disappeared into the house. In no time she was back, and, resuming her place beside me, took something from her pocket, told me to stretch my hand out, and placed it in my palm.

"On your life, don't drop it," she said fiercely.

It was an oval miniature, set in brilliants, backed with sapphire blue velvet.

"That's my mother."

Long curving neck. Bare shoulders, bosom swathed in blue chiffon. Dark hair elaborately piled and puffed out in lateral wings. Eyes painted a melting violet, skin snow-white with faintest wild-rose cheeks. She smiled mysteriously. She was Mrs. Darling. She was a French New Year card angel-face, set in tinsel and blossoms. She was every child's dream of a beautiful mother.

"I found it the other day in the drawer of the cabinet, in the drawing-room," said Maisie. "What do you think of it?"

Her voice was casual, edged with a quiver of triumph.

"Lovely," I breathed. "Was she *really* like that?"

"Exactly like that," declared Maisie. "At least, in evening dress. She wore evening dress a lot. She was the most beautiful person I ever saw." She took the portrait from me, and curled her hand hungrily round the frame. "Wish I dared pinch it. I wonder if she'd miss it."

"Ask her if you can have it."

"Never. I'll never ask her for *anything.*" She glared.

"Truly and honestly," I said, "won't you ever stop hating her?"

49

What I had in mind was the awkwardness of my own position. Though by now I was prepared to think Mrs. Jardine might—must, somehow—be wicked, I was powerless to resist her magnetic influence. So soon as I was in her presence my whole being churned with passion for her. And now I had been elected best friend, and must receive suggestions detrimental to Mrs. Jardine. If only Maisie could have been indifferent to or bored by her grandmother I could have preserved my loyalty intact; but Mrs. Jardine obsessed her; she felt the pull as strongly as I did. Any day, any moment she might abandon the harsh, gruelling strain in the opposite direction, and collapse, and flow all yielding into her orbit; but she never would. Any hour, hate might tip over and become love; she would never permit it.

Setting her jaw, she said grimly:

"Not as long as I live. It would be letting Father down. He talked to us before we came. He said she'd been trying for years to get hold of us, but he wouldn't let her. But now he'd got to go into hospital for this treatment, he didn't want to leave us alone with Auntie Mack, because she was very run down from having such a lot to do after he got ill. And there wasn't enough money to send us somewhere for a nice holiday—so he'd decided we'd better come here for a bit." She fell silent; then went on in a stifled but resolute voice: "He said he'd been feeling . . . if anything happened to him ever, it might be a good thing to have a rich relation to take an interest in us. He hasn't got any relatives, or any money." She swallowed. "I said I didn't need anybody, but he said the others—Cherry anyway. . . . He said what I told you—never to believe anything she said. . . . He talked about Mother, he hasn't ever before. He said she had *ruined* her."

A shiver went down me.

"How?" Ruin was a terrible word, almost as terrible as dead.

"She left her when she was a little girl."

"What, ran away from her?"

"I don't know. But she did, he said. And then she tried to get her back, and she couldn't. Father said that ruined her. I don't quite know why, but it was something to do with her having to be brought up in a—in an unsuitable way. He said he wasn't going to have us ruined. I was all right, he said, and he was placing Cherry in my charge, and I was to watch out for her." She brooded. "How I do wonder what happened when she turned up at the hotel that time. . . ."

"Do you think . . . Don't you think perhaps *your* mother will turn up again sometime . . . soon?"

"It *would* be queer." I could see her concentrating, as she must have concentrated a thousand times before, upon a vision of the meeting. "There's just *one* thing, one rather unkind thing, I mean, I should have to say to her."

"What?"

"That it would have been better if she'd taken Cherry. It wasn't fair on Cherry never to have had a mother. She was only a baby and she can't remember her at all. It wasn't so bad for Malcolm and me—we were a sort of pair—more on Father's side."

"Didn't you love her then?"

"Yes, I did." Her sudden anger wounded, alarmed and shamed me. "And she loved us. If you think she didn't, you're wrong. Anybody who thinks she didn't is a fool and I'll murder them." After a few moments, she put the whole bag of toffee into my lap, and said mildly: "What I meant was, we take after him more —we're more his. Cherry's different."

I said humbly:

"Yes. I see."

"She didn't have the same start as us. She was born after we all came back to England. We never went back to India after that time. I don't quite understand what Father did out there —I know he was quite important. But he gave it up. I have a sort of feeling it was because Mother said she wouldn't go back. Anyway, he came home and we all went to live in Newcastle. We seemed to be rich in India, but since then we've been poor. Father got a new job, teaching in a big school—the one Malcolm goes to. Newcastle isn't very nice, but Northumberland's lovely. Oh, I adore it! In the holidays we go to the coast, or to a little farm in the middle of the moors. And I ride." She glowed. "I wish I was there now. With you. I could never tell you how happy I am there. We could ride together."

I was afraid of the very shape of a horse, and my riding lessons had been given up as a bad job, but I was ashamed to tell her so, and agreed with enthusiasm.

"It's the middle of September now," she said. "Father told me he'd send for us as soon as he could. I wonder when he will. . . . He told me to write once a week, and of course I have. But I'm a hopeless letter writer—I never can think what to say. I just say we're all well and having a nice time. . . . Because we are. I said Harry was kind and the house and garden were very nice. I haven't said anything at all about *her*. As a matter of fact, it all seemed so difficult, I didn't know what to say. . . . I told him about you."

"Did you honestly? What did you say?"

"Oh—what you're called, and you came to play, and you were nice."

The indistinct figure of Mr. Thomson appeared to me for a moment, fitted with the head of a plain sort of horse, receiving news of me in a hospital bed. Hitherto, my impression of him had been a gloomy, unsympathetic one, but now I began to warm towards him.

"He only writes back a few lines," said Maisie. "It's ten days now since I had a letter at all. . . ." She rolled over on her stomach, and stretched herself out along the branch with her head laid sideways on her arms. "You know," she said, "we can make anything happen if we want it to. Do you know that, or don't you?"

"No," I said. "I didn't know." I hesitated. "Do you mean—praying?"

"No, I don't mean praying. I mean *yourself!* If you want something with *every scrap* of you, you'll get it."

The moment she had said it, the idea seemed my own. It had the simplicity of all great revelations. A megalomaniac certitude coursed through me like draughts of ginger beer. Of course!—I could, I would have everything I wanted! I had only to want it.

"For instance," said Maisie, "I *know* Father will get better."

52

She lay perfectly still along the bough for another few moments, then sat up. She was still holding the miniature in her hand, but now she thrust it into her pocket.

"I must put this back," she said. "Cherry said she had toothache, so she's taken her to the dentist in the car, but they'll be back soon. Come on."

We lowered ourselves from the tree and walked together over the lawn.

"I heard her tell Harry our teeth had been shockingly neglected and we ought all to be taken to a proper dentist immediately. There's nothing wrong with our teeth."

"We're made to brush ours night and morning. Are you?"

I hoped my tone did not imply how unlikely, judging from appearances, this seemed.

"I brush them quite often enough," she said. "Anyway, this everlasting brushing's all rot. Natives never brush theirs. She's not going to take *me* to have all my teeth pulled out by any of her dentists—with her standing over me and gloating."

# PART TWO

I T was not long after this conversation that Tilly came for her pre-autumnal visit. She had suddenly grown much thinner—even we noticed this—and her face was as shrivelled and yellow as the dried kernel of a walnut. The sickly smell of age that always hung about her was more than ever noticeable. She was so light now, we could lift her round the room as easily as we could our giant baby brother; but when we told our mother what fun this was, she forbade it, saying that Tilly had not been very well and we were not to bother her. After that we realised that everything pointed to Tilly's imminent death, and we avoided her for a bit, feeling that she emanated some nameless infection. Then, a few days having passed during which we saw her trotting up and down stairs to meals as usual, and kneeling to cut out a new cover for the schoolroom ottoman, the miasma that enveloped her faded away, and we mounted to her magnetic room to sit with her as usual. Never had her flood of reminiscences poured out in such unbridled spate.

She wore a crocheted cross-over, grey with a border of violet, over her black alpaca while she sat and sewed. She said she was feeling the cold this year. This seemed strange to me, as I looked down from her high window at the parched lawn and the dull, prematurely shrivelled leaves of the grove of chestnut trees. September was wearing away, the drought continued; but she said the summers weren't what they used to be when she was a girl and our grandmother made her bring her sewing out under the trees of a hot afternoon. She wouldn't be surprised if those roasting summers weren't over and done with: our grandmother —she was a great one for a bit of education thrown in while you worked—had said that as time got on the sun would give off less and less heat. At the recollection of these bits of education, the chuckle rattled up out of her throat, more witch-like than ever.

"Tilly, do you remember a lady called Mrs. Jardine?" I said.

She was manipulating a sable collar of my mother's. She had been apprenticed as a girl to a Polish furrier and knew everything about the skins of animals. She dropped her work and considered. Her *tic*, so much more pronounced now, made her head shake above her boned collar with rhythmical violence, like one of those Chinese mandarin ornaments that you set nodding by a touch. No, she didn't recollect any such person. A film came over her eyes, clouding them with a sullen melancholy. I felt accused of forcing on her proofs of failing memory. She'd met a good few in her time, she said; it stood to reason she couldn't call to mind every Mrs. This and Madam That. . . .

"I only asked," I said, "because she lives at the Priory now, and she's got three grandchildren and we've made friends and one of them, called Maisie, says when she was very little they lived in a London hotel with their mother, and you came and took them out in the Park."

"*Me?*" She fairly squawked at me. "Take strange children in the Park? I never. The very idea! She can't be right in 'er 'ead."

"And to the Zoo. Oh, Tilly, I do think it was you. She remembers your name and what you wore and everything. Shall I show her to you next time she comes to tea? You might recognise her. Her mother was Mrs. Jardine's little girl, who had a funny name: Ianthe."

At this word Tilly's little frame seemed suddenly to contract, then expand. I saw memory strike her, then pour all through her.

"Miss Ianthe," she said in a flat, automatic way. "Oh yes, she was godmother to '*er*.'" I understood that "she" referred to my grandmother. "That was Miss Sibyl's child. . . . Mrs. Herbert, I should say. That was her married name. Knowing her as a girl, Miss Sibyl always come more natural. That's one of them Greek names, ain't it?—I-anthe? That's what *she* said. 'It's a bit of a tongue-twister,' I says. 'Nonsense, Tilly. It's as simple as it's beautiful. It's one of the most beautiful of all the Greek names. It means——' somethink or other, I forget now what she told me.

'Greek to me,' I says. She never minded a bit of a jokey answer. She knew it was just my way."

Her voice trailed off. She looked vacant and foolish. The pouches under her chin wobbled, her earrings tinkled faintly as her head nodded, nodded up and down. I waited, digging pins into her red emery cushion made in the shape of a big bursting strawberry—immemorial part of Tilly's personal luggage.

"Now do you remember her, Tilly?" I ventured at last.

"Remember 'oo?" she said, rather querulously. "I dare say I do. What of it? I 'adn't 'eard yet my mem'ry's failin'—though there's some a bit nearer than Marble Arch would be glad to make it out, no doubt, to suit their book. It's peculiar what jealousy can demean a man to. But there! *Man!*"

She pointed an unspeakable meaning with a venomous snort and chuckle. I saw the old dragon—her feud with our butler—about to rear its hoary head, and said hastily, to distract her:

"Tell me about Miss Sibyl. What was she like?"

"Oh, she was a Beauty, was Miss Sibyl. The Young Beauty of the season," said Tilly, smiling, musing. "There was more beauties then too. There was Lily Langtry—the Jersey Lily. But she wasn't the only one. . . . I stood on a chair in the Park to watch *'er* drive by."

"Who? Miss Sibyl?"

"Certindly not. Whatever would I want to do that for, when she was in and out of my room all day? Yes, and dressed 'er for 'er first ball. She did look a picture that night, I will say. 'I shall never care for Society, Tilly. It's all a trumpery sham. I want to do something different—something to show I've a brain as well as a face. . . .' She was 'igh-spirited, that was all. She needed guidin'. She was a orphan, of course. I dare say that 'ad somethink to do with it. She'd 'ad a funny bringin' up from all accounts. There was somebody was 'er guardian—the name's slipped me—no better than 'e should be. Well-connected too. One night there was a ring at the front door and in she flew. 'Madrona, will you take me in?' That was the name she called 'er—Madrona. She'd run 'alf across London in 'er evenin' gownd and sating slippers. She did pant. I never 'eard the rights of it

56

—there was a lot of talk. But there she stayed. Of course she'd often stayed before, just for short visits—the families 'ad been friendly a long way back, I fancy. She'd be goin' on nineteen then. Oh, she was a wild thing! She did what she pleased and she said what she pleased—but I never thought there was no vice in 'er—just 'igh-spirited; and didn't 'er eyes give a sparkle like, if anybody crossed 'er!"

At this evocative stroke, I felt my inside turn over. Oh yes, I knew Miss Sibyl. Something came up in my throat and almost suffocated me. Tilly went on:

"But she never tried no tricks with '*er*. It was: 'Yes, darlin' Madrona, certindly, sweetest Madrona'—as meek as milk. Talk of love and gratitoode—she went on as if she fair worshipped 'er."

"You mean she fair worshipped Grandma?"

"That's what I said."

"She still does!" I cried in triumph. "She's always talking about her. Oh Tilly, you *must* see her! Her name's Mrs. Jardine now. Did she have another husband who died?"

"Not as I know of." A complicated expression crossed Tilly's face. "Oh, 'e died in 'is own good time, I dare say," she added cryptically. "I don't know nothink about that."

"But you said she was called Mrs. Herbert——"

"And so she was." Tilly closed her lips sharply. "I'm not likely to forget that—considerin' she married 'im from your grandfather's house. Mr. Charles 'Erbert. I'm not one to put names on people that don't belong to 'em."

I realised that my approach was faulty, and that I must be wily and devious until the tide flowed up again and overwhelmed such scruples as appeared to have risen.

"Can I thread your needle?" I said.

She handed it over to me, and I threaded it and gave it back to her; and she told me to look in her left-hand top drawer if I fancied a fondant. When I had eaten it, I said:

"Did Grandma love her too?"

"She did." Tilly laid down her work and mopped her eyes. Tears often rolled out of them nowadays—tears of age and weaksightedness. I had got over thinking them tears of grief. "There are some natures," she said, "that's treacherous all through. They bites the 'and that feeds 'em. They do it once, and it's forgiven and forgotten. But the time comes they done it once too often, and you can't forgive nor forget. Never trust no one, not even your own flesh and blood, that's once done you a wicked wrong. One day they'll do you another, you may be bound."

"Did you ever know any treacherous people, Tilly?"

"I've come across one or two in my life. And so did your grandma. To 'er scathe and sorrer."

The rhythm was re-established now; the scratch of needle on thimble, the hands' unconscious, faultlessly delicate movement over and through their work, the voice tick-tocking on with a sort of regular rattling beat in it, calling up in the camphor and time-smelling room the presence of my grandmother, so sharp, so faint, so quick, so dead—a presence more composed of sounds —her laugh, her music, her way of putting a thing—than of images.

Once, long ago, at a Christmas party, someone turned out the lights and switched on a gramophone with a tin horn. A nasal goblin voice rasped out the words: *Edison Bell Record;* and then, with a shiver down my spine, I heard the voice of Henry Irving in *The Bells*. Tilly was like one of those antique gramophones—a shaky, trivial, wheezing medium reproducing skeleton dramas over and over again. The body of human life was drained out, yet a mystery, another, piercing reality remained.

"What happened?" I said. "Was she—treacherous? Miss Sibyl?"

"She brought 'er own ruin on 'er," said Tilly. "And tried to bring down others in 'er fall."

I leaned back, feeling weak. I tried to summon up Mrs. Jardine, with all her kind, considerate, fascinating ways, presiding at the tea-table, bandaging us, resting on her sofa with all the thoughts of her solitude, that I had so often tried to imagine, secret behind her calm, stern, noble face; or strolling with the gardener along the herbaceous border, round the kitchen garden, into the greenhouses, energetically discussing, as I had so often heard her, what was to be altered, what planned and planted.

58

But this humane, matronly figure, with all her richness stored in her, distilling quiet, had vanished into limbo. Groping for her, I saw, instead, an icy fiend: Miss Sibyl. I saw her snaky arms coiled round the pillars of the house of my grandparents, great blocks of masonry cracking, about to crash down on her, on all. I remembered her stroking my arm once, saying: "Pretty arms"; adding: "When I was a girl, I had arms like white snakes." Here was this word again: *Ruin*.

"Ruin?" I said shakily. "How did she . . .? What did she . . .?"

"She went wrong," said Tilly in a stony voice. "That's what she done. She flounced off to lay down on a bed of red roses, and many's the time I've thought it turned out nettles and brambles under 'er. Many's the time I've said to myself I wouldn't be 'er, tossing in the watches of the night—not if the Emperor of India stepped down from 'is throne and offered me the ruby from the middle front of 'is crown."

She was silent, brooding. No feed line occurred to me.

"Of course," she went on presently, " 'e was a sober sort of a gentleman. Methodical. All books, book, books, and fiddle, fiddle with 'is precious china, and tinkle, tinkle, tinkle on the 'arpsichord. Not like a real man—for all 'e was a 'andsome well-set-up sort of a feller. A good bit older than 'er. Very 'igh educated, and money—plenty of it. That was a lot to do with 'er takin' 'im, I wouldn't be surprised—though she would 'ave it it was 'is blessed mind. 'He's got the most distinguished mind I ever met, Tilly,' she says. 'A mind I can really respect. I can learn from him. I can look up to him. I could never have married a young man—they're all so silly.' She used to sit and chat as it might be you children—only she was more of a grown-up young lady, of course—and I was a bit younger in those days. 'He's never cared for female society, you know, Tilly,' she says. 'He says women don't understand ideas.' 'They understands one or two when it comes to gettin' married,' I says. 'After, if not before.' It was just my fun—though I 'adn't ought to of made so bold. Lor', she didn't know no more than this reel of cotton what I was after. She'd stare you straight in the face out of them great blue eyes of 'ers; they made you feel small—though it was only my fun. She was as ignorant as a blessed curate, for all her talk and 'eadstrong ways. That was 'er trouble—nobody couldn't never 'elp 'er nor teach 'er. She thought she knew it all. It was others 'oo needed teachin', accordin' to 'er way of lookin' at it. . . . Well, she married 'im, ideas and all."

Tilly fell silent, and I timidly hazarded:

"Who was it she married, Tilly?"

"This Mr. Charles 'Erbert I'm tellin' you about. It was a lovely weddin'. Oh, she was a beautiful bride!—it made your inside work to see 'er. They went off to live in Paris. 'E was in the Dip —whatever the name is—Dippermatic. And that was the last 'appy sight we seen of her. No, she never run in to number fifteen all up on her toes and lovin' and sure of 'er welcome again."

"What! Did Grandma never see her again?"

"Oh yes. She sor 'er again." Tilly's head jigged with increased violence. "When others 'ad cast 'er off, she sor 'er. Till the deed was done that put a finish to it all. Yes, and after. For she sor 'er on 'er deathbed. . . . Ah, you can wipe out the score when it comes to the last, but you can't unplay the game that was played and never should 'ave been."

This doom-fraught speech, delivered with appropriate power, penetrated me like a probe, exploring depths that terrified me. With passionate reluctance, I insisted:

"What did she do, Tilly?"

I must have it, the worst, the Sin, straight out. But Tilly was creating drama. She had no intention of destroying her suspense to gratify a child's banal curiosity. She busied herself with the fur, turning it this way and that, looking haughty and malicious. Presently she thrust obliquely at her object, from a different angle.

"I was never one to set myself up to judge the rights and wrongs of a thing. Leave that to the preachers and all the old nosey-parkers that trots off to church in their best bonnets to pray for sinners of a Sunday. Forgive us as we forgive them—ha! the whited sepulchrums, I know 'em! They gives out a nasty sickish sort of a smell. *I* can smell 'em! What she wanted was a flesh and blood man to govern 'er. Break 'er and make 'er. Mark my words, 'e was better furnished in the top storey than 'e was elsewhere, was that joker."

A convulsion of laughter seized Tilly. Aware of its lewdness, I wrestled fruitlessly to attach nameless implications to a whirling composite picture of wardrobes, chairs, tables, beds, and, at the very tip-top of a perpendicular staircase, one well-set-up gentleman tinkling with china fingers on the harpsichord.

Tilly continued in a meditative way:

"It would come over 'er like, gradual, unknown to 'erself at first, I dare say, she could do with a bit less in the attics and a bit more in the basement. She'd dwell on that—only natchral—I been through it myself. And she'd plenty of time on 'er 'ands. Sooner or later it would stick in 'er mind there was somethink wrong. *Somethink wrong!—tra-la—somethink wrong. . . .*" A cracked midget's voice came out of Tilly's throat, piping and humming. "There was a music 'all song went like that when I was a girl. . . . Ah dear!" She mopped her eyes.

I smiled politely, but said at once, to re-direct her wavering grip:

"*Was* there something wrong?"

"That's as may be," she answered primly. "It's accordin' to 'ow you might look at it if you wasn't one of them Saintly Sammys throwin' up their soapy 'ands and rubbin' 'em over a pretty woman gone wrong. Not that it didn't seem all peace and purrin' on the 'earth at the first. The baby come along—pretty prompt, I will say—and oh Lor'!—the letters that was wrote then! You'd 'ave thought the Queen of England 'ad give birth to the Second Comin'! And what 'er eyes and 'er ears and 'er 'air was, somethink never seen on earth before, and she took the breast like a blessèd archangel. And Mr. Charles as proud as a dog with two tails, dandlin' 'er in 'is arms and singin' 'er to sleep. The 'appiest couple in Christendom they was now. And bless you, the bringin' up she was to 'ave. She was to stand godmother, of course——"

"Who? Grandma?"

"That's what I said. And they'd picked on I-anthe, because any one called that was bound to grow up into a beauty. . . . Ah dear!"

A human expression softened Tilly's face. She leaned back; and her myopic eyes, charged as I had never before seen them with pity and retrospective sadness, stared out of the window towards the treetops.

"She did get to be a pretty little thing too—winnin'. She favoured 'is side—and they was a good-lookin' lot. Oh, 'e thought the world of 'er. 'E 'ad 'is natchral feelin's, I wouldn't wish to deny. It broke 'is pride when she 'opped it. It turns a man sour when a woman breaks 'is pride. You couldn't expect generosity of 'im—though she did. She would."

"Miss Sibyl?"

"Yes, Miss Sibyl. Whatever she done was always right, and oh, the surprise when others didn't see it that way, and raised objections!"

"She broke his pride?"

"Ah, you could tell that's where it got 'im by the way 'e took it. I'd never go so far to say there was much love spilt when *that* tray was dropped—not at the end. A broken 'eart's more easy put together, and don't leave such nasty jagged edges where the break's been stuck. 'E was the proudest feller—gentleman—I ever struck. She took and crushed 'is pride."

I saw that dual figure, the dove-girl-Mrs. Jardine, wrench something hard, like a seal or a charm, from the breast of a shadowy male figure, and crush it into fragments with the strong, short, ringed fingers I knew. In doubt and perplexity I ventured:

"She did it when she hopped it?"

"She did."

"How did she do that?"

"Oh, she tucked up 'er flouncy skirts and was off one summer's evenin'."

"I see," I said, untruthfully.

" 'E'd give a ring at the bell. 'Where is Ma*dame?*' 'E'd be all ready dressed up, you see, to take 'er to the opera or the ball. 'Oh, Ma*dame?* She went out some hours ago, Moossew. She left a note for you in 'er boodwar.' " Tilly minced, rolled her eyes stagily in the style of an imaginary French lady's maid. 'Ah, thank you, Maree. You may go.' *'Oui, Moossew. Mercy, Moossew.'* Up the stairs 'e'd walk, very slow and dignified—smellin' a rat, I wouldn't be surprised. There was the letter propped up on the mantel—scented and sealed. 'E opens it. *Gone,* 'e reads. *Gone with the one I love. . . .*"

"Oh!" I gasped, fatally interrupting. "Is that what she really said?"

There was a dead pause; then Tilly said peevishly:

" 'Ow should I know? I wasn't there, lookin' over 'is shoulder, was I?"

But presently, observing my mortification, she relented and said:

"I'll lay my best seal jacket it was somethink after that style, though. 'Igh-flown. 'Owever she put it, that's what she done."

"She went with the one she loved?"

"Well, you can put it that way. No doubt she would. And mean it at the time. 'E was a nasty bit of work."

"Was his name—was it a gentleman called Major Jardine?" I asked, trembling.

"No, it wasn't nothink of the sort. What's come over you with your Jardine? Gentleman indeed! Is it likely? It was one of them furriners. I can't lay my 'ands on 'is name. Best forgotten too. An artist, or one of that sort of lot, so I 'eard."

"Did Mr. Charles—was he very sorry?"

"Ah! . . . sorry . . ." Tilly shook her head dubiously.

"More cross?"

"What she'd done, you see, she'd caught 'im a slap clean across the face in front of the 'ole world. And 'im in 'is position! Somethink stronger than sorry 'e'd feel. I'd 'eard a bit about 'er before the scandal. There was a young girl, lady's maid to Lady—the name's gone—out there at the time. Swiss, she was, a nice steady girl. She come over to England with 'er lady, and 'er and me scraped up an acquaintance when yer grandmother visited. She told me what a lot of talk went on. I was ever so grieved and shocked to 'ear it. Of course, mind you, she was a beauty. I dare say the flattery turned 'er 'ead—though I never would 'ave thought it in the old days. She might 'ave wore 'er face back to front for all the notice she took of other people's noticin' it. You couldn't spoil 'er . . . so I'd 'ave said. But she changed. It's a funny thing, but some girls do when they gets to be married —in partickler them innocent, wild-spirited sort—all over the place and up in the air—straight out of their schoolrooms. Anythink for a sensation!—that's what three years' 'igh society done for Miss Sibyl. The more eyes was on 'er, the more outrageious she'd act—just to give 'em somethink extra to wag their tongues about. Like as if it was strong drink and sent 'er frantic. And spend, spend, spend! . . . Them French dressmakers aren't too bad; they got 'er up to advantage, I dare say. She was short built, but all in proportion, and carried 'er 'ead like a queen. I'd like to 'ave seen 'er in some of 'er toilets. And goin' about with a white monkey or some such nasty mucky animal on 'er shoulder. And parties. Gettin' that little mite—I-anthe—up out of 'er cot in the middle of the night—winter, mind you—in a bit of gauze and spangly wings, to be set on the table in a basket and lifted out as the Spirit of the Noo Year and made to throw rose petals, or some such silliness. But it was all show-off, if you understand. She caused talk, but I'll lay my oath she never done anythink she shouldn't. Though she 'ad the men all round 'er. 'E couldn't master 'er, so 'e let 'er 'ave 'er 'ead. It came like a thunderclap at the end. She run off with a nobody."

"Did she take Ianthe with her?"

I had a vision of a white form, all veils and flying flounces, running in the night through city streets with a naked winged cherub on her shoulder.

"No, that she didn't."

Though tempted, I refrained from asking: "Did she take the monkey?" and after a pause, Tilly continued in a bitter voice: "No. She 'ad other fish to fry. Any little 'elpless 'angers-on wouldn't 'ave suited 'er book just then. No—she didn't give it a lot of thought at the time—it and its precious upbringin' and that extra special future it was to 'ave."

"Fancy leaving her own little girl behind!" For the first time I felt shocked.

"Ah, you may well say." Tilly shook her head, fetched a brooding sigh. "Ah, and it turned out a serpent to bite 'er, that night's work. It's against nature to forsake your own flesh and blood, and when you go against nature, nature pays out. And once you done it, it's done. You can declare till you come out like a 'Ighland tartan you didn't mean it, and done it for the best, it won't butter no parsnips. You don't get back the child you've lost."

At these fatal words, tears, real ones, from the depths of her unstanched woe, began to pour down Tilly's cheeks. I got up and hugged her and gave her a kiss. I knew the phantom of the Little Feller had risen, troubled by this contemplation of maternal shortcomings.

"God took him, Tilly, you know he did," I urged in broken tones.

"Ah," said Tilly perfunctorily. "No doubt."

God took him, I said so because she always said so; but it seemed, not for the first time, as if these comfortable words administered no comfort. God took him because He loved him, because He wished to confer distinction on Tilly by selecting her little one to go before, and await her in the Better Land. Oh yes! —he was in a Better Place, she'd meet him by and by. . . . No. God took him to spite her, punish her for neglect or ignorance, something she'd left undone that might have saved him to grow up like other women's sons.

"I never left his bedside day nor night. 'Put on your coat, Mammy,' 'e says, all of sudden. 'Let's go out.' 'When you're a bit better, my duck,' I says. ' 'As Dadda wound the clock?' 'e says. Fancy 'is little mind bein' on that! 'E always took an interest in that clock. It was one of them cuckoo-clocks—come from Bo'emia. It was carved pretty—just what would take a child's fancy. ' 'As Dadda wound the clock?' 'e says. Them was 'is last words. A bit after that I saw the change. 'E never struggled. Just let out one sort of a sigh. And breathed 'is little last."

Often and with passionate attention I had assisted at this deathbed, extracting with Tilly the bitter-sweet savour of every harrowing detail. But to-day, time pressed: I could not linger at it. So soon as her voice told me that emotion had begun to be recollected in tranquillity, I eased her tactfully back on to her true course.

"Fancy Ianthe not having her mother there if ever she was ill and wanted her."

"Ah," agreed Tilly. "You got the marrer of it there. They all said what a blessin' she's only a baby—she won't remember 'er nor miss 'er. But I know different. I sor it. It left its mark. She was a funny little soul. The questions she'd ask!—You couldn't answer 'em. It's my belief you never know what a child won't remember—without knowin' it remembers, like. And she 'ad enough to remember!—what with that, and what come on a bit later. Sometimes, the more a child 'as too much to remember, the more it won't let on. But it left its mark."

"How do you know, Tilly? Did you see her?"

"Yes, I sor 'er. At one time. See 'er? I should think I did." Tilly spoke with a mixture of emphasis and reticence. "But an end was put to *that*."

"Did you go and stay with her—like you do with us?"

"In a manner of speakin'."

"I expect," I suggested, "she was very fond of you."

"Well, she took a sort of fancy to me."

"All children take a fancy to you, Tilly. I don't see how they could possibly help it." I spoke with sincerity and guile.

"I was bright," said Tilly judicially. "I could sing a bit and dance a bit in those days. Children like a bit of larkiness. It makes a change for 'em."

"And didn't Miss Sibyl ever, ever come back?"

Tilly laid down her sewing altogether. She folded her hands in her lap. Never before in all the hours on hours of dramatic monologue had I known her perform so epoch-making a gesture.

"One day," she said, "a letter come. In Miss Sibyl's 'andwriting. I reckernised it. I took it in with the breakfast tray—I see 'er snatch it up to open. When I come back for the tray she was sittin' up with 'er shawl round her, with a look on 'er as if she'd got 'er marchin' orders for the North Pole. 'Tilly,' she says, 'you must help me pack at once—I am going to the South of France. I have heard from Miss Sibyl, and I am going to her.'

" 'Yes, Madam,' I says. 'What luggage will you be requirin'?'—not another word—and sets about my job. It would be August or September—about three months from the time the scandal occurred. Of course we'd 'eard rumours at the time, but she never would open 'er lips about it, leastways not to me. They was all tryin' to 'ush it up. I think she 'ad a few words with your grandfather about the journey—ladies didn't travel alone in them days, and she was delicate. But she'd made up 'er mind, and when she'd made up 'er mind you couldn't move 'er. Next day 'e sor 'er off. She was away a week. Then she come back. 'Oh, Tilly,' she says. 'I'm worn out.' I put 'er to bed."

Tilly had a fit of coughing, and took a lozenge from a little box she always carried in her apron pocket.

"You got to dissolve them gradual," she said. "They wriggles right past the erritation if you crunches 'em up."

I allowed her half a minute and then said cautiously:

"What happened?"

"Next mornin' I could see she'd 'ad a good night's rest and was fresh. So I chooses my time and says very quiet: 'Is there anythink you could tell me, 'M, about your journey?' 'Oh yes, Tilly,' she says, very matter-of-fact. 'I was meaning to—I know how fond you are of Miss Sibyl and what an interest you take in all that concerns her.' 'Yes, indeed, 'M,' I says. 'She was like one of the family.' 'Well,' she says. 'I saw her. She met me at the station, and gave me a most loving welcome. She'd got me such a charming room at the hotel. She spent all day with me. We had some long, long talks.' She stops there, and lets out a great sigh. I went on tidyin' 'er things and presently I says: ' 'Ow did you find 'er?' 'She was looking very beautiful,' she says. 'More beautiful than I've ever seen her.' 'I suppose,' I says, 'you wouldn't 'ave seen *'im?*' 'No,' she says. 'She begged me to, but I refused. I thought better not.' She was right, of course, but I was a bit disappointed. . . . Then she says, very decided: 'She looks happy, Tilly. And she is happy.' It seemed a shockin' thing to 'ear, but I didn't doubt it. Never been so 'appy in 'er life. They'd got some sort

of a little poky, leaky place—villas, they call 'em out there—and 'er
doin' all the work and goin' to market—fancyin' 'erself a proper
'ousewife and workin' woman at last." Tilly gave a chuckle.
"That was 'er latest ambition. But she 'ad that bee in 'er bonnet
as a girl. 'Have a cottage, Tilly, and do all my own work: look
after my husband and children myself. That's a life a woman
could respect herself for.' 'You try it,' I says. 'It ain't all 'olly'ocks
by the front door and rosy faces round the 'earth of a winter's
evenin'. It's scrape, pinch, worry, worry, old before your time.
One fine mornin' you thinks to yourself: It's time I 'ad a good
long look in the glass. . . . Oh dear, dear, dear! Where's my
pretty face got to? When your 'usband comes 'ome 'e wants to
know what you're snivellin' for. You try it!' Well. . . . It wasn't
'er first choice, when it come to it. But I suppose it went on
gnorin' at 'er. You never could make 'er see sense."

"So then what did you say to Grandma?"

" 'That won't last,' I says. 'No, Tilly,' she says, 'it won't.' Oh,
she did look grieved. 'I tried,' she says, 'to persuade her to give
up her lover. Even if it was very, very hard. Even if it seemed her
heart would break by doing so. She rounded on me as if I was
insulting her.' 'Go *back*, Madrona? Me? Go back to that miserable, senseless sham of a life? Can't you see I'm *happy*? Can't you
see that what I've done is *right*? Can you see me creeping back to
ask my husband's forgiveness for wronging him—wouldn't he
please thrash me and take me in again for charity's sake? *He!*
Why, he never loved me. He doesn't know what love is. . . .
Why, Madrona,' she says, shocked, 'I did think you'd see it from
my point of view.' 'Sibyl,' she says, 'you loved him once.' 'I never
did,' she says. 'I see that now. Now I know what love is.' So then
she says: 'Sibyl, I put it to you. Weigh it well,' she says, 'as if it
was life or death—which it is. Are you prepared to give up your
own child?' 'What!' she says, openin' 'er blue eyes wide and starin'.
'Give up my child? Why, Madrona, the very idea! Whatever do
you take me for? Of *course* I won't give her up—no question of it.
My own daughter. Every child needs its mother above all,' she
says. 'As soon as we are settled, I shall send for her. She shall be
brought up to the chance of a decent life.' 'Sibyl, I warn you—

*68*

it's my duty,' says the other, 'If you don't go back, you've lost your child.' 'Oh, has he sent you with that message?' she says, blazin' out. 'No, he has not. I came on my own, without a word to any one, as your friend who loves you, to save you, if I can, from drinking the cup of bitterness to its dregs.' " Here Tilly got irretrievably carried away. She delivered the rest of the speech in the vernacular and her richest histrionic style. " 'I know what I know. You can't 'ave your cake and eat it in this life 'ere below. Swaller your nature—go back and make a fresh start—it's not too late. You've give yourself a crool 'andicap. But you ain't chicking-livered;—you'll come up again, able to look the world straight in the face. 'Elp one another to forgive and to forget. 'E'll do 'is part, I'll answer for it. 'E's a good man. 'E'll learn as well as you, —'e'll cherish you. You've a bitter path to tread, but you'll 'ave your reward. A better love will grow.' " With intense missionary fervour, a somewhat sickly sob in her throat, Tilly pleaded and exhorted. "Oh, she spoke beautiful!—she always did. Never settin' up to judge nor preachify—no 'you're a sinner, I'm a saint' kind of a thing; just *true*—and kind—but not soft with it."

I said with enthusiasm:

"Oh, she *did* speak beautiful, didn't she? Were those her very words?" For this phrase was a customary punctuation to the reminiscences.

" 'Er very words. Or if not, as near as makes no matter."

"And what did Miss Sibyl say?"

"Say? 'Stuff and nonsense, Madrona!' she says. 'Why, what a disgustin' idea! You don't understand at all,' she says. 'What, play my lover false 'oo trusts me? Never! Bless you, 'e don't want me back,' she says. ''E knows we're better off apart. Of course,' she says, very generous, 'I wouldn't wish to deprive 'im of I-anthe altogether. That wouldn't be right. She shall pay 'im visits reg'-lar,' she says. 'I've just written to 'im about it. We'll both act fair in the matter. I can trust 'im for that—and 'e knows 'e can trust me.' "

"And did he act fair?" I asked anxiously, my customary feeble grasp of right and wrong leading me to hope that all had turned out to her satisfaction.

Tilly uttered a ruthless chuckle.

"Oh, 'e acted fair enough!—accordin' to '*is* lights. They was a bit different from young Madam's—that's all. Oh dear, oh dear, what a surprise!"

I waited, but nothing came forth. Tilly was preoccupied, savouring with smiles, sniffs and headshakings the limitless folly and vengefulness of human behaviour. To do down: to be paid out; to be done down: to pay out; there was nothing she more relished than examples of such sequences of stroke and counter-stroke. I thought it politic to lead her back a bit, and said:

"What else did Grandma say to you?"

"Not a lot. 'It's no use, Tilly,' she says, turnin' 'er 'ead aside on the pillow. 'You know what she is.' 'I do,' I says. 'She'll be set on 'er woeful way, and nobody can't turn 'er. What might she be livin' on?' I says. 'Tilly,' she says, 'she hasn't a penny. Only what she took away with her in her purse. She left her pearls and rings and bracelets all behind—deliberately—all except the little ring I gave her. She still wears that—and a curious heavy black ring the which, I suppose, *he* gave her.' "

"Was he rich?" I said.

"Rich? 'E 'adn't a farthing to bless 'isself with. But that didn't trouble 'er. 'E was a genius, accordin' to what she told your Grandma. Every one would be all of agog to buy 'is pictures before long; then the money would come rollin' in. 'And in the meantime,' I says, ''e's livin' on 'er, is 'e?' 'A mere pittance,' she says. 'And when that runs out——' 'I wouldn't worry, if I was you,' I says. 'She won't starve. She can't live on love, whatever she thinks now. She'll soon change 'er tune.' 'Ah,' she says, 'I don't know so much. She's got the pride of Lucifer. She'll never beg.' 'Mark my words, Madam,' I says. 'When the money's gone, that'll be the end between them two.' 'Oh Tilly,' she says, with such a sigh, 'money or no, the end will come. They've acted violent. It'll be seen to they never find peace in one another's arms.' 'If ever there was a wicked villain,' I says, 'it must be 'im.' 'No, no, Tilly,' she says, almost severe. 'I don't expect so. More likely just a weak, wild boy who's lost his head. He's only twenty-two,' she says."

"Older than Miss Sibyl?" I said.

"Well, they'd be much of a muchness. I could see she'd never let it pass 'er lips to weigh out blame, but what she meant was, it couldn't all be laid at '*is* door. 'We parted lovingly,' she says. 'That's one blessing. I told her if she ever needed help that I could give, to let me know. And to remember I loved her. She promised. . . . Now, Tilly,' she says, brisk, 'not another word of this. We won't speak of it again, and I trust you not to pass it on.' Of course she could trust me. From that day to this. It don't matter now. It's all over and done with. And then," added Tilly, in further justification, "you take after your Grandma a bit."

"What happened after that?" I said inexorably.

"Oh Lor', what a one you are for questions. It must be near your supper time. You'd best run down or somebody will be after you."

"I will soon, I promise. But, Tilly, ducky, beauty, just tell me *one* thing: what did happen when—when he acted fair according to his lights—like you said? About Ianthe. Didn't—did Miss Sibyl come back for her? Or what?"

"Oh yes!" said Tilly, with a nasty laugh. "That's just what she did do. She come back for 'er."

"And didn't . . ." The words died on my lips. Insist as I might, Miss Sibyl-Mrs. Jardine and her child would not get themselves reunited.

"It was the nurse told me, the one that brought 'er over to England. She wasn't a bad sort of woman—reliable—but she 'ad a dismal way with 'er. It seems the time went on without 'em writin' to tell 'er 'ow 'earty 'e agreed with 'er plans. I don't know when it was, but one fine day she gets a letter from a solicitor—that's a feller you pay to dror up your will and write your secastic letters when there's been a quarrel. It said would she kindly take notice 'is client, Mr. Charles 'Erbert, couldn't 'old no further communication with 'er on the subjeck of their daughter nor any-think else. 'E wished it to be understood their daughter was remainin' in 'is charge 'enceforth and for evermore, and no argument. It would all be put in peculiar language so you can't get

71

round it. Oh, I know 'em! They're artful. Well, that was a facer for 'er."

"What did it mean?" I cried in fear.

"What it meant: don't you dare come botherin' me any more after that child or I'll 'ave the law on you."

"*Oh,* but how simply awful! What a *beastly* man! How could he? She was hers just as much as his. Wasn't she?"

"Hers that she'd deserted," said Tilly, with venom.

"Yes, but she never *meant* to. She *told* Grandma she was coming for her."

As if all were still happening, could yet be changed, as if now, this moment, the half-visionary figure was being devilishly threatened and deprived, I fought with passion to justify her, to give her her own.

"Meanin's 's one thing, doin' 's another," said Tilly primly. "What would you say if your mother was to run off and leave the lot of you one fine night? Would you say she was considerin' you and your welfare when she done it?"

Between violent and conflicting emotions: on the one hand to assert: "Yes, I could," on the other ferociously to repudiate so infamous, so unimaginable a supposition, I felt about to burst. By these words, Tilly had committed cold-blooded desecration of the innermost shrine, and I shrank from her in superstitious loathing. I managed to say faintly:

"I'd want to go to her."

"Hmm," said Tilly. "No doubt."

"And I know she'd want me. . . ." In the voice of an expiring marionette, I added: "And I expect Ianthe wanted *her*. And they wouldn't let her. . . ."

"It was for the best," said Tilly.

With a revival of spirit, I squeaked defiantly:

"It can't be for the best when anybody doesn't—doesn't have their mother."

I knew what Tilly didn't: I knew the maternal goodness of Mrs. Jardine: her lovingness, her patience, the way her hands could tend and soothe; the certainty she inspired that she would know in a flash what to do if you were frightened; above all, her *accuracy*, that made you feel important, equal, respected. I had no words for all this; but I realised with despair the birthright that Ianthe was losing.

"That depends," said Tilly. "Look what she went and done. Don't tell me a mother's feelin's caused *that* bit of play-actin'. A mother—that *is* a mother—studies 'er dooty to 'er child, and acts accordin' to the best of 'er abilities. No matter 'ow near she might be drove to it by excruciatin' circumstances she'd never go and do a deed like that—roused up out of its first sleep, frightened out of its little wits. No, it was spite. And will. Fair means or foul, she'd 'ave 'er way. But she didn't that time."

"What? How do you mean, Tilly? What did she do?"

"Kidnapped it," said Tilly. "That's what she did."

*"Kidnapped it! ! !"*

The room looked all at once hateful. The sun coming in through the partly-lowered red blind poured out a sudden murky glare, as if a dragon's jaws had opened. Fixed in this glare, every familiar object fastened upon me a baleful, watching face. I saw the schoolroom bookshelf, and in roaring letters a foot high one title: KIDNAPPED; and that engraved illustration, dark boat, dark water, white face of evil I never dared to look at. A hammer thumped in my ears. Through it I heard Tilly give a long low of cackle of laughter.

"I'd 'ave given somethink to been there."

"Mm," I agreed feebly.

"The coolness! . . . First, what does she do? She stands and waits at the corner till she sees the pram go out for its afternoon walk; then along she comes, up the steps, a ring at the front door bell, cool as you please. 'Oh, *Madame! ! !*' 'Bonjoo, Maree. I've come to fetch my petty fee. Take 'er to the sunny south for the winter.' 'Oh *Madame*, this is a surprise! Would Moossew be expectin' you?' 'No, 'e wouldn't. I'll just step inside for a bit. 'Ow's your dear old parents and your brother in the Army? I've brought you a little present, Maree. I know you'd like to do somethink to oblige me.' 'Certindly, *Madame*'—the double-faced thing. Not that you can blame 'er reelly. She was between the devil and the deep sea, like—and them French girls is flighty."

73

As this dialogue developed, I felt my sanity returning. When Tilly paused, musing, I was able to prompt her to continue.

"Well, she got round the girl to 'ide 'er till the evenin'. Yes—up in 'er own boodwar, where nobody never set foot no more, except to air it and dust and shut up—the key turned on 'er for safety, like a thief in 'er own 'usband's 'ouse—which she was—where all society 'ad flocked once to fawn at 'er feet. Bidin' 'er time. . . . I wonder what 'er thoughts was, alone there."

I saw a figure, alone, stretched on a couch. I knew how it looked in solitude, the stone thoughts moulding its face. Shivers pricked me, and I said quickly:

"What was she biding her time for?"

Now, I thought, now it's coming. I was braced to bear it all.

"For when the child would be tucked up in its cot in the night nursery. That was 'er only chance of gettin' at it unbeknown to the nurse. Between seven and eight, when she was nicely off, the nurse would pop down for a bit of supper—not long—three-quarters of an hour, say. Well, round about then, this girl Maree—she was on the watch—come and unlocked the door. 'See voo play, Ma*dame*, now's your chance. 'Urry. She's just gone down.' 'Good. And Moossew, Maree? Nowhere about?' ' 'E come in and changed and gone out to dine. Ma*dame*. I 'ad it from the valet.' 'Thank you, Maree. You may go now. 'Ere's your little present. Buy something to remember me. But mind—you ain't seen so much as the whisk of my skirts—see? Keep your mouth shut and you won't get into trouble. You've done nothink wrong. You've only 'elped me to what's my own. I'm takin' 'er far away now, where nobody won't never find us. Good-bye and thankin' you. I'll never forget you.' 'Nor me you, Ma*dame*. Le Bong Dew bless and keep you.' So she gives the girl a kiss and sends 'er off. Then up she creeps to the night nursery, takes that mite out of its cot, wraps it up in a blanket—and sets off down with it."

"Did she wake up? Did she know her mother had come for her?"

"Whether she woke up or not, she never cried out. The woman said she couldn't 'ave. She said it was like as if she always left one of 'er ears up in the nursery, and would 'ave 'eard 'er. Down the

stairs she goes, quiet as a mouse, with it in 'er arms. Reaches the
bottom stair. All quiet. Starts across the marble 'all. When all of
a sudden comes a step outside on the pavement, a man's step. It
stops. Next moment comes the scritch of a key in the lock. The
front door opens. And there 'e stands—face to face, on the doorstep."

I heard myself give a groan.

"Mr. Charles?"

"'Er 'usband."

"But how could it be? He'd gone out to dinner, you said. *Why*
did he comes back?"

"You can call it Providence," said Tilly. *"I* don't know what 'e
come back for. I dare say 'e'd forgotten somethink—but come 'e
did. Oh, the scales seemed tipped for 'er all right—right to the
last momint—but she wasn't meant to win *that* game. And she
lost it."

"What did he say to her?"

Tilly paused, seemed to wrestle with the dramatic instinct, and
momentarily victorious, replied:

"Not 'avin' been present, I couldn't tell you. Not: Welcome
back to my ancestral 'ome—that you may be sure. You can picture
it,—'im and 'er facin' up at one another like a couple of wild
beasts ready to spring—'er clutchin' on to the child. She was
caught, see?—fair and square. All I know is, the 'all bell give a
ring downstairs fit to wake the dead, and the valet went to answer it. Next thing, 'e come runnin' back like as if Old Nick was
after 'im. 'Nurse! You're wanted at once double quick in the 'all.'
So up she tears, and 'Oh Lor'!' she says—you could 'ave knocked
'er down with a feather. It made 'er come over queer to see 'em.
Gashly white, deadly quiet, 'e was, and 'er standin' there by the
bottom step, leanin' up against a great statute they 'ad there—a
naked great marble figure of a female, so the Nurse said, 'oldin'
up a torch, and that mite wide awake, pokin' its 'ead up out of
the blanket to stare first at one, then the other, not makin' a
sound. 'Who let this woman in?' 'e says, cold as a blessèd iceberg.
'Not me, sir!' 'Nor me, sir.' Then she spoke up and says: 'None
of your servants is to blame, Charles. I found my own way in.

You refused me my own child, so I have to come and take her.' 'Frances,' 'e says, takin' no more notice of 'er than a fly on the wall, 'Frances'—that was 'er name, Frances Donkin—'take Miss Ianthe at once. Take her back to the nursery.' At that she gives a look round like a trapped thing and starts to make for the stairs. 'E gives one spring and ketches 'old of 'er by the shoulder, and that pore mite starts off a-sobbin' and 'owlin'. 'Take your hand away, Charles,' she says, very dignified. 'You are frightening I-anthe. . . . There, I-anthe, there, my child,' she says. 'Here, take her, Frances,' and 'ands 'er over as careful and tender as if she'd just 'ad 'er down to say good-night to. 'There, take her back quickly,' she says. 'Don't cry, I-anthe. . . . You know,' she says with a bit of a smile, 'I wasn't going to take her travelling through the night in her nightgown. I had all her clothes ready, waiting in a little trunk at the station—I made them myself.' 'Er who'd never so much as wound a ball of baby wool since the child was born! 'Good-night, Frances,' she says. 'I-anthe has grown a great deal. She looks healthy.' So she couldn't do no other than say: 'Good-night, Madam,' and off she starts upstairs with 'er legs sinkin' under 'er like a pair of feather bolsters. But she 'ad the mite to soothe, and that got 'er on. She was fond of it in 'er own way—that I will say. When she gets to the first landin' she stops and listens. She 'ears 'im say, deadly quiet: 'Now leave my house.' 'Yes, I will go now,' she says, as if she was tired like. 'And if ever you attempt to set foot in it again,' 'e says, 'I will summon the police and have you arrested.' 'No need to threaten me, Charles Herbert,' she says. 'I'll not give you cause to take a step so contrary to the chivalrous instincts of an English gentleman'—she meant it spiteful, see? 'But be sure of one thing,' she says. 'Be it soon, be it late, I-anthe will come back to me. I will have her love. And she will HATE her father.' And with that she sweeps out like a queen, and the front door slams be'ind 'er.''

Now she was in the dark street alone, defeated. She was standing still, wondering where to go, what to do next. Now she was walking away with the step I knew, vanishing, swallowed up in the night beyond reach of my imagination.

Hate, *hate,* HATE, went the hammer in my ears.

She should win, and he should be cast down and hated.

Tilly chuckled.

"Oh, wasn't there a kick-up in the 'ouse that night! Along a bit later, 'e sends for 'er. 'Pack at once, Frances,' 'e says. 'You and Miss I-anthe will be going over to England to-morrow. I shall follow later.' And that girl—that Maree—'ighstrikin' all over the place, lettin' the cat out of the bag, 'ow she done it, and she 'adn't known what to do for the best, and she didn't want the money, she'd do anythink for M*adame,* lay down 'er life, she worshipped 'er, and 'ow she'd give 'er a kiss, and I don't know what all. She was sent packin'. But 'e give 'er 'er reference—'e was just. Bless you, Miss Sibyl could get round anybody. All but one. She never got round *'im.* And the next evenin' they turned up at number fifteen, with ten pieces of luggage not countin' the cot and the pram."

"Oh!" I cried in delight. "They came to Grandma!" For now, surely, Grandma would send for Miss Sibyl, and re-unite her to her little girl.

"Yes. We got a telegram—could they stay till 'e'd made 'is arrangements. You see, there wasn't no relations to speak of on 'is side neither, and she'd been a good friend to 'im too before the marriage. They stayed a month. She was a funny little soul—very takin'."

Tilly fell silent, looking tender and amused, as she always did when she spoke of children.

"Where did they go after the month?"

"Oh, 'e bought a place in Kent, and they went there to live. 'E give it all up—'is Dippermatic, I mean—and the divorce went through, and 'e got it fixed legal the mother would be forbid all access to the child till she was turned eighteen years; and 'e shut 'isself up and grew as stiff and awkward as an old 'orned crab in a shell. It was a shame. 'E was a feller with plenty of brains—and in 'is prime—not much over forty. She broke 'im all right. It was 'is pride. And then 'e'd been a bachelor too long before she got 'im. 'E opened up too late. It was like a weak stomach 'avin' a fancy sudden to come off a diet of milk and soda and take a feed of 'ot lobster. One good go and 'e was finished. It seems as if that night give 'im a sort of a brain storm—and 'e never shook it off. 'E got it stuck in 'is 'ead she'd come for that child and get it by 'ook or by crook. That child was watched day and night. Never let run free to play by 'erself in the garden. Bars on all the windows. Oh, 'e was 'ipped! It wasn't no life for a child. No wonder she went the way she did."

I said quickly:

"How did she go?"

"Wild," said Tilly. Again she looked wandering and astray. "I don't know. It was 'earsay. I lost sight of 'er later."

"Did you go on seeing her *then*—when she was little?"

"Bless you, yes. I see 'er reg'lar. 'E trusted me—and that was a funny thing, too, why 'e did, I never fathomed it. For 'e got so 'ipped 'e wouldn't trust no one after a bit. That Frances, she stayed some years, then 'e got suspicious she was correspondin' with the mother on the sly—and *she* 'ad to go. It was over some little frock or somethink that come from America—addressed to the child—no name or message inside: 'e guessed 'oo it was from and 'eld 'er responsible. Then it was one governess, then another. If 'e didn't give 'em the sack, they sacked theirselves; they couldn't stand it—the watchin' and the worritin'—it got their nerves all of a jangle. But if ever 'e was stuck between one goin' and another comin', 'e'd bring 'er up and leave 'er in our charge. And many's the nice bit of 'oliday she 'ad that way."

"Did you look after her? Bath her and all that?"

"Yes. I'd bath 'er and keep 'er clothes nice. Many's the little frock I made 'er. It was a understood thing your Grandma should see to that. Madrona she called 'er, like the other. Oh, the things she'd say! She did talk strange sometimes. 'You know, Tilly,' she says once, 'everybody has a mother. I've got one. She's not dead. But she told so many lies my father had to send her away, or she might have taught me to tell lies too. But the queer thing is,' she says, 'I do tell lies sometimes, I don't seem able to help it. So I think she must be watching me somehow, and putting them in my head.' Fancy that from a child! It sounded shockin'. 'My father says,' she says, 'if he found me out in a lie it would break

78

his heart. He doesn't mind me being stupid or rude or disobedi-
ent or anything else,' she says, 'only that.' "

A terrible echo stirred. This same paternal threat, expressed in
even direr terms—I had heard it only a short while ago from the
lips of another child. It seemed that this thing went on and on,
like a curse. Liar begot liar; and all their road, forward and back,
far back, was cratered with disastrous pits of guilt, haunted by
ruinous voices crying vengeance. Lying was not like anything else.

But now, I felt, and trembled to feel, now at last I was getting
back to the beginning. The moment was approaching when I
should light on the link I sought, and, with one click, hold the
whole circle in my hand.

Instinct led me to say:

"Did you take her out in the Park?"

"Many and many a time. Through 'Yde Park into Kensington
Gardens. With a bag of crusts to feed the gulls—she'd never go
without that. Nasty scrawkin' ravengeous things—I 'ated the sight
of 'em. They'd come all round 'er—and the sparrers too. It was
there," said Tilly casually, meditatively, "I first sor 'er. One
bright windy autumn day."

"Saw who?"

"It was by the Round Pond—I'd seen a woman, lady, that is to
say, standin' a little way off under a tree, as it might be watchin'
us. But I didn't take 'er in much, except to remark she 'ad on a
funny sort of a blue cloak wrapped round 'er. But when it was
time to go 'ome we passed 'er quite close. . . . And then I thought
to myself: Now where in the world . . . and then what with 'er
chatter I put it out of my mind. Next day, bless me if she wasn't
there again, standin' still and just watchin'. I thought: Well,
that's funny, you do take an interest, I wonder why. I didn't quite
like it. There's plenty of people watches the pretty fashionable-
dressed children in the Park, and this one was worth a look too,
she 'ad a cherry corded velvet coat and bonnet that year—but this
seemed a sort of special watchin'. She 'ad a bit of a cold for a day
or two after that and we didn't go out. But the next time—there
she was again! And the child says to me: 'Oh, look, Tilly,' she
says, 'there's the lady in the blue cloak again.' She 'adn't let on

before she'd even noticed 'er. And oh Lor'! it all come over me then. I felt myself go like a bath of cold water runnin' down the plug 'ole. I thought: Whatever shall I do if she makes to come and speak? But she didn't. I made some excuse it was later than I thought for, and ketches 'old of 'er 'and and starts to scurry off 'ome; and she just stood there a little way off, like a statute, not budgin' a inch to foller us. My 'eart was bouncin' in and out of my throat like a rubber ball, and I says to myself: You daft idiot you! Where's your brains and where's your eyesight? But I was always a bit short-sighted. And it was close on nine years since I last see 'er. And oh, she 'ad changed! Thin!—she was a skelinton. And 'er 'air done different—that changes a woman. So when I got back I goes straight to your grandmother. She listens and she thinks; then she says: 'You have acted quite rightly, Tilly, in mentioning it, but I think you must be mistaken. When I heard of her last she was far away the other side of the world. You look quite upset,' she says. 'Go and get yourself a nice hot cup of tea in the kitchen at once. If you're nervous,' she says, 'I'll take her out myself for a few days and see what I make of this blue-cloak lady. Anyway,' she says, 'she's to go to tea to-morrow with Mrs. Venables' children. They're calling for her in the carriage, so she'll be quite safe,' she says, smilin'. So that night I felt a bit easier in my mind."

"And *were* you mistaken?" I said in agitation.

"Ah!" said Tilly slowly, drawing out the suspense. "Was I or wasn't I? Next afternoon the carriage come about three as arranged, and off she went, ever so worked up. Whenever it came to a little treat or a party she'd light up and go off like a packet of squibs. She'd be like a little mad thing. It was the dull screwed-down life she led—and she was volatile by nature. I thought: Well, I've got the afternoon free—I'll pop down to the kitching and do my ironin'. Round about four comes a ring at the front door bell. As Fate would 'ave it, Stevens was out for 'is afternoon. 'There!' I says. 'That'll be from the dressmaker. It was promised for four. I'll run up and take it in.' So up I run—I was very light and quick on my feet in them days—opens the door—and there she stands! In that blue cloak. Pale. Oh, I nearly fell down in a swoond on the mat. I 'ung on to the door-'andle, and: 'Oh! Miss Sibyl,' I gasps out, 'whatever 'ave you come after?' I forgot myself, see? She gives me a smile—she did 'ave a lovely smile, it was enough to melt a stone. 'Tilly, Tilly,' she says, 'don't look so scared. I'm not a ghost—or a tiger escaped from its cage. I'm the same Sibyl you used to know. How wonderful,' she says, 'that you should open the door to me. It's like coming home again. You haven't changed a little bit.' 'Oh, Miss Sibyl,' I says, 'you 'ave.' She 'ad 'old of my 'and. Mind, she was a beauty still—but she wasn't a girl no longer. She 'ad a look on 'er . . . as if she'd seen a lot and learnt a lot—not all pleasant neither. You couldn't call it exactly 'ard—more stern. Slow to brighten up. 'So it *was* you in the Park,' I says. 'Yes,' she says. 'Forgive me if I frightened you. You see, I felt I must watch Ianthe first from a little way off—before I came close to her. So that I'd take in all the outlines of her nature—*feel* what she was like. So that when I touched her she wouldn't feel strange at all to me; and that would help her, on her side, to know me quickly—*remember* me quickly, I should say.' I've never forgot those words she spoke."

Tilly sank into reverie, as if amazed, half incredulous all over again; then with a heavy sigh and a shake of the head went on!

"There I stood gawpin' at 'er, not knowin' what answer to make to 'er. 'Tilly,' she says, 'it was so *extraordinary* to see you two together. Yet so natural—so right. It was like waking from a fever and seeing the ordinary sweet day. My dear, *dear* Madrona! I knew she was the one person in the world I could trust—however long I had to be away.' With that she steps inside and says: 'Shall I go and find her, Tilly, or had you better prepare her? I don't want to give her a shock.' And at that very moment your grandmother came down round the bend of the stairs, just up from 'er afternoon rest, and see 'er. She stops like she'd been shot. '*Sibyl!*' '*Madrona!*' she cries out. And she lets 'er cape fall on the floor and runs into 'er arms."

I felt my eyes and throat smart intolerably, and saw Tilly's tears fall down.

"'Five years,' I 'eard one say; and the other: 'I told you I'd come back.' I see them sort of wander off into the drorin' room

with their 'eads down, leanin' close, and not another word spoke.
I 'ad to mop my own eyes, I can tell you. But all the time I was
sayin' to myself: 'Thank 'Eavens, the child ain't in the 'ouse.'"

"Why?" I said painfully. "Didn't you want her to see her?"

"No," said Tilly stiffly, "I did not."

"*Did* she see her?"

"No. She didn't see 'er." She was silent; then: "It couldn't be,"
she said. For a moment, strong emotion charged her old crackling
voice with depth and richness. "I'll see 'er like that on my deathbed."

Silence. I stared out of the window and saw the chestnut trees
lift, blow upward ecstatically all together in a gust of evening
breeze. The setting sun was gilding their trunks from somewhere
out of sight.

"Like how, Tilly?" I said at last.

"At 'alf-past five I was due to start to fetch back Miss I-anthe.
It was just a little walk across the square, up into Oxford Street
and over into Manchester Square; and we was to take a cab back,
of course. I run up the area steps and come out on the pavement
just by the front door—wonderin' to myself would she be gone
or not when we got back, but I'd 'ad my orders, and nothink
different said. At that very momint the front door flies open—
and out she comes.

"She stands there at the top of the steps; and 'er eyes seemed
to pierce right through me—enough to freeze your marrer. Talk
of wild tigers—that's what she put me in mind of. *Glarin'*. She
stands there with 'er 'ead up—it was gettin' on for dusk, but I
could see 'er face all stiff and white. Then she comes down the
steps and away she goes, like as if she was sleep-walkin', in the
opposite direction to me.

"'Gawd 'elp us,' I thought. 'There's murder in that face.' I
was in two minds to go on, or to run back and take a look in the
drorin' room, but I says to myself: 'Mind your own business,'
and puts my best foot foremost. Well, I got there and fetched 'er
and back all right. She runs in to say 'er good-nights as usual.
Then she comes up and I sees to 'er and puts 'er into bed like I
always done. She was very good considerin', a bit over-excited,

*82*

but no trouble. Then my bell rings upstairs—meanin' I was wanted in the bedroom. So I goes along. She was settin' at 'er dressin'-table. I took one look and saw she was upset. She showed it very quick—she was always delicate. She looked wore out. 'The black tea-gown, Tilly,' she says. It was velvet with cream Valanceens lace in the neck. It suited 'er. So I brought it, and the slippers to match. 'Well, Tilly,' she says, 'you were quite right, you see.' 'Oh, Madam,' I says, 'I been ever so worried. It's been on my mind, per'aps I ought to 'ave said you wasn't at 'ome.' 'No, no indeed,' she says. 'I should have regretted it bitterly if I had not seen her.' 'What a change in 'er!' I says. She lets out such a 'eavy sigh. 'Since that time I saw her in France,' she says, 'she never sent me one single line or message—not one. I guessed it was because I'd warned her what would happen; and because my warnings had come true. I thought she had chosen to cut the whole past clean away from her, and turn forward to build a new life. I thought it would have been like her to root even I-anthe right out of her and bury her with the rest of her dead marriage; and pass on. She never could bear a failure. . . .' I went on brushin' 'er 'air, and after a bit she says: 'For five years she'd had one idea, *one,* fixed in her mind: to get Ianthe back.' 'Ah,' I says, 'I knew it.' 'Did you?' she says. 'How little I understand people. I quite misjudged her.' She stops there. I didn't like to ask too straight out what 'ad passed; so after a bit I say: 'Might she still be livin' with that one, then?' 'Oh no,' she says, 'that finished long ago. And unfortunately she has not married again.' I thought to myself: if not married, not livin' in what you might call single strictness, not by a long chalk; but I didn't like to say so. 'She's had a bad time, Tilly,' she says. I looked at 'er in the glass, and saw tears in 'er eyes. 'She told me she'd *starved.*' Well, I thought, per'aps she did, per'aps she didn't. What some calls starvin' is a square meal to others. . . . All the same," said Tilly reflectively, emerging from reminiscence, "per'aps she did. I wouldn't put nothing past that one."

"*I* knew," I said, in the ensuing pause, "she'd never forget Ianthe. Of course she wouldn't. I knew she'd come for her."

83

"Ah!" said Tilly. "Fair means or foul. She'd lost 'er chance by the one—so she laid 'er plans to come at 'er by the other."

"How do you mean by the other?"

"Accordin' to what your grandmother told me—and it was strict confidence I've never broke—'er idea was—believe it or not —to see the child, secret from 'er father, whenever she come to stop with us; as she did, reg'lar. And 'ow was it to be kep' from 'er father? You may well ask. 'Why, Madrona, you wouldn't betray me, and I know Tilly wouldn't, and I shall explain the whole situation to Ianthe. I shall tell her her father must never know, and that I trust her. Children never, never betray confidences, if you give them serious reasons not to. Which I shall.' So that child was to 'ave that burden put on 'er. Not to speak of the under'and ways she was to be brought up to till they was second nature. *Nor* to speak of the crookedness your grandmother and me for the matter of that was to be willin' partners in. Oh no! All that wouldn't trouble 'er. She saw just the one thing: what she wanted; and that was the right thing."

"Did Grandma think it was—it wasn't the right thing?"

"She knew it wasn't. And so would any one else 'oo knew the meanin' of the words actin' straight, and wouldn't stoop to deceit and all it leads to."

I was abashed; but I felt now, in my moral fog, so hopelessly committed to the side against the angels, to my partnership in obliquity and obsession, that there was nothing for it but to continue stubbornly in my shamelessness. A complex of feelings about Ianthe knotted itself within me; indignation on her account that she should be denied her chance of conspiracy; jealousy that so stupendous, so unique a chance should be offered to another. How unfathomably I would have kept the secret! How I would have thriven on it! What I would have discovered about truth, to strengthen and keep me straight in my crookedness!

All through this maze I had held tenaciously to one thread: Miss Sibyl had clung to it, and so would I. I said almost tearfully:

"But Grandma did tell her to come if she ever needed help. It was a promise. Grandma wouldn't break her word."

"No, she wouldn't," said Tilly sharply. "She never broke 'er solemn word in all 'er life. But that's what was laid at 'er door. . . . I never in all my days see 'er so shocked and 'urt. What come later was only the consequences of that day—and didn't cut so keen. Though it went on gnorin' at 'er, I knew, like somethink chronic in 'er vitals. But this was face to face. From one 'oo'd been part daughter, part younger sister. And to come to such words straight on top of the joy of seein' 'er again! . . ." Tilly drew in a hissing breath.

"What words?" I said heavily.

" 'She threatened me,' she says. 'But I hope and pray when she has had time to think it over, she will see I could do no other.' 'Of course you couldn't,' I says. 'The idea!' 'She kept saying,' she says, ' "But I've not come to steal her or corrupt her. This is *right*. This is *just*. This is *human*. Not the law of cruel men. The law of humanity. My own child! . . ." Oh, Tilly, it was so terrible. It nearly broke my heart. . . .' I thought to myself: Trouble, trouble—and more trouble to come. I couldn't a-bear to see 'er so grieved. It seemed she 'ad to out with it to someone. She couldn't speak of it to your grandfather, see? 'E was strict in some ways. 'E wouldn't 'ave 'er name mentioned after she run off; 'e'd thought the world of Mr. Charles. So I says to 'er: 'Dear Madam, try not to take on so. You did what was right, may Gawd in 'eaven be your judge.' 'Oh, that's so *little* consolation,' she says. 'To see 'er face change from such joy to such dreadful disappointment and bitterness! "You too, Madrona!" she said. "I thought, no matter if the whole world casts me out, you would still be with me." "And so I am, Sibyl!" She laughed—a terrible laugh.' I says, to take 'er mind off the laugh, like: ' 'As she come to settle in London then?' 'I don't know what she'll do now,' she says. 'She arrived from America a fortnight ago. I don't know what life she's been living these last years, but she told me she was independent now. She had worked hard—and at last she had saved the money to come back and have a home where the child could visit her. . . .' Ah, dear!" said Tilly. "Pore Miss Sibyl! She'd seen the seamy side all right. Toured all over the world in low-class theatrical companies, she 'ad—if she was to be believed; and writin' things for the newspapers, and I don't know what. As a girl, she was always one to go on about women's rights—and they should all be trained up to perfessions like men, and be the equal of 'em. Equals! She got 'er bellyful all right. Ah, well. . . . There's some people in this world you can't 'elp; and she was one. She 'ad a kind, generous offer made 'er that time too. But no. . . ."

"Did she?" I said eagerly. "What was it?"

"Your grandmother says to me: 'I told her,' she says, 'that although I *could not* allow her to come here or help her in any way to gain access, I would most gladly keep in touch with her —come and see her—tell her all I could about the child, write to her if she decided to go back to America; so long as she gave me her word not to interfere with her, or lay plans to see her behind my back. I told her I should make it clear to Mr. Charles I was going to do this; with a full sense of my responsibility,' she says, 'because I knew her word to me could be trusted; and because I wished to pave the way to a better understanding between Ianthe and her mother by the time she was grown up.' That was on account she 'ad to sign a paper swearin' she wouldn't interfere with the child till she was growed up—like I told you."

'What did she say to Grandma about that offer?"

"Scorned it! Thank you for nothink!—that was the way she took it. She didn't want no charity news—bits and pieces as others thought it wouldn't do no 'arm for 'er to know, and no power to influence the child 'erself, so's she'd grow up into the kind of young woman she wanted 'er to be. . . . Pity she didn't think of that a bit sooner. 'Do you think,' she ends up. 'I want to hear from *you?*—knowing, *knowing,* as I do now, that you are hand in glove with that cruel and con-temptible man?' Well, that was the finish. 'Go,' says your grandmother. '*Go.* Go quickly, before more is said that you will regret for ever. . . .' 'My worst fear was,' she says, 'that Ianthe would come running in. What then?' 'You could trust me for that,' I says. 'Well, Tilly, no more of this,' she says. 'We won't speak of it again. It can never be put right. It's all over between us, and I shall never see her again.' 'Not if I know 'uman nature,' I thought. 'Nothink's ever over when it comes to this sort of a circus.' Besides, I seen the look on 'er face. I knew she meant mischief."

There was a brooding pause. Tilly told me to switch on the light; she couldn't see to work any more. I did so; and then said: "Did she mean mischief?"

"Two or three years passed away," said Tilly. "There never came no sign. I could tell she fretted sometimes, but she never spoke of it. Then there was a book wrote. . . ."

Tilly's voice was so ominous, the news she imparted on so totally different a plane from anything I was braced for, that my spine, latterly immunised to shocks, shivered again.

"A book?" I bleated.

"A wicked, shameful book. Wrote and printed. Signed with the name on the outside. Anstey 'er maiden name was, and that was what it was signed: Sibyl Anstey."

"What was it called?"

"It slips my memory what the title was. I sor it owin' to because your father brought it into the 'ouse. 'E was gettin' on to be a man then, and ever so bright in 'is 'ead. 'E used to write bits about books for the papers, for all 'e was only young. 'E'd be at Cambridge College at the time. 'Mother!' 'e says. 'What do you think I've been sent? A book by a woman called Sibyl Anstey. Surely it must be the same,' 'e says. 'E'd recollect 'er from a child, see, though 'e 'adn't seen 'er nor heard 'er name spoke for years. '*Really?*' she says. 'What is it like?' It was up in 'er room. I was makin' your aunt some little light frocks for the summer, and she'd come up to give an eye to the fittin'.

" 'What is it about?' she says. 'I don't know yet,' 'e says. 'It's only just come. From the glance I've had, it looks like the intimate life story of a wronged woman,' 'e says, jokin' like. 'I bet it's auter——' what's the word?—about 'erself 'e meant. 'Jolly strong stuff it looks like. She was a bit of a flyer, wasn't she?' 'I must read it,' she says, quiet. 'Let me have it when you've done with it. I do hope it's good,' she says. 'She was always ambitious to be a writer.' Well . . . She read it."

"And what was it about?"

"It was about a woman what was wronged all right," said

Tilly, with dramatic scorn. "Wronged by men. Wronged by a woman she trusted, one 'oo turned out a false friend, and stabbed 'er to the 'eart."

"Do you mean *murdered* her?"

"No, I don't mean any such thing. I mean: played 'er a treacherous trick. The smooth, double-faced kind she made 'er out, 'oo'd been a enemy in disguise from first to last."

"You don't mean . . . you mean: made *Grandma* out?"

"If you can credit it. I never read the thing. I wouldn't of demeaned myself to open it."

"Did Grandma tell you about it?"

"Never. Not one word ever crossed 'er lips. No, I 'ad it from Stevens. 'E was a reader. I never was. Oh, it was wrapped up cunnin', of course, so you couldn't lay your finger and swear that's 'oo was meant. If she'd 'a been faced with it, she could 'ave acted innocent. 'Why, Madrona, good gracious me, it's only a story made up out my 'ead. Your 'air's dark, Madrona, and the one in the story's fair. 'Owever could you fancy such a thing?' Ah, no doubt she would 'ave, given the chance. Yes, that was 'er thanks for all them years of love and care. That was 'er revenge; and I 'ope it come back to sting 'er like a viper. It was the first time I ever see your grandmother give in—the first and the last. Not even when your grandfather died, she didn't. But she did then. It broke somethink in 'er. She 'ad an illness—not a long one; but when she got up from it she'd aged. She never looked ten years younger than her 'age again, like she done before."

Silence fell again. Two irreconcilable sets of facts confronted me. Miss Sibyl was an authoress; she had written something horrid and unkind about Grandma. Yet, turn the wheel, and she was Mrs. Jardine, who loved Grandma so much that her voice altered when she spoke of her; who loved me for being her grandchild. I could only suppose that grown-ups were like that.

"Lor," said Tilly at last, "your grandfather did create. I don't know what 'e didn't want to do to stop the book and show 'er up. It went like 'ot cakes for a bit, I 'eard. It was wrote clever, and there was some spicy bits in it—not what a lady should know. But of course it was only dignified to turn a blind eye to the nastiness; which they done. 'E was a 'ot-tempered gentleman, like yer father. One thing she did let drop to me—she 'ad to: 'e forbid 'er ever to 'ave Miss Ianthe to stop in the 'ouse again. 'You'll rue it,' 'e says. 'If you don't now, you will in a few years' time.' 'Is idea was, nothink but trouble ever come from 'avin' anythink to do with the 'ole lot of 'em. 'If it doesn't change *your* feelings to her,' 'e says, 'knowing whose child she is, it will mine. I shall loathe the sight of her. See her where and when you choose, so long as it's not here. She *shall* not come here.' She wiped a few tears away when she told me, and I'm sure I did. I was fond of that child, and I felt it as much as she did pretty nearly—losin' touch; more for the child's sake, you understand. But no doubt 'e was right. Thank the Lord it was all took out of our 'ands. For Mr. Charles got wind through that book of 'er bein' about again, and 'e saw 'ow it was with yer grandmother, and 'e give up the 'ouse and went off to Italy or some such foreign place to live. Where 'e died, some years after."

"Died? What happened to Ianthe then?"

"Oh, I never 'eard much. I dare say she got along some'ow. She went on sendin' me picture post cards for quite a time. Reg'-lar on my birthday and at Christmas. And I'd do the same. Then all that stopped. She got growed up, see, and 'ad other things to occupy 'er mind. I did 'ear somethink. . . . But I never took much notice. I dare say it was all a lot o' lies. She got married in the end—I do know that, and went off to India to live. She 'ad some children. . . . I did 'ear that. . . ." The wandering look made her face droop again.

"Yes, yes!" I said eagerly. "Maisie and Malcolm. I *know* them! And did you take *them* in the Park too? Like you used to take Ianthe?"

"Oh, *them!* . . ." I saw some petrified layer break up in Tilly; something struggled up through it to the surface. Her memory, for the old days microscopically accurate, had well-nigh ceased to function with regard to the events of the last ten years; but I had somehow at last managed to tap where buried forms and voices could still be heard, alive, tapping and calling back from underground.

"Bless my soul," she said rather weakly. "Fancy your mentioning them! They were a job lot—nice little things, though. Yes . . . I got a card one day. It 'ad been sent to yer aunt's address—of course, I'd retired then, but they forwarded it to my lodgin's. 'Tilly, do you remember Ianthe? Please do come along to the Somethink 'Otel and see me and my children.' So I thought I'd go. I asked for 'er at the desk by the name she'd gave me—it's slipped me now. And I was showed up. Oh, she 'ad got a lovely woman! But them two!—like something off of a jumble stall— to *look* at, mind you; they was nice-mannered children—I'm not sayin' different. I don't know 'ow ever she come by 'em. 'E can't 'ave been no oil-paintin'. 'Oh, Tilly dear,' she says, 'you haven't changed.' That was all my eye. 'I did want them to know you when they came to England. I've told them how you used to take me to the Round Pond when I was a little girl. I do want them to go in the Park with you,' she says, 'as I used to. Nobody knows how to make it fun like you do.' " Tilly chuckled. "She wanted them off 'er 'ands a bit, I think. . . . 'Well, it's over twenty years back,' I says. 'I'm not so quick on my feet as I was. If they offers to fall into the Pond, I couldn't fish 'em out.' 'Oh, they can swim like fishes,' she says. She was off 'and with 'em—a bit abrup' . . . Well, I took 'em a few times, just to oblige 'er. She made a lot of fuss of me that time—but I didn't see much of 'er the other times. She'd be gone out, and them two sittin' waitin' in that dismal 'otel bedroom as good as gold. Of course they was like all children: they liked to be told what their mother done and said when she was a little girl. . . ." Tilly mopped her eyes. "Fancy them comin' up! I wonder what became of 'em, pore little souls."

I hesitated. But the thought of repeating for the third time that I knew them, they were Mrs. Jardine's grandchildren and were at this moment but a mile or so away, made me feel hopeless; ill-mannered as well. I had only a moment or two left. It was my supper time. I decided to go back to Miss Sibyl, and I said:

"So you never saw Miss Sibyl again?"

"Never," said Tilly. She sighed. "When your grandmother was

on 'er deathbed, she says to me sudden one afternoon when the nurse 'ad gone out: 'Tilly,' she says, 'I've seen Miss Sibyl. I'm so glad,' she says. 'It was such a comfort. I thought you'd like to know.' 'I *am* glad, Madam,' I says. She was dozin' like; I couldn't bother 'er with questions. I've sometimes asked myself if she was wanderin'. . . . No, I never sor 'er with me own eyes again." She mused. Then, once more a tremor ran over the hardening crust. "But that was a funny thing too," she said. "It only shows . . ."

"What was a funny thing, Tilly? Only shows what?"

"What a shock that time must 'a' been, to stick so in my mind. Believe it or not, one day when I was with them two by the Round Pond, bless me if I didn't fancy I see 'er again, watchin' from a little way off. . . . It was the way she stood. . . ."

"Was it—was it just your imagination?"

"I 'ad to pinch meself," said Tilly. "It give me quite a turn. I believe I'd always been on the look-out for that there blue cloak, ever since. . . . But this was . . . oh well, I dare say it wasn't nobody special. Just a grey-'aired woman—a lady, you understand. Pale complexion. Dressed very nice——"

"Nobody you knew?"

"Oh, but she 'ad got stout, though!" said Tilly. "I'd never 'ave credited . . . It's not always a 'ealthy sign, not by no means, when a woman gets stout." Her head jigged up and down. "No," she said vaguely. Then: "I did 'ear some time ago she'd married again and settled down respectable. I don't know what she changed 'er name to if she did."

I said softly:

"Mrs. Jardine."

But Tilly seemed not to hear. She drew her cross-over round her, and said it was a chilly evening: she'd been glad of a bit of fire last night, and she'd be the same to-night. She told me to run along do, she never knew such a child for getting her talking.

I kissed her good-night, and felt that she was going to die soon, and that she knew it. I went downstairs with my heartache, and it was so horrible and so enormous, that it was like carrying a bag of stones tied on to the bones of my chest.

# PART THREE

TILLY left us a day or two later. She said she'd be more herself when she got back to her own place in London, where her landlady studied her ways and the girls were bright: it was the country made her feel low—she never could abear it. She was mulish, vacant, sullenly melancholy. My mother tried to persuade her to see the doctor, and after that Tilly refused to speak to her any more, and left without saying good-bye. There was nothing my mother could do except to write to the landlady, asking to be kept informed of Tilly's condition, and offering any assistance within her power. We were relieved to see the dolman and bonnet disappearing round the bend of the garden path towards the station. The garden boy stumped ahead of her with her portmanteau; and that was the last we saw of her. She was not our Tilly any more; she was an inauspicious old fairy, ill-wishing our hearth. Unable to rid myself of the suspicion that my afternoon with her was responsible for her final disintegration, I felt a double relief at her departure.

Maisie was to have come to tea that very day. I expected her at two o'clock, and we had planned to plot out the garden in Grand Variety Cycling areas. I was already practising my technique for Bicyclists' Dashing Hill—a piece of frantic momentum-gathering pedal work, then a free-wheel swoop from end to end of the long sloping path between the lawn and the kitchen garden—when I saw the large yellow car of the Jardines coming up the drive. I rushed; but when I reached the front door, there was no Maisie. The chauffeur had already delivered a parcel and a note, and was preparing to drive away again.

The parcel was addressed to me in Maisie's tumbledown, dashing but uncertain hand. The note was addressed to my mother by Mrs. Jardine; delicately branching, sharp-jointed coleoptera, transfixed upon a rectangle of violet vellum.

I opened the parcel. It contained a perfect specimen of ammonite wrapped up in a piece of paper, on which Maisie had written:

*"Dear Rebeca.—I cannot come to tea to-day because my father is dead. Auntie Mack came yesterday to tell us and fetch us for the funerel. We are going by the night train, not Cherry, only Malcolm and me. It was her who said not Cherry, and then Auntie Mack quite agreed. She said to come back imediately after and Auntie Mack too, but I don't know. Here is a fossell for your museum. I found it in the quary the day before yesterday and I was going to bring it to tea, so here it is.*

*"Love from*

*"Maisie."*

I took the other note from Mossop and went to find my mother. She read it and laid it down and reflected, looking faintly wary and ambiguous. My father was in London. Her manner suggested that Mrs. Jardine had confronted her with a critical social problem. Then she said:

"Mrs. Jardine wants to come and see me. About her grandchildren, she says."

"I've got a letter from Maisie," I said. "Her father's dead, so she can't come to tea."

"Poor children," said my mother. "Poor Maisie." She sighed. Maisie's orphaned state, her uncompromising simplicity, the kind of forlorn toughness there was about her made a special appeal to my mother. She was touched by her, and always took particular pains to encourage her when she came to tea. In return, Maisie bestowed upon her an almost reverent devotion; seeing her, no doubt, as a satisfactory embodiment of that abstract Good Mother figure of which her life was deprived. Watching her glow and expand in response to my mother's welcome, it seemed impossible to believe that she was the same girl who twisted and shrank, physically shrank, in the presence of her grandmother.

"What is to become of them now . . .?" said my mother. She

93

took up the letter again, and murmured it through disjointedly. "'. . . *to whom you have shown so much kindness, and whose affection and confidence you have won . . . your advice . . . Friday next at 3-30 should that day and time be convenient to you.*'"

"Shall you say yes?"

I felt tense. The time had come for Mrs. Jardine to advance, to establish another bridgehead. I was aware through all my being of her plan, her timing. We were in her house, but she not yet in our house. I saw myself in dual motion, running ahead of her, running to meet her, cutting a hopeful but rather feeble figure both behind and before.

"I'll see," said my mother. "I have to be very busy this Friday."

"When does Daddy come back?"

"Not till Saturday."

She told me to run out and play, and I went and bicycled gloomily in the kitchen garden. Jess had gone riding, Isabel was out with Sylvia and the pram; a suddenly blank, lonely, mortal world oppressed my spirit.

About half an hour later, my mother's voice called from the drawing-room window. She had a note in her hand, and asked me if I would like to walk up with it to the Priory.

"What have you said?" I inquired nervously.

"That I shall be delighted to see Mrs. Jardine on Friday. Just ring, and when the bell is answered, say: 'Will you please give this note to Mrs. Jardine?' That's all you need say. And then come straight back."

I set off with mingled alacrity and reluctance, feeling that the magic grove would be different, disenchanted, and that I was coming with sadly diminished status to ring the bell and hurry furtively away again. But when I came through the blue door in the wall, whom should I see at the end of the herbaceous border but Mrs. Jardine, wearing a white cape embroidered in peacock blue and gold thread, and cutting dahlias. She kissed me warmly and read the note and said: "Ah! . . . Thank you, my darling"; and went on cutting dahlias. I held the big shallow basket, and she laid the red, tawny and lemon heads in one by one with love and care.

She looked replenished, full of energy and power, as I had not seen her since our first visit: as if she had thrown off something that had been muffling her, behind which she had been suppressed, though watchful. Latterly she had been of another, a remote generation—the children's grandmother; but now we were equals again, and the sense of a time barrier between us was once more abolished.

"Is your father at home?" she said.

"No. He won't be back till Saturday."

"Ah! . . ." She held up a great crimson-black head, and murmured: "What a cup of beauty!" and laid it in the basket.

"Mummy was pleased when she got your note," I said. "I'm sure."

"Yes. We should meet." She paused, staring into space, snipping the air rapidly with her scissors. "I want advice. She found the knack with that girl."

"Maisie?"

"Yes. Maisie." She repeated slowly: "Maisie—Thomson."

"I think—I suppose—Maisie just sort of—took a liking to her."

"Ah. Hmm . . ." She looked at me reflectively. "Yes. I failed with that one. It was inevitable. Yet it still seems odd to me. I cannot get accustomed to failure with human beings—particularly the young."

"It seems odd to me too. I don't see how anybody could *not*—with you."

"Could not?"

"Love you," I said bashfully.

"Oh, do you feel that?" She spoke as if considering an impartial judgment. "My dear, as it happens, you are entirely wrong. I can be hated. As you have seen for yourself. No doubt," she added casually, cutting another dahlia, "she discussed it with you."

"Well, yes," I murmured, embarrassed. "A bit."

"She has violent passions, that girl. All torn up by the roots. All jangled. All destructive. Most dangerous. What is to become of her?"

"It's because——" I stopped.

95

"Yes. We must speak of these things." She moved to the next clump of dahlias, and made as if to start cutting again. Then her arm dropped to her side, and she said in a voice of strong lament: "She has had too much to bear! And so shuttered a nature. So righteous, so dogmatic. She is not a vessel fitted to receive suffering. It will only corrode her, petrify her. How can I endure to be responsible for such a being?"

I said finally, with thumping heart:

"Do you think—now—perhaps—her mother might come back for them?"

"No." She drew in a hissing breath; then began once more to cut and fill the basket. "No. Ianthe will not come back. She has never wanted her children."

"But I thought . . ." I stumbled. "Maisie said . . ."

"What?"

"She loved them."

She was silent; then said with compassion:

"Unfortunate girl. There!—you see again: the distortion, the violence of the will. Malcolm knows better. He has undergone the crisis, and surmounted it. He is safe. Boys have, on the whole, more moral candour than girls. He has a lot against him, that boy. Singularly undistinguished appearance. Impoverished outlook. He has been taught, my poor fellow, to see himself with dislike and shame. Once his confidence is restored his looks will improve. Besides, I shall deal with his jaw. My dentist appears to be the only man in this country with any grasp of bridge work. Oh, Malcolm is decent human material. He will do. As you know," she added, "these three children are now, for all practical purposes, orphans. The charge of them devolves upon myself. . . . Upon Harry and myself."

She squared her shoulders, flung back her cape, and, chin lifted, stared towards the house. Her eyes sent forth electric rays. At last! cried her heroic and challenging pose. At last she had snatched victory out of the long years of plot and counter-plot, of ambush, espionage and surprise; of mortal episodes of frontal combat. She had outwitted and outlasted. She would bring her flesh and blood back into her home.

96

"Harry will want Malcolm to go to Winchester," she said. "That is where he was educated. Cherry will, of course, remain here with us for the present. She needs the discipline of an intelligent, emotionally sane governess. It cannot be *altogether* impossible to find such a woman. Cherry is shockingly backward in every way. Later we shall take her to the south of France for the winter. Her health requires the sun. She troubles me, that child. Her vitality has suffered some natal or pre-natal injury. The source rises in her—then flags and wavers down again. It is not stable. That is *her* inheritance." Again she drew in a sharp breath.

"The source?" I said, puzzled about the spelling, following her with the blossoming basket.

"The source, Rebecca! The fount of life—the source, the quick spring that rises in illimitable depths of darkness and flows through every living thing from generation to generation. It is what we feel mounting in us when we say: 'I know! I love! I *am!*' Do you understand me now?"

Her voice vibrated as if speaking waters ran through it. "Yes," I breathed, bewildered by a flying vision of streams and fountains, and myself borne along, dissolved in their elemental welling-up and flow.

"Sometimes," she said, "the source is vitiated, choked. Then people live frail, wavering lives, their roots cut off from what should nourish them. That is what happens to people when love is betrayed—murdered." Her eyes flicked. Then looking at me sternly, she said: "One day, Rebecca, women will be able to speak to men—speak out the truth, as equals, not as antagonists, or as creatures without independent moral rights—pieces of men's property, owned, used and despised. It may begin to be so in your lifetime. What am I saying?—it has begun. When you are a woman"—her smile broke over me, full and tender, "living, as I hope and believe you will live, a life in which all your functions and capacities are used and *none* frustrated, spare a thought for Sibyl Anstey. Say: 'She helped to win this for me.'"

"Sibyl Anstey?" I said, trembling inwardly. "Is that you?"

"That is my name. We will speak of these things a great deal more one day. Look, these six dahlias are for you, for yourself. What colour are these two?"

"White."

"No. Look more carefully. You must learn to be more accurate. If you were painting them you would mix green for them—faint, faint green that would make the white luminous. A green thought. Can you paint? When I was young, I painted flowers very beautifully. There, two of these. Two citron. Two blood-red. I hope you will grow up with seeing eyes, my love."

I took them from her, and laid them in a corner of the basket by themselves, feeling grateful but abashed, as if I were under charges of inaccurate observation and lack of talent for flower painting, and therefore unworthy of the gift.

I followed her down the herbaceous border. She strolled and stopped, examining, casting busy speculative glances about among her plants, as though her mind were on them, and what she had been saying mere background accompaniment to practical horticulture. But I saw the electric storm passing through her, shaking her.

I said, timidly:

"I knew your name was Sibyl Anstey."

"Ah, did you?" she said briskly. "It was my maiden name. Also my stage name, and the name with which I signed my books. When I was younger, I was a very well-known writer. I wrote three novels, and then I stopped. I had said what I had to say: I made room for others. My books are forgotten for the moment—but they will be read again. I suppose your father told you?"

"No. It was Tilly."

"Who?" She stood still, looking at me in a startled way.

"Tilly. You know—Grandma's old maid."

"Yes, yes, I know."

"As a matter of fact, she told me a few days ago. She's been staying with us."

"I thought she was dead." She took a deep breath and walked slowly on again. "*Staying* with you. Tilly. *Well!* . . ." She seemed agitated.

Once more I gave an account of our relations with Tilly, and concluded by saying:

"Mummy says she doesn't think she's going to live very long now."

"I must go to her," said Mrs. Jardine. "As soon as possible. This is most extraordinary. I sent her a letter a few years ago. It was returned to me. On the back of it some uneducated hand had printed: *Address not known. It is to be feared as Mrs. Svoboda as passed away.*"

"Who *ever* could have done that?" I said, appalled.

"I think I can guess." Mrs. Jardine uttered a brief chuckle. "How foolish of me not to guess at the time! Well! . . . I must go to her. As soon as possible. Your mother will give me her address. What a little *dea ex machina* you are proving, love. To think that this might have been left all unresolved, a cruel discord . . . as I thought indeed it had been. It was a stroke on the heart for me. Well . . . I can see her once more. Seven years —yes, it must be—since our last meeting. How time gallops!" Her eyes widened to embrace an unseen horizon. "So Tilly spoke of me to you."

"Yes. Well—a bit. Maisie remembered her too, you see, so I told her about us being friends. She did just remember Maisie; but she's forgotten about most things, except, and this is so funny, what happened a long time ago."

"Ah, so she remembered Maisie," said Mrs. Jardine meditatively.

"She calls you Miss Sibyl," I said, hoping to make her smile.

She did smile; but the tears, which came so simply and with so much beauty, brimmed over and slipped down her cheeks.

"Oh, Til!" she murured. "Tiny carapaced beetle on the stalk of life. Still living. . . . What tenacity! I think it probable that she was the only human being Ianthe ever cared for. A *grain* of genuine feeling. I will not dignify it with the name of a disinterested love." She sniffed. "Ianthe was born with a face like a flower, but she has no heart."

Struck forcibly by this declaration, I could think of nothing to say but:

"Tilly told me she looked after her, sometimes, when she was a little girl."

"And afterwards," remarked Mrs. Jardine. "Yes. She looked after her well."

"Oh no," I said, anxious to clear the situation. "After she went abroad, to Italy, I think, she never saw her any more. She said so. Except that one time with Maisie and Malcolm in the hotel. And she doesn't seem to remember much about that."

"Possibly," said Mrs. Jardine in the same dry tone, "possibly she remembers more than she discloses. Tilly is a very cunning woman. Some old people, you know, are deaf, and not so deaf: as it suits them."

Tilly's face and manner, vacant, sullen, rose up before me under a different light to dismay me.

"Her memory is bad," I insisted. "Sometimes she doesn't remember our names and muddles us up. And she really seems to forget Boy is born at all. When she saw Isabel wheeling him in the garden a little while ago she asked her who he belonged to."

Mrs. Jardine chuckled.

"Belonged to, indeed! From what you tell me of that one he would not lightly overlook such affronts to personal dignity."

"I never knew she was cunning," I said tentatively.

Once more in this caressing garden as in Tilly's familar room, intimations of desolation brushed me, made me shiver. The worm was under the leaf. "Cunning" echoed in the same land as "ruin," "treachery," "fall."

Mrs. Jardine, pausing at the end of the herbaceous border, mused. For the first time in her actual presence the sense pierced me directly: that she was wicked. A split second's surmise. But when next moment I looked up at her, there was her profile lifted beautifully above me, serene and reassuring as a symbol in stone.

"When we are children," she said, "we do not see the people close to us as themselves—only as our need for them, our habit of them. When something happens to make us realise that they have an enormous life going on apart from us, we feel rather resentful. Perhaps rather frightened. Do you understand what I mean?"

"Yes," I said truthfully.

"It is the mystery that frightens us. Once the mystery is explained, quite simply and straightforwardly, we can digest it; and then we feel satisfied, confident again. Children have very strong stomachs. What they cannot deal with they will spit out again; and no harm done. There is always a way of making a puzzle comprehensible. It is sheer idiocy," she vehemently declared, "*criminal* idiocy to blinker children, to refuse a decent explanation, or to explain falsely, to pack facts in cotton wool, or smear them with treacle . . . or with mud. That is what is amiss with your friend Maisie. She has been alternately starved and sickened by a repellent diet." She paused for breath; then rattled on briskly: "The same diabolical policy was practised upon Ianthe. With the inevitable disastrous results. I was powerless."

She had been declaiming out into the garden as if to an invisible audience ranged along the wall: but now she turned to me and, fixing me with her brilliant eyes, said:

"My dear Rebecca, I will always answer, truthfully, any question you care to put to me. Truth is my foible. But what you ask me and what I reply is a matter between us alone. I will respect your confidence and you must respect mine. Do you understand?"

"Yes," I said, appalled.

"You want to know, do you not, why I called Tilly a cunning woman. But you did not like to put the question directly?"

I nodded, swallowed, uneasy about the strength of my stomach.

"It would be wrong of me to make such an assertion without giving you my reasons."

But she still paused; and I felt rather than saw the ague shaking her. I knew the great question that I wished to ask, the question that summed up all: "Why do you tremble?"—could neither be asked nor answered.

When she spoke at last, her words, from their unexpectedness, came as a profound shock.

"Did Tilly never tell you about a journey she made to Bohemia?"

"No. I knew her husband came from there when he was a boy.

101

She told me that. And he brought a cuckoo clock with him. But I don't think *she's* ever been there, because when I said I wished we had one just like it, a cuckoo clock I mean, she said I'd have to go there one day and find one for myself, it was too far for her. Are you *sure* she went?"

"Oh yes. All that way—right into the very heart of Europe."

"When was it?"

"Nearly twenty years ago."

"Before Grandma died?"

"Not long after. Your grandmother died young, you know. Comparatively young."

"Did she go alone?"

"She went with Ianthe."

"Why?"

"Ianthe called upon her for help. She was in great trouble."

"What was the matter?"

"She was going to have a child. She was eighteen. She was quite alone. She asked Tilly to help her."

Mrs. Jardine's voice was quiet, conversational. She walked on slowly to the white wooden bench beneath the wall, at the end of the border, and there seated herself, motioning to me to come beside her. She sat bolt upright, with her cloak folded around her; and I noticed how queer her little feet looked in their flat-heeled paste-buckled shoes, planted squarely side by side. I had seen old nurses and cottage women sit like this, solidly, their knees a little spread.

"We will not sit here for long," she said. "There is a chill in the air. Are you quite warm? At your age one is always warm. Let us enjoy these beauties for ten minutes. I am extremely fortunate in Gillman. He has real sensibility. An artist. See how he has dealt with the masses of the Michaelmas daisies."

I looked down the feathery perspective, its many-coloured birds'-breast plumage softly burning in the rich sun of summer's end, and tried vainly to summon a conception of taciturn, grey-whiskered Mr. Gillman dealing with masses.

"Do you mean—was it Maisie she was going to have?"

"Oh dear me no. If it had been, it would make Maisie nineteen years old, would it not?"

"Yes, I suppose so," I agreed, totally adrift among mathematical and biological calculations. "Then—she had another baby before Maisie?"

"Yes."

"Maisie never told me."

"I presume that she has never been told."

"Where . . . What happened to it?"

"He died. He was denied his life. My eldest grandson."

The bitter woe in her voice alarmed me. I put out a timid hand and laid it on her lap, and she took it up and held it in hers, beneath her cloak.

"These things are for your ears alone," she said quietly. "Lock them up in you. Such extravagances are not fit for common eyes and ears."

Half dreading the weight of what was to come, I said, to prepare myself, to delay the moment of impact:

"Does anybody else know?"

"No one knows the true facts."

"Not Harry?"

"Oh Harry, yes. Yes. He knows. We have not spoken of it for many a long year."

"Grandma you'd have told, if she hadn't died?"

Her pause disturbed me; her answers had been coming so pat.

"Circumstances," she said at last, "separated Laura and myself. A tragedy for me. For her too I dare to think—I know—a deep sorrow. If there had been no—no gap in our intimacy, who knows how much of all these disasters could have been avoided . . . ? Do you know what goes to make a tragedy? The pitting of one individual of stature against the forces of society. Society is cruel and powerful. The *one* stands no chance against its combined hostilities. But sometimes a kind of spiritual victory is snatched from that defeat. Then the tragedy is completed. . . . Yes. Love proposed. *Man* disposed between Laura and myself. As to your question," she added crisply, as if suddenly recalling the terms of our pact: "The answer cannot be a simple yes. *If* she had been

alive, *all* that happened—the whole course of events—would have
run a different course. Tilly would not have been able to hatch
her fatal plot alone—your grandmother would have had to be
consulted. She—she with all her sense and sensibility—would
have taken control. She would have found me, called me—ME!
. . . I know she would—I know it. She would not have left me
at the mercy of a conspiracy between a vulgar, vengeful old
woman and an ignorant, corrupted, desperate girl. *I* should have
been there. I should have won back Ianthe. He—*he* would
have been saved!"

Fiercely riding the climbing crest of her passion, suddenly she
broke, collapsed. Bowed double, plunging her face into her
hands, she burst into sobs. Dry, labouring gasps tore her body.
She rocked herself back and forth in primitive female lamenta-
tion.

It was all over in a minute or two. She sat up and straightened
her shoulders, and through ashen lips drew in one long, deep,
steady breath.

"It was Tilly's revenge," she said in a weak, calm voice. "She
should have called me. She would not."

"Perhaps," I said, "she didn't know how to get hold of you
—how to find you."

"Oh yes, she did." Mrs. Jardine smiled disdainfully. "Yes, yes,
she did. I came to see your grandmother when she lay dying.
All was understood; all was made beautiful again between us.
There was only love. We did not say much to one another, but
every word was truth, and holy. When I left her I knew that I
should never see her again. So did she. I wrote down my address
and put it in her hand. She said she would give it to Tilly, and
enjoin upon Tilly to call me if the need arose. We envisaged
circumstances in which, perhaps, tidings of change in Ianthe's
life might reach Tilly before me. We knew they still corresponded now and then. That is so extraordinary. I have never
been able . . ." She broke off; then murmured vaguely, as if
speaking to herself: "That I should have envisaged it so clearly
then . . . yet later, when the time came. . . . However . . ."
She went on now in her former grave, simple manner: "The

dying can make promises too. Your grandmother promised me that. It was my first great—oh, huge!—consolation for many a long day. You see, she trusted Tilly. But Tilly hated me so much that she betrayed even her."

I said with false innocence:

"Tilly hated you?"

"Yes."

"But she told me," I said, "nobody could help loving you when you were—when she first knew you; you were so beautiful and you—and everybody loved you."

She took up my hand again and kissed my fingers.

"Ah, Rebecca!" she said, smiling. "You are one who will be too lavish with the sweet oils of life. It is your grandmother over again. Beware! It must be cemented, this honey nature, with something firm; an essence of the experiencing, time-resisting *mind*. Yes, Tilly loved me once. Later, it was no longer so."

"Why not?"

"She thought . . . Most mistakenly, she conceived the suspicion that I had injured your grandmother. We will not go into that now. Sow ignorant doubts at random on these harsh natures and you crop flints and thorns. Their hearts are choked, choked with stony loyalties, with lacerating malice. After long years of waiting, she was granted the opportunity to strike me down. She took it. Who is to blame her?"

Stretching an arm above her head, Mrs. Jardine plucked a sprig from the late-flowering creamy rambler profuse on the wall behind us. She divided it and gave me half, and held hers to her nose, inhaling the fragrance.

"What did she do?" I asked, sniffing at my bit in a perfunctory way.

"You must know," said Mrs. Jardine calmly, "that I left Ianthe's father when she was a very young child. Our marriage had become a wretched affair—without tenderness or communion. There remained nothing but convention to keep us together. Convention is another name for the habits of society. When a habit is bad it should be broken. A bad marriage is the most detrimental, most vicious of habits—and one of the most difficult for a man or a woman to break. Society sees to that. It is very powerful, and people are mostly weak, and fear its judgment. Do you follow me?"

"Yes," I said. "I don't know all the words, but still——"

"Tell me which you want explained."

"Oh no," I said hastily. "Please not. I like hearing the ones I don't know. I mean, I do understand them, even when I don't."

The importance of the unknown words she used, the excitement of apprehending their meanings, the fact that she never diluted her language to fit the infirmity of my understanding—all these things formed a major part of my joy in her company.

"I am not weak and not afraid." She stopped, and then said: "In those days I was not afraid. I judged others by my own standards, and trusted in their good faith. When I left the man I had married I took the only course that could save us from a life of self-contempt and spiritual dishonour." She drew in a hissing breath, and continued rapidly: "Unfortunately he was a man not sensible to such considerations. He had *once* been capable of nobility, or naturally I would not have married him; but his spirit had petrified. The sole concern of that man had grown to be his position in the eyes of the world. I took a step which destroyed his prestige as a man of property. I was his property: he had lost it. Therefore he would destroy me."

I stole a glance at her. Her nostrils were dilated, her expression dramatic but composed. Her words came so smoothly, with such precision of timing, it was impossible not to feel that she was presenting a part she had rehearsed a hundred times. I experienced a curious moment of disabused vision, and thought I saw myself not as uniquely privileged, selected after a lifetime to receive her secrets, but as one of a long shadowy series of confidential audiences, all gazing, listening, as spellbound, as gratified as I.

"He was a man," she went on, "in whom violent and strangled jealousies took the place of heart. A creature incapable of disinterested love. Yes, yes." Her eyes flicked. "I pity any being delivered over to Charles Herbert's passions."

"Didn't he love Ianthe?"

"Love her!" Her mouth stretched disdainfully. "Oh, he loved her so devotedly he must make a prisoner of her, deny her the light of day and the fresh springs of freedom. He must cut her from her natural roots. Not enough that she should grow up outrageously deprived of a mother. No! She must be taught to link the name of mother with all that is the enemy of truth and goodness."

"He—he taught her to think you were horrid?"

"He did."

"How beastly of him!" I cast my eyes down and inquired: "Couldn't you take her with you, then, when you went away?"

"He refused me that."

"Her own mother!"

She nodded.

I felt Tilly's revelations, and consequently my duplicity, weighting my tongue; but if her suspicions had been aroused or were kindled by the disingenuous manner which accompanied my next inquiry, she passed them over.

"Not even *part* of the time?"

"Not for a day. Or for an hour."

"Poor Ianthe."

"Yes. Poor Ianthe."

"Was he kind to her? Did she love him? I suppose she must have, as he was her own father."

"Oh, they fastened upon one another," she said coldly. "They battened."

This time I recoiled from the meaning of her words. She made them sound disgusting.

"How long was it," I said, "till you—— How long before you saw her again?"

"I never saw my child again," said Mrs. Jardine.

"Oh, but the Park!" rose to my lips. I bit back the reminder. There was silence; then she added:

"I have seen Ianthe. I have stood at a distance and watched her. I have spoken to her. But I have no daughter."

She got up and drew her cloak around her, and together we started to pace over the lawn towards the nearer lime alley. We passed through one of the arches into the clipped, leafy enclosure, and she went and stood before the stone figure of a graceful, nude, meditative young man with a cap of curls, and said, smiling faintly up at him:

"This is the temple of Apollo. I brought him from Italy. He is safe here. He is worshipped."

Unearthly, incandescent, their mysteriously harmonious heads answered one another within the green light. Then she looked round and stooped to pick up a bicycle pump, some string, a doll's tea-pot, and a match-box lined with scraps of checked cotton stuff and cotton wool.

"Untidy children!" she exclaimed with maternal sharpness. "That boy assured me, positively assured me, that his pump had been stolen from the shed on Wednesday by some master padlock-picker. He shall be well scolded when he comes back. Careless fellow. . . . Cherry likes to play here by herself." She fingered the match-box with a tender expression. "Harry has taken her on the river. They will be back before very long. Let us go in. You must stay and keep me company at tea. We will send a telephone message to your mother that I am sending you back in the car as soon as it returns from the river."

She began to stroll up the lime alley, drawing in luxurious breaths of the leaf-scented air. Tension had vanished from her manner; she appeared collected and alert.

"So when they come back it'll be for good?" I said, walking beside her with the flower-basket.

"Oh yes, certainly. This is their home. That woman Flora Mackenzie—she is an excellent woman. But she has no natural sympathy with children, or understanding of them. However, I believe her to be perfectly good-hearted and scrupulous."

"You mean Auntie Mack?"

"That is their name for her. She is merely a distant cousin on the father's side. Yes, she has been good to them, according to her lights."

"Will she be coming back with them?"

"I have offered her a home for the present. She has been under a severe strain and is greatly in need of rest. It will not be a permanent arrangement. It seems that her ambition is to share a cottage at Bude with a woman friend, a retired schoolmistress. Harry will provide her with the means to compass her ambition. A lifetime of care for others—and then to be left elderly, solitary, penniless; without prospects or qualifications. . . . No. Such cast-off members of society are not enviable. There are thousands in similar case. Where do they creep to, to drink cups of tea, and starve and freeze by fireless grates, and preserve their rags of gentility in camphor, and wait in the night for those clawing pains they dare not own or name . . .? Distressed gentlewomen!" Her voice and eye grew full with pity, scorn and indignation. "It was very pleasant," she added, "to be able to reassure her about her future. We had a long talk yesterday evening. Most interesting. She is a sensible, simple, responsive woman."

I saw them pacing the paths in earnest *tête-à-tête*. I felt the firm magnetic pressure of Mrs. Jardine's hands at work, manipulating Auntie Mack, softening her out. . . . Then the deeps quaking—opening—yielding up all: all the difficulties, doubts, devotions of a lifetime impetuously, rejoicingly exposed.

"As a matter of fact," said Mrs. Jardine in a casual way, stooping to pick up a screw of grubby paper—a crumpled sweet bag —"we have corresponded, at long intervals, for some years. Since Ianthe left the man Thomson, to be precise. So soon as I discovered the fact, I wrote to Flora Mackenzie, requesting a private interview. It seems that she consulted her conscience and came to the conclusion that, situated as she was, a dependent beneath the man's roof, under an extorted vow to him to preserve them from all possible contact with their mother or their mother's family—she came to the conclusion that it would be both un- ethical and unsafe to comply with my request. On the other hand," continued Mrs. Jardine in her crispest expository man- ner, "being a woman of feeling *and* a prudent Scotswoman, she was unwilling to jettison what chances of happiness remained to those young creatures by depriving them irretrievably of my support—Harry's and mine. She foresaw the need that would arise—the desperate situation. She explained all this to me. She offered to keep in touch with me to the extent of two letters a year—begging me neither to write back to her nor to write to my grandchildren, for fear of interception. I promised her this in exchange for a promise that she would inform me immediately of any major crisis. We kept our pledges. Twice a year she wrote me bulletins. She does not carry a soul in her pen, but still . . . Up to a point it was satisfactory. Oh, yes. I owe a debt of gratitude to Flora Mackenzie. I am the first to acknowledge it. It shall be repaid. The moral conflict must have been a heavy burden for a woman of her strict religious principles."

Needless to say, no suspicion of irony then struck me; and even now, looking back, summoning her voice in memory, I detect no ambiguous ring. I told myself that Auntie Mack must have taken this—this too—to God. But how account for the simultaneous impression that visited me: a consciousness of the spiritual rewards of guilt—the pride, the romance, the sense of secret power and peril—which must have sustained her through those long years of uncongenial duty?

So Auntie Mack had been in the plot all the time. I pondered on this. How far, how tenaciously the net had been flung, and flung again; with what cunning and singleness of purpose; what strange and various fish had been netted!

I said:

"So when their father got ill, she wrote and told you?"

"She did."

"Did she think he wouldn't get better?"

"She knew he would not."

"Soon . . .!" I heard Auntie Mack whisper, twitching on the end of her line. And then: "NOW!"

"She put it to him," continued Mrs. Jardine briskly, "that it was his duty to attempt some provision for his otherwise destitute children by an appeal to me—their only close living relative: certainly the *only* one with means. She offered to spare him a distasteful task by making that appeal herself, on his behalf. At first he vehemently refused. At late last he yielded; and their visit to me was arranged. She must have used considerable tact and patience. He was a bitter, stubborn man. However," added Mrs. Jardine, "no doubt his illness weakened him. And no doubt his responsibilities lay heavy on his mind. It seems he cared for them, after his own dour fashion. He had nothing to leave them. They had scraped and pinched along on his inadequate salary as a schoolmaster; and that would, of course, cease with his death."

"So they might have starved?"

"Well, naturally I should have come to the rescue in any case, after his death, if not before. And in the event of my dying before him, I had made provision for them in my will. But I did not choose that he should know that. No. As it has been, it has been for the best. He yielded to death at last in tranquillity of spirit. He even sent me a message with his last breath."

"What was it?"

"He thanked me. He confided them to my care."

Again Mr. Thomson rose before me—sad horse, trying to get on his legs again. I had seen one once in the village street, a huge, prone cart horse, colossally struggling to rise, urged on by human goads and shouts. As his head sank convulsively at last between the shafts, Nurse had hurried us away.

"Did you write and tell him you would—would look after them?"

"I had already done so. Yes. Yes, of course." Mrs. Jardine drew a heavy breath. "One cannot let a human soul go out utterly uncomforted, no matter how poor in grace it has been, if one is granted the power to soothe it. I sent him four lines. I told him I loved them; that all three had magnificent appetites, and the glow of sun and health; that all had put on weight; that Malcolm and Cherry had become effortlessly at home beneath our roof; that Maisie's character and loyalties should be treated with the respect they deserved."

"What a good thing you did that," I said, nearly choking with emotion.

"I am glad you think so," said Mrs. Jardine, as if a little surprised. "God knows I have no reason to honour the memory of Robert Thomson. But I see him now as one more unfortunate, unequal to his destiny. A small man. He undertook what only one of exceptional stature could have carried out. And even

*111*

then . . .! Well, now the wheel has come full circle. In my end is my beginning. A sort of miracle. Only I am old, not young."

Again she drew a heavy breath, lifting her head to gaze in triumph and desolation at what was hidden from me. We had emerged from beneath the lime tunnel and were in the sun-flooded loggia, facing the expanse of lawn. Calmly she stared into the full light; and now, I told myself, now was my moment to release what I had all this time been holding and clutching in anxious preoccupation: the carrier words that would float me —me too—back into the beginning from which, since her out-burst, we had so strayed. I said:

"She did what Tilly didn't, then?"

She looked at me, raising her eyebrows in inquiry.

"Auntie Mack. She sent for you when—when you were needed. Not like Tilly."

"Ah, Tilly. . . . Poor Tilly, she was—is, I should say—an emo-tionally frustrated woman. It was not to be expected that she should have vision beyond such an extravagant opportunity for paying off a score. 'You alone,' said the child. 'Tell no one.' "

"If Ianthe said that . . . said it was a secret, I suppose she thought she had to keep it?"

"That is what she would tell herself," agreed Mrs. Jardine. "That would be the common level of behaviour—the world's level. Wisdom and magnanimity are not attributes of the world. I bear Tilly no grudge at all. I will explain."

She leaned against one of the pillars of the loggia in an un-familiar pose: relaxed, informal. She said:

"You must imagine Ianthe a beautiful girl of sixteen, living in an Italian city called Florence, having for well-nigh sole daily companion a sick, elderly man: sick in body and in spirit. They chose to live as exiles, so it seems: let us say in the manner of a dispossessed monarch and his princess daughter. In pride, isolation and sterility."

Measured, abstract, her voice fell, weighing out syllable after syllable into the air. No drama coloured it now, no calculated effects of presentation; and the unstressed words began to build a formal elemental pattern, weaving my attention into it in a repetitive design of interrogation marks.

But she did not long sustain the impersonality of her once-upon-a-time manner. After a brief and vivid description of the beauties of Florence, she replied to a question of mine as to how the pair passed their days with a distinct lapse into dryness.

"Between doctors, collectors of art objects and priests," she said. "It seems that Charles Herbert sought support and consolation in the bosom of the church. The need came on him, I presume, subsequently to our separation. I detected no symptom of it during our married life. I should have said, indeed, that he was notably indifferent to the evidences of Christianity—or to religion in a more general sense." She sniffed.

"He'd got sort of religious?" I inquired with anxious hope. For surely if I took her meaning this must mean an increase of goodness in Charles, despite apparently unfavourable omens.

A faint smile crossed her face.

"Oh yes. Undoubtedly he had. And Ianthe was his Snow-white Virgin, his dedicated Lamb, his unspotted Daughter-Bride." She spat the words out. "Oh yes. They flourished together in a *hot bed* of sanctity."

Her lips coarsened with their expression of nauseated contempt.

"Except," I suggested in the ensuing silence, "*he* didn't flourish really, did he? I mean—if he was sick?"

She looked amused.

"Well, there are ways and ways of flourishing," she said. "Sickness can put forth remarkable sprouts." But then, as if deciding it was high time to soar again, she continued with an alteration of tone to simple gravity: "I am not mocking at religion, Rebecca. Heaven forbid that I should descend to such loathsome and imbecile vulgarity. No. . . . I am no bigot in agnosticism. One must have the humility and the imagination to honour all deep human experiences—not least those one has never come near to sharing. How often have I wished for the experience of faith!—of God pervading all, like the heart beating, the breath

*113*

drawn in and out. But this is to be dowered with a special genius, rare as any other kind."

"Don't you believe in God, then?" I inquired, shaken.

"I neither believe nor disbelieve. I am *ignorant* of God. I know only the mystery. *That* has not faded out, at least."

"Jess believes in God," I said. "She knows exactly what He's like. She's told me. But I don't seem to imagine Him the same."

I dared not admit the difficulty: the inability to rid myself of an early identification of Him with the Toby jug on the school-room mantelpiece—a rubicund grotesque with nut-cracker profile, falsely benign leer, and grey wig beneath a three-cornered hat.

Mrs. Jardine turned upon me a meditative glance.

"I rather doubt your ever becoming one of the faithful," she said. "One can never tell; but I doubt it."

There was no vestige of criticism in her voice, but I felt disappointingly classified and hastened to cover my chagrin by re-directing the weight of her judgment to its original objects.

"But no. Ianthe has not the temperament for God. No harmony, no discipline . . . no dedication. Ianthe grew up sharply brilliant, graceful, morbid, self-absorbed to a pathological degree. Given the circumstances, this was inevitable."

"If you—if you didn't see her, how do you know she was like that?"

"Oh, I had means of discovering," said Mrs. Jardine. Calmly she smiled into the distance. "Years of practice made me an adept in the art of seeing unseen. I stood at street corners. I strolled with the crowd in parks and gardens. I attended religious services. I was an English lady-tourist in picture galleries; a frequenter of operas, concerts, lectures. I learned where to look for my cultivated daugher. Oh yes!—I will give him his due: he devoted much care to her education. She was well read and unusually accomplished. Yes," she said, after a pause, turning towards me, "I saw her quite often, in one place or another. At a distance, you understand, always at a distance. Fortunately I have very long sight. And in time I acquired the technique of suppressing my personality—of becoming as it were blank, neutral, dissolved into my surroundings: invisible indeed. So that I was never recognised. I have often thought what useful lessons I could give to a detective . . . or to a murderer."

She smiled.

I took in her meaning at last, with all its implications; and a shiver went through me. The lady in the blue cape: the middle-aged woman nicely dressed (but oh! she had got stout); and in between, how many others, impressive, inconspicuous, utterly exposed and disguised, posted solitary at their selected vantage-points, in deadly concentration?

"I watched her carefully," continued Mrs. Jardine. "It was necessary that I should understand what material I should have to deal with. Oh, I grew to know her—through and through. I saw what she had become."

"What?"

"A mirror-haunter."

"What's that?"

"She had built herself a room of mirrors. She never looked out straight into the light, at objects, at other people's faces. She looked into these mirrors and saw the whole of creation as images of herself thrown back at her. On them she brooded, adoring, fearing what she saw."

"I wonder why she did that," I murmured, confused by the concrete, Lady of Shalott scene presented to me.

"She was afraid of the world. That is why. When people are afraid they dare not look outward for fear of getting too much hurt. They shut themselves up and look only at pictures of themselves, because these they can adapt and manipulate to their needs without interference, or wounding shocks. The world sets snares for their self-love. It betrays them. So they look in the mirrors and see only what flatters and reassures them; and so they imagine they are not betrayed."

"Fancy you noticing all that just by watching her from far off!" I said admiringly. "I can't think how."

"It was plain, all too plain, to the seeing eye," said Mrs. Jardine. "And who should see clearer than I? My own flesh and blood."

"What did she look like?"

"Tall. A long full neck," said Mrs. Jardine dreamily, staring before her. "She carried her head . . . down. Drooping. Sidelong inclined, like a wilting lily. As no doubt she was pleased to see herself. His lily maid and all the rest of it, I dare say. Ach! He was always a sentimentalist, as all cruel people are." Her eyes dilated.

"Was she pale?" I asked enthusiastically. Though pallor was, I knew, not healthy, it was a quality I much admired.

"Strikingly so."

"Like you." I gazed at her with a voluptuous eye.

"Yes, she inherited that from me—though in build and feature she resembled her father's family. Such a complexion can be a great beauty. It was so in my case—glorious. I had a white glow, incandescent. A great poet who loved me praised it in one of the poems he wrote for me. But she had no glow. However, her skin had its own quality: a mushroom texture, smooth and thick. Her eyes were fine—but too full. They looked dark, because the pupils were unusually large. The iris was blue and melting. She made great play with her eyes. But they took in nothing, no one. They were *bound* to herself." Mrs. Jardine brooded. "That was disquieting enough; but there was something else. During the times when she was *not* rolling glances around, demanding to be observed and admired, her eyes did not relax: they appeared to me to remain *taut;* fixed in an inward rigidity of contemplation." She made a brusque movement, drummed with her fingers on the pillar. "I have noticed a seed of the same thing in Cherry," she said abruptly.

"So have I," I said. "If you mean—staring at nothing—and Cherry's eyes look black too, don't they?—with blue round."

"Oh, you have noticed it too, have you?" she said, throwing me a sharp glance, as if my powers of observation were this time unwelcome. "Ah well—that can be dealt with. There is time, ample time. If I live—and live I must—Cherry shall have her freedom. It cannot be an irrevocable inheritance, a congenital . . ." Her fingers tapped violently. "No. . . . Such symptoms are the result of criminal mishandling; the ingrowing reaction

*116*

of an exceptionally egotistical nature, obstructed in its development. Physical beauty makes, of course, for an additional menace. . . . But I have noticed with such natures that beauty itself, of a particular type, seems as it were an external symptom. They seem to put it forth mysteriously, abnormally, as consumptives do."

Taking the flower-basket from me, Mrs. Jardine lightly lifted and redistributed one or two dahlias.

Presently I said:

"Had she got a smiling sort of face?" And added hastily: "Or not?"

"What would you expect?" said Mrs. Jardine, encouraging me to make a psychological judgment.

"Not."

"Quite right."

"More sad?"

"Unhappy. There is a difference. Sorrow can beautify. I have seen it regenerate and purify an old coarse face. But unhappy faces are merely distressing. Faces that cannot forget themselves and flow outward freely, generously to meet their fellow beings. One is apt to see that look on adolescent faces, but it is generally accompanied by something else, which makes it exceedingly moving: some passion of anxiety and longing, as of a prisoner struggling to be free, to communicate. Some hope, some question: 'Is it time? When will the time come? Is this the way out of the tunnel? Can you be the person who will help to set me free?' . . . But in her face, that fitful spark, that young life gathering its forces to burst out was missing. Her mouth was a displeasing feature, although the lips were well shaped. It looked cramped, ungenerous, *repudiating*. Yes. I had to see my daughter preparing to *repudiate* life. To *unfit* herself. To be an invalid."

"An invalid? Ill?"

Mrs. Jardine put her fingers to her forehead.

"*There.*"

She was silent, and so was I. It was the sign for insanity, I knew. Ianthe was a mad girl, then; was that what these accumulated hints portended? I saw her with a wreath awry on her dishevelled locks and a straggle of broken flowers in her hand, like the picture of Ophelia in my illustrated Shakespeare. Then suddenly the miniature Maisie had shown me slid before my mind's eye. So concentrated had I been on the portrait Mrs. Jardine was building up, that this image had lain dormant. But now it struck me that this phantasmagoric Italian princess, that Christmas Annual mother were one and the same person. Between these two incompatible figures, where, apart, from their equal mystery and fascination, was the connection?

Almost in the moment of presenting myself with this dilemma, I found the solution. It came over me with the same huge wave of relief and pleasure that I had experienced when at the age of six, between one despairing hour of guess-work and the next, the power was granted unto me to make sums give the right answers, that obviously no person was one and indivisible—one unalterable unit—but a multiplicity; so that everything about a person might be equally true and untrue, and I need no longer be puzzled by the badness of good people, and the other way round; and so on.

Confident that from now on I should be brighter, less dumbfounded, I was emboldened to say:

"Do you think it was *really* true, what you saw—that she was like that? Or only that she looked like that to you because——" I foundered. "Because——"

"Yes?" said Mrs. Jardine, expectant.

"Because you wanted——"

"Because I wanted to think so?"

"Well, not really, of course, but sort of."

"That is a perfectly legitimate point to raise," she pronounced judicially. "A woman in my position might well, out of the bitterness and frustration of her feelings, create distortions. She might so have made up her mind beforehand that this influence she loathed was ruining her child that she would inevitably project her will in all its falsity upon the child. But no. I cannot be deceived. I have lightning in my eyes. It strikes without warning, often to my own discomfiture, into dark places—a blinding flash. And then I *see!* Doubtless the world saw her as a charming and interesting creature in her spring-time bloom. But beneath her young roundness and smoothness she was sick. Life sick. Love sick." She drew a sharp breath that turned into a shudder all through her frame. "I saw the invisible worm."

She uttered the last words without emotion, but they exploded in me with a colossal reverberation. Compulsively I averted my eyes from the sky where, so it seemed, her fabulous gaze rested upon portents and monsters. Another moment, and its candid and impenetrable depths would be rent for me—me too; some dire apparition, some mythical reptile would appal my sight. I looked attentively into the loggia at some basket chairs piled with gay cretonne cushions.

After a while I said feebly:

"I wonder why she went like that."

"That is what I had to ask myself," said Mrs. Jardine. "What I had to discover. What canker was eating at her adolescence. I had become cut off from any effective source of information about the intimate aspects of her life. My intuitions were strong —and I had never had reason to mistrust them. But it was not till later that I ascertained certain facts, and knew that my suspicions had been all too well founded." She paused; then in a vibrating voice burst forth: "Wretched hallucinated creatures, both! Sick indeed! Criminal father! Ah, there is one corruption above all that stinks to heaven, and that is the odour of sanctified perversion. Which he died in."

"What is perversion?"

"Perversion, in the sense in which I use the term, is an abnormal love," explained Mrs. Jardine in a painstaking way. "That is, a bad, harmful love."

"Is that what theirs was?" I said, gloomy.

"Yes. Any love whose demands are excessive is a bad love. I mean, when the aim of the lover is to swallow up its object and possess it entirely, body and soul. *That* is the sin against the Holy Ghost."

"Oh, is *that* the sin against the Holy Ghost?" I exclaimed with interest. "I heard Mr. Grigsby read it out in Church, and we both wondered. Why is it a sin? Is it because—because it's wrong to force another person to do things they don't want to do?"

"That is partly the reason."

"*Bad* things, I suppose, they might have to do?"

An analogy struck me: Alan, our handsome and admired boy cousin, urging us to steal peaches for him under threat of the disfavour he knew we could ill endure.

"They might well. It is an abominable enough thing in a married relationship. But when the obsessed pair are father and daughter. . . . This subject cannot be ventilated. I touched on it in one of my novels." She broke off, looking scornful and indignant. "The outcry!—laughable if it were not so menacing. 'Indelicate,' 'outrageous,'—'indecent' even; those were the epithets. 'Miss Anstey's cynical pen does not spare the most sacred ties of human life. She dwells on them only to degrade and to debase them.' That was the lofty tone of my male critics. Ach! Hypocrites! Humbugs! Yes, and abusive letters. 'Having just removed a filthy contamination from my household by consigning your book to the flames——'" She laughed harshly. "Ah, but a few thanked me. That made the rest a gnat-bite—less." She broke off again and laid a hand on my head. "Dearest! Do not trouble your head with all this. It is immaterial. I was speaking my thoughts aloud. I am so much alone—I speak so much to myself." She added slowly: "*The thought runs through—through— yes, through . . .*" Then: "Later you will understand, though not, I hope from experience—I have no reason—oh none!—to think so—what crimes are committed in the name of parental love."

She turned over her little watch and consulted it. "They should be back by five from the river," she said vaguely; and I felt her beginning to make preparations in advance to readjust the equilibrium, to stabilise herself.

"Oh, please go on," I said anxiously, fearing to hear her say we would speak of these things another time.

"As I was telling you," she went on in a lighter way, "Ianthe's father became a singularly abnormal man. Normal people send their energies and emotions out through a number of channels.

He ceased to do this. He turned from life which had so disappointed him, and concentrated his whole being upon two objects; his daughter and his God. Naturally," she said dryly, "the two got somewhat mixed up. The world was not to breathe upon her. It was to be a kind of spotless union—a Trinity. She was not to know any other fulfilment. He taught her that the natural love between a man and a woman, the love that makes them wish to live together and have children, was loathsome and degrading. Yes, he taught her that wickedness! He and she for God only and each for God in one another: that was how it was to be . . . every variation upon that theme. It involved——" She paused. "It seems that it involved watching over her day and night: a total absorption. Not one word or thought, not one instinct was to escape his possession. Waking or sleeping, she must be his—guarded—his miser's treasure."

"Did he have her to sleep with him, then?" I asked, astonished at such intensity of fatherly concern.

"Yes. That is what he did."

"Did he think—was he afraid someone would get in and steal her, do you suppose?" I asked, assuming incredulity: thinking of Tilly, of Paris, the nursery windows of Ianthe's childhood barred—I knew against whom.

We did not meet one another's eyes. She gave no sign; but I felt her divination flicker over me.

"It may have started," she said calmly, "with some such fantastic notion. As she grew older, nearer to the time when a child normally begins to leave its parents' care and influence, his crazed love grew. At all costs he must isolate her from any future she might reach towards for herself—or that might open out for her through *me*. That was at the back of it all, of course. So he devised this union, this marriage in God. Oh! on the highest plane of spirituality and innocence . . ." She was talking to herself now. Disgust made her lips thick and heavy. "The sleep of the blessèd angels. Let me not appear to hint at a monstrous——" She stopped short.

"She was rather old, wasn't she," I observed, "to sleep with somebody else?"

"But in the ferment of adolescence!" she exclaimed, still thinking aloud, and disregarding my suggestion. "The awakening instincts of sex all crushed, distorted——" She broke off; then addressing me once more, continued: "Well now. Round about the time of Ianthe's seventeenth birthday, his health began rapidly to fail. He had long been a sick man—but this was mortal. The time was at hand when I should have what is called, in terms of the law, access to my daughter: that is, when she was eighteen I was to be permitted to see her occasionally. You can imagine, Rebecca, how I was preparing myself, what plans I had made, hoping against hope that it was not too late, that I should be able to apply purges and balms to drain away fifteen years of poison and make her whole again. There is a great saying—it is in Latin but I will translate: *I believe, because it is impossible.* That has always been my faith. Now, knowing he must die, what weighed most upon this father's mind?"

"What would happen to Ianthe?" I hazarded; thinking how all the crises in this family history seemed to follow the same pattern.

"Exactly. He saw the way open for Ianthe to come wholly back to me. A hideous dilemma for him. He was determined that his last act on earth should be to prevent that. He had already seen to it pretty thoroughly—but this was a practical act. He made a will. In this will he left all his money to various scholastic and ecclesiastical foundations, apart from a sum which would furnish Ianthe with an extremely modest yearly income—a mere pittance. This was to prevent the temptations of the world assailing her. She would otherwise have been an heiress—exposed, through me, so he chose to assume, to the predatory schemes of unscrupulous males. At the same time he appointed a guardian for her—an Englishman, a friend of his—not a friend, he had none—an acquaintance rather, one of the few regular visitors to his house. A man in whose high moral character and religious principles he recorded his utmost trust." A violent snort came from her. "Now, I knew nothing of all this. Just at this time I had met Harry, and married him. I was far away, on my honeymoon voyage, when I received the news of Charles's death."

"What was he like—the Englishman, the guardian?"

"Oh, an interesting type. At some stage in a chequered and dubious career—I subsequently traced it—he had regularised his position by taking Holy Orders."

"You mean he was a clergyman?"

"Yes. A clergyman of a sort."

Then surely it must be all right this time. This at least must be a good man.

"He then proceeded further to advance his interests by marrying a rich woman—a doting, devout spinster, considerably older than himself. He had been some years in Florence and had established a reputation for charm, culture and saintliness—with a touch—oh, just that touch!—of worldly wisdom, of deep sensual experience now foregone which makes the blend so irresistibly attractive to women. And Charles had much of the woman in him. Yes, he had much, this man, to commend him to Charles Herbert. A taste for art. A collection of china. A knowledge of music. Besides, they shared and indulged together a passion for the sensuous trappings of devotion—images, candles, crucifixes and the rest. All that gave them enormous satisfaction."

I had learnt, I scarcely know how, when irony and malice were intended. Sometimes there was a sniff; but the edge of her voice never sharpened. Perhaps it became, if anything, a shade more matter-of-fact.

"Well," continued Mrs. Jardine with a light sigh, "he died and was buried. And I was on my wedding journey. Harry and I were travelling round the world. I was in a time of peace and hope. When at last the news reached me through my solicitor, I turned in my tracks and started with all haste for Italy. Terrible weeks those were of agitation and suspense, with no information but a bare few lines saying that she was under the roof and guardianship of this unknown man."

"Did Harry go with you?"

"Harry naturally accompanied me." She paused. "Arrived in Florence, I behaved with the utmost correctness. I wrote to the man's wife asking for permission to call upon her."

"And she said yes?"

"No. The request was refused. My letter was the appeal of one woman to another, for understanding, if not for sympathy. I received in return a cold, curt note, dictated, no doubt, by *him,* stating that no useful purpose could be served by such an interview. Their duty to Ianthe consisted in discharging their trusteeship in the letter no less than in the spirit: and this they were doing and would do." Her lip curled.

"And did they?" I said weakly.

"Then," said Mrs. Jardine, "I wrote again. I said I was aware that my first meeting with my daughter was not due for another few months, but as I had re-married and expected to be travelling abroad during the whole of the coming year, I should be grateful for one brief interview, in order to explain to her my new circumstances. If they could not see their way to acceding to my request, my alternative would be to write to her, fully explaining my plans for our future. I added that I should remain in Florence until this question was decided. They evidently concluded that my pen was more to be feared than my presence. Or possibly," she added with a sardonic inflection, "they conceived the odd suspicion that I might cause them embarrassment if thwarted—make a spectacle of myself—get up to *mischief.* Be that as it may, the man appeared next day at my hotel to call upon me. I had fifteen minutes in which to sum him up. I saw him for what he was."

"Was he nice?"

"Heat in his eye," she murmured. "Aloes upon his lip. A mesmeric animal irradiation . . . one cannot mistake, it however veiled. . . . A dangerous man to women. Oh yes, we understood one another." Something seemed to flicker in her eyes, in the long corners of her lips. "It was in its way a remarkable head —intellectual pride was in it, æsthetic sensibility, passion, the marks of suffering. But the effect was most distasteful."

"You didn't like him?"

"He proposed to me that he should bring Ianthe to my hotel and that the interview should take place in his presence. She was shy, he said. An ordeal for her, naturally. She would shrink. He would be able to oil the wheels, as he delicately put it. Her con-

124

fidence in him was such . . . I answered that I preferred that his wife should accompany her. I should feel, I said, less artificiality and constraint with another of my own sex. I was curious, of course, having summed him up, to see the woman. He was obliged to acquiesce. That being arranged," said Mrs. Jardine in a brisk voice, giving a few light busy touches to her dress, "he was prepared to stay longer."

"He'd got to like you!" I exclaimed triumphantly. He'd thought he wouldn't, but of course he had. She had done it within fifteen minutes: I wondered by what words and looks.

"Oh, it was to discuss my daughter," she said, in mock expostulation. "The sacred trust reposed in him to foster her happiness and welfare. The rarely guarded creature that she was, the casket of treasures. He had been in a special relation to her for so many years—as it were an *uncle*"—she stressed the word venomously—"that the break and transference had been accomplished with the minimum of pain. Natural grief there had been indeed —the tie had been as I was possibly aware of *peculiar* strength. He would not presume to attempt to fill the place, and so on and so forth, but he dared to say that she was happy, at peace. He relied fully upon my doing nothing to—— I cut him short. I told him I understood my daughter and her needs. I dismissed him." She paused, then gave a loud sniff. "Not before he had expressed the view that I had the eyes of a mystic."

"And what did you say?" I asked with satisfaction, presuming this a compliment.

"'You are mistaken, Mr. Connor,' I said." Her voice was dramatic, rhetorical. "'I am in love. The visions I see are of earthly love and truth, and account for the light you are good enough to remark upon. Also,' I said, 'I have suffered; and will *never* be resigned or be defeated. That helps to keep a woman's eyes alive.' He shook his head wisely, sorrowfully, as if to say: 'I know you. Could I but help you to know yourself!' Oh, we might have got far, very far." She looked contemptuously amused. "But I was not interested. I am not a person to be flattered by the impertinences of professional understanders of women. So we met and parted, for the first and the last time."

"What you said—about being in love," I interposed. "You meant—you did mean Harry?"

"Of course. Harry and I were deeply in love with one another. It was very unfortunate for Harry, the whole thing—very hard. I was preoccupied. The sense, which had been falsely—oh, falsely! —lulled to rest during our first months together, of myself pitted against a malevolent fate—this sense had become fiercely active again. I *could not* forgive myself for relaxing my vigilance."

"What does that mean?"

"I mean, I had been mad enough to allow Fate this new chance to strike . . . by forming new ties, by allowing myself to be persuaded—momentarily persuaded—to forget; to spread my wings in heedless happy flight, far from my one true dark path. . . . All this made for difficulties between Harry and myself."

"Was he there too when the man came to see you?"

"No. I preferred to be alone. Oh no. Harry would not have tolerated speeches about my eyes. He would have knocked him down. Harry was—is—impetuous, strong as a lion. He could never stand humbug. He is so true himself, he can never be taken in by what is false and meretricious."

Her voice had its customary ring of aggression when Harry was in question. I thought, not for the last time, that she spoke of a man who has died and is remembered heroically. I would say now: she spoke in obituary notices.

"No, he was not present on that occasion," she continued. "Or on the next day when a strange pair drove up to the hotel. Ianthe and her guardian's wife. I received them in my private sitting-room."

"Was she pleased to see you?"

"What would you expect her to have felt?"

I dragged out a deep reflective pause, fearing to expose an abyss of inadequacy.

"Excited. And shy, like he said," I ventured at last. "A bit afraid."

Mrs. Jardine nodded and remained silent, brooding.

"What did you wear?" I said.

I had in mind some vague conception of mother clothes as

distinct from lady clothes. My own mother wore the former, and they would, I felt, have inspired confidence. Mrs. Jardine might have chosen to set off the extravagant and therefore unmaternal quality of her beauty by wearing something on the queer side. Ianthe might have been put off by this.

"I see what you mean!" she exclaimed approvingly; and, smiling, she laid a hand upon my hair. "I wore a white frock. I remember it so well: long, simple classical lines, narrow ruffles of lace round neck and wrists. At that time I had all my clothes especially designed for me, as all beautiful women should. And I nearly always wore white. Dear me, what a *divinely* pretty dress it was! I can still feel the texture of the material—like apple blossom petals. I asked myself: what will most charm this child?—and that is what I chose. I thought: if things go awkwardly we will speak together of clothes."

"And did you?"

"No."

Pause.

"I do wonder if she liked it."

Mrs. Jardine shrugged her shoulders.

"Oh, she was far too busy with her own effects to take *me* in. Hmm. Most extraordinary. Perhaps I should have been prepared. We all know that girls of that age are frequently a mass of affectations and imbecilities. But being singularly straightforward myself I was *not* prepared."

Her manner was the one she used for speaking of Maisie: an appearance of strict critical impartiality combined with an element of detached surprise.

"Do not misunderstand me," she went on. "I did *not* expect her to greet me with eagerness or affection. No. I *had* expected some such feeling as interest—curiosity, let us say. To put it at its lowest. Nervous?—almost certainly. Unfriendly?—suspicious?— very possibly. Oh, but *direct, genuine!* Something to be acknowledged between us, and respected."

"What was she like?"

"A boy now," continued Mrs. Jardine, pursuing her own train of thought, "under similar circumstances. . . . Dumb, tortured, embarrassed to the depths of his soul. But *underneath,* there would have been the desire, pure, intact, to find his mother. I *know* this! I should have known what to say. With a feather touch, little by little, I should have lifted his burdens from him. I should have felt his relief, his dawning trust, his *gratitude.* Then he would have looked at me. He would have seen me as beautiful and been glad. Before he left me, I should have won a smile from him."

"Didn't she smile at you?" I said, shocked; for she sounded indignant at having no son to appreciate her; and I felt the comparison, so much in favour of boys, as a reflection upon myself. "I do think—I'm almost sure—some girls would. Most."

"You asked me what she was like," burst out Mrs. Jardine with a grand sweeping turn towards me. "Oh, most gracious!—keeping, of course, the distance suitable between us. Carrying off a social misfortune with the utmost sang-froid and condescension. The black sheep relative, the blot, the skeleton in the cupboard emerged after many years' concealment, to everybody's discomfiture. . . . Oh, I must be dealt with, of course, for convention's sake—but firmly kept in my place. My role, that of grateful recipient of her patronage."

"Perhaps she *was* shy, really," I hazarded, despairing.

"Oh, you think so? Shyness can take many forms, I am aware. Perfection of social poise is an unusual one." Her voice clanged harshly, a cracked bell. "She controlled the conversation admirably. We chatted about Florentine architecture and painting, if I remember rightly. She was a blue stocking, and like all the breed, wished to drive home that desolatingly boring fact."

I had never heard her display such uncontrolled exasperation, and dared not interrupt to ask the meaning of this fantastic word.

"And her voice!—cold, high, pedantic, drawling. . . . To hear that heartless high-heeled voice from my own daughter; I who consider the most important part of a girl's education is to learn to speak, to *breathe*—nobody knows how to breathe nowadays—to pitch the voice, to develop and make flexible its modulations, to love words, to *feel* them, to be—ah yes!—a person of feeling! Oh God, voices, how I have suffered from them!" She shuddered.

"I know what I am talking about. I taught myself to use mine properly. I was, of course, gifted by nature with an instrument of great range and richness. But I would have seen to hers somehow, poor material as it was. She inherited it from *his* side—they all squeaked and whimpered and clipped their syllables. Oh yes, I should have worked on it. And possibly improved her character into the bargain." She inhaled a prolonged sniff, and wheeling round on me again, said dramatically: "You asked me if she smiled. Yes, she was prodigal of smiles. That is, her lips stretched —she showed her pretty well-brushed teeth. Her great eyes, rolling aside, around, were empty of smiles." She brooded; then added in a thoughtful way: "No, I said to myself, afterwards: that is a most unpleasing girl."

I hung my head, in utter dismay and dejection.

"And all the time there sat that woman in the corner, stiff, upright on the edge of her chair, a length of lead-piping in a coat and skirt and toque, clutching her parasol—dumb, goggling at nothing, coming out in liver-coloured patches all over her face and neck. *Aunt Hilda,* as she called her—wretched, paralysed, unhappy creature." Her voice vibrated with a sort of raging pity.

"Didn't she say anything?"

"What could she say? A provincial commonplace Englishwoman, loveless, victimised, *hypnotised* into obedience. Gracious heaven, how distressing! Like seeing a tone-deaf woman hoisted on to a concert platform under demented instructions to give a recital in place of Madame Patti. Most painful. . . . Yet," she murmured, "I could have made that woman love me. I could have loved her. She was *capable* of truth. Unlike that polished artificer, her lord and master. I have no doubt that she suffered extreme cruelty at his hands."

"What did he do to her, do you suppose?"

"Oh, snubbed, exploited, terrified her," she answered rather impatiently. "Ah, what a contribution to human experience from such strangled lives, could their secrets but be laid bare!" She reflected a moment; then a look of bitter triumph lit her face. "There was just five minutes of reality. At the last. Yes, I had the last word. Precisely one hour after their arrival, the woman consulted her watch and rose: obedient to instructions, no doubt. 'Good-bye, Mrs. Connor,' I said. 'I ask your forgiveness. You have been obliged against your will and through no fault of yours to witness a most unhappy occasion.' Ianthe glanced at me sharply —the first direct glance she had vouchsafed me. The other made nervous flustered sounds and gestures. 'Believe me,' I said (her manner was her most superb), 'I have been deeply conscious of your distress, its nature and extent. I respect it. I understand it. But of *mine* you can have no conception. I am too experienced a woman, too realistic by nature, to be easily prone to shock or disappointment at human behaviour. But I must confess to you, I part from you and my daughter with these sentiments uppermost. Three female beings have been gathered together in this room upon a human occasion of the utmost gravity. What has occurred? A drawing-room comedy, a farce I might say, without interest, without sense or sensibility—without even the bare extenuation of a first-class performance. You are blameless. You have all my sympathy. But Ianthe should not have so disgraced herself and me. You are right—let us be done with this outrage. I am *bored!*"

"So what did they say then?"

"They were abashed. That poor creature—she became dusky, congested. Her mouth opened. No words came."

"What about Ianthe?"

"Terror," said Mrs. Jardine meditatively. "Her jaw dropped. The mask fell off. It had not been in her programme, you see, that I should assume control. She had no resources. She was perfectly transfixed with terror."

"How awful it must have been!"

I saw her icy, venomous, the serpentine Miss Sibyl of Tilly's legend; and could not forbear to pity Ianthe and Mrs. Connor.

"It was an insult, the whole abominable business," snapped Mrs. Jardine. "I am not so poor-spirited that I can be humiliated with impunity."

"So then did they go away?"

" 'Good-bye, Ianthe,' I said. 'You look charming in black. Once when you were a very little girl I made you a black velvet frock and sent it to you from America. I made it myself. Did you ever wear it?' She shook her head. 'What a pity!' I said. 'But that was, of course, a festive frock, not a mourning one. It had a slotted sash, the colour of a dark red rose, and I saw your face flowering out of it like a white rose *just* tinged.' She glanced at me then—a ghost of attentiveness—not knowing what to make of *that*. 'I hope,' I said, 'that you will soon feel a natural wish to discard this conventional uniform of grief. What can we do to love and honour the dead except to join their lives to ours, inwardly, to fructify and enrich us? It never seemed to me that the outward signatures of dyers and dressmakers were necessary to mark this poignant communion.' "

For the first time, but not the last time, it struck me that, privilege though it would be to be the child of Mrs. Jardine, this status might assume the nature of a formidable burden. So many noble conceptions, so much wisdom and originality, demanding so exhausting a standard of behaviour, presented with such implication of critical reflection upon one's disabilities . . .?

"Did she look at you, *then?*" I said.

"No. She tossed her head aside—pouting—a sulky schoolgirl. 'Good-bye, Ianthe,' I said. 'As time goes on we shall understand one another better.' And then to the woman I said: 'Mrs. Connor, you are afraid. I beg you not to fear me.' " Mrs. Jardine's voice sank, deepened into a quiet fervour of earnestness. " 'We are fellow women. You cannot say something to me that you would like to say. I know what it is. Do not think me impertinent if I tell you that I understand your situation. Let me ask you to believe that you can trust me—*as I am going to trust you.*' Then I shook hands with her."

"What did she say to that?"

"Ah well, poor woman, it was not the kind of appeal that could be answered out of hand. It was too much. She could not endure it. I was cruel, I pierced her without warning. It was deliberate on my part. I knew I should not regret it."

"So she didn't say anything?"

"Oh, she adjusted her toque and drew on her gloves, all painful flurry and agitation, and hurried away."

"With Ianthe?"

"Yes. Like a distracted hen, dragging a wing out over her, thrusting her along." Mrs. Jardine smiled. "But those words drew me one last look from Ianthe—one wild brief wondering look from her great eyes."

Her voice died away, soft and lingering as if in tender recollection. I saw that pair making off, all in disarray, hastening to escape from the eyes and tongue they could still feel stabbing between their shoulder blades. I saw Mrs. Jardine turn slowly in a swirl of white folds and walk to the window; alone again; the silence quivering still with the violence of her triumph. Strange, I thought, or half thought: so many last-moment routs to her score; yet the battle seemed always lost.

"Do you think," I said, "Mrs. Connor was fond of Ianthe?"

Mrs. Jardine paused. Then she looked at me, and I felt in her glance, for the first time, some doubt, some scruple perhaps, about my fitness as a vessel.

"No, she was not fond of her," she said gravely. "You see, she wished her husband to love her, and he did not."

"Did he make more fuss of Ianthe?"

"You might put it like that."

"She was afraid he was—was more fond of her . . .?"

"Yes."

I quite saw the reasonableness of Mrs. Connor's antipathy. The thought of her neglected state distressed me.

"When you said that—about her wanting to say something to you and you knew what it was—what did you mean it was?"

"*Take her away. Out of my house. Quickly.* That was what she was saying. All the time."

"Oh . . ."

"I guessed beforehand that it would be so. It did not take me many minutes of her company to be certain. Her personality was strong and fierce, though stifled. We were—fellow conspirators, you might say. I wished to make it clear to her that I *was aware* . . . and that she could count on me."

"Did she understand?"

132

"The event," said Mrs. Jardine, drawing a long breath, "proved that she did."

"What happened?"

"Harry and I left Florence and returned to France. We had bought our château, near Fontainebleau, not far from Paris, before our marriage; and now we had a busy time decorating, furnishing it, moving in. Naturally my first duty was to Harry, to prepare his home, to fill it with beauty, make it a place of peace, joy and comfort for him and for his friends. We both had so many friends. They flocked to us. We hoped very much to have a child. I——" She paused. "But we were disappointed. That was a grief. But all the same we were happy in our new life together. I wrote regularly now to Ianthe—sending my letters always in a covering envelope addressed to the woman, in order to be sure that they were not intercepted. I knew I could trust her to deliver them. She did. A note came from her. It said: *'Your daughter is receiving your letters.'* Nothing more."

"Did Ianthe answer?"

"Never a word. I wrote nothing personal or controversial—merely friendly letters giving an external picture of the beautiful home, the interests I hoped that she would one day share. *My* circle was, of course, musical, literary, artistic, the most distinguished Paris could offer. Ah, and that was something in those days! I felt all that would appeal to *Miss.* I spoke, too, of Harry's tastes and hobbies. He was a passionate ornithologist—that is, he knew all about birds. Did not you realise that? You had not noticed the library in his study? Oh yes, Harry is one of the finest amateur ornithologists in England. Horses were his other great interest. He bred them and raced them. Harry on horseback was a glorious sight. He planned to buy her a horse of her own: it was to be ready waiting in the stables when she came for her first visit. I told her this."

"Wasn't it kind of him!"

"Harry is the soul of generosity. Oh yes, I wrote with every intention of making our assets clear to her, of tempting her with fair prospects. She might be a prig and a pedant; but worldly enough, I could see that. I tried deliberately to enhance my value to her in terms of worldly goods."

Mrs. Jardine consulted her watch.

"We will go in now," she said. "I need my tea. And you, my poor child, are, of course, famished."

She led the way through the garden door which opened on to the loggia, and we walked together down the print-hung pot-pourri-smelling passage. We went into what she called the flower-room, a kind of closet next door to the pantry, and she took the basket from me, ran water into the sink and plunged the dahlias in. "I will deal with you later," she said to them. Then she called through the pantry hatch a message to be telephoned to my mother; and we went back to the drawing-room. The tea-table stood spread in the bay window, a bright white and silver block in the subdued glow of chintzes, Aubusson carpet, polished wood, crystal bowls of roses, dahlias, Michaelmas daisies. She busied herself with the spirit lamp and said:

"A few months later I got another note."

"What did it say?"

"It said: *'Your relative called upon me this afternoon. In the absence from home of my husband, your daughter and I received him.'*"

"What *did* she mean?"

"I had a great friend." Mrs. Jardine measured out tea from the caddy, poured boiling water from the kettle into the teapot, and allowed me to put out the flame with the long silver snuffer. "A man of rich experience," she went on. "Brilliantly talented, extravagantly handsome. He had been devoted to me for many years. He was, as a matter of fact, a second cousin on my father's side. He knew my life—my troubles. I confided in him . . . in a way I could not confide even in Harry. In a sense, Harry was too simple, too uncompromising a nature to take in what was involved. Honest men are no match for knaves. Indeed," she added in a different key, "to see a typical English gentleman trying conclusions with a sinuous, subtle-witted adversary is one of the most painful, most ludicrous——"

She broke off, bade me help myself to scones and guava jelly, then continued:

"As I was saying, I laid the whole matter before this man, my friend. Whom I trusted." She spoke these last three words with sudden brusqueness, almost with violence.

"Was he old or—not old?"

"He was—let me see, in the late thirties. In the prime of life. He found occasion to visit Florence. He thought it would be interesting—amusing is how he put it—and of service to me to . . . to spy out the land there."

I had never heard her use anything in the nature of a colloquialism before. It made me suspect—I did not know what. She went on speaking in this deliberately flattened way, lapsing occasionally into what, from her, amounted to a vulgarism, and still —since now the crisis of the drama seemed at hand—still, I did not know why. But now I know. Even she could not endure a high-level presentation for the last act; what scorched her heart must be slipped lightly, spitefully off her tongue. She must belittle the tragedy, and despise—not scorn—the actors.

"Did you think," I said, "it was a good idea?"

"An excellent idea," she said, with a peculiar little laugh. "Oh, excellent! Why not? An unusually attractive man, one to whom no woman could be indifferent; one who in addition to everything else could offer the tie of cousinship—such an ideal one between the sexes—covering as it does so much romantic emotion without arousing detrimental comment." She laughed again. "The initial familiarity of blood is there—the mystery is not impaired. Oh, a cousin can provide most valuable experiences."

I thought of Alan and realised the truth of this.

"What did he—what did you want him to do?" I timidly inquired.

"Want him to do? I? Oh, my dear child, I am no cunning schemer and plotter. Do you imagine that I exploit human beings for my own ends?—set them cynically to partners—for sport, to see what will happen?"

Snubbed, I felt the hot blood flooding over me.

"No," she said more gently. "Such sport corrupts the player.

Besides, it is too dangerous. God knows what will be started up."
Her eyes gave a flick. She stared across the tea-table. "Dear me,
no. Though naturally I was anxious to wean her away from the
detestable and morbid influences surrounding her. *Such* a messenger, I thought, signed with such richness, such wit, such effort-
less prestige. . . . What a privilege for the girl! Not so much a
messenger from *me,* you understand . . . though possibly I
counted on his tact, his devotion to me to do me a bit of good
with her. . . . Oh yes, that did occur to me!—but something in
the nature of an appetiser . . . or a medicine, strong, sweet-
tasting, to sicken her of her unwholesome diet. That was his function—if any function I proposed—to myself, I mean . . . we had
too intuitive, too pervasive an understanding to——"
She sounded agitated, almost confused. In the surprise and
interest of observing this, I recovered from my humiliation.
"Oh, and to teach her a few lessons—most necessary lessons!"
she snapped out viciously. "I knew what he could do if he had
the mind. I was reluctant to be socially embarrassed by a smug
censorious little fraud. . . . In France, where the duties of par-
enthood are taken seriously, wise fathers personally select a suitable woman to educate their young sons. It is not left to casual
and more often squalid opportunity. The result is that French-
men understand how to treat women, how to cherish them. Have
you noticed how Frenchwomen put a natural value on themselves
—as women?"
"Well no, not really," I murmured, realising that she had forgotten she was talking to me, but feeling that some non-commit-
tal fill-in was required. I considered Mademoiselle. Perhaps, I
thought, that accounted for her. Perhaps I ought to view her in a
more reverent light.
"What *few* Englishwomen have reason or occasion to do, poor
wretches—few indeed! Englishmen dislike women: that is the
blunt truth of it. I have no son. If I had, I should have seen to
*him* all right. But why should a girl not receive a similar education? Oh, what an outrageous, what an indecent proposition! Do
not you know that in England it is considered immoral to teach
a girl the needs of her heart and body? . . . Dear me, dear me!

Sometimes one is really led to conclude that material vindictiveness is at the bottom of it—imposed inferiority has bred it—as it will. 'Let her go through what I did. Let her be unhappy, disappointed, shocked. She will get used to it. I had to: why should *she* not?' That seems to be the sort of idea. What a pass to be brought to! How long, I wonder, will ignorance spell purity and knowledge shame? . . . Ah, well! Why should *I* care? I do not, any more."

She fell silent, breathing deeply. Totally adrift in the storm, I continued to eat scones.

"But in those days," she continued, speaking as if with indulgent self-contempt, "I was still young, fervent, hopeful: I wished to equip my daughter with what at her age I had so pitifully lacked: some sense of proportion about the other sex. Women need men, you know. They cannot live without them. But are they taught their most important lesson—*how* to live with a man? —what to go for, what to avoid? How to please, how to keep their men? Oh dear me, no! I was determined that *my* daughter, at least, should not be flung into marriage ignorant, unprepared."

"Oh, you wanted him to marry her!" I said enthusiastically, light dawning at last.

"No, I did not," she said shortly. After a pause she added: "I wanted him to knock the nonsense out of her."

"I see."

"Take her out of herself. Shake her up. It was time she fell in love. Quite right and proper at her age." Her manner momentarily heightening, softening, she went on: "It is the beginning of growing up. The hearts of the young are enclosed in a crystal case. It is this that breaks when they first fall in love. Then the heart is set free to grow, to be moulded into human material. Remember that later, when you think your heart broken by your first love. The heart does not break: only this cold isolating crystal. The heart is exposed for the first time, and of course that is painful: just as a baby finds it painful to be born and cries out in distress at its first nakedness. Oh no, no, no, you do not crack a heart with one stroke. . . ."

We seemed together again, and I ventured to say, though diffidently: "You wanted them to—you hoped they'd get to love each other?"

She shrugged her shoulders, and said lightly:

"Love is a serious word. I should not have objected to a little romance. I was not planning a grand fireworks display. Heavens, I was not *planning* anything! The situation aroused his curiosity. So did she. Because she was my daughter. He never would believe in her," she said, smiling in a way that made her suddenly seem like a girl, "although he heard of her often enough, God knows. He loved so to hear *all* my life. This meeting in Florence had so passionately interested him. I discussed her with him, of course. 'She is a frostbitten kind of creature,' I told him. 'And a minx besides. But beautiful—possibilities of *great* beauty. Intelligent. Not without temperament, judging from her eyes.'"

"And what did *he* say?"

"He laughed. She shall be saved, he said."

A figure printed itself suddenly upon my sight. For an instant before it vanished, it was precise, actual as a distant figure caught in a powerful telescope. Though I could not have begun to describe him, I saw the man whose very words these must have been.

"Oh!" I said eagerly. "He was going to take her away from those awful people—bring her to you?"

What I thought an unamused smile crossed her face.

"Oh, do you think so?" she said, with apparent seriousness, as if pondering the suggestion. "I wonder. I wonder if that is what he had in mind. It seems rather a naïve conception, and there was nothing naïf about Paul. In fact, innocence was what he most disliked. It exasperated him. He accused me of it—many a time."

For a moment she seemed another person, speaking of herself dubiously, almost ruefully, as if for once permitting herself to be objectively reflected through the eyes of another person. In years to come I was now and then to hear her repeat strictures on herself, but always with a kind of surprised indignation, an immediate counter of dogmatic self-justification. This time, this once only, was different. She was recalling a memory with a taste at least as sweet as bitter.

138

I know now what he meant by her innocence. He must have understood her well—the elemental paradoxes of her nature. Whether she also understood, whether she accepted, from him, the soft words' double edge, I was never to know.

But I told myself even then, floored though I was again, that they must have been great friends, very fond of one another.

"No," she said. "He was a *man*—a man of stature. He was not concerned with womanish interferences, apportionings of desert and blame—with Sunday School prizes for merit and black marks for bad behaviour. Ah, he belonged to a richer age than ours! An Elizabethan he was, all ferment, all fire. He wanted everything. The world was his oyster. How wonderful he was!—the curiosity, the exuberance, the prodigious appetite. . . ." Her eyes swam, grew luminous with tears.

"Is he dead?" I timidly inquired.

"He is dead. He shot himself one day. Just like that. Without one message, one single scribbled line to any one. So, to account for it, his friends exercised their ingenuity in the usual ways. But when I heard, *I* knew why he had done it! His was a nature that must always challenge itself—higher, higher! and that was the last, the ultimate challenge. He must *choose* death, not wait for it." She spoke with rapid intensity, almost with joy; then relapsing into quietness added: "One day I will show you the poem I wrote for his epitaph. But that is all another story. This thing of his in Florence—it was one of his side lines. He hated waste, you see, fumbling, vain expense of spirit—anything on a shoddy level. Struggles with cobwebs, shadows, echoes from the cruel hollow tyrannical dead: he would tear through all these. He wanted— one might say to burst open the furtive situation. He thought . . . he thought I was mismanaging it. He thought my timing fatally wrong." She faintly smiled; and again the rueful look about her brows made her personality unfamiliar. "God knows! It may have been so. One should act always from one's inner sense of rhythm. Sometimes I have asked myself: *could* that have received some damage, unknown to oneself? Could disastrous strokes have so impaired it that one's actions—movements—have become . . . grotesque?" She tapped her fingers on the arm of her chair. Then she poured out a cup of tea, and said, as if suddenly remembering to answer my question: "No, no. He did not want to bring her to me. That would be an absurd view. He wanted her for himself."

I said: "Oh."

"That was it. Quite simple."

"Only he did say—I thought you said—about saving her?"

"Oh, what he said! My dear child, that was a joke. People who are very intimate always tease one another. Surely you know that?"

"Yes," I agreed humbly. It struck me that she and Harry never seemed to tease one another. Perhaps they did when they were alone. "I wonder a bit, though, why he wanted her when he didn't know her, did he?"

*"Mon Dieu, cela n'empêche pas,"* she murmured, looking amused, though not in a pleasant way. Then, agreeably: "No. He did not know her. It was *not* simple. Nothing he did was simple. But sometimes it happens that a man—a person—can want two things at once: to do something out of love for another; and at the same time to do something out of—something *against* another. Both are something he must do for *himself:* perhaps to feel free again where he has felt bound; or to prove to himself, it may be, that he is master—still has power over the other. Perhaps to make up to himself for some deep hurt. Do you understand?"

"Yes, I think so," I said truthfully.

"I am speaking of him and me. Possibly he may have felt my marriage had—estranged us. Not that there had ever been question of marriage between us. Oh no! That would never have done. No, when I decided to be Harry's wife, he wished me all happiness. Yet. . . . Who knows?" she said low, speaking her thoughts aloud. *"Le coeur a ses raisons. . . .* Were we blind? Were our eyes open? Both. Certainly we knew what we were doing. But, you see, we chose always to live on the tragic level. We took notable risks. 'I shall lay dynamite,' he said. 'They will all be blown up. It will be a lot of trouble—all for your sake. I tell you now, beforehand, I lay the victims at your door.' 'Oh, my dear boy, victims!' I said. 'It is what they are waiting for.

They are desperate characters, all of them.' 'You will do yourself no good,' he said, 'in your *new life*. I suppose that does not worry you?' 'Nor you,' I said." She uttered the ghost of a malicious chuckle. " 'I might get a shaking myself,' he said. 'That would annoy you frightfully.' 'On the contrary,' I said. 'I expect you to get a lot out of it. Would I be likely to send you on an altruistic mission?' 'You mean,' he said, 'you are prepared for *anything?*' 'I *want* it,' was my reply. He looked at me—a peculiar look. I have often recalled it since. . . . Ah, he could not get used to such levels even from me! That was it. 'Very well,' he said. 'We will see what we will see.' That was the last time we were together."

A faint wind began to agitate the listening room, breathing upon us through the open pane the first premonitory chill of autumn. She got up and closed the window, then stood in the embrasure, drumming with her fingers on the window-pane.

"Yes—yes—yes," she muttered.

I writhed in my chair, pierced by a chilling thought. Could Mrs. Jardine be—not quite right in the head? . . . And I alone with her?

There was an old woman in the village, Mad Mary the children called her, shouting it at her through the hedges, then running away with hoots and squawks. She lived alone in a filthy tumble-down cottage at the top of the village, and kept a lot of birds in cages. Sometimes one saw her padding up and down in front of her house with one or two perched upon her shoulder, wearing a long loose ragged burberry, smeared and stained with bird-droppings. Her feet were wrapped up in newspaper tied with scraps of knotted string; and a sort of skirt of sacking and paper crazily stitched together protruded in front and behind from the coat's gaps. Stabbing at the earth with a stick, impaling straws and scraps of refuse, round and round she went, talking to herself in a low vibrant monotone broken with shouts and chuckles. Sometimes she counted rapidly, running up the scale on an urgent mounting cry; sometimes she uttered a sort of humming snatch of tuneless song: exile as solitary, as absolute upon her patch of earth as any castaway adrift upon a raft in boundless wastes of ocean, never to be picked up, re-united with humanity.

Isabel liked to walk that way. She would stop for a good look through the starved and broken hedge while I clutched her hand, half loth, half enthralled. Once I heard her mutter: "Yes. Yes. Yes"; and she struck the earth with her stick.

"Pore soul, she's harmless," said Isabel placidly. "It's only her daft fancies. She was done wrong to by her plighted true-love and it turned her brains. All in her bridal white she was, at the altar by his side, and when the parson come to just cause or impediment, up rears a veiled woman at the back and speaks out she was his lawful wedded wife. At least that's the tale. If so, it was a good long time ago. But it stands to reason a shock like that would turn a person funny. It seems as if she couldn't get no rest, like, with what's working in her."

Frequently after these expeditions Isabel would render *The Mistletoe Bough* with strident fervour while she washed up the tea things.

All this returned now to cause me anxiety: that three-fold affirmation, that tranced monologue. . . .?

She continued to stand at the window, watching the still sun-brimmed but now faintly troubled garden. All in a moment, it seemed, the first crack had run up the golden lustre bowl. The weather was going to change. As if a veil had been soundlessly rent, the transfixed archaic presences upon the lawn shook off their legend. They were two fine old trees, no more no less, subject to time, triumphantly, grievingly preparing to resist, to accept through all the intricacies of their giant organisms, one more ineluctable decay and death.

"I am not happy about that copper beech," she said quietly. "Nor is Gillman. He thinks the roots may have penetrated to something deadly. If so, it is not a tragedy I can face with equanimity."

I said, with relief, that it would be an awful shame.

She came and sat down again, and started to sip her tea.

"Ah well," she remarked, "as it turned out, nobody did themselves any good that time."

"Didn't they—didn't he and Ianthe make friends?"

"Oh, dear me, no," she said, with mild thoughtfulness. "Nobody made friends. Everybody lost a friend that time."

"*Every*body?"

"First came this note from Mrs. Connor, as I told you. Then, a day or two later, a long letter from him, very much in his manner, describing his reception. Deliciously amusing. Then, about a week later, another letter, dashed off hurriedly. It was somewhat cryptic. '*The plot thickens,*' he said. He wrote jestingly of one of two futures yawning before Ianthe—the nunnery or the——" She broke off. "He saw her daily, she confided in him, so he said. Perhaps I would be interested to know what foundations her father had laid for her purity and peace of mind. He described them. '*I incline to think,*' he said, '*there is more to come out with regard to le beau C. She wears a vacant look and turns the conversation when his name crops up. But give me time: all will be made clear. She is a terrible girl,*' he said. '*I would prefer to make love to Mrs. C.—but that there is a touch in her which that heroine lacks. She absorbs me. I would like to be damned by her, and saved by Mrs. C. But Mrs. C. won't save me. Not she.*'"

"I wonder what he meant."

She shrugged her shoulders.

"Oh, it was his usual vein—making sport of himself, playing with allusions. . . . It did not disturb me. Or scarcely. Apart, I mean, from those revelations. *They* were a facer."

"It was just his joke?"

She disregarded this.

"A few weeks passed. Blank. Then came two lines."

"From him?"

"From him."

"What did he say?"

"He said: '*It is all coming along admirably, just as you planned. I am getting a lot out of it. Everybody is.*'"

"I do rather wonder what *that* meant," I ventured obstinately but uncertainly.

"I wondered too. Ah, then I *did* wonder! I was prepared, of course. Wherever that man went, he was bound to start something. There was some force he generated which made for—the full orchestra. Sometimes I have thought—it has kept coming over me—that letter—the fact that he wrote *at all*—meant: *Come*. An appeal. . . . Perhaps." She began to seem confused again. "It would have been characteristic of him to put it in this way. I should have known. There had been other times between us. . . . However. . . . Be that as it may, I made the wrong decision. For once. I should have gone to Florence. I did not go—against my instinct. Scrupulousness restrained me. I waited. I told myself: Whatever happens—*whatever* happens, he is to be trusted—on our level. I was right—as I see it—as I shall always see it. *The drop of anguish*—it burns me now, but what of that? There was *nothing* ignoble in the design. Call it playing fast and loose if you will—that is just a phrase the petty-cautious use against the fiery ones, the risk-takers—— But what possibilities—glorious! *The tried intent of such a truth as I have meant. Such* a truth! *He* meant it too. How often has my life pointed those words for me! But poetry is not to be lived, except for the few to whom it is more important than self-preservation. One can present people with their opportunities. One cannot make them equal to them."

Floundering in all this, I began to feel, as I ate my way on through scones into sponge cake, how unequal I was proving to my own opportunities. I was not going to be told—or maybe I had been told, and had not taken in a word of it. Perhaps it had been the same with Ianthe and Mrs. Connor; perhaps their chances of illumination, of bettering themselves, had been presented to them in so rare a way that they had not even noticed them. But I was wrong about Mrs. Connor.

Almost I could have prayed, now, for the cup of honour to be taken from me and transferred to some more worthy recipient. But I must not give up—I must see it through.

"I wrote another note to Mrs. Connor," she said presently. "I asked merely after Ianthe's health and well-being. A few bare lines. Of course I knew by then that there was a rumpus going on."

"A rumpus?"

"He had told me, hadn't he, more or less plainly, that he had fallen in love with the girl?"

144

"Oh! . . . Of course he had. And her with him?"

"Ah." She meditated, as if about to discuss a debated historical point. "Who can say? Not I. She must have had—a *movement* towards him. A movement of some violence. That is the way with such natures under urgent pressure. There is no organic growth or gradual unfolding. Passive, opaque, self-contained, unimpressible as cats; then a convulsion, a leap—half panic, half craving . . . and cold, yes, cold in its rapacity. Then it is over. They drop away, furtive, secret, before they are cornered. They can neither sustain emotion nor face the consequences of their own actions. Poor Ianthe. Trapped! By the time I got to Florence it was too late. The die was cast."

"You did go to Florence?"

"I received a telegram from that woman, in answer to my letter. It said: *Come at once.* I took the next train and went straight from the station to her house. She was waiting for me. We had our second—and last—interview."

"Was Ianthe there too?"

"No."

"Nor *him*?—Mr. Connor?"

"No."

"I wonder where they were."

"Ianthe had gone."

"You mean—run away?"

"Yes."

"Why? Wasn't she—were they unkind to her?" Then realisation broke; and with a rush of relief at seeing my own lights spark once, however feebly, I gasped: *"Oh! I see! Him* and her—they'd run away together!"

"Precisely. Vanished."

I was seized with sudden apprehension, and was obliged at the risk of irrevocable disgrace to falter out:

"You do mean *Paul* and her?"

"I do. But how perspicacious of you! I myself was uncertain beforehand. It was a huge relief."

Over-encouraged, I said:

"You were pleased?"

145

"I had no time," she said curtly, "to examine all my feelings on the point. It was a moment of the utmost *immediacy*. The shock was no trivial one, even at the best. I had to summon all my resources. I had to deal with *her,* the woman, first. We had something to say to one another: more *not* to say. That was understood on both sides. She was not a clever woman—on the contrary, she was an ignorant woman of lowish mentality; and a hard-pressed one, and a frightened one. Hysteria might well have broken loose and swept away the boundaries of what was permissible between us. However, she kept her self-control—I was obliged to admire her. Congested, taut-necked, gobble-eyed as a hen-turkey; but preserving the decencies. Oh yes, we made a decent fighting end."

I saw them, the two, in a foreign room with green shutters. Since it was a kind of room totally unfamiliar to me, yet plausible and clear in all its details, I can but think that she was projecting from her own vision on to mine the very room they met in. Sun came through the closed shutters in narrow bars, and there was a general stone-grey look, and a lot of china cabinets and stiff brocaded furniture. They sat facing one another in high-backed chairs, hands folded in their laps, still as tigers; one cased in black, like a Victorian lodging-house keeper, the other all light and flowing elegance.

"What did she say?" I asked.

"She said she would protect her husband. I mean, that was the essence of what she had to say."

This was unexpected.

"I didn't think grown-up men had to be protected," I said finally.

"Ah, naturally you would think otherwise. You would think it was a man's part to protect; to guard with a father's solicitude the young girl committed to his care?"

"Yes. Because that's what he said to you, didn't he?—about a sacred trust and all that. Hadn't he guarded her?"

"He had behaved—as I had guessed he would. I told her so. Had not we both known it, I said? Was not that the reason of our secret pact? I thought I could be as direct as that. But she would not answer. Dumbness came up and darkened her, choked her. 'She is a bad girl,' was all she said. 'I wanted her out of the house. She's gone; and good riddance to her.' I presumed, I said, that her husband had gone in search of her. 'He may have,' she said. 'I don't know where he is. But he'll come back. And he won't bring *her*. He knows he can't, after what's happened. It would never do.' That was the way she spoke: the vocabulary of a refined housemaid. It was not for me to suggest that he might, in his desperation, have done himself some mischief, but she read my meaning. 'He'll come back,' she persisted. 'I know he will. He knows I know what went on; but he knows I won't let it come to a scandal. I told him I'd see it didn't, and he knows he can trust me. If there should be any rumours, we'll live them down,' she said. I suggested that this might be difficult in view of the circumstances, but she replied: 'If you give me away, I'll give you away. And if you give *him* away I'll tell it out to all the world what that girl was. We're respected here—more than respected. He's looked up to by all, worshipped pretty nearly for a man of God. What's happened? She's gone off with a man. What will they say if I tell them that? They'll say: Bad blood will out.' . . . Yes, she was very forceful."

All this had been spoken without a trace of passion, as if in mild amazement at such a manifestation of human behaviour.

"Inconsistent," she added in a thoughtful way, "but extraordinarily forceful. 'A fortnight's passed,' she said. 'Any questions I've been asked I've said she's gone on her first visit to her mother, as arranged. That's good enough: and that's all I shall say. Any questions about her return, and I shall say it's been agreed she shall finish her education in England, with relations of her father.' She told me, and I think she spoke the truth, that my letter had come to her as a shock and a surprise. She had assumed that they would come to me. 'You sent him for her, didn't you?' she said. 'I took it for granted you knew what you were about. I don't suppose you sent him for *my* sake.' " Again Mrs. Jardine marked the thrust with a mild raising of her brows. "She was right there, of course; I had no interest in attempting to deny it. 'You did your part,' she said. 'And I did mine. If it was for *her* sweet sake you wanted her out of my house—well, she's out. It's not my fault if it hasn't turned out as you meant it. My part was to see they had their opportunities—which I did.' It seems the man Connor had had to make some journey or visit just about the time that Paul arrived. That greatly facilitated matters. It was a strange intervention of Fate—I cannot but see it so. But it was a strange mix-up, all of it, from the beginning. *Who* started *what?* I ask myself. Who was responsible? Sometimes I seem to see us all as *taken charge of.* The stage set and empty, the threads drawn all together, the knot tied. . . ."

"Did they run away while he was on the visit?"

"It seems not. It seems he came back, discovered what was afoot. Some fearful scene took place, I fancy—but she would not tell me. Whether Paul faced him, accused him, I do not know—whether after this they went hand in hand out of the house; or whether . . ."

"What?"

"It could have been as the woman said . . ."

"What did she say?"

She did not answer me, but continued in a muttering, staring way:

"An act of hysteria—cunning?—unpremeditated? . . . She was *trapped.* She must be released—no matter how. . . . Yet I do not know. He had enough experience of clamouring women—he was very nimble, he could look after himself. No. I have always been sure he fell *deeply* in love with the girl. And one must take into account her hatred of Ianthe, her raging jealousy."

"She really and truly hated her?"

"Yes. I have told you why. I presume that as time went on her position grew more and more desperate."

"She felt more and more left out?"

"You could put it in that way."

"I don't suppose Ianthe meant to be unkind."

"Her language with regard to Ianthe was extremely strong," remarked Mrs. Jardine in the same surprised way. "I have more than once been astonished by the grossness of vocabulary such so-called gentlewomen are capable of. Where do they learn it?

. . . The gist of it was that Ianthe had insinuated herself, wily, predatory; had wound herself round and round this husband of hers; then when the next man came along, had flung herself at *his* head."

"It must have seemed queer—not very nice—hearing her say nasty things like that about Ianthe. To her own mother!"

"It was curious," agreed Mrs. Jardine. "But interesting. Another light on Ianthe's character. Allowing, of course, for prejudice, and for the crudity of an inexperienced old maid, I could not altogether dismiss the possibility of an element of truth in what she said."

"How do you mean?" I said, surprised at her slip of the tongue about Mrs. Connor's married status, but deciding to let it pass.

"That Ianthe was corrupt."

*"Bad?"*

"Bad. Something amiss with her moral nature. A warp. The hypothesis is plausible. How indeed should it have been otherwise? Her instincts over-stimulated, directed into unnatural channels. . . . At the same time enjoined to loathe her body's functions and desires. Imagine the confusion, the shame for the wretched girl." But she was addressing herself, not me. "Next, the other gentleman! Ach! I know the breed. He would enfold her, no doubt, in a pestiferous miasma of sanctified sensuality. Have her helpless under his magnetic eye and hand. I saw his hands! White, sinuous, hirsute. Long padded finger tips. Hmm. . . . Adept to place the secret mark upon her, the honourable stigma. The sin, the bliss, the expiation. . . . Oh, ecstasy and terror to be thus chosen, set apart! Ah, he would groan over her no doubt—repent—pray—*fall* again." Her fingers tapped on the tea-table. "Or I have thought—a different initiation. Cynical. Brutal. Anonymous. Threats. Bribes."

I had planned to finish up with shortbread biscuits, and began now to complete my design. Mrs. Jardine had fallen into brooding; but after a while she continued on a different note:

" 'I did not give birth to a moral delinquent,' I said. 'I made her without a flaw. She was torn from my hands. Who has made her the sick creature you say she has become? Two masterly practitioners. One was my husband. Shall I name the other?' 'Are you insinuating,' she said, 'he's done anything *wrong* with her? He never would have—never! He wanted to guide her. She tried her tricks on him, she tried to tempt him—I saw her game. No man's a plaster saint, not even the best. She ruined his peace of mind.'" Again Mrs. Jardine brooded. "I dare say she did," she added dryly. "But what pitiful rubbish!"

"Did you tell her you thought so?"

"No. I said little. My duty was to *hear* as much as possible. I had to have every available light. Whatever conclusions one was led to, it was clear that Ianthe's future presented a grave problem."

"Didn't you answer back anything at all?" For it really seemed as if, this time, she had actually let someone else do all the talking.

"I asked practical questions. I wished to find them, you see. But she had nothing useful to tell me. The day before it happened, she had seen him for two minutes. He had come suddenly into the room, looking pale, she said."

"What did he come for?"

"To say he was going to take her away. Those were his words, she said. 'I am going to take her away.'"

"What did she say to him?"

"Nothing. 'It was his look-out—and yours,' she said to me. 'I washed my hands of it. I liked him,' she said. 'He had very pleas-ant manners. He knew my home, where I was born—I should have liked to talk to him more about it. If he was weak like all the rest, the slave of a pretty face, it wasn't my business to tell him so.' No, she could give me no clues at all—she was quite genuine in this. So I left her."

There was a prolonged silence.

"Did you find them?" I said at last.

"No."

"What did you do?"

"I went back to France, to my home."

"And told Harry all about it?"

"Yes, I was obliged to tell Harry."

"What did he say?"

She paused.

"He was angry." Her eyes flicked. "He wished to take violent measures—denounce—expose—institute immediate police inquiries. But I could not have that. How could I have done that to them?" Her voice became a poignant cry. "Set the police on their tracks, make them a public scandal? Harry could not understand. He did not know all the—the labyrinth, the complications. Oh Paul! Ianthe! What could I do now for them but let them alone, permit them their choice—to be lost to me, to ignore me, leave me in the outer darkness of lonely suspense and anxiety? Their only chance. Mine too, perhaps. I fought him for it."

"Harry?"

She nodded. Shaking, she leaned forward. The opaqueness of flesh and bone seemed to drain out of her face, leaving it in the half-transparency of a white lamp; and over it slipped that shinning fall of tears, so phenomenal, so inhuman in its unchecked profusion: as if an object, a holy relic, should flow suddenly, weeping absolute tears for the world.

I waited for them to stop, but they did not; so I said with rather nagging insistence, to try to stop them:

"What did you think would happen, really and truly, in the beginning, I mean, when you arranged it?"

She dried her eyes and cheeks with her little handkerchief.

"Oh, arranged! What did I arrange? I was hard pressed too. They think me made of steel and ice, a flail—I am not so. I wanted my own. Tear a mother from her child—they shall see what devils they raise." She leaned back, her lips blue, and began to relax. "Rebecca, it comes over me again, again. That child was hard pressed. She had too much to bear. She needed her childhood,—a long blank abstract of time by the seashore, digging castles in the sand, picking up shells and stones, exploring the rock pools. How I loved that!—do not you?—better than anything else in the world. I still do. Ianthe would have loved that. . . . Or a piece of earth to make into a garden. Making things grow —flowers and fruit and vegetables. That would have been good too—I have done all these things myself, and been healed by them. Instead, what did I do? I put *man* between us—again, again! . . . as if that sword, that alone, had not separated us from the beginning; as if she were not wounded enough by *that* already! I matched them with calculations as cruel, as sterile as their own. I sent her *man*—his arch-type—a whole *world* of man —to complete her desolating knowledge. I sent her that one."

She wiped her lips, her forehead on which the sweat stood in beads.

Out from beneath her voice swung two long lines of figures, linked hand in hand, singing in chorus: *We'll send Paul to fetch her away, fetch her away, fetch her away.* . . . Mournfully, gaily, forward and backward, forward and backward. Out stepped two figures. Advancing, solitary, through a great stillness, towards one another, they stopped face to face. He was in armour; she was the Greek virgin on the vase, bare-foot, bare-breasted. His arm of steel shot out, he caught her hand. One tug. . . . Away she flew, whirling in white through the air. The figures drew her in, obliterated her with laughter and clapping.

"It was a terrible mistake," said Mrs. Jardine, calm once more. "I tell you so—nobody else. *She flung herself at his head.* Those are the words I cannot forget. I have seen a small trapped animal fling itself straight upon the trapper. One last blind bid for liberty. . . . There is another thing I will tell you. I think of it often. Something that woman said. 'I heard her knocking on his door,' she said. 'In the middle of the night. He opened, and I heard her tell him *she was afraid to sleep alone. I* heard her!' I see her there often, knocking."

Silence. I told myself I supposed it might well be so, though very babyish. A girl who had never been allowed to sleep in a room by herself. . . .

After a while I said:

"Don't you think he was kind to her—after he took her away? Paul, I mean?"

"Oh, I should think so, certainly," said Mrs. Jardine, sharp, judicial. "He was capable of extraordinary tenderness—unlike the majority of men. But when two people unite, kindness must be mutual, or shocking things will happen. What could *she* give *him?*—that is the question. Was she capable of cherishing him? Unlikely. I cannot picture him sustaining the role of mediæval knight-champion of romance. He was not given to notions of rescue, chastity, dedication to the ideal. It must have been an *extraordinary* infatuation, no doubt of that. I could only *hope,* with all my heart, it would turn out to their advantage.

"What did I expect, in the beginning?" she said, suddenly reverting to my question. "Not *that.* It was my folly, innocence, vanity if you will, that I did not see that danger. It did not occur to me that he was—packing his bag. Perhaps he did not realise it either—not consciously. But being what he was, he would, of course, choose the most distinguished, the most sensational exit. What more final than to pack my child? Really though," she said lightly, "how *odd,* when you consider it! He had never been attracted by young girls. They bored him. . . . No. I expected that he would come back to me with news, clues—valuable to me—as a spy might come back. I had become so used to conducting a secret service—oh, with such rare, such picked agents!—you could count them on less than the fingers of one hand. I was too prone, no doubt, to view those few I trusted in that light. A mistake. Did you know that nobody can stand more than a small dose of being of service to his or her fellows? It turns their stomachs, one way or another. The moment comes when they revolt from the notion that they are in the power of another; being made use of, they call it. Then we say that they have betrayed our trust."

The corners of her lips turned down in a bitter smile; and she said with an irony I could not fathom, though I see now its target was her own delusion: "I thought we would *talk it over together* —the experience, in all its aspects, for him, for her; what might come of it for me."

She sighed as if almost bored, and exclaimed suddenly:

"Dear me, how I have talked! What a listener my darling is. What do you make of it all?"

I simpered rather feebly, and said I loved it, would she go on, please?

"Some months passed in this suspense. Then at last a letter from him."

"Oh, good! What did he say?"

"He said: *'Ianthe and I are in love with one another.'* "

"Just as you thought!" I cried joyfully. "He *was!* They both were. Were you very relieved?"

"He wrote: *'You will laugh cynically when I say that this is different. For me it is like a re-birth.'* "

There was so much in her voice I could not understand, that I remained silent.

" *'I shall marry her,'* he wrote, *'directly she feels able to consent to be my wife. Don't come after us, will you?'* "

"What? Didn't she want to marry him? Why not?" I was confounded.

"This letter," said Mrs. Jardine, "filled me with the gravest alarm. So unrealistic. So *idiotic.* Not like him. And so unmannerly too. He could not marry her without my consent. And how, I asked myself among other things, did they propose to *live?*" She made a rhetorical pause, and there flashed into my mind the figure of my grandmother in a French hotel, asking Miss Sibyl the same question. "He was dependent for his income upon an allowance from a much older brother, the owner of the family estates. He was supposed to assist in the management of them and to look after the library: not an arduous career, as he pursued it. But I could not see this brother disposed to continue that allowance indefinitely with a Bless you, my dear old fellow, love is best. As for Ianthe, she had nothing. Her pittance was in the hands of Connor, until I could get control of it for her, which, of course, I did later. No, I was infuriated. He was no green boy, to think bread and butter bestowed magically on lovers. As for her *feeling able to consent*—what nonsense did that imply?"

"Did you write back?"

"Yes, I wrote back. He did give me an address. I thought that possibly significant. Only care of the Post Office, some small place on the shores of the Adriatic—but still it seemed to mean that he wished to leave a thread between us in case of need. I sent some money for Ianthe. I wrote: *'Come back to me, both of you, so* soon as you wish to receive my consent to Ianthe's marriage. You will be welcomed with love and joy.' It was all I could do."

The room was getting to look sadder and sadder. Brightness began to drain away from all the surfaces. Haze, spreading from the west, advancing like a total world of negativity, dissolved the sun, precipitated into the air's lambent texture a soft, greyish sediment. Soon all the bloom and iridescence would be blotted out. *No,* whispered every object—*No. No.* In the vacant light she had a paper face, scored with criss-cross lines, thumbed here and there into shallow smudged concavities.

"They didn't come?" I said at last.

"No."

"Write?"

"No. Not a word. A year went by, a dragging year. I was lonely. I had nobody to speak to."

"Not Harry?"

"Harry was with me. And others, of course, besides. I did not lack company. Harry did not even tell me when he sold the little mare he had bought for her to ride. Harry took it hard; it bit into him. He had built a lot on welcoming her for my sake. And for his own; he loves young people. But all that could never be discussed. He blamed me." She drew a sighing breath, and added rapidly: "So I was not able to tell him when one day, towards the latter half of that year, hope left me. Yes, between one day and another. My instinct, which was all I had left to trust, which I spun out incessantly towards her through the dark—my instinct turned sick. One spider's thread lifeline. It shrivelled, rotted away. Something terrible had happened."

"What was it?"

"I could not tell. There was only this void, this *unconnection.* All I knew was, some adverse influence had set in. I thought: it is over. Mangled. I waited on in the desert. I hope you will never need to go into that place. Day and night, the stones grind one's heart. You search the scorching wastes for pools; but when you find them, the rats have been before you. Their swollen bodies float in them. . . . Then, one day at the close of the year, the oppression began. *Here.*" She put both hands on her body, pressing them in under her breast. "How can I describe it? *The symptoms were not mine*. They were part of my body, but outside it; so that I could not accept them, recognise them in order to deal with them. When you have hurt yourself, you know how all your nerves cry: *Pain!* Immediately you fight it with every fibre of you. You are *filled* with pain, and with resistance to it. But this brown suffocation is the opposite: it is a helpless subjection. A wasting out. I struggled to draw breath. I knew what it meant, I could not be mistaken. I had been in *that* place too, before, when as a child she had a serious illness, and I was far away the other side of the world. I knew that her life was in danger."

I could only gasp.

"Many mothers have this kind of experience," observed Mrs. Jardine, on a didactic note. "I cannot remember that it has ever been described. Curious. Possibly it is so physical that it is thought an indecent subject." She sniffed. "You see, to have a child means that a living body has come out of one's own. I suppose you do know that?"

"I suppose so," I said, embarrassed.

"Once it is born, and the cord is cut, it is free of one's own flesh; yet in a sense it remains for ever part of one. So when it is badly threatened one is bound to get some warning. If one is far away the warning can only take the form of this blind dull drag towards it. Once one has *got there*—oh, then one can recharge it with life again from one's own; as one did before it passed out of one's body and became separate. The birth miracle will happen over again."

"It didn't happen like that for Tilly's little boy," I said. "She was there all the time, she never left him, and he breathed his last."

She looked faintly taken aback.

"Yes," she agreed quickly. "Poor Tilly. I had forgotten—for the moment. Yes, I had forgotten." She seemed to meditate. "Of course it is not always so. I was indulging in a dream. What do I know of this other experience, the positive one? I have never been called to come. It was perhaps the worst feature of my separation from her, the hardest to bear, I mean—the haunting fear that death would stretch a hand for her, grasp her before I could reach her and draw her back. As I felt—I *knew*—I had the power to. For whatever they do, they cannot do that: they cannot cut the invisible cord."

I feared that the mutter was about to begin again; but to my relief she broke out of it and said with decision: "However . . . *No* suffering I have ever endured is to be compared with Tilly's. Ianthe did not die. I waited about in this fog, dreading, hoping for a summons. But none came. For several days I did not even leave the house. Then the fog lifted. So I knew at least that the danger was past. *Now,* I thought to myself, now is the time to take action. I cast about in my mind; and after a while what should I light on but this very Tilly! I must go to England, and ask Tilly to help me to find her. As soon as I had got all this clear, I was quite at peace. My instinct was whole again. I remembered what your grandmother had told me that last time: that she still sent Tilly picture postcards. Of course I had never actually forgotten it. But it had seemed to my blindness a piece of information without significance. Now I saw it for what it was: the *path.* That child had wanted, had needed to keep a track open back into her childhood. She wanted to have an old nurse. Tilly had helped to nurse her through that pneumonia. Now, I thought, if she is sick, in trouble, who might she turn to?"

"Tilly!" I said, triumphant.

"So I went to England. Alone. Harry stayed behind." She said this hastily, to forestall, I suppose, my customary query. "I had found out long ago, from your Aunt Sylvia, the address of Tilly's lodgings. I went there. Oh, as I rang the bell, a *wild* thought came to me. This is the end of my journey, I thought. *She is here.*"

"And she was?"

"No. She was not there. Nor was Tilly. But she had been there. They had gone away together."

"Where to?"

"The landlady was reticent at first; but I thawed her. The young lady had come a few months ago. A lovely young lady. She seemed to be in trouble." Mrs. Jardine paused. "But, said the landlady, she didn't know anything about that. Mrs. Svoboda was always one for keeping herself to herself: and *she* never meddled in what wasn't her business. She understood Mrs. Svoboda had been nurse to the young lady as a child. She'd stayed some weeks in these very lodgings, and to the best of her belief she never saw no one all that time but Tilly. She'd stop in bed all morning, and then they'd take a walk out together of an afternoon. So drawn and sickly she looked and so sad with it it wrung your heart. Haunted like. But they seemed ever so thick together; and sometimes she'd hear them laughing up in her room. Mrs. Svoboda was such a one for a joke. She'd watch them from the window sometimes, going off down the street. Such a funny-matched pair they looked—the one so tall, the other such a tiny body. The young lady never wore nothing else but a long loose black cloak, which seemed a bit funny. So *old* like. You'd expect a young lady so high-bred from the looks of her to have a trunkful of fashions." Mrs. Jardine paused again. "Then one day Mrs. Svoboda sprung it on her she was going off for a bit to foreign parts to visit her late husband's people out in a place called Bo'emia. They were always on at her to come, she said, but somehow or another she'd never found the opportunity, not since her honeymoon; and that was a fair long time ago. She'd make it a proper stay while she was about it, and drop a postcard now and then to let them know how she got on. She wanted her lodgings kept, and she paid up four months in advance for the two rooms. Well, you could have knocked them all down with a feather, knowing what a one she was for London and her own little place, but there, she knew better than to waste words on the ins and outs of it. 'Well, you have got a spirit, Mrs. Svoboda,' was all she said. Then they packed their bags and off they went. 'Good-bye, Mrs. Pringle,' said the young lady, she was ever so sweet-spoken when she did speak. 'I've been so comfortable in your nice homely house.' A couple of postcards had come, lovely views, not saying much, just: 'Having a nice time.' She'd forwarded anything that had come, like she'd been told to. Nothing for the young lady. . . . I gave some plausible reason of old friendship for wishing to get in touch with her, and she gave me the address. So to that address I went."

Mrs. Jardine sighed, as if the memory of that long journey still fatigued her.

"And you found them?"

"It was a big farm house on the outskirts of a village, not far from a beautiful old town called Prague. That is the capital of Bohemia. I wonder, can you picture it? A village of coloured houses, white, pale blue, pale pink plaster, with wooden balconies filled with flowers—mostly red geraniums. So clean, so bright, so extraordinarily pretty. At the top of the village, on a little hill, a white church with a round green dome, the shape of an onion. And beyond, green hills and the pine forests. I could smell the forests as I walked down the wide village street. It was like walking into a fairy story. Flocks of geese wheeling off this way and that as I came along. So I came to the farm where Tilly's husband was born. Jinric Svoboda. A very handsome man. They were an exceptionally handsome family—tall, splendid cheek bones, so much dignity. Jinric's parents were dead now. His two brothers and his sister lived on there, with their families. Imagine pert Cockney Tilly among them all!—like a London sparrow bouncing and pecking round a team of noble cart horses. But they adored her —they thought her fascinating. She was giving them English lessons,—shouting at them, of course, as we English always do to make it easier for poor weak-witted foreigners to understand us. They repeated words after her so painstakingly in their soft slow voices, and their faults of pronunciation caused her to cackle with laughter; and the more she laughed at them, the more they delighted in her amusement. I saw them all through the window. They were sitting round a big wooden table eating their evening meal. It was like a picture of peasants by a Flemish master—the bright, spotless wooden kitchen, the shining pots and pans, the circle of faces half lit, half shadowed. There were some children in pinafores. It was only a glimpse. I saw no one precisely. Naturally I could not press my nose to the window and stare in. I moved noiselessly and put myself out of sight in the doorway, and heard this lesson going on. The laughter. Then I heard a different kind of voice speak a word or two in English: a well-bred voice, high-pitched, not unmusical from a distance. 'My —mother—has—blue—eyes,' it said slowly, clearly."

"Ianthe!"

"Ianthe. She was repeating it for a child, and a child's voice lisped it after her. She went on patiently repeating simple words —my kitten, my spoon, my plate, my baby brother; and I heard Tilly say: 'Mudder, brudder—'ark at 'im, bless 'is 'eart! Oh, 'e'll get 'is tongue round it before any of you.' It was a strange experience for me. I would have liked to stay there for ever listening. After a hundred years of anguish, to have arrived at last beside this well, and find her there, drinking peace with a peasant child from a white cup. . . ."

Her voice faded out like sad singing. It made me want to cry.

"And to hear her say that first of all, about blue eyes, as if she was talking about you," I said shakily.

"Yes. Did that strike you? It struck me too."

"Did you go in?"

"No, no. I could not break in. It came to me suddenly as I stood there that if she were to see me unexpectedly she would——" Mrs. Jardine stopped dead; then said calmly: "I *heard* the scream that she would give. I slipped away, skirting the wall, and took a field path back to the inn. I asked for a room, and then I had a delicious supper."

"What did you have?"

"A kind of junket called yoghourt, with brown sugar; we should be a healthier nation if it formed part of our diet; and brown bread and butter and coffee; *good* coffee. Then I wrote a note and asked the landlord's little daughter to take it to Tilly for me."

"In English, did you ask?"

"Of course not. How could she have understood me? In German, her mother tongue, which I speak perfectly."

"Tell me what you said."

She told me; and added rather severely:

"I hope your mother will see to it that *you* are taught to speak it properly."

"Oh yes. She says we're to have a German governess next summer holidays," I said, depressed. "So then what happened?"

"I went and sat at a little table under an apple tree in the inn garden, and waited."

"And Tilly came?"

"She came."

"Was she pleased to see you?"

Mrs. Jardine smiled.

"No. She was not. There she sat, a most singular sight, in her bonnet, and—what was it called, that cape thing she always wore. . . ."

"Her dolman?"

"Ah, yes, her dolman. Does she *still* wear it?"

"Oh yes. Always."

"She does!" Mrs. Jardine chuckled, sighed. "Oh, Tilly is an unique experiment of Nature's. We shall not look upon her like again. There she sat, clasping her reticule—I remembered *that* from twenty years ago—looking fixedly into the apple boughs. She would not look at me. Excessively dignified she was. Seeing as I'd put it how I had in my note, she said, she'd felt it no more than her duty to come along. What had I to say to her?"

"How had you put it?"

"'*In the name of one whom we both loved,*' I said, '*who on her death bed promised you to me in case of my need, and enjoined on you this promise, come immediately.*'"

I nodded, deeply stirred.

"'What I want, Tilly,' I said, 'is the information you owe me.' She didn't know what I was driving at—information, was her answer. Since it seemed I'd ferreted it out somehow that Ianthe was with her, all she could say was Ianthe had turned up at her front door one day, as was very natural, her being in England again and considering the old days. It wasn't her business, she said, whether *I* knew Ianthe's whereabouts or not. She wasn't to suppose I troubled myself much, not from the way Ianthe spoke. Not that Ianthe ever mentioned me at all. What was the harm, she'd like to know, in her paying a visit to her own husband's people that were always asking her, and Ianthe coming along too, seeing

*161*

she was looking peaky, like she needed a holiday, and there was nobody seemed to trouble themselves about her, and remembering how fond Madam had used to be of her as a little thing, and sorry for her too to be deserted like. Oh, a rigmarole! and her eyes popping at the apples; and rather impertinent. Yes, I must say, her whole attitude was one of impertinence. 'Enough of this, Tilly,' I said. 'Answer me plainly. *Is the baby living?*' She looked at me then." Mrs. Jardine drew in a long loud breath. "Her face mottled like old blotting paper. Whatever in the world was I insinuating? Baby? . . . Then I will frighten you, I thought. So I did."

The rap in Mrs. Jardine's voice, sudden, icy, made me jump.

"I threatened her with the law. In no uncertain terms I threatened her. It did not take me long to break her down. She broke into hysterical weeping. I sat by her and held her hand. Such a warm sweet starry night was coming down. There were other people sitting out in front of the inn, drinking their evening beer. Somebody had a violin. He played it very sweetly—old German airs. After a while they called good-night to one another and began to go home. We were alone. Tilly began to grow calm. 'Oh, Miss Sibyl!' . . . she sighed out at last. So then I knew we could speak to one another."

"Was she more polite then?"

"Much more. 'The baby died?' I said. I knew it, of course, by that time. Until I saw her, I had been nursing a mad hope that all was well. It was hearing her voice in that kitchen, so calm and contented. Listening, I had thought: perhaps she has just fed him and put him in a wooden cradle. A foolish piece of self-deception. She was contented because she had become a child again among children, without responsibilities, protected."

"The baby was dead?"

"The baby was dead. A boy. Born dead. So she assured me."

The controlled intensity not only of these sentences but also of the pauses between them appalled me far more than her former outburst of tears.

"*Born* dead?"

"A month ago. Never brought to birth." Mrs. Jardine's eyes,

her whole face, dilated for a moment as if about to explode. "The whole story came out bit by bit. How Ianthe had arrived one day, without a word of warning, having travelled alone from Italy. Had asked Tilly to take her in, hide her and help her. She was like a trapped thing, said Tilly. Half out of her wits. Saying she'd do away with herself, acting so queer some-times—suspicious-like—making out there was somebody after her. *Gasping fits* and that. Other times she didn't seem to take in nothing. 'She'd chatter like a child.'" Mrs. Jardine drummed sharply with her fingers. "Hysteria, I dare say. . . . But it is true that an actual seed of mental instability will germinate at these times. In any case her behaviour, her actions appear to have been those of one—at least temporarily unhinged. All Tilly could elicit from her—or rather, all Tilly told *me*—was that Ianthe had been happy for a time in her new life——"

"Her life after she ran away with Paul?"

"Yes. Had *intended*—that seems to have been the way she put it—had *intended* to be happy. Then, after a time, had been over-taken by a mounting horror of him—had turned against him with such an uncontrollably violent repugnance. . . . 'She went on how she hated men,' said Tilly. 'Hated and loathed them.' So one fine day," said Mrs. Jardine briskly, "it seems that she was seized by an over-mastering desire to—attack him."

"What? Hit him?"

She shrugged her shoulders, then nodded.

"Badly? To hurt him?"

"I do not know what happened. I heard that when he died— he died far away, alone, in a hotel bedroom—he had on his fore-head, above one temple, a terrible scar. He had no scar upon his beautiful brows in the days when we were together. I under-stood then. . . ." Her voice trembled. "I understood why he had never let me look upon his face again." Then rapidly: "Yes, we will assume she wanted to hurt him badly. Or let us not put it in so crude a way. Let us say an *impulse* seized her; that there came the bursting point of a complexity of hideous fears and pressures. I can well imagine . . . I can remember . . ." She drew another labouring breath. "Aghast she fled from him, leaving in her panic and confusion no trace behind her. If Tilly is to be believed, she did not appear to realise her condition. So possibly—I think certainly—she had not informed him." Another hard breath. "When she *did* realise, that a child was on the way, I mean, it seems that she became frantic."

"She didn't want to have a baby?"

"She did not want to. No doubt Tilly did her best for her," said Mrs. Jardine, dry as gunpowder—I could not think why. "I did not inquire. Time went on. Tilly devised a desperate plan. She would take her abroad to this obscure far-away village where nobody would recognise or follow her. There the child would be born. Beyond that she had not looked. If the worst came to the worst, she thought, the child could remain there. They would bring him up as their own. I would not have objected to that. It would have been a good life, a happy wholesome life; perhaps the wisest solution in the circumstances. If she had seen where her first duty lay—to inform me—I would have given that scheme my blessing and furthered it with all my powers. But Ianthe, she said, had pledged her with threats and prayers to secrecy regarding me; and she considered that enough. Enough indeed! I should say so. No need, when you place the long-sought weapon in a person's hands, to beg her to strike home with it. . . . Yet it was a difficult situation for Tilly; I am the first to admit it. . . . So this journey was undertaken. She had enough money—your grandmother had left her a little annuity, as perhaps you know —Ianthe had what I had sent her. It is some comfort at least to remember that. So off they went. Ianthe grew calmer there at once, she said. They made her welcome, cherished her, and asked no questions. Ah, they must have been good people. I think of them daily with love and blessings. 'She never seemed to worry no more about nothing,' said Tilly. 'She left the worrying to me.' So she had this time of healthy, peaceful, vegetable existence —all as it should be. 'But,' said Tilly, 'not even near the end she didn't seem to take it in what was coming. She wouldn't talk about it nor make its little clothes nor nothing. She just took little walks and played with the other children and ate hearty.' This sister-in-law was the village midwife: that is, the woman who looks after poor mothers when their babies are born. Then it came to Ianthe's time. Everything went very badly, as badly as possible. Ianthe nearly died."

"Like you guessed?"

"Yes. They saved her life. They could not save the child. A fine big boy. . . . 'If I had been there,' I said to Tilly, 'he would have been saved.' 'It was better so,' said Tilly. 'She didn't want him.' '*I* wanted him,' I said. 'He was mine.' I said no more. What use? It was all too late. That beautiful child had been denied his life. Paul's child. He would have been glorious."

"What a shame." I wiped my eyes on the back of my hand.

"All this was a month ago. Ianthe, with the vitality of youth, had made a rapid recovery. She had never spoken of her baby, never shed a tear for him, or asked for any token—not even one word of description—by which to remember him. 'It seemed unnatural,' said Tilly."

I decided that Mrs. Jardine was quite right: Ianthe was a very horrid girl.

"It was clear that Ianthe wished to cast off the whole experience, force it to be undone and erased altogether. She had reverted, in appearance at least, to her former state of blank childlike contentedness. She liked to sit in the kitchen where there was talk and bustle going on. She would not be alone. She slept in Tilly's room. 'Very well, now, Tilly,' I said at last. 'All we have left now to discuss is the future. What is to be done with Ianthe? Is she to remain here for the present? Or for the rest of her life? Or what?' Tilly said it was a funny coincidence I should mention that. It was only that very morning she'd brought the conversation round to that very self-same topic. For her part, she was sick and tired of the place. She wanted to get back to London and have her own things round her and hear people talk civilised. She never was one for the country—and as for *foreign* country, the very look of them pine forests turned her up—nasty great black creepy things."

"Oh, that's just like her!" I exclaimed appreciatively. "I can just hear her say it. She hates everywhere except London, she always says."

"In fact," said Mrs. Jardine, with a sniff, "she had decided by now that my turning up when I did was a blessing in disguise. She'd told Ianthe straight it was time she pulled herself together and thought what she was going to do to get on with her life. What was over was over. They'd had a lot of kindness showed them and paid their way and now they must think about getting along back. They were a good-hearted lot here, but ignorant!— you'd never credit. Why, they'd never been to the seaside nor seen a street of proper high-class shops or so much as put their noses inside a music-hall, believe it or not."

These impressions of Tilly's style, breaking recurrently into the classical form of her narrative, were accompanied by an uncanny facial transformation. It was as if the ghost pattern of Tilly's features kept intruding, diffusing Tilly's alien spirit through her own mask of flesh. Since then I have noticed young children's faces alter in this way after they have been staring for some time in total unselfconsciousness at someone. She had "got" Tilly to the life, at some deeper level than mere imitation.

"Did Ianthe want to stay on with them?"

"Ianthe had taken it a bit on the queer side at first—turning her head aside sharp and staring out at nothing. But she wasn't going to stand no more nonsense from her, she'd humoured her long enough. After a bit she'd talked her round. 'Another week, then I'm off back to London,' she'd said. 'And you're coming along with me. But not to settle in them lodgings with me and droop and drift in and out like the Pantomime Fairy Queen, and be looked at old-fashioned and insinuendos put out you're hard put to it to answer back to. For one thing, I got myself to think of. I got my own life to lead. At my time of life it gets on your nerves tagging someone else around when you want a bit of peace and quiet at last on your own. For another, it wouldn't be right. You're getting a big girl now. Are you going where it's only right you should—back to your own mother and tell her the truth of what's been going on or are you not?"

"Oh, she *did* say that!" I exclaimed, triumphant. "You see, she *hadn't* forgotten you."

"That was Tilly's version of the conversation," replied Mrs.

Jardine with dryness. "The monologue, rather. She rendered it with fine dramatic fervour. 'What's more,' it seems she said, 'to the best of my belief your mother can have the law on you. She's your lawful guardian till you come of age. And a nice figure *I'd* cut in the courts, had up for aiding and abetting you and harbouring you against her wishes. You'd best go back, you know, and make a clean breast of it and ask her to forgive and help you live it down.' "

Mrs. Jardine leaned back in her chair and let out a long deep chuckle. She shook her head and sighed as if contemplating Tilly with helpless relish and amusement. Not seeing the joke, I smiled politely and said:

"And what did Ianthe say?"

"Oh, Ianthe said she'd rather be seen dead in a ditch than on my doorstep," said Mrs. Jardine lightly. "She created so Tilly wouldn't answer for the consequences if she did happen to set eyes on me, face to face, and got it in her head I'd come after her. When pressed by Tilly for constructive proposals, she had confessed to a determination to earn her own living and be independent. 'Very well, Tilly,' I said. 'That is perfectly sensible on Ianthe's part. Most right and proper. Now how does she propose to implement her determination? How is she going to set about it?' "

"How was she?"

"It came out that Ianthe cherished a passion for the higher education. She wished to fit herself for an academic career. She'd got it in her head, said Tilly, she'd like to go to one of them new-fangled Cambridge colleges for women."

"Oh," I said dubiously. It seemed a come-down—eccentric without being romantic; dismal.

"She had a pedantic bent, inherited from her father. But it was from me that she derived the wish to strike out on her own, to use her intelligence to make something of her life. I was glad. To me personally it was not a sympathetic idea, but that was immaterial. I was relieved—proud—glad. I thought: the girl has something sound in her. 'Very well, Tilly,' I said. 'Teaching is one of the most honourable of professions. I am glad to say that there is increasing scope in it for educated women. I shall make it my business to inquire into every practical means of furthering her wishes.' "

"Did Tilly thank you very much?"

"Oh, dear me, no! She was outraged. Ianthe, a lady by birth and breeding, to lower herself so, and I abet her! Ianthe make herself a figure of fun, aping what should be for gentlemen only, and then turn schoolmarm or governess. Nothing else Ianthe had done or undergone appeared to have outraged her moral sense: this did. She had only repeated it, she gave me to understand, to show me how sorely Ianthe stood in need of moral guidance. There was no point in wasting breath. I gave her my orders. 'You will take Ianthe back to England in a week's time,' I said. 'Expect to hear from me in London shortly; and when you do, come at once to receive my instructions.' Then I closed the interview and bade her good-night. Next day I returned to England."

"Didn't you see Ianthe?"

"No, I did not. I had no wish to see Ianthe. None, none." She drew that hissing breath. "Then I busied myself with necessary inquiries and interviews. Finally I arranged for Ianthe to enter the family of a university coach. He was a schoolmaster, retired on grounds of ill-health, with a decent wife and a large family. The mistress of Girton College, that is the first college for women to be founded in Cambridge, recommended him to me. She was a remarkable woman. I have the most impressive recollections of my interview with her. Then I paid *him* a visit, and said and arranged what was necessary. Then I summoned Tilly and gave her my instructions. First she was to take Ianthe to the doctor I had selected, to see that her health was properly re-established. So soon as I had received his report, which was perfectly satisfactory, I conveyed, through Tilly, a letter to Ianthe, containing in the briefest and most businesslike terms my offer. She was to prepare herself for her examinations and enter College as soon as possible. Her fees would be paid and she would receive in addition a small but sufficient allowance for herself. Her vacations should be spent—not with me if she chose otherwise, but under my indirect supervision and control. That is, I should insist on being kept informed of her whereabouts and plans. It was made plain to her that my only remaining wish with regard to her was to help her to attain an honourable independence."

Mrs. Jardine's energy was beginning to peter out. She spoke in a weak, light, rapid way; the voice of one hurrying to reach a bare conclusion before her forces should be altogether spent.

"I received an answer to this letter. She accepted my offer, and added the words, thank you. As I thought, she proved to have unusual abilities. She passed her examinations with distinction and entered College the following autumn. She studied languages. Each term she wrote me one letter, containing news of her studies and her progress. It caused me a strange disturbance always to see her handwriting—small, neat, precise as a don's, with here and there a touch of nervous weakness and uncertainty. As time went on, these letters became a shade more human and confiding. She was happy. I saw her once, at a distance, emerging from a lecture hall. She was wearing spectacles, and looked rather drab and plain—it was a cold day, which did not suit her complexion, and her clothes were unbecoming—but solid. I was reassured; though something about her gave me the notion of a person deliberately suppressing three-quarters of her personality."

"And in the holidays, did she . . . ?"

"No. She chose to spend them with this coach and his family. She established friendly relations with them. It was all perfectly suitable, harmonious and domestic. Really, she seems to have done nothing for three years but apply herself voraciously to study. And at the end of three years she acquitted herself brilliantly. Yes," said Mrs. Jardine, with a sort of ironic pride, "she took a double first in her final examinations." She paused, brooding; then added: "However, those intellectual laurels were all discarded—thrown away."

In the ensuing silence I heard Harry's Cadillac change gear loudly at the bottom of the hill, and begin to moan slowly up.

"I wrote to congratulate her. I thought it on the cards that we might now meet; but she chose otherwise. This man, this coach, whom obviously she regarded by now in the light of a parent, was sailing for India with his wife. She sailed with them. She removed herself as far as possible from me. She obtained a teaching post for herself in Calcutta. Quite soon she met the man Thomson, and for some reason married him. A respectable middle-aged man, a civil servant, Inspector-General of something or other to do with the Police."

The car changed gear again with its usual noisy grunt of protest and touch-and-go moment of possible refusal. The moan became a bellow.

"Curious," said Mrs. Jardine, but now as if she had no more strength to mark any surprise emphatically. "After her marriage she appears to have assumed yet another personality. She became a beauty again. And other traits became predominant. Frivolity. Extravagance. Passionate absorption in dress and in society. I see it as an attempt on the part of a person with no true centre to try out yet another character with which to face the world. She had those two children—as rapidly as possible one after the other. Curious. That seems to have gone off without the emotional disturbances one would have apprehended. She left them entirely to nurses and stuck on them the most perfunctory of names, and kissed them in the morning and at night, and danced and danced. And led Thomson a pretty dance. Then one fine day she took the two children and sailed for England. She did not come back. So he threw away his post and his pension and followed her and found her. . . ."

The car stopped at the front door. I heard Cherry jump out and call something in her high penetrating treble.

"Ah!" exclaimed Mrs. Jardine. "They are back. We must make some fresh tea. And you must go in a few minutes, dearest. Yes, you must go."

"May I go and get my six dahlias?" I said. "I know which they are."

"Ah, yes," she said, pleased with me, leaning back and smiling tenderly at me out of a transparent face. "Yes, love. Go and fetch them."

I got up.

"About Mr. Connor," I said. "Did he come back to Mrs. Connor?"

"Oh, dear me, yes, of course he went back. Respectable men always go back to their wives, you know. I cannot tell you in what frame of mind he returned, for my only further communications with him were through my solicitor, with regard to Ianthe's money."

"Perhaps he got nicer to her . . .?"

"Ah, yes. There may well have grown up between them a deep and terrible tie. She died, I heard, about ten years ago; and then he relinquished the world altogether and joined some religious order dedicated to prayer and contemplation. He became altogether a saint."

I heard Cherry running through the hall, and I said in a hurry:

"Where is Ianthe now?"

"I have not the slightest idea," said Mrs. Jardine.

# PART FOUR

THAT day she came to call upon my mother for advice we hovered in the drive to see the car come round the bend. She alighted, formal and elegant, in a dove-grey cloak lined with lilac silk, long grey gloves and a shallow wide-brimmed silvery straw hat girdled with blue and mauve ostrich feathers. She kissed us affectionately, but she was different: that afternoon she was not for us, or we for her. Next moment Mossop had opened the door, and she swept on into our house and left us behind. We yearned after her retreating back; but we recognised it for the banishing back of a lady parent come with ceremony to discuss her responsibilities with another. What they were about to reveal to one another with so much mutual tact, deference and affability dashed us from any notions we might have held of high estate. We were but little children weak.

We mounted our bicycles and went and rode round the lawn, and showed off a little at a discreet distance from the drawing-room windows. We caught an earnest glimpse of her sitting forward in her chair, hat and cloak inclined towards my mother; but we did not approach her again. She stayed for an hour and then she drove away. When we dashed in to ask why she had not stayed to tea, my mother replied that Mrs. Jardine had regretfully preferred to get back to pour out tea for the Major. This had been her unfailing custom during the whole of their married life, and he counted on her presence and ministration.

Restraining our passionate anxiety, we asked in a casual way: "Did you like her?"

My mother said with care but without condescension that she seemed a charming person.

"She is very fond of you children," she added, with an ambiguous glance at us, part gratified and willing to gratify, part deprecatory; even, to my guilty conscience, a shade suspicious, as if speculating upon lines familiar to us. What, said the glance, had we been up to with Mrs. Jardine, so to impress ourselves upon her affections? My mother did not completely trust her little girls.

"What did she say——" I wished to say: "about us," but thought better of it, and added instead: "about Maisie?"

My mother closed her lips. Then she said guardedly: "She had a suggestion to make to me about Maisie."

"What was it?"

I saw her begin to draw down the blind, and I went on:

"She thinks you're a good influence on Maisie. She said you'd found the right touch. Maisie's never got to like her. But she loves you. She told me so."

"Poor Maisie," said my mother again. She sighed. Then she said, almost against her will, almost as if we were all sisters:

"Mrs. Jardine's idea was that Maisie should share lessons with you. Perhaps live here. . . . At least during term-time."

"*Live* with us? What did you say? Can she? Did you say she can? Would she share Mamselle? What room would she sleep in? Can she sleep with us?"

While we shot out questions, Jess stood still, watching my mother closely; but I began immediately to cast my limbs about and clap my hands in lunatic abandonment.

My mother told me not to be foolish.

"Well, what *did* you say?"

"I told her," she said firmly, "that I must think it over. I rather doubt . . . I think myself it would be a wiser plan to send Maisie right away to boarding school."

These words tolled leaden in my ears. To me they were as if a judge should assume the black cap and pass sentence of death. I made a sickly protest.

"I'm sure Maisie would rather come to us."

"Maisie is the type of girl who would do well at a suitable school," said my mother, inexorable. "I should always recommend boarding school for a child without a satisfactory home influence."

"I don't think she'd like it."

"Oh, nonsense. Maisie is a most sensible independent girl. A nice school would provide the best possible atmosphere for her development."

I felt the ominous subject of character-building begin to breathe its threat upon me. I wiped my eyes: the eyes of a girl lacking sense and spirit, clamped as voraciously to a state of dependence as an octopus to its prey.

"In any case," said my mother, "I must consult your father. I told Mrs. Jardine so."

"Dad'll say no," said Jess.

"Well, we must see," said my mother.

"Did she say anything about Tilly?" I inquired.

"Yes. She asked for Tilly's address." My mother looked rueful.

"Did you give it to her?"

"I gave it to her, of course. She is anxious to go and see her, but I fear it is a mistake. She seemed to think it might do Tilly good—rouse her perhaps—but I very much doubt it. I heard this afternoon from the landlady: poor Tilly is very, very feeble. However . . . Mrs. Jardine is going up to-morrow. She said she couldn't rest until she had found out for herself whether there was any little thing she could do for Tilly's comfort."

"Is the landlady's name Mrs. Pringle?"

"Yes."

"I thought so, only Tilly was always forgetting it, or getting it wrong. Isn't Mrs. Jardine kind to want to do something for Tilly?"

"Very kind. Now run along and put away your bicycles."

My father said no, without hesitation and with considerable emphasis. He did not say it in our presence, but we took the sense of his reaction from my mother's telling us on no account to pester him about Maisie; he had decided against the scheme, and that was all there was to be said. The following week he was absent in his constituency; and in accordance with my usual practice of inspecting any letters my parents might leave about

174

upon their desks, I found occasion to read a note from him to my mother. The main contents, dealing with some matter of local liberal politics, lacked interest for me; but the postscript was enthralling. It said: *"I trust you have been perfectly firm with that woman, and made it clear, ONCE AND FOR ALL, that the plot is OFF. It was like her impudence."*

It was, I suppose, made clear beyond a doubt; but no light ever shed illumined for Mrs. Jardine a prospect of defeat. Next day a letter in violet ink lay on my mother's table, and cast its own rewarding rays upon my tenebrous but doggedly pursued path. It said:

*"My dear Mrs. Landon,—I entirely understand your position, and indeed feel persuaded of the accuracy of your analysis of Maisie's temperament and educational requirements. I shall now pin all my hopes upon a suitable school. Discipline and kindliness combined with a broad and progressive intellectual outlook are what I require for her. It cannot be impossible to discover such a combination; but as I am now out of touch with the trends of modern education, I should be deeply grateful for your advice before making a final decision. Will you not bring your two to tea on Friday next? My grandchildren returned yesterday with the relative, Miss Mackenzie, who has had the charge of them during these sad and difficult years. I should so much like to give her—poor devoted woman—the pleasure of meeting you. We could have a conversation, and the young ones could play in the garden. I will reserve a full account of our dear old Tilly until I see you. I have visited her twice. She is sinking rapidly. I shall not go again. A quoi bon? I can now say to myself with conviction. I was able to satisfy myself that she was receiving every reasonable care and attention. She did not recognise me. She is in a merciful stupor, far beyond reach of human communication. Her passing will be easy, painless. I sat long by her bed each time and held her hand, and said farewell to one more link with the past. How thankful I am that my meeting with you should have given me this poignant opportunity!*

*"Sincerely yours,*

*"Sibyl Anstey Jardine."*

Whether or no my mother hesitated, who shall say? It may have been the word education, ever acting upon her ears as the trumpet upon the war-horse, or the promptings of a natural curiosity to see the Jardines at home; but I think myself that it was another weight that tipped the scales. It was the spell of the spell-binder, no more, no less. My mother was prudent and incorruptible, but she too was drawn, irresistibly drawn, to look upon, to listen to Mrs. Jardine once again. So we went to tea on Friday next.

The ladies took tea in the drawing-room, and we had ours apart, a proper schoolroom spread, in the dining-room. I had expected Maisie and Malcolm to be in deep mourning, but they were not. Maisie wore a black band round her arm, Malcolm a black tie. Maisie told me later that her grandmother had laid specific injunctions upon Auntie Mack to refrain from buying her a mourning outfit. This was an added grievance. She herself had insisted upon the black band and sewn it on with crude, uneven stitches. I had also expected hushed voices, funereal gloom; but everything seemed more or less normal. Maisie pounced on Cherry for blowing bubbles in her mug of milk, and Cherry wailed, and was first upbraided for babyishness, then immediately consoled by Malcolm and Maisie together. She began to blow bubbles again and to giggle through them, and next moment we were all bubbling, giggling, and humming God Save The King into our mugs, in competition. Malcolm did best, the milky froth came up right over the brim and clung to his nose. We rolled about with laughter. Then the door opened and Harry came stalking in and sat down among us.

"Couldn't face it," he said, jerking his head in the direction of the drawing-room.

Cherry sprang on to his lap, and the rest of us poured out his tea and plied him with buns, anxious to welcome, spoil and comfort him. He looked round at our milky lips and noses, but he said nothing. Cherry crumbled his bun and fed him by hand, kissing him repeatedly. He cast rather a silence, but no shadow. Once more I noticed the complicated and pleasing smell which

176

always emanated from him: honey and flowers, I think, tweed and brandy.

"Was it devilish in there?" said Maisie. "Did you try?"

He shook his head.

"One peep through the window," he said. "Saw 'em at it." He sketched a gesture with his hand. "Stirring the cauldron. Dropping you all in—bit by bit—legs—ears—noses—liver and lights——"

We laughed in hearty appreciation to encourage him, and Cherry flung herself back on him, rolling her curls on his shoulder and shrilling affectedly:

"Oh, you funny, funny man! Oh, you do make me laugh so!"

"I'm the one they won't digest," said Maisie. "Oo-o, I'll give 'em such a stomach-ache."

This always amusing word, uttered with particular grimness and gruffness, had never seemed more strikingly humorous. We collapsed in hysterics. Gratified by her success, Maisie perceptibly expanded. She had been addressing her attention to Malcolm and Cherry, practically ignoring Jess and myself, just as she had the first time we ever came to tea. It was, I see now, her way of expressing her sense of the need for family solidarity. Exposed and isolated as they were by trouble, she must bind them all together in one group. But now, temporarily at least, she relinquished them. When tea was over, she came and put her arm through mine and said:

"Come on. Let's go out."

Harry began to pour milk into a saucer for his cat. I saw with anxiety that he was not going to be able to manage without spilling most of it. Cherry took the jug from him, saying:

"My pet, you're a bit too shaky to-day."

She took up the saucer of milk and went trotting out after him towards the study. The rest of us went into the garden.

Malcolm was to go to a crammer the following day, with the idea of an intensive preparation for entry into Winchester the following term. He was fourteen, and backward. In order that no time should be lost in the initial stages of laying him open to the proper influences and traditions, a gentleman resident in Winchester, an ex-tutor of the college, had been found to receive and coach him. Mrs. Jardine had been startlingly active. What with his prospects and the fact that Harry was to accompany him on the journey, he was in a somewhat oscillating and nervous frame of mind. He took Jess off to present her with his old stamp album. Maisie and I were debating which tree to climb when the french windows opened and the ladies came out and called to us.

"Damn," muttered Maisie; but we advanced obediently to the terrace.

"So this is Maisie's little friend."

It was Auntie Mack, none other, who addressed these words to me in a penetrating and genial whinny. A very large hand gripped mine and wrung it hard. She was a tall, protuberant, bony person, with a carelessly assembled frame. She was dressed in a black jacket and skirt, both of unusual length, fusty, dusty, threadbare, trimmed with wide black braid and voluminously flared below the waist and knees. Her black blouse was secured at the throat by the largest cameo brooch I have ever seen; and in addition she was hung with chains of various sizes and designs. Her narrow flat chest broadened to an abnormal convexity combined with meagreness in the hips. Her legs and feet were elephantine. Her bundles of hair, striped sandy and white, were done up askew in plaited circles secured by formidable steel prongs. Desultory wisps hung round the expanse of her face and forehead like a tacked-on oddment of frayed and faded trimming. She had a flourishing sandy moustache and long pinkish-yellowish cheeks patched with freckles, bulging sad green eyes edged with white lashes, and a big solid yet somehow vacant assortment of features. She was just the type of figure—knocked about, unsuspicious, mildly monstrous—with whom a child is instinctively at ease: perhaps because it represents, for a child, some truth about the world. A clown's truth. I felt an instant affection for Auntie Mack.

"Maisie," said Mrs. Jardine, "Rebecca's mother and your aunt and I have been talking about you."

She did not make it sound portentous: indeed her manner was

particularly gentle and unambiguous; but Maisie flushed black, and her whole person took on a lowering bison stance.

"We have been asking ourselves and each other what kind of school you would like to go to. And it seemed to me rather wrong to make any final decision without consulting you."

Maisie lifted her head and looked cautiously first at her grandmother, then at my mother. What was the catch in this?

"Come indoors with us a little while and let us talk it over. We have the prospecti of several schools and we can look at them together. You can tell Mrs. Landon, can you not, what strikes you about them; and Mrs. Landon has made us such a kind offer. When we have selected one or two, she will take you to see them before we finally decide. Then you will not have the feeling that you are being sent out blindfold, against your own will and judgment. Will you?"

Silent, Maisie hesitated. My mother put an arm around her shoulders. She dashed the tears from her eyes with the back of her hand. Still circled by my mother's arm, she was drawn back into the house between the two imposing ladies.

"Meanwhile," said Auntie Mack to me, softly, slowly, trailing her syllables, "you and I will take a wee stroll, shall we, around this glorious garden?"

I placed a docile hand in the hand she held out to me, and we started off across the lawn at a confidential meandering pace.

"Will Maisie be long?" I said.

"Oh, just a little talk with those two kind motherly advisers," she said vaguely. "Just to settle things up and point the way for her."

We paced on.

"Beautiful!" She stopped dead, and, face upraised, eyes closed, sniffed voluptuously at the air. "Delicious! Glorious! Oh, it's a morrtal treat to smell grass and trees again."

It seemed to me so odd to apply the olfactory rather than the visual sense to trees that I took an anxious glance at Auntie Mack. Could it be that she was Afflicted, and that Maisie and Mrs. Jardine had omitted to mention the fact? But next moment she opened her gooseberry eyes and cast them dreamily up and down over the landscape. I realised that she was deeply savouring the beauties of Nature.

"I am a country woman, borrn and bred," she said. "For seven years I have looked out of sad windows and seen a row of grey houses opposite, tram lines between. I have waked to the clamourr of the firrst tram and laid my head down upon the pillow to the clang of the last one. Seven long yearrs. I am like a wee birrd let out of a cage. A caged birrd free at last."

I was interested in her vowels, her l's and r's, and by the whole unfamiliar distribution of stresses in an accent I did not then recognise as lowland Scottish.

"It is nice here, isn't it?" I agreed.

"Oh, magnificent! A magnificent properrty. A real precious gem in the crown of old England." She turned with the slow uncertain sweep, as of a craft swinging at anchor, which characterised all her movements, and surveyed the house-front. "Yes, yes, yes. A privilege to be beneath this historic roof. And a morrtal treat"—she pressed my hand—"to meet so many kind new friends."

"Mrs. Jardine's awfully kind, isn't she?" With every speech of Auntie Mack's, I felt my heart expand further towards her.

"God bless her and the Majorr too!" she exclaimed in tones half-stifled with emotion. "If ever there lived a true English gentleman, it is the Majorr. When you have mentioned that, you have mentioned the finest type of man the Creatorr ever turrned His hand to."

I was struck by this view of Harry, which so corroborated Mrs. Jardine's own.

"I have discharrged my duty to the best of my ability," proclaimed Auntie Mack, wheeling back slowly and continuing our linked pacing. "To the best of my ability I have discharrged it. I leave them now in his care. I told him so last night—over our coffee. Delicious coffee! 'Majorr Jarrdine, I leave these three orrphaned children in good hands—I may say pairrfect hands. The burrden of care has rolled off my back and you have taken it up. May God make it light to you. May He rewarrd you.' "

"What did he say?"

A tender smile played over her face. She shook her head. "He was most touched," she said. "Worrds failed him altogether. He is a man of a few worrds—he is not one to waste them. Perrhaps you have remarrked that."

"Oh, yes. He never says anything."

"That is the true British tradition. 'But regarrding the measure meted out to *me*,' I said, 'I cannot speak of it. My hearrt is too full. I must be dumb. Gratitude does not reside upon the lips alone. Its properr home is *heerre*.'" She pressed her hand against her bosom.

"Did he say anything to that?"

"No, not a worrd. He just hurried away."

I realised that she had fallen deeply in love with Harry, and could not help feeling that Mrs. Jardine must have imposed upon her an over-inspired conception of him. I thought it my duty to say:

"You know, I sort of think Mrs. Jardine will have most to do with looking after them. She does everything."

"Yes, yes," was the lilting reply. "She is the executive parrtner, I am aware of that. His true helpmeet. A pairrfect marriage. An example, that is what they are. An example."

"I like Mrs. Jardine very, very much. Don't you?"

"Oh, a wonderful specimen of womanhood. A remarrkable woman. It is a privilege to be in her society. Such a brilliant converrsationalist."

"Oh, I love her! She's my best friend really. At least—Maisie is, I suppose, but that's different. Mrs. Jardine is my best grown-up friend."

"Ah yes, no doubt," said Auntie Mack in a vague way, musing. She did not seem to take in what I wished to convey: that she could freely confide in me; so I added, in a spirit of encouragement:

"She tells me everything really."

"Yes, yes," repeated Auntie Mack, still rapt, I presumed, in dreams of Harry. "She has told me what a jolly friendship has sprung up between you all. It has helped Maisie. Malcolm has been helped too."

I saw Jess and Malcolm emerge from one of the lime alleys and approach the swing. He steadied it while she seated herself, and then began with ardour to swing her; and I felt it only just to say:

"It's Jess who—who's been a help to Malcolm. He likes her much the best."

"Malcolm has a lot of good in him. Quite a lot," said Auntie Mack, screwing her eyes up to take in the pretty boy and girl picture they appeared to present. "He takes after his father, pooorr boy. A rough diamond. But with the instincts of a gentleman. Bringing out is what he needs. The Majorr will do that for him. He will smooth off the raw edges and add the polish."

I could not help feeling her expectations of Harry a shade immoderate. In any case Malcolm, whether considered in his present crude state or in his future, purged of the base and flashing from every facet, remained for me a bore. Romance was all; and I could not bring myself to believe that he would emerge a more romantic figure from all the chiselling, refining processes which he was about to undergo. I re-directed Auntie Mack's attention.

"Maisie doesn't like Mrs. Jardine," I said.

My brusqueness shocked her. She wagged her head reproachfully.

"Oh, there you are too strong. Too strong altogether. Love has not triumphed yet, but love will come. I tell Mrs. Jarrdine not to despairr. Maisie will rise on stepping stones—but it will be gradual. Maisie has been through deep waterrs. Oh, the pity of it all! I cannot but see it as a happy release. Poorr fellow! He wished them sent away. We agreed on that. He thought it right they should be spared the end. But it seems she cannot forgive us."

"Forgive you for what?"

"You will not credit it, but she accuses me of *plotting!*"

"Plotting?"

"That is what she calls it. *Taking sides* with her grandmother to deceive her. Did you ever! I have quite lost Maisie's confidence. Oh, quite! It is all very difficult. I feel the irron has sunk deep into her soul."

Favourably impressed by the power of her metaphors, I looked up attentively at Auntie Mack. She was rolling her eyes in a mild but distraught way at the distance, and looked altogether in a state of contemplative perplexity; as if the puzzle were beyond her, just above the garden wall somewhere, and she had neither will nor way to catch up with it and straighten it out. The sun gilded her moustache with a placid gleam. Then she frowned. A look of anxious expectancy concentrated her features. She put a hand delicately to her mouth and gave utterance to a deep and prolonged eructation.

"Excuse me, dear," she remarked, after an interval. "I am such a sufferer from indigestion, a reeal martyrr. The Majorr's lavish boarrd has quite upset my stomach. I must be more careful. I over-indulged at tea. The sight of that dewy golden butter!—and all those fresh baked scones and dinky biscuits. . . . I *could not* refrain. Oh dearr, dearr me, I made a thorough pig of myself. I must suffer the consequences."

"Nurse takes bicarb. for her indigestion," I said.

"Ah, is she a sufferer too? Just fancy! There's no remedy like bicarb. It breaks up the acidity. I must go in soon and beg a glass of hot water."

We paced on and turned into the right-hand lime alley, through which I had so lately walked at Mrs. Jardine's side. Auntie Mack did not pause to smile at the nude Apollo. I thought, indeed, that she passed him rather hurriedly, with head averted.

"Does Maisie think you ought to have told her he was going to die?" I said.

"Yes, she thinks that. She has told me she will *never forgive me!* Since then she has scarcely deigned to open her lips to me. I'm sure I only acted from principle, and with her good in view."

She spoke with the wounded loyalty of a faithful employee smarting under unjust reprimand.

"The thing is, she was sure he was going to get better. She told me so."

"Ah, and Maisie doesn't like to be wrong. That's the core of it. Maisie will *not* endure to be wrong."

For a moment, as I hopped along by Auntie Mack, striving to

match my step to her raking stride, I felt a little peculiar. Time and place shifted, I was back in the upstairs room, listening while another authority passed a like judgment upon a different girl: different, yet kindred, it seemed, in more ways than one.

"I should have thought she'd see you did it not to spoil the summer holidays," I said, sympathetic. "She couldn't have enjoyed them if she'd known he was dying, could she? Still, perhaps she feels if she'd stayed with him he wouldn't have died."

"Ah, she'd have that bee buzzing in her bonnet," agreed Auntie Mack, in tones of resigned exasperation. "Maisie's the girl to work miracles against nature—she always was. Flying in the face of what's plain as the nose on it. Oh, she knew all right, but she wouldn't have it—not she. Malcolm, now, he was on to it. There was no need to put it to him or keep it from him. He had bowed his head meekly to the Lord's will before he came away. And afterwards—he took it like a man, did young Malcolm. But Maisie —oh dearr, dearr, dearr, what a commotion! And if you'll credit it, it wasn't only us, it was herr fatherr came in for it, poorr dearr dead creature, with the breath scarce out of his body."

She shook her head, appalled; and a grisly picture rose before me of Maisie, red and savage, pouncing on the corpse and shaking it.

"She seems more or less the same as always now," I suggested. I thought hopefully of Maisie's unaltered look of robust freshness, and of the hand she had slipped in a spirit of rough affection through my arm.

"Oh, she'll be harrbourring up something," said Auntie Mack, with what seemed a certain irresponsible satisfaction. "Maisie's not the girl to give in. 'I am quite in favour of boarrding school for Maisie,' I said to them both when they requested my opinion —what a charming woman your motherr is, to be sure!—'quite in favour of it. But what will be the outcome of it? That is, if I may say so, another question. I have had five years' experience of that child, and headstrong is no worrd for her. As I see it, she is nothing but a wild colt—a wild untamed mooorrland colt. Break her and make her—that has been my watchworrd with Maisie girrl.

184

And altairrnatively, make her and break her, if you take my meaning.' "

This was, I knew, a deep saying. I tried to fathom it, sparing a moment to note how frequently her metaphors seemed drawn from horses. There was a rather vacant meek look about her, as if she were being dragged down helpless by the weight of her reflections.

"Did they take it?" I inquired.

"Beg parrdon?"

"Your meaning."

"Oh, yes, yes, they took it. 'It all depends upon the *approach,*' I said. Firrm but kind. Kind *and* firm. That is the approach I would suggest to the headmistress selected to mould her. She is a child you can influence, but *cannot forrce.* On the other hand, once let her get the bit between her teeth and you will rue it. Steel true and blade straight, that is Maisie. But oh dearr! . . ."

Heavily she wagged her head and sighed. Maisie appeared to me in madcap guise, complete with gym tunic and black stockings, on the cover of a book entitled: *The Rebel of the Fourth,* or *The Worst Girl at St. Monica's.*

"Mrs. Jardine is going to start telling her the truth now," I said. "She told me she would. She thinks that'll sort of make Maisie feel better. She always tells people the truth, even children."

"Ah!" Auntie Mack seemed faintly perturbed. "Mrs. Jarrdine has her methods. They would not be everybody's. I am all for the broad view; but surely, as I ventured to say to her, it must be temperred to fit the individual capacity? Oh, I was quite fascinated by her converrsation! Such a bold thinkerr. It was quite a thrill. Such a wide knowledge of the worrld—yet so unworrldly with it, if you take my meaning. Have you noticed what a way she has of putting things?"

"Yes, *rather!*"

"All her own. Most stimulating. 'Miss Mackenzie,' she said to me, 'those children are the most *undernourished* trio I have ever encountered.' For a moment I was quite taken aback. I have always been most particular—a plain wholesome diet and plenty of it, that was my watchworrd. Second, even *thirrd* helpings never grudged. Penny wise, pound foolish, I would say to Robert when he questioned the grocer's bill, or it might be the dairyman's. I will *not* stint their growing frames. Sugarr, butterr, milk may be up a few pence, but doctorr's bills are a thing unknown. Cherry had her little upsets, but doctorr's bills were a thing unknown. He would bow to my judgment. So between you and me I *was* just a *wee* bit taken aback. Just for the moment. Till I took her meaning."

"She didn't mean they hadn't enough to eat?"

"Oh, dearr no, that was the last thing she meant. She explained to me that she was speaking in a spiritual sense. It was just her unusual way of putting things—I wasn't quite quick enough. To tell you the truth, I rather fancy my wits have got a wee thought rusty lately. A deal of worry makes a body slow. 'Well, Mrs. Jarrdine, that is quite a new point of view,' I said. 'I am a Believer myself. I have been punctilious about their prayers, and I neglect no opportunity to sow the seed. God is Love, I tell them. And so forth. . . .' They asked me such awkwarrd questions at the time, particularly Maisie. What could I say but that these were things beyond our underrstanding? . . . that we must trust. . . ."

Auntie Mack was getting agitated. She took out a large black-edged handkerchief and blew her nose.

"At *what* time did they ask questions?"

"Oh . . ." she gasped. She flapped a faint protesting hand.

"When their mother went away?"

"Yes, yes, yes. Oh, the things children think of! I was not accustomed to children. Perhaps anotherr would have given a wiser lead. I did my best. They have been unnaturally deprived—no need to tell me that. It stands to reason I could not make up to them. . . ."

We walked on. She put away her handkerchief and strode with equine dignity, a wounded figure.

"I'm sure Mrs. Jardine didn't mean to blame you for anything," I said. "She told me how awfully kind you'd been to them."

"Oh, good gracious me, no; nothing was furrther from her

thoughts than blame! She made that pairrfectly clear. We had a nice long cosy chat. It was a morrtal treat to pour out a bit to such a dear understanding pairrson. And so good!—so really good. That is what I would so have wished him to know."

"Mr. Thomson?"

"Yes. Pooor dearr suffering creaturre."

"Didn't he think she was good?"

"Oh dearr, dearr, dearr, I don't say he didn't. But—well, he had not seen fit to make the opporrtunities for pairrsonal contact with the matairrnal side. He was a wee thought set in his ideas, you might say: you couldn't shake him. Nobody knows but me what that man had to put up with. And so proud! A sympathetic worrd was what he would *not* stand. It was sealed lips, sealed lips to his last morrtal breath."

"I wonder if Mrs. Jardine quite realises what a lot he had to put up with. Did you tell her?"

"Dear, oh dear!" she gasped again, as if really children nowadays, and how was it I—she—both of us seemed to keep on overstepping the mark and offering one another these fatal opportunities, when set a guard upon thy tongue had always been her watchword, and there were so many sad, difficult things best kept from children?

"Naturally," she continued in mild reproof, "I did not toss about and make play with the family affairs—his side of them *or* hers. It would have been an impairrtinence in me." She paused, brooding; then, irresistibly, she was led to add: "But I felt it no less than my duty to say it to her, and I did. 'Oh, Mrs. Jarrdine,' I said, 'no one knows but myself what that man went through!' In justice to the departed, I felt obliged to say it."

"And what did she say?"

"Oh, she saw the forrce of it." Auntie Mack waved an evasive hand. "She quite saw it. She did not wish to dwell. Naturally she did not, to a stranger. Not that *I* can consider *her* in that light. I make so bold as to say she has become a *friend*. From the fairrst handshake I felt it: heerre is a friend, I said to myself. Robert is at peace now, we must not repine; but I do grieve, I cannot otherrwise, that it was not granted to him to become acquainted with her—and with the Majorr too. It might have meant the worrld to him. He cut himself off so. Oh, he was a lonely fellow!"

"I *am* glad she wrote to him before he died, aren't you?" I said, much affected.

"Ah, I see you are quite her little confidant," exclaimed Auntie Mack, rolling a dubious eye at me. "Yes, yes. It was a consolation. Well, poorr fellow, he is in a better place. I for one will not repine."

"Perhaps," I suggested, "Maisie'll stop repining soon."

"Maybe," she said, vague. "Maybe."

We emerged from beneath the limes and started across the lawn at an angle again. Jess was still with Malcolm underneath the tree. They were now standing face to face on the swing. Over and over again he crouched low, then drove forward, straightened himself, urging his freight to giddier heights. It looked somehow a joyless, business-like performance. Silently he laboured; and her response seemed utterly silent. I wondered if she felt sick and did not like to tell him so. She would feel that on his last day she must be a sacrifice.

"We will keep our distance from the terrace," observed Auntie Mack. "I would not wish their colloquy to be disturbed. We are approaching a milestone in Maisie's life. All depends upon the approach. One worrd with your mother over the tea-table, and I knew I could depend on herr for that. She is motherrly tact itself."

I threw a furtive glance at the french windows, imagining I knew not what portentous confabulation: maternal wings, a couple of pairs of them, spread ominously over Maisie; maternal voices, earnest, benevolent, tolling each its alternate dirge-note in her ears: *This school? That school? SOME school. WHICH school?* Inexorable chime and counter-chime.

"D'you know what I think Maisie will do as soon as ever she's grown up?" I said. "She'll go off and look for Ian—for her mother."

Had I remarked that Maisie planned to go off and run an opium den, the effect upon Auntie Mack could not have been more electrifying. She stopped dead in her tracks. Her eyes winced, then focused suddenly, as if shocked back to attention from years of dream and *wanderlust*. For the first time she took me in with a full and dwelling look.

"What makes you think that?" she said, in quite a sharp realistic way.

"Oh, it seems like the sort of thing she would do," I said, rather unnerved.

"Does she speak to you of her mother?"

"Oh yes. At least she did once. She told me about—you know, about the postcards coming, and then stopping."

"Ah, she told you that."

"And a few other things."

"Pooorr Maisie," said Auntie Mack softly. "She suffered. Oh dearr, dearr, dearr, how she did carry on! It was the same identical carry-on then. She *would not* have it. Oh, she was for taking the next train to fetch her back and I don't know what. I had to watch herr. At her age!—seven or so. Oh, I did have a time! It seemed wisest not to dwell. Least said soonest mended is what I told myself. She seemed to give up after a while. I would answerr as I judged best—I would never refuse herr an answerr—but oh, I was thankful when she stopped! And thankful when those postcarrds stopped. They were nothing but cruelty in the cirrcumstances—yet I asked myself: of two cruelties which is the greater? —withhold? or not withhold? . . . I may have made the wrong decision. I may have. . . . Then they stopped. Well, maybe they tided them over a wee bit, I thought. Now, Time is the great healer. A child's sorrows are brief. She looked bonny enough with it, and ate well all through. But, as I told Mrs. Jardine, Maisie's is not a nature to alterr. Faithful unto death, that's young Maisie, but it has its awkwarrd side. If she's got that fixed in her mind still . . ."

Seeing that Auntie Mack was off again, I made bold to say: "Wouldn't she be able to find her?"

"Better she should not. Better far. Far better."

I could only have said, "Oh"; and I did not say it. There was that in her voice which brought to mind low hissing conversations through the night nursery door. *So she said: 'I'd sooner see her dead at my feet,' she said he said"*; and similar pregnant passages. Crime and passion were, I knew, in question. I said, after a pause:

"Were you living in the house before—before she went away?"

"Yes," said Auntie Mack, speaking with simplicity. "I came at Robert's request when Cherry was a wee babe in arms. There weren't many pennies to spare in that household, you know, and my dearr father had just passed on. I had no home ties remaining of my own. Robert offered me a home: on the understanding, of course, that I should take parrt of the burden of domestic responsibilities off his shoulderrs. Oh, he was bowed down with them!" She broke off, heaved a huge sigh. "Oh dearr, dearr, dearr, they were all at sixes and sevens. He was harrd put to it to know which way to turrn."

"I suppose she was too?" I suggested. She looked blank; so I added: "*Her*—their mother. Hard put to it."

"Oh, yes. She would be too. Of course." She was vague. "But there it was. She was not quite able to pull her weight. It all fell on him."

"Wasn't she very well?"

'Her health was delicate. Cherry was a mistake. Quite a mistake. There was a lot of lying on the sofa, and so forrth. She needed—oh, constant looking afterr."

"Who looked after her?"

"Her husband," said Auntie Mack, solemn and emphatic. "He looked after her."

"He does seem to have had a lot to put up with."

"A marrtyrr that man was!" The words burst forth. "A positive marrtyrr. I would *beg* him to relax, to . . . to make other arrangements——" She broke off, catching her breath in a gasp of horror. The eye I could see rolled frantically, accusing herself. "He would not," she added, reticent.

"I suppose he loved her very much?"

"In all my borrn days," she declared, emotion claiming her again, "I never saw a more beautiful creature. Oh, it was nothing but a tragedy! A tragedy, that's what it was."

"Did she love Malcolm and Maisie very much? And Cherry?"

"Well . . . She was not the motherr type, if you take my meaning. She loved them, of courrse, afterr her own fashion. It would not be everybody's fashion. They would get on her nairrves, you know, on her bad days. She would get to be—not quite in control of her nairrves. It would be best to keep them away. But in between times—oh, they'd be clustering round her, you know, just as it might be you and your sisterrs round yourr own motherr's knee."

"And my baby brother."

"Oh, you have a wee brotherr? Fancy! What a joy! What a joyous day *that* was forr yourr parents, I'll be bound! Three little girls and last the boy. The son and heirr! Just to round off the family. At least—unless——" She caught her breath.

"They wanted me to be a boy," I said. "And even more when it came to Sylvia."

"Ah well, they will see it as all for the best now. And his sisterrs will train him up in the way he should go." A sort of jocose whinny developed in her voice. "Oh, I dare swearr they will! There'll be nothing for the wee man but to walk the straight and narrow path."

We wheeled round and started back across the lawn in silence. I was occupied in wondering how to re-direct the conversation when she stopped, laid a hand upon her diaphragm and mildly groaned.

"Oh dearr, dearr, dearr, this flatulence! I cannot seem to master it. My stomach is positively taut. It strikes me now it would be the melon at the midday meal. *Always* fatal. I should have refrained. Oh, I do ask myself, how will my digestion stand up to the climate at Bude?. All that strong airr off the sea, you know —it is bound to be liverish. We must hope forr the best. Oh, the sea!—it is the love of my life. Picture it! To pairrch upon the cliff top at sunset, and just let the wind stream through my hairr . . ."

Rapt, she gazed forward into dreamland, beholding illimitable horizons: a battered figurehead, sand-and-salt-streaked, stained with time and the world's inclement weathers. I gazed at the unco-ordinated fantasies of her coiffure and strove to picture it.

"I expect your hair's lovely and long when it's down," I said.

"Below my knees, dearr. But oh, I am quite out of conceit with it: it has altogether lost its sheen. It was my fatherr's pride. 'Flora,' he would say to me, 'others may beat you to the winning post forr forrm and featurre, but for a woman's crowning glory you can knock spots off them all.' You must excuse me now, dearr. I must positively go in and sip a glass of hot waterr and bicarrb. Why not run and join the others for a jolly swing? Up like a birrd—into the tree-tops!"

"I'll just walk with you as far as the house," I said politely.

"Ah, some little girrl has been taught pretty mannerrs!"

She took my hand again and gave it a squeeze. I simpered. We walked on. I said:

"Did she ever come back for them after she went away?"

"Who, dearr?"

"Ian—their mother. Did she—sort of try to get in and fetch them?"

Auntie Mack stared at me, dumbfounded at the things children think of.

"Good gracious me, no! Neverr. Oh, dearr, no."

"I suppose he wouldn't have wanted her to have them."

"Indeed he would not have. At least—dearr me——! But there was no question of it, you know. He knew that, poorr man, when —when she finally deparrted from his hearrth and home."

"Oh, I didn't mean Mr. Thomson so much. I meant"—I nerved myself—"the other man."

"The other——?"

"That she went away with."

Again our progress was arrested. She dropped my hand; she turned on me a face: an inexpressibly shocked grown-up's face.

"Who told you?" she said rapidly.

"Who told me what?"

"That she went away with—with anybody?"

"Well . . . Maisie." I was embarrassed. "At least she thought so. She thought—we thought—people generally do, don't they?"

"Oh!" she gasped. "What a terrible thing! People gen—— Oh, good gracious me, *where do* children—— A pairrfect sink their minds are, that's what they are. Perrhaps it is not altogetherr to be wondered at. Little pitcherrs. . . . I said so more than once. 'It will be brought into your verry home one day,' I said to him. 'Then what?' Oh dearr! A bitterr black day it was, but a mairrcy in disguise when——" She gave the wildest gasp yet. " 'Mind,' he said. 'Never a hint so long as you live. Swear it.' I swore it on my mother's bible, and he was satisfied. As for them, he called them to him and he said, once and for all, they would go on loving her; but never speak of her together. *Never*. I don't know how he put it to them but that was what it came to. And they neverr broke their worrd to him. They were so sorry for him they'd have bit their tongues out rather than—— They pitied the man. I saw it, —those mites. Making allowances if he flew out. Oh, it was a morrtal shame! I wonderr now, could Mrs. Jardine be right in saying a dose of the bitterr truth will do no harrm . . .?"

"She thinks it does a lot of good," I interposed.

"Ah . . . Well. It is out of my hands now. Let come what must. *No*," she added with intensity, turning on me again. "*She went away with no man*."

We began to walk on.

"She just went away?"

"She just went away."

I pondered. It made it no better, even more mysterious, more cold, more desolating. I thought, if I were Maisie I would feel even worse, thinking of my mother simply wandering away alone. In any case I would not dare to repeat to her this conversation: she might accuse me of plotting, and tear me limb from limb: I was receiving the confidences of one who had quite lost her confidence. Nor could I throw out to her the suggestion with which I had just been visited: that her mother had attacked Mr. Thomson and then bolted. I wondered if he had died with a scar on his brow. I gave up.

"And to think," I sighed, "poor Mrs. Jardine doesn't even know where she is."

She made another half turn towards me; checked herself, gasped, but feebly.

"Ah," she said, nodding.

I saw the french windows open. Maisie emerged and came galloping down the terrace towards us. Mrs. Jardine and my mother appeared within the entrance.

"Come in, Miss Mackenzie, come in," called Mrs. Jardine, peremptory and courteous. "Rebecca and Maisie will play together now. Come in and join us."

"Ah," murmured Auntie Mack, leaving me, all gratification and alacrity. "Then the bicarrb must wait."

"Don't disappear," called my mother, smiling. "Fifteen minutes, Rebecca, then we must be getting home."

Running at full tilt, Maisie passed Auntie Mack without a glance and slithered to a halt by my side.

She seemed in an aimless mood. She bit her thumb and stared around her, frowning.

"We don't want to go with *them*," she said. She narrowed her eyes at the swing, now at rest, with its occupants idly stretching themselves against the ropes. "We haven't got to stay out if we don't want to. We're not babies to be told to play in the garden. Come on in."

We trailed up to her bedroom. She flung herself on the bed, crossed her arms under her head, and whistled up at the ceiling. I said:

"Have you decided?"

"I have decided."

Her voice made me start. Was it an imitation of Mrs. Jardine? —or her own spirit speaking? It sounded brisk, harsh, matter-of-fact, self-willed. Her eyes were fixed, wide open, on a crack in the ceiling, and nothing gave her away.

"Where?"

"Oh, you wouldn't know. You're not going away to school, are you? Ever? I'm going to see two delightful schools next week; one quite near, one quite a long way away. Your mother's going to take me—it's jolly decent of her. I quite like your mother, I must say. But I have already decided."

"I do hope you'll be coming here every holidays."

"Oh, I don't know. I'll see."

194

She turned her head sharp aside. We were silent. I watched her waggling the toes of one crossed foot. Then I glanced at her face. I thought how pretty it looked. Laid back on the white bedspread, the big hard prominent features fell into relaxed childish lines. Her eyes were two long green-glinting slits, and her thick black lashes met the high, glowing, carnation curve of her cheeks. The pose of her head on the pillow lifted her upper lip and exposed the edge of her regular teeth. Even her springy upstanding mop of hair had lost its aggressiveness and fell down in a soft tumble. I wondered if anybody else had ever had the opportunity to notice how much like a pretty girl she could look.

She squinted down at her feet and pushed off one gym shoe.

"Lying on the nice clean bedspread with your dirty shoes on!" she exclaimed. "Will I never learn the manners of a lady?"

One shoe dropped on to the floor, but she left the other on; and presently she swung herself up violently and hopped over to the dressing-table. Opening a drawer, she fumbled at the back of it and brought out a large white cardboard mount with a photograph pasted on it. She handed it to me.

It looked queer because one part of it had been cut off. It was the full-length photograph of a solid stocky bald-headed man with a heavy dark moustache and large undistinguished features. He was smiling a bit, and he wore a tail coat, light grey dress trousers, spats, and a white carnation in his buttonhole. In one hand he carried a top hat. In the crook of the other arm lay a white-gloved hand; but the arm and everything else belonging to the hand had been cut off with a blunt pair of scissors. There seemed a portion of white tent behind him.

"Is that him?" I said, terrified.

"That's him. It's the only one I could find. It's not a bit good of him."

"He looks frightfully nice."

"It was taken out in India. It's a wedding group. I cut the rest off."

We heard Mrs. Jardine calling us from the bottom of the stairs.

She snatched the photograph from me and stuffed it back into the drawer.

# PART FIVE

## I

NEXT day came a telegram announcing that Mrs. Svoboda had passed peacefully away. We were with my mother when Mossop brought it in. She said: "Girls, poor Tilly is dead." Then she sat on at her writing desk, holding the orange envelope, looking out of the window with an unfamiliar expression of sorrowful solemnity. We said nothing. I tested myself expectantly for tears; but there were none: not one. I tried to picture the ascent of Tilly into Heaven, the Little Feller scampering to meet her at the Golden Gates; but it seemed more like imagining a black small bird, a crow, say, giving a little croak and a flap of its wings, and, still flapping, go up, up till it faded into a black dot and vanished. There was this crow ascending, and also there was Tilly, her life-like yet already unreal figure, unostentatiously vacating the sewing-room and composing herself in her coffin. Neither of these images made sense.

"I must let Mrs. Jardine know," said my mother with a sigh.

She left the room to telephone. We went out into the garden and rode round the lawn on our bicycles, and said never a word about our sad loss. But that night Jess remained longer than usual in prayer by her bedside, and I guessed that she was mentioning Tilly, and felt that my own perfunctory devotions and light-hearted spring-up from the kneeling posture showed lack of proper feeling, and made for invidious comparisons. In bed, I screwed my eyes up and said to myself: "Oh Tilly, I will always remember thee in my heart." My voice rang hollow in my ears.

Two days later my mother put on a black coat and hat and

196

went up for the funeral: my father was joining her in London, she said, and she had ordered two beautiful wreaths, one from us children. She gave Jess a card and told her to write on it in her best hand: *With love to dear Tilly from Jess;* and then I followed after and added *Rebecca;* and then Sylvia concluded the ceremony with a piece of tipsy printing which incurred my mother's disapproval. While I was making my signature I began to cry. That card with its message and our names affixed, so tender, so simple, so final, was pathos itself. Jess asked if Mrs. Jardine was going to the funeral, and my mother said no. Mrs. Jardine had said on the telephone that she had bidden Tilly good-bye at her bedside, and with her own hands arranged on the table a great bunch of roses, the whole late glory of her garden.

"I hope," I said, strangled, "Tilly knew they were there."

"I expect the scent of them came to her, anyway," said my mother, mildly optimistic.

"Did she know Mrs. Jardine had come to say—good-bye?" I gasped out, feeling hideously hit below the belt by the word.

"No. She didn't know that." Then she added, more to herself than to me: "At least . . . who can tell?"

But I thought, and think still, that if in any recess of Tilly's mysteriously shuttered being, some breath had come to her with the breath of roses of her old enemy, old love, Tilly would have peered through one last chink and made a sign. What was it that Mrs. Jardine had wanted of her, waited for? The *Word over all, beautiful as the sky*—the Reconciliation? Something, just possibly something more that Tilly had shut her lips on all these years, that might flutter forth with her last sigh? Too late now. Tilly had slipped for ever from her grasp.

I saw Mrs. Jardine once more that autumn. It was about a week after the funeral, when we went up to say good-bye to Maisie before she went off—a late new-comer—to her boarding school. Lessons had begun again for us, and to our bitter resentment an era of stricter discipline had been inaugurated. To pay us out for the general aroma of frayed moral fibre which she had sniffed on her return, Mademoiselle had persuaded my mother that it was in the interests of our health and education not to permit us to go out to tea during term-time. It interfered, she said, with her programme of conversation at the schoolroom tea-table, and with our subsequent hour of mingled entertainment and instruction with the Bibliothèque Rose. So it was a dismal case of making our adieux and coming straight back. At least, though, we managed to leave Mademoiselle behind with her weekly migraine.

Once again we toiled up the green sheep-cropped slope, damp now and fading dun under the touch of the season, and went past the churchyard and in by the blue gate. Maisie was upstairs, helping Lucy, Mrs. Jardine's maid, with the packing. One quarter of her pile of new underwear had been apportioned to her for the sewing-on of name tapes; and she was sitting on her bed, performing this task with a huge needle and a heavy frown. We inspected her wardrobe, serviceable rather than ornamental except for one poppy-red frock for Sundays and occasions—a special present from her grandmother. I was enraptured with it, and shocked by the off-hand way she grabbed it up to show it to us, then flung it aside again. Everything now at last was stamped with radical change. That Maisie who had sat with me in the walnut tree, sharing sweets and placing in my palm the secret shape and substance of her human destiny in a miniature frame of blue velvet and brilliants—that Maisie had gone into the past, as irrecoverable as the halcyon weather in which she first appeared before me, saying: "Friend"; and which now still contains her, along with Mrs. Jardine's rings and her enamelled pansy watch and the portraits and the dahlias and the silvery rug folded at the foot of the mauve couch; and emerging and dissolving through all these, one electrifying figure over and over again, in gauzes, in wraps, in embroidered art garments, doubled sometimes with an apparition—ice-maiden, Snow Queen—white, in a blue cape, behind its shoulder. At the very centre, pinned to the season's core by that one centripetal force, is Maisie's face, framed in intricate branches and lucent in walnut leaf light.

She was not unfriendly; but between us was the sense that we had neither part nor lot in one another any more. Her past had been wrenched off from her, raw, exposed, unmentionable, and she was in the wilderness, her future the undesired inevitable unknown. Snug and sheltered, for our part, in our continuity, what could we say to her?

"Who's taking you to school?" we said.

"Oh, good Lord! I'm taking myself, thanks all the same for inquiring," she said rudely. "Do you suppose I'd let anybody in *this* house——? Not likely! Auntie Mack feared it was her painful duty to conduct me to my fate, but I managed to pack her off to Bude yesterday. Dame Lucy here is going to be given half a crown —aren't you, Luce?—and Lucy's going to give it to the guard— mind you do, Luce!—and that kind guard's going to see I'm not kidnapped, all for two and sixpence, and he'll help me step out ever so carefully at the right station, and there—*there*. . . . What do you think?—a schoolmistress with a nice kind face will be waiting, and she'll say . . . Oh, she'll say: '*Can* this be Maisie Thomson?' . . . And she won't be as clever as you think, either; she'll know me by this smart school chapeau—see? But I'll have spotted her before she spots me. You bet! It's all as simple as pie."

She tweaked Lucy's ear, and then gave her a hug; and Lucy responded to the embrace with one of those eloquent compressed looks I had observed on the faces of the dear maids at home when one or other of us was in trouble. 'It's a downright shame, that's what it is, and I don't care who hears me say so,' were the unspoken words behind the look.

"Oh, and Madame Jardine says you're to go and see her for a few minutes. Only a *few* to-day. She's not quite up to snuff," said Maisie, pronouncing her grandmother's name with a heavy pseudo-Gallic accent.

She took us along the passage, knocked, and when Mrs. Jardine from within said "Come!" (never 'Come in') she opened the door for us and left us to go in by ourselves.

Mrs. Jardine lay on her sofa, propped on several pillows, the rug over her knees, her lips blue. She was gentle and loving; a little short of breath, she said: she had perhaps been doing too much. This must be good-bye for a while: next week they were going back to France with Cherry for the winter. She was trying to garner her strength for the journey. She told us that Malcolm and Maisie would spend their holidays on a farm in Devonshire with a former devoted parlourmaid now married to a prosperous farmer and particularly fond of young people. They would get Devonshire cream, and ponies to ride on the moor; it seemed ideal. We would all meet again in the spring, she said. She would think of us often, often, and of the strange happy summer it had been. She took a hand of each of us and kissed it. "Don't kiss me to-day, loves," she said. "I have not a cheek fit for young lips." She wiped the faint dew from her forehead with her little fine handkerchief. She charged us to give grateful and affectionate messages to our mother.

"She went to Tilly's funeral," I said. "So did Daddy and Aunt Sylvia and Uncle Fred. There were some lovely wreaths."

"Ah," said Mrs. Jardine. "That is what Tilly would have wished—that the family should see her to her last resting place."

"And she's left all her money to Boy," said Jess. "A whole hundred pounds! It's going to be put in the bank for him."

Tears brimmed from Mrs. Jardine's eyes.

"That is very touching," she said. "The savings of a lifetime. . . . Naturally she would have the feeling that it would crown her dignity and value to leave this solid sum in the family."

"That's what she said to Daddy when he helped her make her will," said Jess. "She wanted her property to remain in the family. She left Aunt Sylvia a gold watch and an amethyst brooch that Grandmamma gave her."

We did not like to mention that we had been pierced with a sense of incredulous outrage and indignation on hearing that our infant brother had acquired a fortune overnight. Were we so much as mentioned in the will? We were not. He, Boy, sprawling at ease, without care or conscience in his perambulator, had casually tossed in the claim of male superiority and bagged the lot. Sylvia had voiced the feelings which our own years forbade, or took at least the sting from, when she bitterly remarked, the morning the news broke: "I bet I was never called Girl when *I* was a baby."

I said:

"I've never been to a funeral."

"Nor I," said Mrs. Jardine. She paused; then with an access of energy: "No, no. All should be said and done before the end. They who are about to die should be heaped round with flowers and friends and words of love before the end. That is the sacred moment. When it is over—it is over. Oh, I have watched, many times watched, beside the final mystery. But afterwards?—no! I will not, *cannot* be a party to those inflated falsities, those competitive displays of public handkerchiefs, those grotesque, commercial, *vulgar* trappings, those . . ." She broke off; then went on to say with a smile: "I thought: could but the body dissolve, simply, purely, automatically, so soon as the breath is out! Could one but watch it grow transparent, evaporate from stage to stage until there remained only. . . . *What* would remain? One inextinguishable spark? I wonder!" she heaved a sigh, shook her head, fell silent, her eyes dilating, fixed. "Dear me, what a wretched awkwardness it is, this problem of disposal! It will be out of my hands, no doubt. The whole thing will be botched, I must resign myself. There is no one—now—whom I could select with confidence . . . who would see any profound point in according me a last graceful gesture. I must be huddled off with the least possible display and trouble—as everybody else should be."

She was talking to herself; and while Jess noiselessly examined the crystal bottles on her dressing-table, I took a last look at Ianthe's portrait. The room was partially darkened, and in the obscurity the face's pale oval was barely to be distinguished. I tried again to think of her as real, this child in a dark velvet fitted jacket and a high fur cap, looking over her shoulder, hand on hip, graceful, formal, like a lady. But all the Ianthes, represented and imagined, were equally fantasy figures.

Then we said we must be getting back, and she bade us au revoir till the spring and told us not to forget her. We returned to Maisie, and Maisie accompanied us as far as the blue door, and we said: "Well, good-bye"; and she answered: "Good-bye." Then, when we had turned away and started down the hill, she called suddenly after us: "Race you to the bottom!" and came thundering full tilt past us. We swooped after her in panic ecstasy, our breath caught squealing in our chests, our legs galloping off away from our hips like demented pistons. Just as the railings began to rush on us, we collapsed in a tangle in the grass, and lay on our backs, panting, groaning and shaking with laughter. Then we got up.

"Crikey!" said Maisie. "Fancy having to sweat to the top again! Could it have been worth it?"

She made a grimace and started straight off up the slope at a steady march. When we got to the turn of the park road we looked back; at the same moment, near the churchyard gate, she also stopped. We waved to one another.

# II

NEXT time we walked that way was on a blackberrying expedition with our father. This was an annual event. Each of us carried a walking stick with a crook handle to pull down the higher brambles, and an enamel mug to pick into. My father held the big basket: this was the ritual. We went along the road that swept round Priory Hill, past the drive gates and on, over a stile, to merge into grassy pastures set with bracken, gorse and brambles, and backed by ramparts of beech, still green, but beginning here and there to kindle. The wrought iron gates were closed. Mr. Gillman, who lived beside them in a flint and brick cottage with dormer windows and a garment of clematis and roses, was digging in his front garden, and touched his cap as we passed.

"Good-day, Gillman!" called my father, waving the basket with jovial implication.

Gillman responded with a meaning jerk of the head. If he had spoken he might so far have committed himself as to say: "Ah . . . That's where it is": thereby acknowledging that the season, the family parade, the blackberry and apple pudding, with all that this meant in the way of simple milestones and traditional pastimes and pleasures, had now come round again. But he did not like speaking, and he plunged his fork once more into the ground as we passed on.

"The Jardines must have gone to France," I said.

"No doubt," said my father.

Christmas brought us a large parcel from Paris: inside it a resplendent box of candied fruits sprinkled with crystallized violets and rose petals. New Year brought us each a card rioting with nosegays and gold stars and white lace and silver-winged cherubs, and inscribed with loving messages from Mrs. Jardine. I slept with mine under my pillow, and each time I drew it forth to gloat on it I was thrown into a strange voluptuous ferment, half physical, half æsthetic. My mother received a long letter, as from one lady friend to another, with news of health, weather and domestic occupations, together with an account of Cherry's general improvement under the care of a superlatively excellent young governess, Tanya Moore by name, handpicked for various stated moral and intellectual reasons by Mrs. Jardine from among a dozen candidates. She was the daughter of a Russian dancer, who had died in giving her birth, and of an Irish father, a painter, of dissolute habits, living an irregular and promiscuous life in Dublin, and indifferent to the interests of his only child. She had left this most unhappy and unsatisfactory guardianship and come to Paris at the age of nineteen to study music at the Conservatoire. Her money had become exhausted; and not wishing to return home or to appeal to her parent for financial assistance, she had made up her mind to find some way of earning and saving the means for the resumption of her studies, when her path and Mrs. Jardine's had miraculously converged. Her spirit of honourable independence, her artistic sensibility, the absence in her character of all that was banal, cramped, grasping, oblique —all this Mrs. Jardine found intensely sympathetic. She had seen in this young creature the image of her own solitary youthful struggles for self-determination. Nothing could exceed the perfection of her touch with young children. Her natural candour and equability had given Cherry an instant sense of confidence. "*To sum up,"* wrote Mrs. Jardine, *"Tanya Moore has no cruelty in her. She can do a child no harm. Of how many guardians of the defenceless young could one say as much?"* My mother was rash enough to read this message aloud to us, and Jess, smarting from her latest *punition,* saw her chance and took it with bitter and economical emphasis. My mother told her not to be ridiculous.

Mrs. Jardine said also that she had thoroughly satisfactory reports of Maisie and Malcolm, and was hopeful on their score. They had been taken *just in time.*

It was plain from this budget of news that relations between Mrs. Jardine and my mother were now established upon a firm basis of mutual matronly interests. I do not know if she showed the letter to my father. Certainly she answered it without delay, for I posted her reply myself.

It was in March, that month of baleful stars, unpropitious to humanity, that there came another violet envelope: inside, one flimsy sheet. Three nights ago, it said, in the mid hour of night, a cry: *"My head! My head!"* Cherry. Sickness, delirium, then convulsions. The best children's specialist in Paris summoned posthaste: *"But naturally,"* it said, *"I knew already.* Cerebral-spinal meningitis. *Now she is blind. She neither sees me nor knows me. While there is life there is hope.* Priez pour nous." The handwriting was firm and finely formed as ever, her signature showed all its customary formal idiosyncrasy. She must have laid down her pen, then, in a paroxysm of anguish, seized it again; for at the bottom of the page she had scrawled: *"I know I can save her. I can do this";* and underlined it twice, with trembling ferocity.

*"Deeply distressed,"* wired my mother. *"My thoughts are with you."* Two days went by. Then came a telegram. Flushing, she tore it open, scanned it, sank back in her chair, her colour fading. It said: *"She died at dawn."*

"This is a terrible tragedy," said my mother, pale.

She went out of the room.

Some weeks passed before a letter arrived. After reading it, she sat as if thunderstruck; then, handing it to Jess, said in a stifled voice that we could read it. It was always curious and unpredict-

able what areas of experience my mother would see fit to un-
cover to us, naked, what conceal.

We read:

*"It was a comfort to hear from you. I knew that you would be
able to enter into my agony—you who are such a loving mother.
Yes, from the start we were told to nurse her without hope of saving her. There was nothing to do but watch the remorseless text-
book forward march of the disease, in superficial ways to alleviate
her distress, and to be thankful when her tormented little body
sank at last into a coma. I sat for twelve hours and watched the
breath flutter in and out, lighter, lighter, slower, slower. Harry
had sunk asleep exhausted in the armchair by the fire. One
breath. . . . Another. . . . Another? . . . No more.*

*"Mary Landon, how can this be? One moment ago she was sing-
ing by the piano while I played.* Trempe ton pain, Marie. Sur le
pont d'Avignon—Malbrook—*and I said to myself: 'Tanya is right.
This child has music in her: an ear for the dead centre of the
note, and* ecstasy *in those small pure bird-sounds. That is what is
pressing in her for release. She is rare, she shall be cherished and
brought whole into life.' It was the evening of the night when, lying wakeful, I heard her cry. A moment ago. Aeons ago.*

*"How is it conceivable that our treasure should be thus sought
out, stalked, struck down? No epidemic, not one other case in the
neighbourhood, near or far. Her only companions the healthy
brood at the home farm. One journey to Paris to buy her a pretty
winter wardrobe . . .?*

*"I thought I could save her, my lamb, my own flesh and blood
—and I could not. The virtue has gone out of me, I suppose.
Nothing has been spared me, nothing. I am mocked by day and
by night. An old barren woman. Must I be taught to die, while I
still draw breath, that I am thrust again, again—and now* irrevocably—*into this pit where all experience is a proof of* nothing
—no warmth, no light, no colour, no happiness, no love? Like a
wounded snake I drag my slow length along. I should be allowed
to die, with my TERRIBLE knowledge locked in me. But I must
exist a little longer, in case Malcolm should need me.*

"Harry is broken utterly. We can do nothing for one another. He adored this lovely child, they were inseparable. It would break your heart to see him. He has not even my wretched bare resource of speech. He cannot endure to speak of her, or to hear her name mentioned. Since her death he has only once broken silence: it was to say that he wished her buried in her place—a spot at the south end of the grounds where a small grove of willows by a pool make a kind of temple, and where she loved to play. Her almost dæmonic imagination had named each tree with a name of her own invention, and made of them creatures with half-human, half-magical attributes. Harry—he alone—was the recipient of these fantasies, which once or twice I overheard, and which seemed to me to bear the wild stamp of visionary genius. So this was done. She was taken from beneath the coverlet of snowdrops which I picked and wove for her, and laid in a white coffin. It was the first spring-promising evening when Harry and Antoine, his faithful friend and valet, carried her through the garden and laid her in her place. In the autumn I shall plant winter-flowering cherries along the path that leads to her; and one day a sculptor—could I but find now a sculptor equal to the conception—shall make the memorial I have planned for her there. When, if ever, I am no longer physically prostrate, I shall go in search of him.

"Malcolm and Maisie did not come. What use? For Malcolm, better to remain where he is, among his new interests and activities. For Maisie best too, and in a more positive sense, to remain away from me. Shall I tell you what you will know already? She will blame me for this death. Indeed, as I lie here, the thought runs through: how far back and in what dark tangle of monstrous roots lies the undying worm—the GUILT? What expiations, for what crimes, are still in store? Here lies the innocent, the victim, born rootless, unearthly flower of disease and drought, blooming for a day." Here two lines were scored out indecipherably. "These are bad thoughts. No more of them. Tanya Moore, the charming girl to whom I had entrusted a portion of Cherry's education, went immediately to England at my request to visit the other two. She is a creature of unusual tact, insight, and sensibility. *She has spoken to them of their little sister, of our life here; of all that was done and will be done. She is still in England. She will have been a comfort to them. She wishes to continue to live with me, to be of service to me in some capacity. We shall see. In the event of her being successful in winning Maisie's confidence and affection, I might conceivably try the experiment of a long summer holiday here for both children, with Tanya as their companion. Tanya writes that she found the unhappy girl frozen at first and stubborn, but that by degrees she has penetrated to deeper feelings, that Maisie had wept natural tears at last, questioned and listened in a spirit of simplicity and trust, and accepted, she thought, her offered friendship.*

*"I must relate to you a curious incident. The day after we had consigned our child to the earth, the village priest came to call upon me. He is an excellent man, shrewd, conscientious, well-loved in the parish: a man of some parts and education. Distressed as he was by the unconsecrated place and manner of burial, he came to offer his condolences and to ask my permission to bless and say prayers above her grave. I gave the priest my permission. Why not? Prayers from a good heart will not make my darling's sleep less sound. Harry, with his detestation of R.C.'s, would have peremptorily refused his consent, as I was obliged to make clear to him. In this one matter, I told him, you must share with me the responsibility of practising a deception. To be brief—and this is what I wished to tell you—he left me with these words: 'Ah, Madame, consolez vous! Ne voyez vous pas que le Bon Dieu lui a épargné un destin funeste?' There was that in his tone which arrested my attention. I inquired of him what could cause him to see in the cutting down of this beautiful, precious and gifted child a merciful dispensation. 'Madame,' was his reply, 'pardon my frankness. Is it possible that you with your acute and penetrating sensibility had not detected for yourself . . .?' 'What?' I asked. 'The symptoms in this child of abnormality?' 'Certainly,' I replied. 'She was conceived and reared in circumstances of ill-omen. I had undertaken it as the work of my remaining years to counteract the symptoms you perceived and restore her to a normal and a fruitful development.' 'Again*

207

*pardon me,' he said with sorrowful firmness, 'you could not have succeeded. My young manhood, passed in hospitals, in asylums, has made me familiar with many forms of tragic inheritance. Do not imagine that I seek to pry into the secrets of your family history. I saw this exquisite grandchild but once. It was enough. I could not be mistaken. She exhibited in her personality the seeds of a congenital mental instability. In one form or another, this would have increased in her, inevitably increased, as she grew towards maturity. Believe me, Madame, she and all who loved her have been spared untold grief and pain.' He added, 'There are many who would be mortally affronted by this directness of mine. You, I know, are made of a stuff that can endure the exposure of a cruelly wounding truth.'*

"Was not this a curious experience?—an extraordinary thing to hear?—to be told? I have no reason to think him a charlatan: the reverse, indeed. He spoke with an earnestness as blunt as it was genuine. These things are for your ears alone.

"Blessings, my dear, dear friend. I know you think of me; and I think of you: a patch of freshness for me in my parched heart. Keep your four safe beneath your wing.

                                        "*Sibyl Jardine.*"

My first thought was: no wonder my mother had appeared dumbfounded. It was as if she had been obliged—she so temperate—to drain at one draught a bottle of spirituous liquor of stunning potency. *These things are for your ears alone.* I had heard these words before. In this letter, I thought, Mrs. Jardine was at her old trick of speaking her thoughts aloud; or speaking over my mother's head, as over mine, or Jess's or another's, to that sole listener capable of all, equal to the drama's whole extravagance: that listener she had once had . . . or never had? In default of him, it must be told out, to the vacant air; it must still be told. But in this case, I felt, Mrs. Jardine really should not have done it—not to my mother. It was all right to do it to me; but to attack my mother's reserve and inexperience with such violence was almost outrageous.

My mother locked the letter away in a drawer of her bureau, where she kept papers of particular privacy and importance.

# III

THEY did not come back that year. Mrs. Jardine wrote saying that Harry could not face the Priory empty of his darling. He had fallen, she said, into a fixed melancholy, most painful to witness. But Malcolm and Maisie were to come out to them for the summer holidays; and perhaps the company of young people would raise his spirits. *"Harry is a family man,"* she said. *"And he has no family. That is the tragedy."* Tanya was still with them, and the greatest comfort. It was almost like having a grown-up daughter about the house. She—Tanya—and Maisie were in regular correspondence. She appeared to have won Maisie's heart; and it was entirely owing to her influence that Maisie seemed now prepared to consider the château as a possible home. *"I hope much from the relationship,"* wrote Mrs. Jardine. *"I owe Tanya Moore a deep debt of gratitude."* For the rest, after exhaustive inquiry and research, she had *discovered* a young sculptor fitly equipped to carry out the memorial for Cherry. Born and brought up in South Africa, he was of mixed ancestry. Celtic and Scandinavian strains had combined to produce a being of *genius*. She had found him in Paris, working as pupil and assistant in the atelier of an old and dear friend of hers, one of the masters of modern sculpture. To this great artist she had, she was proud to remember, posed as model (for the head) in various symbolic groups some thirty years ago. *"Directly I set eyes on this boy,"* wrote Mrs. Jardine, *"it was as if I recognised him. I told myself I had found the one I sought. We established an immediate sympathy—rare joy for me in these bad*

209

*days when so often the sense overcomes me that all is falling into the sere and yellow—the leaves shrivelled, the branches brittle, hollow—and no fresh shoots in me or around me to put forth fresh buds. The contact with this brilliant and fertile young intelligence was an exhilaration for me, and gave me food for hope that the breed I knew was not altogether departed from the earth. His work, what I have seen of it, has inspiration; and in addition, a power and certainty of execution far beyond his years. I ask myself what happy conjunction of stars has shaped him as he is, steered him to where he is—healthy, beautiful, confident—without confusion or disaster? What manner of person was—is—his mother? He will come to live in the old mill-house, long disused, by the weir at the end of our property. There he will be quite independent, and will remain and work for a time; for I think the influence of the place will help to create for him the best conditions in which to produce what I hope for and expect: a masterpiece. There was much reconstruction and alteration to be done, and this I am personally superintending, with great enjoyment. I have designed for him an ideal studio."*

At long but regular intervals throughout that year, budgets of news continued to arrive. She wrote of the successful outcome of the summer holidays: Malcolm greatly improved in looks and bearing, beginning at last to find himself, Maisie more considerate, more tractable. Affection was perhaps too much to hope for, but restraint and civility were *not*—and these Maisie had not withheld. She had actually permitted the wheels of family life to revolve without *grincements* or breakdown. For this blessing Tanya's mollifying influence must be held responsible. She had attached herself to Tanya with all her customary violence of concentration upon one object. The days had been diversified with excursions, picnics. Harry had sometimes been persuaded to be of the party: this had taken him out of himself, and done him so much good. Gil Olafsen, the young sculptor, had taken possession of his studio, the stone was there—a glorious lucent alabaster block—the work in progress. He had proved a great favourite with the children—he had become like an elder brother to them: the benefit to them would be incalculable. She too was deriving true happiness from his presence and companionship. He had a radiance of life, a *crystalline* quality. It was a huge source of satisfaction to be able to provide him with such ideal working conditions. He had been living in Paris in poverty and deprivation: *not* that it was detrimental to young people to be poor— on the contrary; but he had reached a point where country air, nourishing food and temporary financial security were more than a luxury. Her heart was still troublesome, she was confined to her sofa. He carried her up and down stairs, he read aloud to her; for hours on end they would converse. *"After many dark years,"* she wrote, *"once more, miraculously, I have someone to* speak *to. I am not dumb by nature!"* she gaily exclaimed. *"You will understand what this means to me."*

No, the end was not yet for Mrs. Jardine. Like the phœnix she was renewing herself. Beneath the chatty, matron to matron tone of this and subsequent letters, ran a stirring warmth, a glow, almost palpable to my fingers, as of embers about to break in flame, as I took the envelopes by stealth from my mother's desk and spread out the fine rustling pages and breathed the mysterious fresh scent that came out of them. Perhaps, if I had asked permission to see Mrs. Jardine's letters, my mother would not have objected. I did not ask. My passionate nostalgia and curiosity preferred a secret nourishment.

The year passed. It was spring, 1914. They did not come back to England. Better not to risk it for Harry. He had taken a hopeful turn. Gil and Tanya between them had succeeded in giving him an increased sense of local attachment. Gil was a great gardener, and Harry had become interested in helping him to plant a garden round the mill-house. Then, too, he liked to watch Gil at work; and to listen while Tanya played the piano. Tanya had persuaded her, too, to re-exercise her stiff fingers, so long disused, and sometimes in the evenings now they played duets for two pianos in the big music room. *"One should never let any talent lie fallow,"* she wrote. *"Invariably the time comes when one bitterly regrets it. I was once, I think I may say without self-deception, a first-class amateur pianist."* And Gil sang. He had an exquisitely true though untrained tenor voice, and he sang the

*211*

old folk airs, English, Irish, Scottish, which so moved Harry. Apart from consideration of Harry, it would be excellent for Malcolm and Maisie to spend another summer in France. They had so profited last year in health, not to speak of the advantages to them linguistically. Could not my parents be persuaded to part with us, Jess and Rebecca, for a month? No need to say how joyfully we would be made welcome, with what care supervised. She thought she could promise us a happy time; and even our exceptionally good accent and vocabulary would be bound to benefit.

My parents could not be persuaded. My father's ruling brooked no appeal; our sense of grievance was bitter to the point of flagrant unfiliality. Then it was August, 1914. What a mercy, said my mother, that we had not gone to France and been caught there. We could not deny it. Equally, we thought, what a mercy that Mademoiselle had been caught in Belgium. Poor woman. More than a year later a letter reached us, describing the horrors of occupation, of bombardment and starvation, of weeks spent underground, in cellars. Jess said it was a judgment on her. We never saw or heard from her again.

Time passed. Very occasionally, a letter arrived from Mrs. Jardine. Fragrance still came out of it; but that other emanation, that tingling current rising from the page—of that there was no trace. She had had a serious illness, a complete physical break-down, she said, during the first weeks of the war. But she had made a satisfactory recovery. They had offered the château to the Red Cross. It was now a British hospital. She and Harry had moved out into a tiny lodge in the grounds, and lived there a life of frugality and service. She did her own cooking—an occupation she had always enjoyed. "Real *cooking*—skinning, truss-ing, *stock-pot and all*: not *tying a wisp of frilled muslin round the waist and tossing up a soufflé once a week. I taught myself to do it,* toute la lyre, *in my young solitary, bare-cupboard days. How thankful I am for a solid self-taught grounding in the art! How much I* hope *you will see that your girls are accomplished in this respect. Let them be good cooks: all the rest shall be added unto them.*" (We were shocked at this low view of our future spheres of influence, and repelled when my mother said that she had always planned courses in domestic economy for us.) Harry chopped wood, dug and planted in their little garden. His health had greatly benefited. She visited the hospital daily, read aloud to patients, wrote their letters, spoke with them of home. She had sat by many a death-bed, performed the heavy task of transmitting many a last whispered message. There were little services that Harry too could render them. Often a few of the convalescents would walk across the park and drink a glass of wine with them. Such small acts of hospitality helped to prevent Harry from feeling that he was useless to his country. Gil had felt impelled to join up in the ranks during the first autumn of the war. So far he was, thank God, safe. He had been in the trenches, but was now back in England on a special course, and was to receive a commission. He had completed the figures for the memorial the week before war was declared; the base, the total design remained half-cut, unfinished. Nevertheless she had had it placed among the willows, where it shone in miraculous beauty.

As for Malcolm and Maisie, she had good reports of them both. Convinced that war must break out, she had fortunately prevented Malcolm from crossing to France at the end of July, 1914. Maisie had actually been with her during the whole of that month, having been removed from school upon medical advice to convalesce after a sharp attack of measles. Luckily she too had got back to England in the nick of time, in the charge of that young woman, Tanya Moore by name, whom possibly she had mentioned in former letters as having been engaged as governess to Cherry, and who had continued at her own request as part of the household after the child's death. Mrs. Jardine had, she said, sometimes regretted the impulse which had caused her to yield to the young woman's importunity. The influence of the place had perhaps been too—how should she say?—*un-commonplace* for a nature inherently weak and dependent. It had disorientated her from the path she must carve out for herself by stabilising her, one might put it, at a higher level than she could support. She had attempted in the house a role to which neither birth nor quality gave her right. *"There is no getting away from it, Mary*

*Landon,*" wrote Mrs. Jardine. *"BREEDING DOES TELL!"* It had been a predicament. Fortunately the war had solved it. Mrs. Jardine trusted that she had seen where her duty lay, and was serving her country in some useful capacity as every able-bodied man and woman should.

A hint—the merest—was thrown out that it would relieve Mrs. Jardine's mind if Maisie and Malcolm were to pass a portion of their holidays beneath our roof. But my father's ban was unrelaxing, and my mother, whatever her private regrets, was obliged to comply. The subject was not re-opened. They spent their holidays on the Devonshire farm, or with Auntie Mack; then in Malcolm's case with a school friend, in Maisie's with one of her schoolmistresses, one Miss Argemone Willis. *"This seems,"* wrote Mrs. Jardine, *"an unusual woman of masculine force of intellect, a true scholar. In addition, she weaves upon a hand loom, has advanced views on women's suffrage, and is a devotee of the nut and fruit diet. Maisie finds her outlook wholly sympathetic. An intense reciprocal attachment appears to have grown up between them."* Did I, did I not, hear a sniff, a crispness behind the violet ink? Impossible to tell.

As the war dragged on, the letters grew fewer. I think it was towards the autumn of 1916 that they ceased. But by that time, though Mrs. Jardine still walked about in my imagination in many a guise, we did not speak of her any more. For us, too, life had taken on a fixed melancholy. My father had set out without complaint upon his slow heart-rending journey into the shadows. Here, there, on every hand, inchmeal, the view beyond the windows of our home contracted, clouded. Our friend's brothers, the big boys who had partnered us in the polka, Sir Roger, the Lancers at pre-war Christmas parties, were being killed in Flanders, at Gallipoli; were being torpedoed and drowned at sea. An unrelenting diet of maize and lentils brought us out in spots, chilblains caused us to limp, the bath water stopped being hot at night.

Nobody except an anxious aunt with sons at the front, or an occasional harassed elderly friend from London came to stay any more. A favourite uncle was a special correspondent in France.

We had looked forward to his visit, in uniform; but it was clouded for us by his eating all the butter ration at one breakfast.

Round my father's armchair, they talked about the war, the war, the war.

# I V

O N E afternoon in Christmas week, 1916, a motor-bicycle roared up to the front door, and a young man in khaki dismounted. From the schoolroom window we saw him run up the steps in a debonair way and press the bell. Who could this be, we asked ourselves, half aghast, so intrepid, so ignorant as not to know that nobody came so lightly to our door any more? Shortly afterwards Mossop appeared in the schoolroom, and announced a gentleman to see us in the drawing-room. To see *us!* . . . We blushed, ran combs through our hair, and in a twitter descended. A tall, fair, pink young man with sentimental blue eyes, an untidy mouth, and an expression of simple goodwill, stood beaming at us. It was Malcolm, in the uniform of a subaltern in the Gunners. He was just eighteen. At seventeen he had decided to leave school and join the army. A month ago he had got his commission, he expected shortly to go abroad. He had a few days' Christmas leave, and Maisie had hit on the notion of their wiring for Harry's permission to spend it at the Priory. So there they were: one wing had been taken out of dust sheets, and they were having a glorious picnic, with Maisie and Mrs. Gillman sharing the house-work. There was a sort of party to-morrow night: some friends were turning up. Could we be persuaded to come to supper and stay the night?

My mother came in at this moment. I don't know how he did it, but, contrary to our forebodings, he persuaded her without difficulty. "Honestly, it'll be almost unbearably respectable," he told her, laughing, coaxing, flirtatious. "Some old friends of ours, a married couple, to chaperone us. And Maisie's a proper dragon, I can tell you. It'll be lights out at ten, and no talking in the dorms." He had a natural ease and expansiveness that would have overcome a far tougher resistance than my mother's. He stayed on and chatted gaily, giving her nearly all his attention, his eye dwelling only occasionally, with respectful appreciation, upon Jess. It was marvellous to be back in the old place, he said. He'd always hated to think of it shut up. Grannie and Harry had told them ages ago to think of it as home and go there whenever they wanted to, but Maisie had never cottoned on to the idea till now. Maisie?—oh, she was turning out a thumping good sort, brainy too—going to be head of the school, he understood—must have got her poor brother's share of grey matter on top of her own—jolly unfair. She still went about looking like a scarecrow, didn't give a hoot: pity, because she was turning out fair to middling in the face. Oh, rather, he was frightfully happy in the army. Oh yes, he heard regularly from Grannie: she was a marvellous correspondent, no one could write such good letters. She seemed to be getting along in France all right. She was a wonder. He hoped to see her before very long—first leave he got after he went out. Rather a good show having relations over there. Poor old Harry, he wondered how he was weathering this rotten war: hoped he still had a few bottles of good wine to see him through.

He offered to come and fetch us away to-morrow one by one on the back of his motor-bike; but my mother drew the line at that. The car should take us up, and return us on the following morning. Then he rode off with a roar and a wave of the hand; and we went back to the schoolroom and stared at each other and gasped and kicked our heels and tried to believe in this phenomenal turn of fortune, this transformation falling magically across our paths like a shower of red roses out of blank winter skies. To-morrow evening, instead of supping on lentil soup and baked apples, and reading for an hour in the library before bedtime, we would have unpacked our suitcases in the Priory spare room and be guests at a *dinner party*.

Later, my mother said what a charming boy he had grown to

be. Only eighteen, and going out to fight. . . . "Let's hope—" she said, and stopped, sighing heavily. Jess and I agreed that, what with his becoming uniform and his well-knit figure and the large blue eyes in his healthy face, he was nearer to glamour than we could ever have imagined possible.

# V

THE night came down in a noiseless eternity of wet, part fog, part rain: a nasty night for the road; and horrors! our mother underwent a dubious period. The suffocation of our anxiety did not relax until we had climbed up and round the sweep of the drive. Then we were standing in the porch, prey to a clutch even more complex and acute; and the headlights, shafts of some silvery, half-solid substance, tunnelling with difficulty through a world of luminous midge swarms, wheeled away. We stood in blanketing dark with our suitcases, and heard the bell peal, and felt the damp stick to our hands, our faces. Then we heard steps coming with a run and a buoyant leap, the door burst open, Malcolm was before us, radiant, solid, reassuring under the five-branched wrought-iron lamp of the outer hall. Once more we stepped in over the blue and white mosaic paving into the body of Mrs. Jardine's house.

"Oh, *grand!*" He was voluble, hospitable, helping us off with our coats. "This filthy night—ghastly doubts were beginning to gnaw me. Do you want to go straight upstairs according to Maisie's instructions? No, you don't. You look as neat as a packet of new pins. Marvellous!"

We stood revealed in our long-sleeved velvets—Jess's sapphire blue, mine claret-coloured, cut by local Miss Midgley with more optimism, fitted and finished with more complacency than the results warranted. We wore our pearl initial christening brooches, and our gold lockets, and our long hair was tied back with wide, stiff, moiré ribbon to match.

"I'm butler-valet to-night," he said. "There's no knowing *what* might happen. My hat, isn't this fun? I've got a gramophone, so we can dance. Maisie's cooking, she said to bring you to the kitchen, I hope you don't mind. We've all been chucking different things into the saucepans—you never saw such a mess. We thought we'd better send Mrs. Gillman home, she was beginning to look a trifle pinched about the mouth. She's presented us with an out-size in Christmas puddings she made last year and never used, so we can always fall back on that. It's fairly stuffed with pre-war richnesses." He led the way along the passage towards the back premises. His hair was a little dishevelled, his tunic unbottoned, his face Leander pink. "I shot a brace of pheasants yesterday," he said. "D'you suppose they'll be tough? Maisie *says* she knows how to deal with 'em. Actually we've torn them in pieces and bunged them into a giant's stew-pot, and Gil poured a bottle of red wine over them, so I don't know," he said again, hilarious, "*what* mightn't happen . . . Maisie! Here they are."

We stood in the kitchen doorway, assailed by what seemed to my giddy senses a roaring pantomime cavern of light and colour. Brilliance, decoration, steam, smells streamed towards us. The dresser was festooned with holly and evergreens, in the middle distance stood a vast table heaped with utensils, with bowls, bottles, loaves, apples, Brussels sprouts, and, surmounting all, a toppling, drifting pile of dark feathers. Over this extravagant composition a bunch of mistletoe tied on a string to a hook in the ceiling spread its chill, glistening, porcelain-bead-studded, abstract convolutions. Beyond loomed a figure stooping over the range: a short stocky female figure swathed in a long cook's apron with a bib and cross-straps.

"Oh, hallo, you've come!"

She looked over her shoulder at us as we advanced towards her, and continued to stir with a wooden spoon in a saucepan. I had the impression of a pair of eyes focusing on me with an absolutely externalised vision: eyes designed solely for seeing objects. She shook her hair back and wiped her fiery face with the back of her hand. A smear of coal dust across her mouth and chin gave her an expression of comical grimness. "Good Lord, you're tall. I wouldn't have known you. Well, well, growing girls will be growing girls, I suppose."

"Vertically if not horizontally," said Malcolm. He gave her a whack on the behind.

"Mind you don't mess up those dainty dinner gowns," she said, disregarding him and continuing to fix us with a sharp eye. "I knew you'd come looking like the maiden's prayer. But can you cook?" She raised the dripping spoon and wagged it at us. "A pretty face is all very well, but it takes you nowhere; a good cook gets her man every time. I got that straight from the horse's mouth. Just think, Malcolm, at this very moment your grandmother is in her apron, skimming the evening broth for Harry. It gave Gil and Tanya quite a come-over when I mentioned it. I wonder does the fragrance of this stew steal to her across the Channel?" She broke off, glared into the pot she was stirring, and hoisted up its contents on her ladle. "It looks rather unearthly," she said, doubtful. "Continental cookery, I fear. Gil would have it so."

"Where are they?" said Malcolm. He had seemed a little uncomfortable during her last speech.

"Dressing up. At least, she is. She's going to appear in an ancestral wedding dress."

"Not really?"

"Really and truly. Her grandmother's, I believe. I suppose nobody likes to feel they're absolute orphan waifs when they get married. It's the time for family rallyings and blessings, isn't it? —and there does seem rather a dearth on both sides. She said her mother brought it from Russia in her trunks. It's about the only thing she had to leave her when she died—that and her silver necklace. She's hung on to it all these years to wear on her wedding day. It's rather upsetting. . . . As for me, I shall sit among you at the festive board just as you see me, my natural self, to remind you all of the shortest way to a man's heart. I'll give them half an hour more and then dish up. You'd better go and blow

219

the fire in the drawing-room, Malcolm. Have you laid the table?
And put out the candlesticks? Take these pretty dears with you,
or they'll lose their appetites. No. Leave me *one*." She looked at
me and grinned. "You can leave me Rebecca," she said.

Jess went away, demure, with Malcolm, and I was left with
this eccentric girl.

She cleared a corner of the table, sat down on it, uncorked a
large beer bottle, tilted it to her lips, and before my incredulous
eyes poured a draught down her throat in great easy gulps.

"God, I'm thirsty. I've been at it since five o'clock. Cooking, I
mean, not the drink. Have some?"

I refused politely.

"Don't you like it? There's champagne for dinner. How old
are you? Fourteen? You must be careful. I don't like to see young
girls drink, but this is a special occasion. You must drink their
healths. I sort of suspect your mother may think we got you here
on false pretences, but I did want this party to go. I wanted someone for Malcolm, to make him feel—to make him . . . He doesn't
know many nice girls, and he likes them. He prefers them, in
fact. He's going out soon." She fell silent, staring at the wall. Her
eyes stretched, gave a kind of flick. "How is your mother, Rebecca? She was very kind to me once upon a time. I ought to
have written to her, but I never did, I'm no hand with the pen.
I should have liked to come and see her, but I thought better
not, in case of ructions with your father. He doesn't exactly share
Sibyl's feeling about re-soldering old links, does he?"

"Do you call her Sibyl?" was all I could think of to say.

"I call her Sibyl." She looked at me, nibbling her thumb. "You
haven't changed much," she said. "It feels rather nice to see you
again."

"You're the same too." Gratified, I blushed.

"Oh, I'm always the same, only more so. Lots of freak-fair
schoolgirls do a transformation scene round about my age. One
evening they lay their nauseating forms down upon their truckle
beds resigned to another hopeless dawn; next morning they wake
up and hey presto! they're *mysteriously beautiful*. Now that'll
happen to you, I shouldn't be surprised. Not to M. Thomson."

"You're not—not plain," I said, not falsely. "I think you're——"
"Wonderful" was the only word that occurred to me, and I
could not utter it. Just as in former days, she riveted my eyes by
the magnetic power she radiated. The blood glowed carnation in
her bony cheeks; her large and brilliant eyes would never, I
thought, open blurred and swollen as mine did in the mornings,
her copper wire hair stood up on end electrically. Her features
had emerged from her face with uncompromising prominence.
The nose sprang out from a high bridge, then took a downward
curve and ended in wide thick nostrils. The mouth also was wide
and thick, grim in repose, but when she smiled, her whole coun-
tenance broke up and warmed with humour and geniality. Her
big teeth were not only regular now but well-brushed and unusually white. Her figure, considered as a woman's figure, was
disastrous: heavily square in the shoulders, thick waisted, her
bosom a solid plateau, aggressive yet unpromising, the lower half
of her squat and sturdy, with muscular thighs and calves like a
footballer's.

Not a line, not a feature recalled her grandmother; but all the
same, each time I looked at her, a baffling echo of Mrs Jardine
brushed my senses. It was what Tilly used to mean when she
would suddenly, at some trivial gesture of one or other of us,
catch her breath and declare with a gasp that that was her to the
life—her very identical way. It was Maisie's stance, feet planted,
head thrown back on the short neck? . . . It was the way she sat
herself down, back erect, knees a little spread? . . . or the thing
her eyes did, fixing and dilating? Or the incisive edge she put
upon her least remark?

"There's something," she said thoughtfully, "that happens to
girls that'll never happen to me. Don't look so bravely expectant.
I'm quite a normal, well-developed female, as you may have noticed for yourself. No. I mean . . . it's something they put out,
the real girls. . . . I always knew it wouldn't happen to me. I intended it shouldn't. And it never will."

Sharply, she turned her head towards the door. Before I could
tell myself that it was not sudden watchfulness, but an unconscious movement of emphasis, a mad notion pierced me: Cherry

was about to come in. Till this moment, I had suppressed the image of the third, the absent one; but now she rose up, sucking her finger, inserting herself obliquely in quarter-opened doorways, hovering, sidling and twining there, nagging for attention; then at first sign of Maisie's awaited pounce, withdrawing with noiseless rapidity and prolonged nerve-rattling exhibitions of mystification on the door handle, from the other side. "Take no notice," Maisie would hiss. "She wants us to think it's a blasted ghost." With terror I thought that if I were to go out now and search through the fabulous shrubbery, I should come upon one of those match-boxes stuffed with scraps of moss, leaf, berry, petal which she delighted to hide there, in mouse-scale nooks and crannies.

"Peregrine," I said. "Is he still alive?"

"Yes, he is alive," said Maisie. "He lives with the Gillmans. Mrs. Gillman says he's twenty-five in January. I suppose he's immortal. I hated seeing him. He didn't look at me, he looked through a hole in space, as if Cherry had never been alive at all."

Silence dropped between us. She got up, shifted a saucepan to the side of the range, opened the oven door and looked in.

"Casserole of pheasants with surprises," she said. "Purée of chestnuts with Brussels sprouts. Plum pudding. Everything's done and everything looks like food. I do know how to cook, actually. I stay in a gnome's cottage on the edge of a wood in the holidays with a woman called Willis, and we do the cooking. She used to live on nuts and grasses, but I've weaned her of them and now her appetite's as virile as mine. I'll go and see if they're ready for me to dish up."

I came and stood beside her, tentatively offering help, while she drew forth her dishes and examined them. She shut the oven door again, straightened herself slowly, looked at me, smiled, and took my hand.

"I shall have a different sort of life from other people," she said abruptly. "I shall never fall in love."

Again the echo throbbed, carried this time from so far, through so many receiving and transmitting instruments, that I could barely reach the original source. "People think I'm just talking through my hat when I say that—schoolgirl swank—but it's true. I got over the whole thing in July, 1914."

"What thing?" I asked.

"I mean, I got to know then what it was, this love business. I had enough of it to last a lifetime. Believe *me*, it's devilish. It's murder. There's been enough in the world of what men and women do to one another. At least there's been enough in one family. Enough harm done."

She went on holding my hand in a warm grasp, just as she used to hold it. It seems to me now that she was unconsciously asserting the depth, the validity of her need for all that her declarations repudiated: reassurance; confident surrender; the seal of mutual possession. In the gesture, we still befriended one another, our affection made common cause in the face of all the inequalities of experience that divided us. The child made the gesture; but yes, the girl, the woman-to-be discarded all that it might have stood for or foreshadowed. She was not beside me; nor was she caught in the chasm whose first fissure had cracked open years ago in our shared territory. Some force had taken her, blown her clean across, and there she stood now, firm-planted on the other side, exposed, protected in an astringent air: an air dry, unfructifying, restorative as salt.

She dropped my hand.

"I understand Sibyl better nowadays," she said, drawing a deep breath. "After Cherry, everything boiled up to a head. Do you know what I decided? To murder her for Cherry dying. I thought. . . . I thought I was being commanded to clean the world of such wickedness. Yes, I did, really. I'd got it all planned. Tanya turned up to be my friend in the nick of time. I suppose if you're not meant to be a murderer something does always turn up to stop the deed being done. Tanya took away my madness. Would you believe it, I began to pity the old girl; and you can't kill someone you pity." She reflected on this, and added: "At least, I couldn't. About Cherry. . . . It pretty well broke her into pieces. You wouldn't have known her. I didn't see her till months after, but she hadn't *begun* to recover. She could only *just* breathe, and every breath hurt. What's that line about drawing breath in this harsh world with pain. . . . It seemed like that. I didn't know suffering, unhappiness I mean, could be like that. She explained it to me. She said if you're a mother and your child dies, you have to—you go on and on trying to give birth to a dead child. Oh, I shall never have one, thank God! She wasn't Cherry's mother, of course, but I didn't point that out. She did obviously have the flesh and blood feeling so strongly that it being one generation removed wasn't making any difference. It seemed to—even something up that *somebody* should feel like that for Cherry . . . although, as things turned out, it was all such devilish waste."

A hard shadow fell across her face. After a moment or two she glanced at me and went on:

"What do you think she said? She said she'd known I'd blame her, and want to. . . . I said yes, but I didn't feel it any more. And as soon as we'd said that to each other, I stopped hating her for good and all. It *was* a shock! It made me feel quite weak in the stomach. I suppose it was awfully crass of me not to have realised that if you have a—very violent feeling about someone there are times when you might feel its exact opposite. And that's when the harm is done." Pacing up and down the red-tiled floor, she drew a deep breath. "You know how I always felt about her. It was war to the knife. She was my enemy. Well then—in a twinkling I had a different sort of surge inside me. I wanted to show her——"

"You didn't hate her?" I suggested, nervous.

"Yes. Do something fatuous, like—oh, I don't know! I couldn't trust myself any more. I thought to myself: this won't do. You've got to know where you are with people; and if you hate them, you can't know. Or—*or* if you love them—in a violent sort of way. It's all the same somehow. Did you know that?"

I said no.

"Well, I do, because—I know. And I know things that make me sure of it."

"What things?"

She hesitated, then said brusquely:

"We must go to the others."

Quickly I said:

"When did you start to call her Sibyl?"

"That time. She asked me to. Also she talked to me a bit about my mother—truthfully for once: I mean, as much as one person can see the truth. For the one and only time."

"What did she say?"

"Oh . . . not much." Evasive, she turned away and began to undo her apron. "We were both in the mood when we could say things, I suppose. Sort of—released." She flung the apron on to the table among the feathers. "Oh . . . she told me something I asked her. And a bit about my mother's girlhood—how she was brought up, and what it had done to her. It sounded quite convincing. And I told her—but only a very little—about what it was like after she went away. It was all right, because she didn't try to sympathise; and she wasn't out for sympathy herself or—making excuses. It was just *saying*. After that we didn't talk any more. I didn't want to . . . because I was *determined* not to let anything go too far. Perhaps she was too. She knows a lot when she's at her best. When she's not on the prowl, she can be grand. Come on. We'll have to clean up later. God knows how."

"How do you mean, on the prowl?" I asked, following her out of the kitchen.

With sudden, startling loudness, Maisie said in the passage: "Plotting to get something she wants. Stalking. In ambush. Then —*pounce!* In with the claws."

We came into the dining-room. Logs burned in the grate, the table was laid for six, above the glass and silver four white china cherubs held up long newly-lit candles. The connecting door into the drawing-room stood open, and beyond it I saw Jess, Malcolm, and two unknown figures standing by Mrs. Jardine's fire.

"Who is here?" I whispered, touching Maisie's elbow with a delaying hand.

"Gil and Tanya are here, of course. Didn't Malcolm explain? You know who I mean?"

"Yes."

"They're married. They were married in London this morning. We went up to be witnesses. He's back from France on ten days' leave."

225

"I see. . . . Does Mrs. Jardine know?"

"I don't know what she knows or doesn't know, I'm sure," said Maisie sharply, stopping to shift the candle sticks a little. "We can ask who we like here. They're *our* friends. Anyway, this is Harry's house, not hers, and Harry'll be delighted." Then as if in further justification, she added: "Besides, Gil will probably be killed, so what's the odds?"

We went on into the drawing-room, and, in a dream, I was introduced to a man not very tall, in uniform, with a big head and face, and a lot of rough hair and massive shoulders; and to a young woman in fancy dress.

# VI

JESS and I were totally unused to anything in the nature of social occasions; but whereas Jess appeared to swim into parties as into her natural element, pleasurably anticipating them beforehand, immediately expanding in unselfconscious ease and gaiety to meet and mingle with them, I disintegrated altogether in the face of any call upon my communal instincts, and was aware only of a whirling, a burning, an alternate dryness and icy clamminess now within me, now about me. Through this combined maze, I beheld the company, my plate and its contents, and all the other objects of the dinner table in a flickering surrealist film sequence.

My reverence for art was intense if incoherent; and here I was, I told myself, for the first time in the presence of a genius. Mrs. Jardine had pre-illumined him with the divine fire. This was enough to make him appear ten times life-size; but, in addition, he was magnified in the candlelight by the effulgence of romance. A genius with his musician-bride; a bride with her bridegroom-genius. They towered and swelled, yet seemed a long way off, portentous as Easter Island effigies discerned through a telescope from the bridge of a storm-tossed vessel.

He did look like an idol. It seemed so then, and later I was sure of it. His eyelids were cut out under his forehead with a striking appearance of plastic symmetry, and the lower part of his face was a massive mask, the lips modelled on it, full, even, with a wide-cut prominent outline: anonymous lips in low relief. His hair sprang up and back from his brow in thick feathery brown wings, and his skin was a uniform pale brown. The eyes themselves were dark, long in shape. They seemed to slip and glance and slide in his head like two fishes flashing and turning their white under-sides. I thought him ugly, terrifying. I could not take my eyes off him.

She wore a dress of stiff white silk flaring round the ankles into wavy rows of pleated flouncing, with an overskirt of white gauzy stuff, swept up to pile all its puffed fullness into the back, and caught here and there among its folds with bunches of blue and white buds. When she moved, it was a swan moving, and the sound she made was of stirred rushes. She had dressed her hair high on top of her head, with one or two curls tapering down her neck: it was dark fine hair and it would not stay in place; and this soft untidiness and the thin long neck and immature bony breast and shoulders framed by the low-cut bodice gave her a delicately amateurish, touching appearance.

What did Tanya look like? I never found out. At the time she was a great disappointment, because she did not conform in the least to my tuppence-coloured conception of a lovely bride. I thought her, indeed, a very plain kind of person. But now recalling her, I suspect that she had the equivalent of beauty; something wild, cool, lucent and subtle; like one of those January twilights that contain, for an hour, all the throats and buds of spring. Her face was long, serious, pale, with slow-moving grey eyes, slightly prominent, and a forehead whose clear square was underlined by heavy straight black eyebrows. She had a mole on her cheek, and her upper lip slightly overhung the under one. The mouth was sensuous, full: it looked vulnerable; and when

227

she smiled she looked extremely amused and mournful, and she showed a space of gum above her irregular teeth. In her period dress, she looked, I see now, like a minor but important character in a distinguished film or play, a type chosen by a sensitive director with an eye for poetic truth. Because of this there was something not quite right, not quite like life. She was the young schoolmistress; or the niece, the protégée in the country house, about to emerge from half light and be loved, about to throw off the shrouding hood of dependence and virginity and walk out acknowledged, radiant, into experience. Only there is something unsensational, irreparable, about to go wrong: it is clear from the casting. She was awkward and graceful; nervous and serene; dull, interesting. She had not a young face, nor a face that one could imagine ageing. She had, I now think, a vocational, a dedicated personality, within whose contradictions she was positive, intact; but all the same she was an orphan of the world, and the unity she expressed would never serve her to find her place—nor seek it either.

Gil, Malcolm and Maisie talked and laughed hilariously, and she joined in the laughter in a subdued but whole-hearted way, and now and then said something quiet which made them double up with amusement. It all seemed in an idiom to which I had no clue, and the jokes were private ones.

There was champagne, and they kept drinking healths. Jess and I had a glass each and were inhibited from accepting more. We took sips and swallowed wryly, almost choked by the tingling in our throats and noses. After half a glass I felt queer. The room started to whizz round, and once when my intention was to prop my elbow nonchalantly on the table, I failed to do so, and was jerked forward with a startling sense of disturbance in my centre of gravity. My cheeks began to scorch. I heard Malcolm say something about Grannie and Harry, and Maisie cried loudly:

"No! Keep her out."

"You can't. She's here," said Gil. "I want her at my wedding. She's the high priestess of——" some word I could not catch. "I hear her prophesy behind the curtains. Now I know I shan't be killed, and Tanya and I will have ten superhuman children."

"This is Harry's house," insisted Maisie. "And when he's allowed to die, it'll be *hers* for her life; and when she dies, if ever, it'll be Malcolm's. Malcolm had a letter from him the other day to say so. Fancy Harry taking up the pen! He has a very pretty gentlemanly writing, only shaky and out of practice. This is *Harry's* party. He'll be so glad when he knows all about it. How can we let him know? We can't write and tell him."

"Why not?" said Malcolm.

"There's no way to put it," said Maisie, incoherent. "He wouldn't be able. You daren't. It would be like—trying to get a message into—into a locked-up, barred, bolted house you couldn't even be sure was inhabited any more. . . . You can't do any sort of—ordinary thing with Harry—or even any polite letter-writing sort of thing. . . ." I thought she was going to burst into angry tears.

"You're cracked," said Malcolm. "Of course we must write to him. He's a great stickler for politeness. He's got very old-fashioned ideas about manners."

"This isn't quite like an ordinary thing," remarked Gil.

"There you are!" said Maisie. "He might be frightfully upset. How do you know? He might be shocked. He's had enough."

"My good girl," said Malcolm, "you're tight. Give over being so damned theatrical. Harry's a frightfully decent, generous old chap, who's had the misfortune to drink himself pickled. Do stop going on."

"Misfortune!" cried Maisie, going on. "How dare you interfere with—judge what he's—he's seen fit to do? Look at his life! It adds up to nothing, nothing, nothing. She's taken away everything from him. Why is it allowed? What, what, *what* can his life mean?"

"I don't know why it's allowed," said Gil. "But I should say it means a lot." He looked down at the table, his fingers closed on the stem of his wineglass. I noticed his big, clear-looking hands, the flexibility and precision in the fingers, the long spatulate thumb. His face in composure looked suddenly noble and authoritative.

"Oh, you do, do you?" snapped Maisie. She stared aggressively

229

at Gil, but he went on looking down, contemplative. Her face became forlorn, and she muttered: "Well . . . *what?*"

"He's not corrupted," said Gil, speaking with care and deliberation. He narrowed his eyes as if scrutinising his own statement in the wineglass. "He still knows what's what."

"A fat lot that helps him. What use is it to a person to know what's what so well they can't stand it and have to drink themselves unconscious?"

"He's not in the least unconscious," said Gil, shifting his glass very accurately. "He's as raw as a child."

"Well, then!"

"So it doesn't matter."

Maisie made a violent strangled exclamation in her throat.

"It's a tragedy," said Gil. "It's not a disgrace. No doubt there's not much comfort for him in that reflection. . . . You never know though. . . . But what his life means is a distinct consolation."

Everybody was silent.

"Well, I wish somebody would tell him so," said Maisie. She blew her nose fiercely. "*Somebody* might have the decency to tell him he's—he's appreciated."

"Nobody had better try," said Gil. "I'd scarcely go so far as to say he was hoping against hope for a pat on the back. No one was less interested in rewards, I should say."

"Everybody would like to be happy," said Maisie, still indignant.

"You can't make Harry happy," said Gil mildly. "All you can do for him, humanly speaking, is—to do nothing. He accepts what's happened to him—in his own way. He doesn't compound with it. I doubt though if he'd thank anybody who made it clear that they understood his point of view or sympathised with it."

"Oh, this is all above my head," burst out Maisie. "Compounding and all that! You're just talking brainy talk—turning people into—into specimens. *Real* people have to have *something,* or they couldn't live."

"He's got *her,*" said Gil, quiet.

Maisie uttered an explosive snort.

"She's not corrupted either," observed Tanya. She had a light, soft, colourless voice.

"I call it corrupted," said Maisie, "to talk that sickening stuff about him. Blowing him up into a sort of Book of Golden Deeds. And all that wifeliness. She's always jawing about what a wonderful soldier he was. What she *doesn't* mention is why—the real reason—why he had to leave the army. I suppose she thinks we're taken in."

"I don't suppose," said Gil, "she thinks anybody's taken in. It's simply a convention she's built up which she chooses that the world should observe. She's made it as artificial as possible; and she sticks to it through thick and thin. I admire her for it."

"She needn't say anything at all. It would be much more—dignified."

"Oh, she's not interested in dignity. Besides, she always has to speak, as you know. And on this subject it would be a real necessity. The more he ruined the performance, the more blatantly she'd have to put it over. It has to be kept going."

"Why does it have to?"

"Because she needs him."

"I suppose you think that's a good reason for—squeezing the life blood out of him."

"Nonsense. He's very much alive, as I said before."

"Well, for—doing what she's done to him."

"Not necessarily a good reason," said Gil, smiling. "But reason enough. Which is as much as you can expect of the reasons why people stay together."

He lifted the wineglass and tilted its contents back and forth. The more the argument developed, the more heated the expostulations, the quieter and more level grew his voice.

"You stay with people because you're fond of them," she said. "And can do something for them—do good to them. If you find you can't, you hop it. Or if you don't you're a swine."

Seizing the opportunity for comic relief, everybody laughed.

"All right, laugh your heads off," said Maisie presently, without rancour. "You wait. I don't know about doing good—but I intend to have it written on my tombstone: Here lies a person who never needed anybody, so she never did anybody *any harm*." She looked at Gil and Tanya and grinned. "Though I suppose it's untactful to say such a thing at your wedding feast."

"You get everything mixed," said Gil. "The word in question is 'need,' not 'love.' They're not always identical, as you may possibly discover for yourself one day."

"Possibly I may," she said rudely.

"It's frequently all wrong when people need one another, but it doesn't prevent it. In this particular case I don't believe it's all wrong. It's the proof of her . . . of how magnificent she is."

"Oh, good Lord! It would be."

"From anybody else in the world," continued Gil in his muted voice, narrowing his eyes at the glass he still held up as if gauging the wine's level, "she gets back—*immeasurable* reflections of herself. It's not deliberate, so it's pointless to moralise about it: it's some property of her nature—some principle. Like yeast. She throws out all she has—her beauty, her gifts, her power over people—and objects—and events; and it works. Each time she tries it out, it works like magic. Up come all these disturbing, magnetised self-images. There's one person, one alone, it doesn't work with, and that's Harry. Nothing comes back to her. And she knows it: she doesn't deceive herself. And she stays with him—*inevitably* she stays with him. He's her resting-place. If that doesn't justify her claim to care for truth. . . ."

I said loudly:

"Yes, she does care for truth! I know she does!"—and heard my own voice like an explosion in the room. Everybody looked at me in astonishment, and nobody smiled or said anything; and willing myself obliterated through the floor boards, I bent to grope for an imaginary handkerchief. When I raised my congested head, Maisie was muttering:

"She cares for money." But she said it half-heartedly.

"It's perfectly all right," said Gil, "the way she cares for it. She understands its value. She knows about poverty. It isn't contemptible, the kind and degree of importance she attaches to money."

"Oh well," said Maisie, with a shrug and an impatient sigh.

"You know her better than I do, I suppose." She stared at him, nibbling her thumb. "Do you think he hates her?"

"No."

"Loves her?"

"I don't know anything about Harry's feelings," said Gil shortly.

"That's something to be thankful for," murmured Maisie, half to herself; then giving her chair a violent heave backwards, she added: "Anyway, we won't drink their healths, thank you very much. Not at this party."

"You're right," said Gil. "It wouldn't be quite the thing."

Maisie got up, saying:

"Now I'm going to fetch the pudding. Kindly pour some brandy into that ladle and heat it on the candles while I'm away."

I think this is the conversation that I heard. I could never be sure. I know that after it the circle soon warmed up again and expanded in frivolity, leaving me out of it, eating Christmas pudding.

# VII

AS time went on I grew more and more sad, uneasy, suspect in Mrs. Jardine's house. I could not get rid of a vision of her, high on the watch tower of a castle in France, directing upon us searchlight eyes over wastes of winter dark and ocean. Her glittering face blazed in the firmament, savage, distraught, unearthly: Enchantress Queen in an antique ballad of revenge.

To brighten the drawing-room, pots of chrysanthemums had been brought in from the greenhouse, and set in stands and bowls; the fire burned uproariously, the piano stood open; but there was something dreadfully wrong. The sterile drained feeling of a room just emerged from sheeted vacancy had not been

233

dispersed; and the dove girl on the blue tub looked dispossessed, mournful as the portrait of a girl who is dead and forgotten. All round me I felt locked untenanted rooms pressing in like icebergs around a liner's lit saloon. We roasted chestnuts and played a rude verse game which made us laugh a lot. I remember Tanya sitting at the grand piano, lightly swaying in her plumage while she played; but what she played I do not know, except that it was something formal, classical,—Bach perhaps—and that she played with authority; and that within the abstract pattern which the music's shape drew round the room, everything lost its separateness and fell temporarily into harmony. Purged of dubious designs the interlopers were simple listeners, innocently devoted, in a quiet interior. At the centre, the white fluid form, stripped of all ambiguities, all stock romantic suggestions, was a colourless vessel from which poured only its essential pure content. While the music lasted Mrs. Jardine sat in our midst, welcoming her guests on her own level: glad without reservations that we should assemble in her house for this æsthetic experience.

Then everything broke up again. Malcolm suggested dancing. He rolled back the rugs and put a record on his husky portable gramophone, and I sat with Maisie while he danced with Jess, and Gil with Tanya. Then, more in the spirit of a courteous host, I felt, than from any promptings of personal desire, Malcolm invited me to dance. We went round and round in a somewhat hit or miss fashion, and he talked volubly, excitably, and I see now that he was rather drunk. Then he went back with alacrity to Jess, and as I stood against the wall, under the dove girl's portrait, Gil suddenly came and put an arm round me, and danced me off. I was startled and flustered; but it was a waltz tune, and though I was ignorant of up-to-date steps, I could waltz with confidence; and in the firm clasp of his arm, held close against the wall of his chest, I felt a sense of whirling, keyed-up safety and exhilaration. After a while he said he was thirsty, and I accompanied him to the dining-room, where he mixed himself a whisky and soda, and I cooled my dry throat with a glass of water. He looked round the room, at the cream-panelled walls, the curtains of magenta brocade, at Harry's eighteenth-century ancestors, in uniforms, in hunting coats, with the long, heavy-jowled faces, wine-skinned, prosperous, of the period; and with a narrow elegant, snow-bosomed, taper-fingered satin wife apiece; and all with those full-bodied eyes, gross yet alert—eyes without questions— which the world made then. He looked at it all and shook his head, and said rapidly, blurring his syllables:

"What do you make of it all?"

I made nothing of it. Quite out of my depth, terrified lest this remark should be the cryptic prelude to a discussion on sculpture, I took a breath and plunged.

"I love Mrs. Jardine," I said.

"So do I."

I said that I was very glad.

"How are you feeling?" he said. "Are you all right? I wonder if it's suitable, your being here. There are some desperate characters loose in this house, you know."

"Oh!" I said, startled by an echo. "Somebody else said that."

"Said what?"

" 'Desperate characters.' Not in this house, I don't mean. It made me remember. Somebody Mrs. Jardine knew . . ." I hesitated: had not those confidences been for my ears alone? ". . . That she told me about."

"Ah," he said, smiling. "That would be Paul."

"Yes, it was," I said, relieved. "I thought she'd probably told you about him."

He was silent; and feeling much more at ease, I went on:

"It was awful that he died, wasn't it? I think she still misses him dreadfully."

He looked at me, reflective.

"Did she talk much to you about him?"

"Quite a lot. And about other things that had happened to her. The story of her life, you know."

"How old might you have been at the time?"

"Well, I suppose . . . about ten." He was silent, smiling to himself in a way that I could not interpret; and I added timidly: "Has she told *you* the story of her life?"

This made him laugh.

"You are so incredibly——" His voice sounded affectionate, unpatronising. He stopped. "Well, it must have been a treat for her, telling you."

"It was a treat for me, listening," I assured him. "Nobody had ever talked to me like that before. . . . Or ever has since."

"I suppose not," he said, serious.

I felt more and more happy. Here was a genius, and I could converse with him in perfect freedom.

"Of course it made me feel very important, hearing it," I said. "It was mostly things people would think children oughtn't to hear. But that was only part of the excitement. We had an old sewing maid who used to tell me stories too—real ones, about my grandmother, and the old days. She acted them, and went on for hours, and I simply adored them. But Mrs. Jardine's were different. It was . . . oh! it was like hearing something *so true* it made everything else I knew—or that I'd been taught—seem like—boring feeble pretences. That's why, when you said at dinner that she cared for truth, I knew how right you were."

Head bent, he seemed still to be engaged upon reflections of his own, and to be only half attentive. Yet the idea of intimacy between us persisted intoxicatingly in my mind, and I continued:

"I know Maisie thinks she tells lies. But Maisie was brought up to think so. She can't quite see straight about her."

"And you do," he said. It seemed more a statement than an inquiry.

"Well, I suppose it's what you were saying at dinner: perhaps nobody can? Only she did so understand everything!" I cried, carried away by nostalgic enthusiasm. "And if she didn't, she never pretended to, or said she knew best: she asked us to explain, and listened to us. She was only sharp, a bit, if she suspected I was saying what I thought I *ought* to say. She wanted me to—well, to care for truth, like her."

He nodded quickly, in an absent way, as if he were intent upon recalling or reconstructing some private conception.

"She would," he said. "She pursues truth with passionate, avid curiosity. She sees the possibility of it in the most unlikely places. She hunts it down. Testing herself . . . experimenting with the

236

design, the reflection that comes back to her, over and over again. Building up the proof, once and for all. She's not sure, you see. She hasn't much confidence."

This last remark puzzled me so much that I could only assume that the word confidence must have another grown-up meaning, beyond my understanding. I was silent; and he said, turning the dark glinting weight of his eyes on me:

"You must have been an interesting experiment for her."

I said, a little uncomfortable:

"You do see, don't you, how good she is for children? Not—*not* a bad influence? It wasn't only me, and my sister Jess too, but Maisie and Malcolm and Cherry. She was wonderful to us all. Only, worse luck, Maisie had to hate her. Sometimes, you know, I could see why Maisie—and other people—called her wicked. Anybody very—strong must seem so sometimes. People are afraid of them."

"And you weren't," he said in the same uninterrogative manner.

"Oh no!" I exclaimed. "How could I be? As if she could possibly have done me any harm. She loved me." This sounded conceited, and I qualified it. "It was mostly because she'd loved my grandmother very much. She lived with her when she was a girl. Then there was a quarrel and they parted, and she didn't see her again till she was on her death bed, and they made it up. I think she felt about us that we were—like part of my grandmother she'd got back again; and that was a comfort to her because she'd gone on missing her so much. She—she wanted to tell me things she hadn't been able to tell Grandmamma."

"Ah," he said, smiling at me again with simple affection, "I think she would feel able to tell you things she would never have told your grandmamma."

"But they were true, I'm sure," I said anxiously. "Surely even at that age one knows when a person's pretending?"

"Oh yes, yes, they were true," he said.

"It's nice to have someone to talk to about her," I said, encouraged. "Somebody who understands. It feels so queer being back here—without her."

237

"Yes, it does feel queer." He glanced round the room, frowning slightly. Then his eyes widened, resting blankly on a portrait opposite. He looked suddenly stricken with depression: I heard him give a heavy suppressed sigh.

"If I'm killed," he said, "and if she talks to you about me after I'm killed—bringing the story of her life up to date, you know—don't believe her if she tells you it was a solution on a low level to take Tanya; or a treachery; or even a fatal *mistake*."

"I'm sure she won't," I said, startled.

"She might well," he said. "She would see it so."

Silence hung between us. I broke it by saying in faltering tones:

"Why . . .? You don't think it's—any of those things, do you?"

"No," he said shortly, but not in the knuckle-rapping way I had half feared. He brooded. "I've married Tanya because I meant to," he said.

"Well, she'll understand that," I said feebly, feeling inadequate.

He shook his head and said with a brief smile:

"It was understood that I was not the marrying type."

"She won't blame you," I said eagerly, struck by a recollection. "She never says anything is a person's *fault*. She tries to see what made them do it—why they had to. She didn't blame Paul when . . . all that—you know. She saw why. Even though it went against her."

He turned his head aside sharply, as if shaking off painful thoughts.

"Yes," he said in that muted voice. "She does like to see meanings. The harder they are, the more she embraces them. . . . Well, that's the only legacy I can bequeath her. The meaning."

He shrugged his shoulders.

"Didn't she want you to get married?" I said timidly.

"No."

"Not—not even to Tanya?" I added, disingenuous.

"Particularly not to Tanya."

He seemed despondent; and wishing to cheer him up, I said: "Well, one thing I know——" But I stopped.

"What do you know?" he said in a soft, teasing way. It was too late to draw back, and with a violent blush I concluded:

"She'll be terribly glad if—when—if perhaps you have a baby. She's so very keen—she loves people to have babies."

"Ah," he said, smiling faintly. "Doesn't she? She ought to have had a dozen. It's what she was made for. It's all been wrong for her. She'd have been happy and glorious. . . . Yes," he said, "yes. I hope I do have a child."

At these words, an extraordinary churning sense of emotion rushed through me. I gazed up at him, and my head swam, and I thought he was wonderful, proud, like a king. His head was turned away, bowed, engrossed, and above his eyes, just between the brows, I fancied a kind of knot of glowing intensity, a radiation; and yet the whole head had, like Mrs. Jardine's, the repose of a statue. Poignantly, I thought of Mrs. Jardine, and saw how they would be—should be—together. I could not bear to think of her deprived of him. I saw the place they would both be able to inhabit, like an almost unpopulated land of immense, of supernatural vistas, where one might be lost; where at any moment some resplendent monster might burst out of the jungle to confront their untroubled gaze.

"It's the war that makes one want it so urgently," he said. "There's no time to wait for a son: everything has to be crammed in. If I live, I shall take him back to Africa and bring him up there."

It was only Gil and Mrs. Jardine that I could see, setting out for darkest Africa and carrying the baby: not Tanya at all.

"I wish I was back there now," he said. "In the place where I was born."

"You will go," I said, my heart thumping to suffocate me. "After the war." I thought with a fearful pang: He will go back to Africa and I shall never see him again.

He repeated:

"If I live, I will." He added, hunching his shoulders: "Or if I'm not altogether ossified, or wrenched out of shape, or broken up along with the rest of my generation."

Perturbed by the bitterness in his voice, anxious to deflect his thoughts towards myself, I said:

"I hope I shall marry and have children one day."

He turned towards me, giving me his full attention, searching my face. The swimming sensation came over me again.

"Yes, you will," he said. "It goes without saying." Suddenly he put his arms around me, bent his head and laid his cheek to mine. "You make me feel homesick," he said.

"Why?" I whispered, through the humming and whirling of Mrs. Jardine's dining-room.

"You remind me of the girls that were round me in the place I lived in when I was a boy."

"In Africa?"

"Yes. Dark and . . ." He stopped. I could feel his heart-beats, even and strong, against my shoulder.

"Native girls, you mean?"

"Native girls. Are you offended?"

"Of course not."

"I know you're a well-brought-up, well-educated English girl," he said. "But all the same, you seem so nice and dark."

"I don't know what I am," I said, strangled. I put up both my hands and clutched his lapels.

He kissed me, his curious lips pressing hard, terrifying on my cheek. Appalled, giddy, I hid my head and went on clutching his coat; while fragmentary moral principles, practices, precepts, protests shot through my skull and exploded there in fruitless chaos.

But then, while I began to despair of disengaging myself without hurting his feelings and at the same time vainly asked myself what a girl should say, do, to retrieve a well-nigh hopeless position, he let go of me with the utmost simplicity. There seemed, after all, no situation.

"Remember," he said, quite as if he had never kissed me, "if the opportunity arises, tell her: *Reconciliation*. It's the great word of her life. She knows what she—we—did to Tanya. She'll take it in."

"Couldn't you tell her yourself?" I suggested, nervous again of wading out of my depth. "Write to her, I mean? I'm sure she'd rather."

He thought a minute; then said, raising his eyebrows:

" 'My dearest Sibyl,—A line to let you know I'm married to Tanya, and spending my honeymoon beneath your roof. . . .?' "

"Well, perhaps," I said, "you needn't put it quite like that, if you think she'll be so upset."

"I expect you're right," he said in a hard voice. "I needn't put it quite like that. I could say that of course it will make no difference: what's marriage, anyway?—a mere convention. And that it's always been understood that no amount of women in my life could alter our relationship. Oh, and that it is she, she only, who taught me the meaning of love—made me equal, at last, to assuming the responsibility of a permanent tie. This knowledge, and my undying gratitude will, I know, be her sufficient reward and consolation. On my marriage night I am thinking of her more tenderly than ever. That's the sort of thing that's said on these awkward occasions, I believe. . . . No, I won't do it. I won't write her that sort of letter."

"No," I agreed, depressed. "She wouldn't like a letter like that."

"It's too simple for her to believe," he burst out. "It's so ordinary she wouldn't accept it. *I've changed*. It's the war. I've been out there. It's regrettable, but all human dealings except the most elementary have become impossible to me. I don't want anything on any—pitched-up level. It's too difficult, too exposed. Furthermore, it's *nothing;* so when I try to contemplate it, I get frightened. I tell myself I'm a plain ordinary chap with ordinary wants . . . and then I feel safer. I don't know why I tell you this, you post-war girl, because you can't understand it; and when *your* time comes, after the war . . . oh, my goodness, after the war! . . . you'll have other fish to fry, all of you."

I felt very miserable. But there seemed nothing now to lose, and breaking a last lance for Mrs. Jardine, I said with weak firmness:

"Even if I can't understand . . . I know she could."

"I've got lazy," he said lightly. "I can't write long letters any more."

I looked at him again, and thought him hideous, repellent.

Hating him, I hated myself, I hated men. I wanted to get away from him, I wanted to stay with him and quarrel, say something outrageous.

"I wonder," I began, "why you did come here, if——" But I could not go on.

"Oh, that's quite natural, isn't it?" he said, not taking up my tone, but replying as if it were a natural point to raise. "Tanya and I are both quite homeless, rootless, in England. These two, Maisie and Malcolm, are our closest friends. We wanted to be all together: there might not be future opportunities, you know. And it was *such* an opportunity, with Malcolm and myself both getting leave. Besides, it's not much catch honeymooning in an English hotel in winter in the middle of a war."

"No. I see."

"I was curious to see what it was like: an English country house. I've never been inside one." He paused. "I only know her French life. I wanted to see—how she would be here. She said so often: My English home. She does feel part of what's traditional." He looked round the room again. "She longed to be back. But I can't find her here—it's one of her delusions . . . one of her affirmations, I should say. No doubt she knows she doesn't live anywhere."

"You wouldn't think that," I said, "if she was here." I gulped. "I keep on thinking about her not being in her room. Upstairs."

He said slowly:

"I know about that. There's nothing there."

The cold-sounding muted drawl in his voice struck me with fear.

"There's a portrait of Ianthe there," I said. "When she was a little girl."

He nodded.

"It's a remarkably fine portrait," he said, in the manner of a critic.

"You've seen it?"

"Yes."

"Is—is the room empty?"

252

"The furniture's all there."

"She used to love to lie and look out of the window."

"Yes," he said. "Yes. That's what she does. There's nothing in the room."

"Well," I said, giving up, "I believe she'll be glad you've been here—when she knows."

"Oh, she'll know. She'll see it as a ritualistic act. The Black Mass . . . or the Purification."

He poured himself out another whisky, and drank it off. There was now a great distance between us again. My sense of being drowned, dissolved in a magnetic tide towards him, my revulsion of loathing, had equally vanished. I watched him dispassionately, noting his physical characteristics, feeling full of knowledge of him yet empty of emotion about him. In later life the faculty for pure violence of abstract experience is lost. It takes longer than half an hour, more than a kiss on the cheek, a touch of finger tips to absorb the entire experience of being lovers and to emerge at the other end. At fourteen, even the no kiss, the no touch, is enough.

I told myself how different newly-married people were from what I had imagined.

"Does Tanya like it here?" I said.

I thought it was about time that he went back to her: I was not stopping him.

"Oh, Tanya . . ." he said. "Tanya has come here to execute a commission for Harry. The child, Cherry: something of hers, or to do with her, that was left here, that he wanted sent to him, or secretly destroyed—I don't know which. She promised him to do it."

I had a vision of her in her bridal dress, peering, hunting through the soaking shrubbery—at this moment?—for what? The match-boxes? . . . But at this moment the door was flung open, Maisie appeared, and beyond her I saw Tanya's white form sitting peacefully on the sofa.

A guilty conscience led me to imagine that Maisie glanced sharply from Gil to me and back again.

"Hallo, Maisie," said Gil in a mild voice. "We were just talking about you."

"Were you indeed?" she said loudly. "What were you saying?"

"I was just telling your friend Rebecca to beware of you."

"He wasn't," I urged, in shocked dismay.

"Quite right," said Maisie. "I was just telling your wife Tanya the same thing. Come on, Rebecca. The party's over for you. You must be taken to the kitchen and sacrificed."

"I'm not sacrificed," I said eagerly. "I'd rather help you wash up than anything."

She passed Gil without another look, and I followed her to the kitchen.

# VIII

S H E surveyed the table and shook her head.

"We'll leave all that," she said. "What does one do with feathers? God knows. Mrs. Gillman might like them to make little pelisses for Doris. We'll just deal with the bare essentials."

We went from kitchen to dining-room to kitchen, to scullery, piling plates, glasses, knives, forks, spoons, bowls, saucepans on to trays and stacking them on the scullery table. Then she hurled on the taps full cock, filled the sink to the brim, flung in soda, rolled up her sleeves, and started to plunge in everything pell mell.

"I'll wash, you dry," she said. "My hands are more toil-worn than yours. How do you manage to keep your nails clean? Mine always look as if they'd been used for knocking into coffins."

The taps dripped, the dish-cloth swirled the water round, the things in the sink made various cool domestic noises of clinking and clashing. I looked at her muscular arms, her brilliant bony cheek, her energetic hair glittering under the light, and felt a glowing sense of comfort, and of attraction to her. I hoped to be able to stay with her alone till bed-time.

She said suddenly:

"What do you propose to do when you grow up?"

I admitted that my hope was to marry and to be an author.

"Menial tasks are what I really love," she said. "This sort of revolting job, and shovelling coke into boilers, and chopping wood. I'd be quite content to do it for my living, but I agree with everybody, it would be a waste of my abilities and education. I intend to be a doctor. Have you a prejudice against women doctors?"

"I don't think so." I considered the project, impressed. Then a disadvantage struck me. "But what about—what about the blood?" I said.

"What about it?"

"Well, you didn't use to like it much. And I suppose a doctor's bound to come across it?"

"Oh, I've got over that," she said grimly. She paused, nodded her head with vigour. "And I don't mind foul smells; and I doubt if dissecting corpses will turn me up."

"Oh, then I think you'd make a wonderful doctor," I said ardently, wishing to express my sense of the vitality and confidence she radiated.

"I come from a line of professional women on the maternal side. My mother taught in a school once—she covered herself with academic distinction, though it's a ludicrous idea if you could see her now. And look at the old girl. If she's to be believed she's the world's greatest loss to the stage, and her novels are sheer genius. Actually she has got brains; but of course she was just a dilettante. I bet her books are trash. Have you read any of them?"

"No," I said. "We don't seem to have them in our library. I believe one of them was about my grandmother and made her rather upset."

"Oh, indeed! That's interesting." She cocked an eyebrow at the saucepan she was scraping. "So that was the trouble."

245

"I think only one of the troubles," I said, with scrupulous intention.

"I must cast a glance over that one of these days. I expect it's got a certain *verve* and *aplomb*. It must be somewhere in the bookshelves here. I'll let you borrow it if I find it."

A complex of fears and loyalties caused me an inward resistance to this offer; but I thanked her politely.

"Why did you say," I said, turning away to stack a pile of dry plates, "a ludicrous idea?"

"What are you talking about?"

"About your mother. If I could see her now, you said."

"Oh, that. Because her present condition is such that the idea of her ever swotting for exams or earning her living or leading any kind of normal life is—well, more than ludicrous."

"How do you know," I said, striving to make my voice as offhand as hers, "for so certain?"

"From having seen her, of course. How do you suppose?"

"Oh, you've seen her," I said, conversational.

"I've seen her."

"When was it?"

"July, 1914. In France." Her nostrils dilated, her mouth turned down in a sardonic smile. "How often I'd imagined it! Hmm. It all turned out quite different."

"So you saw her," I repeated.

"I'd had measles at school, and the doctor sent me off before the end of term to convalesce. If it hadn't been for those measles I'd have missed everything."

"Malcolm wasn't there?"

"No, thank God. He'd have been shocked into pulp. I've never told him I saw her." She turned on me sharply. "Mind you don't."

"Of course not."

"He thinks she retired into a convent and never came out. That's quite a respectable end to imagine for one's mother, I suppose." She chuckled.

"She didn't really retire to one at all?"

"Oh yes. She did. She went in. And she came out again."

"I wonder what made her go in."

"She got fed up with living in the world, I suppose. It was some kind of sisterhood in France. She got ill and they nursed her there, and then she stayed."

"I didn't realise she was religious. Was that why she—why she left you? Did she want to go into a convent so much that she left you?"

"No," said Maisie, "that's not why she left. The religious business didn't come on till some time after."

"I see."

I waited. The moment hovered, passed. Maisie fell to scrubbing another saucepan.

I said:

"I wonder why she came out again."

"Oh, she never could stick to anything for long." She scrubbed away; then added: "She got remorse about us. She had to see us again."

"Did she come to get you?" I said, feeling my wrist go weak as I wiped a glass. "I mean, all to start living—having a home together again?"

"I shouldn't think so. I think she just wanted. . . . God knows . . . to have a look at us, perhaps. She couldn't have known *what* she meant to do." She gathered up a bunch of knives and forks out of the now opaque swamp-coloured water and flung them on the draining board. "That's the lot." She seized another cloth and casting, I thought, a pointed glance at the painstaking tempo of my labours, set to vigorously to help me dispose of what remained.

"Come on, polish them off quick," she said, "and we'll go and put our feet up on the kitchen fender and eat walnuts. Unless you want to go back and dance or something. I don't mind dancing with you, if you don't. I'm always gent at the Saturday night revels at school, and I give the dear girls a rousing time in spite of obvious handicaps."

"I'd much rather sit by the kitchen fire with you," I said. "I don't think we're awfully wanted in there. At least, I'm not."

"I dare say Gil and Tanya will have gone to bed," she said

with simplicity. "I made a glorious bridal fire in their bedroom. I hope your mother won't object to Jess being left alone with Malcolm. He's very gentlemanly and backward. I *may* be wrong, one never knows with one's brother, but I don't *think* his intentions go beyond fox-trotting for hours with the girls he's keen on. I hope Jess won't get bored. He *is* a good dancer."

"Jess is good too," I said, writing them off with satisfaction. "She adores it."

We went back to the kitchen. She plucked a basket of walnuts out of the wreckage on the table and drew two wooden chairs up to the glowing range. We sat down with our feet on the low steel fender. She hitched her navy-blue serge skirt up above her knees and leaned forward, cracking nuts together between her palms and staring into the fire.

"What do you think of Gil?" she said.

"I don't know," I said, hedging. "I've never met any one like him."

"I should jolly well think you haven't. He's higher class than most people by a long chalk. I'll tell you something. He's the only man I could ever—be a fool about—*ever*. And as I haven't been, thank God I know I shall *never* be—about any one."

Incautious, I inquired:

"Did he and Tanya fall in love at first sight?"

"Oh . . . !" She sounded exasperated. "No. Yes. *No.* I don't know. It wasn't like all that rot—holding hands in the firelight and engagement rings and . . . You wouldn't understand."

"I would," I said abashed, aggrieved.

"Well, there's no real reason why you should," she conceded. "He's got different ideas about behaving from most people. It's his philosophy that's different."

I felt that a philosophy of life was precisely what I was fitted to understand, and said that my conversation with him had made it clear that his was different.

"Tanya loves him simply terrifically," said Maisie, abrupt. I was relieved by this positive view of what had appeared to me dubious.

"And Gil too, I suppose," I said. "He loves her like that too?"

"They're not a bit suited to one another," she went on, frowning fiercely into the fire. "Except that they're both so unordinary. . . . She knows she'll only share a bit of his life: she thinks she doesn't mind. She's got her music, of course. . . . But it won't balance out what *he's* going to keep to himself. He's completely independent—what's the word?—self-sufficient; and she's not."

"A—a heartless sort of man, do you mean?"

"No, I don't. He's awfully affectionate and gentle and kind. He makes people feel he's very fond of them; but if anybody, *anybody* seemed to be getting to interfere with his work, *they'd* go—and he'd be all right. What I mean is, his work comes first. But she's different: perhaps women always are. If things go wrong with people for her, she's done for. I've seen it happen."

"Would you say he was very fond of her?" I persisted, returning to the attack on a more temperate level.

"Of course he is. He dotes on her. If you can't see that much, you're blind." She began juggling with three walnuts, throwing them up alternately and catching them in one hand. "His idea is," she said, "that very few people would be capable of appreciating her. He can, so he's going to look after her. . . . Oh, well. What's the good of looking ahead, at a time like this? If they can comfort each other for a few days, it's something." She stopped juggling, and threw me a glance. "What did he talk about to you?"

I hesitated.

"Well, mostly about Mrs. Jardine."

"Oh, he did, did he?" She flung her head back, threw a walnut high in the air, and caught it with a click in her mouth. "Bet you can't do that," she said.

I tried, and I could not, and we spent a few frivolous moments in further competition.

"Don't break your teeth," she said. "What would your mother say if you came back with your front set smashed?"

"Was Mrs. Jardine awfully fond of Gil?" I inquired, when the game had lost its savour and we had returned to peeling and cruching the crisp, milky, convoluted kernels.

"She was mad about him," said Maisie solemnly. "I dare say

249

she thought she'd got him fixed there for ever. But for the war he might have been—for a bit longer. It was rather hard luck on her. He was incredibly satisfactory for her—he's everything that excites her. She could make him up to be a mysterious, unique person that only she could understand. He came from such a long way away and had such an extraordinary beginning. She could swell him up into . . . I don't know . . . a sort of god."

"Where did he come from?"

"From somewhere in the very middle of Africa. His father was a Norwegian missionary, and his mother is a Highland Scottish woman. She went out to Africa when she was twenty-one to teach natives in a mission school, and got married to his father. They lived far away from white people in a wooden house they built themselves, and they were absolutely poor, and worked like slaves to keep alive. Gil was brought up with black boys and girls, Zulus. He was their only child. His father's dead now, but his mother still lives there and keeps a store. You can imagine how impressed Sibyl was. It's the kind of life she admires. She'd have liked to live it. I don't blame her: so would I. How I wonder what his mother's like. . . . I've seen snapshots of them. She looks like a little withered working woman, with a knob of thin white hair, very thin and bony, worn-out-looking—but very energetic too. His father looks like an Old Testament prophet, a giant with a great beard. Amazing." She brooded, chin on palm.

"Did he like living with the Zulus?"

"He adored it. He loves them. He says the tribe he lived among are good and fine and very civilised. He thinks what white people have done to them is awful: taken away their land and shoved them in the mines and made them lose their human pride, he says . . . made them sad. He fairly boils when people call them niggers and talk as if they were only fit to be knocked about and treated like animals, or worse."

As I listened, I felt more and more stirred. Ever since one childhood summer spent on my maternal grandmother's farm in the White Mountains of New England, I had known that I loved coloured people. She had a negro cook called Nathan who taught me to play the zither, and on one occasion during the long hours I spent in the kitchen gazing at the plum-dark spheroids that composed his face, the dazzling split of carved ivory that made his smile, at his round astrakhan cap of hair, at his dusky coral palms rolling the dough, he had lingeringly given back my gaze and softly drawled that there was music in those eyes. This was the sort of approach to which I responded as the pin to the magnet, and ever since, I had dreamed confusedly of a race whose life still sprang unbroken from archaic roots in darkness and sunlight and exposed itself in eternally simple, incorruptible forms of music and movement.

"When he was a little boy," said Maisie, "he used to model animals and figures in mud or clay. The Zulus taught him. He did that before he learned to read and write. When he got older he was sent away to school in Johannesburg, and some rich man or woman, I don't know which, saw some sculpture he did and got interested in him, and gave him enough money to leave Africa and go to Paris to study. He was only eighteen, but he'd done so much, so many different things already, according to what he's told us . . . He wasn't a schoolboy, he was a man." She mused again; then said: "That thing he did for Cherry, the memorial —it's not her. It doesn't look like her, I mean. It's a very queer piece of work. It's a group of two figures." She put both her hands to her forehead, pushing at it with her fingers till it was all lumps and furrows. Under it, her eyes contracted, tense with the effort to give me the image. "One's sitting, all weighed downward and stiff and heavy-looking, all shrouded close, its head bowed forward and this sort of shroud covering its face. You can see the moulding of its face and body under the drapery, but it's not like a human man or woman. It's—it's just a *being*. Its thighs are spread apart, and it looks—done for, somehow, like a broken-open shell or husk. And this other figure, which is a child, is rising up between its knees—stretched up, naked, with it might be a smile on its face, and its eyes shut. It's not a bit what nurses call a bonny child: thin, with a *sad* sort of body. It's got a broad, listening sort of face . . . or waiting. . . . Oh, I can't describe it. It's not an English child—not a child of any country, I shouldn't think. It's more like an *idea* of a child, if you see what I mean. Do you?"

"Yes," I said, following her with dumbfounded attention.

"It gave me a shock when I saw it first. I thought it was hideous. I felt awful about it: I told Sibyl it was a monstrosity. But when she'd talked to me about it, and told me to empty out all my second-hand notions of what statues *ought* to look like, I began to see the point. And after a bit, whenever I saw it I took it in more. And I can't forget it. . . . He certainly is a queer sculptor, but I suppose he's a pretty good one. Sibyl would be likely to know."

I said:

"Did your mother see it?"

"She saw it," said Maisie, short. Silence. "Just imagine," she said. "Till she came out of that place she didn't know Cherry was dead."

"Good gracious!" I said, inadequate.

"She wrote to Auntie Mack for news of us, and Auntie Mack had to tell her. Poor old thing, she's always had all the unrewarding jobs. I saw her afterwards. She said she'd always known it would happen—that Mother would turn up again some day and present her with a problem beyond the fathoming of human reason. It was her fate, she said."

Maisie chuckled, and I felt bound to do likewise.

"What on earth did she mean?" I asked.

"Oh, whether to reveal our whereabouts to Mother, or conceal it. And whether to tell Sibyl Mother was on our tracks or keep it under her hat. You see she had a pact with Sibyl, it seems, to keep her posted. Oh dearr, dearr, dearr, she was pairfectly distraught."

We laughed more and more.

"What did she do?"

"She took it to God." Maisie caught my eye and we doubled up with mirth: we were no longer children. "And God advised her to tell Mother the truth, and to make a vow of secrecy with Mother not to breathe a word to Sibyl. So there she was, with a double noose and plenty of rope to hang herself. She wrote off

252

a letter to Mother, saying where we were and breaking it to her that there was no more Cherry. After all, as she said, she felt most strongly that Mother had given us birth and had a right to the information. On the other hand there was this sacred pact with Mrs. Jardine. And yet *again* there was Mother telling her on her life not to sneak to Sibyl. Oh dearr, dearr, dearr! . . . She showed me Mother's letter. It was perfectly sensible and to the point." Maisie stopped short, oddly.

"So," I said, after a pause for nut-cracking, "she turned up?"

"Talk of midsummer madness!" exclaimed Maisie suddenly, tilting herself back with such violence that her chair legs yelped on the floor. "When I think about it now I feel as if the war started then—all roaring armies marching against one another and land mines bursting under everybody. When the real war started and every one else was in a state of chaos, it seemed to me a mere rumble on the horizon. Everything had happened for me."

She clasped her hands behind her head and stared absently at her legs, flexing and unflexing the muscles of her calves.

"Maisie, what did happen?"

She said slowly—and I knew she had begun at last:

"Do you know what this place in France is like? It's very exciting; not like anywhere else. The house itself is a great high plain block built of white stone. It looks somehow ominous, with dozens of long dark windows flat on its face. It's perched up so high, and it's a landmark for miles. It's all very stony and solid, outside and in. It's called The Tower of the Doves. There's a big round stone dove house in the courtyard. It's very old and it's got a lot of local history attached to it. Sibyl knows it all, of course: I don't. She's made it perfect, I must say: she does know how to furnish houses. All round the park is a high wall. The church is the other side of the wall, with a graveyard. . . . A French graveyard has to be seen to be believed. And there's a glorious old farmhouse and some barns as well. The grounds go down and down in a long steep slope to the valley, and there's a little river there, and a weir, and an inn, and boathouses, and an old white mill where they don't mill any more. Harry owns it all. Oh, that river! Parts of it are so matted up with water lilies you can hardly get a boat through. People row up and down in ridiculous little flat-bottomed boats like water beetles. On Sundays French chaps come out from the town and spend the day fishing for tiddlers. They don't throw *one* back. They're all taken home in the evening and made into a fry. Their wives tippet about on the bank in high heels, crooning sillinesses to naked-looking dyspeptic little pinky-white dogs with black blotches on them and rolls of fat in their necks. And they peep into the chaps' fishing jars and flute out: '*O, Georges, regardes-donc! Quels amours de petits poissons!*' They do sound asses. But they're all so cheerful and polite and pleased with themselves you can't help feeling drawn to them. When the chaps call out to the women their voices come out so ringing from their chests. . . . They sound so—so full up with life."

This picture of French society impressed me vividly. It was not what I had been led to expect from my studies; yet it could not have been invented. I saw the French now as a connubial nation of aquatic holiday-makers, sonorously hauling up minnows and piping on flutes to unresponsive lap dogs.

"There's this ripping inn," went on Maisie, "with a garden on the water front and a roofed-in sort of summer-house by the landing stage where you can have meals and read or write. Sometimes Sibyl and Harry, or just Sibyl went down in the evenings and had supper there with Gil and sat by the river till it was dark. A couple called Meunier who were once her cook and butler run the inn, and they adore her, of course. They're both jolly decent."

"Where was it Gil lived?" I asked.

"Gil lived in the mill, on the other side of the river. You go across by a narrow plank bridge. She'd opened part of the old roof and put in glass for his studio. It was an enormous high room with whacking great oak beams and pillars in it. Oh, the whole of that place was thrilling—I never hope to see a better. Only," she added slowly, "it was sinister. There never seemed enough air there, down by the river, though you could see the tops of the poplars and willows waving about, and hear the breeze in them. It was so close, with all the trees, it seemed to weigh you down. And the sound of the weir closed you in and made you dizzy. And all those tangling lilies and river weeds. . . . And the mist ghosting up . . . and the mill opposite looming at you with a blank white face. . . . I suppose it's my imagination, but . . . You know the look of a photograph of a house where *something happened*—how it looks different—it has a special secret expression, as if it had been built on purpose for that terrible thing to happen? That's how I think of the mill now. . . . The inn garden was lit with coloured lights strung in loops along the landing stage and all through the willows. It was so pretty and musical-comedy. To think it's all still there!—but no lights in the garden, I suppose; and the inn and the mill are used for convalescent annexes in summer. I wonder if Sibyl still goes down to sit by the river. . . . Oh, Rebecca . . . I can't help thinking of her there. You know how she sits bolt upright with her head and shoulders wrapped up in pale gauzy stuff, as still as a stone statue. That's my last memory of her, sitting in the place she always sat, staring, staring across at the mill. She said: 'Good-bye, Maisie,' and then nothing more, and I left her alone there and went back to the house; and then Tanya and I went to the station to catch the train for Paris."

"Why was she staring at the mill?" I asked, frightened.

"Because," said Maisie, unclasping her hands from behind her head and letting them fall loose in her lap, "that's where everything happened."

I drew my chair a little nearer to the fire. Both of us leaned forward so that our bowed heads almost touched.

"I used to go down to bathe," she said, "and stay for lunch sometimes at the inn with Madame Meunier. One morning, about eleven, I went down as usual and had a swim. I used to sit on top of the sort of stone parapet where the weir went over into the pool. It was lovely. I liked letting my legs go with the turn-over of the water till they almost began to feel dissolved, as if they were pouring over the edge too. It's the most extraordinary sensation—your legs curving downwards and waving in the water as if they weren't attached to you. I specially enjoyed it, because my legs are my heaviest cross. We won't dwell on that.

It was slippery enough to be exciting too, from green weed that grew on the stone—brilliant electric green as if it was lit up from inside. Then I used to slip down and let myself go under into the plunge of the weir and come up again farther along with the drift of the current, and float—float into the calm stream again. Of course it was only a little tame weir, but gosh! it was heaven."

"I can't imagine anything more like heaven," I said, with sincerity.

"Yes. I thought of you once or twice and wished you were with me."

"Did you honestly?"

"Mm . . . Well, I had this bathe, it was a scorching hot morning, and afterwards I went in to the inn for lunch. They have it at twelve in France, you know, and can't they jolly well make vegetables taste good! After lunch I decided I'd go for a row. It was fun steering through the lilies, they lie like great rugs on the water and all their ropy stalks come gliding up on the oars; and I liked nosing around the midget islands of willows and guelder-rose and stuff, and looking at the freakish little castellated houses perched up on the banks. I came out of the inn; and as I went down to the landing stage I noticed a woman in a queer dress: a dark yellow bodice and a long, bright-coloured skirt, sort of magenta, not an English colour, and edged with a gold band, sitting in the summer-house and having her lunch. I couldn't see her face. I poked about on the river and came back about four, and had another swim. I gave Gil a shout, and he looked out of the window and waved to me. To my surprise the woman was still there. She had papers spread round her and she was writing. She didn't look up, but I saw her side-face and I thought she didn't look French. I looked in on Madame Meunier and asked her if someone had come to stay, and she said yes, an English lady had arrived this morning and taken a room. She'd said she was writing a book and wanted to be undisturbed. Madame Meunier said she was very *comme il faut* and spoke French like a native. I went back to the house. It was one of Sibyl's bad days. She couldn't breathe very well, but she was all serene, lying on the sofa. Gil turned up for supper and after-wards Tanya played."

"Is that what she did all the time?—play the piano?"

"Not all the time, but a good deal. She did things for Sibyl when Sibyl was laid up, and was secretary to them both, and went for walks with Harry. He loved her dearly. He wasn't drinking nearly so much and he got quite interested in the farm. What's more, he went riding with her sometimes before break-fast; and a fine sight he looked too on horseback. He's an ab-solutely idyllic horseman. Otherwise she practised hours and hours a day. And she went to Paris twice a week for lessons. Her idea was to study and study till she felt she was good enough to give a concert and start being a real professional performer. Harry paid for her lessons, he insisted; and Sibyl—she depended a lot on Sibyl—she always said Sibyl was *the* ideal person to back anybody in any kind of artistic way. She knew what was first-class and what wasn't—Gil said this too—and she believed so passionately in going all out for the very best and not sparing oneself every refinement of torture to get to it. She seemed to charge Tanya up again when she got tired. In return, Tanya—well, she'd have drunk prussic acid for her without a murmur. It was a pity all that smashed up. Tanya's been teaching music to lumps of girlhood at my school, for her living, these last two years. It's a wicked waste of her. Harry wanted to go on giving her an allowance, but she wouldn't let him. I'll come to all that. Wait here a sec."

She got up and left the kitchen. When after a few minutes she came back, she said:

"I took a peep at Jess and Malcolm. He was just winding up the gramophone again, and they looked very innocent and rosy. I told them we were in the kitchen if they wanted to find us. We might cook an omelette later."

She sat down again, fished two apples out of her pocket, gave me one and demolished half the other in one bite.

"Tanya played," I said.

"Tanya played. It was a wonderful night with the moon full. I mentioned that there was an English lady author staying at the

257

inn. 'Yes indeed,' said Gil. 'She came to call on me. She wanted to know the way to the Post Office.' 'What an excuse!' I said. 'She could easily have asked the Meuniers.' There were some jokes about her having spotted Gil through the window. Sibyl asked what she was like, and I remember Gil said slowly: 'A ruined beauty.' Up poked Sibyl's head at that, and she asked some more questions. 'Might she be an addition to our circle?' she asked, smiling. He said, on the whole he thought *not*. His advice would be to run a mile if we saw her approaching. We teased him some more about wanting to keep her to himself. Then he said quite seriously: 'She's got a dreadful great pair of blood-sucking eyes, and caverns in her mouth.' That's the sort of way he talks. 'I don't know what she's up to,' he said, 'or who's responsible for her; but I have the impression that her book won't find a publisher.'"

"Did she tell him what kind of book she was writing?"

"She told him it was her life story. He said he kept off inquiring into it. She wandered round the studio, he said, looking at things—at some drawings that he'd got pinned up round the walls, and three or four portrait heads in clay that he'd done in his spare time. She came to a new one of Sibyl that he was working on. It was covered with a wet cloth. She asked what it was, and he said it was a woman he knew. 'Beautiful?' she said. 'Yes,' he said. 'May I see it?' she said. He told her no, it wasn't finished, would she please leave it alone: because she would fiddle about and twitch at things and she didn't really seem to take anything in, though she talked, he said, as if she understood something about sculpture. Then she came and stood in front of Cherry's memorial, in the middle of the room. She stared at it; and she said how beautiful it was. You know it's carved out of a block of alabaster with marvellous half-transparent bits in it. The upper part is like that—so that most of the child's figure looks shining; and her whole head shines. The block is so beautiful in itself it makes your mouth water to look at it. It took him six months to find it. She asked what it was, and he said it was for a dead child. She went on staring at it, then she asked him: 'What was her name?' He said: 'Her name was Charity Mary

Thomson. She was called Cherry.' Then she did a peculiar thing. She put out her hand and touched the figure; and muttered something."

Maisie paused. Watching her, I saw her eyes, fixed on the fire, dilate. After a bit she said reflectively:

"I think I guessed then. It's hard to explain. I'm *sure* I tumbled to the whole thing—such an extraordinary feeling went through me. And *then* I knew I'd known all along . . . from the first moment I'd set eyes on that woman in the summer-house. But why, at the time, she'd slipped quite casually on to my sight as if she was nobody in particular—why I didn't get the slightest conscious shock *then*—that's a mystery. . . . Anyway, while Gil was talking, I got a picture of her standing there in her long, bright-coloured skirt; *and I suddenly remembered that stuff.* It was some Indian silk, a sari. She brought home lots from India. I used to look at them in her drawer, and that was the one I loved best. I knew it . . . and yet . . . it was more like saying to myself: It's someone wearing Mother's sari . . . if you see what I mean."

"Did Mrs. Jardine begin to guess?" I said shakily, my heart pinched by terror and excitement.

"No, she didn't. I'll swear to that. She says she always has instincts and premonitions; but this time she didn't. She was too wrapped up in Gil, I expect. She was seeing it all through him —the effect on him—and she was just interested, like you would be if any one you loved told you a strange woman had come to visit him, and behaved very queerly."

"Did she—your—the woman say anything else to Gil?"

"She asked him his name. He told her. Then she said: 'Did you know this child while she lived?'—and he said no, and tried to change the subject, because she began to get very agitated, and to talk about having lost a baby, and to say she knew now that women should stop having babies, it was too terrible to have them, and that sort of thing. He said she had a look on her like one of those crazy women who steal children out of prams. . . . Sibyl lay on the sofa with her eyes very blue and wide open, and I could see that she was worked up—that she'd never rest until she'd come face to face with this spectacular person and discovered if she really had lost her baby and if so, why, how and when, and done something about her. I heard her say some words under her breath: I couldn't catch them."

"I suppose Gil hadn't guessed anything?"

"Well, that was the queer thing that I was coming to. It had never crossed his mind, of course, before, or he wouldn't have talked about her openly like that. *But,* he told me afterwards, suddenly, when he heard Sibyl mutter to herself, something seemed to hit him a great slap across the forehead."

"It all dawned on him!"

"Not exactly. It wasn't a thing anybody could be expected to *take in* at one fell swoop. It was the sort of smack, like a revelation, that I got; and afterwards you think perhaps you're unhinged too. He said it was hearing that mutter, it made a connection with the other one muttering. . . . He'd never heard Sibyl do it before. I had."

"I have too," I said.

"Anyway I did notice he suddenly pulled up short and was rather curt and silent. When Sibyl—or Tanya asked him some more questions, he merely said he'd requested her politely to go away, he was busy."

"Did she go?"

"She went. He could see her walking along the bank, through the meadows, and stopping dead now and then to look at the water. He could see her a long way off in her bright skirt. Sibyl said in that lecturing way she has when she thinks she's been a lot sharper than any one else could be—she said: 'Did it strike you that this unfortunate woman might be contemplating doing herself a *mischief?*' " Maisie grinned.

"Did she mean——?"

"Yes. She meant just that."

"What did he say?"

"He said in a casual, airy way, yes rather, it had struck him forcibly. Only, he said, experience inclined him to the conclusion that people like her were too bent on planning mischief to others to consider themselves. The only thing that had bothered him was whether he ought to rush and pull her out, or let her get out on her own. He knew she'd take care to jump within sight of his window—if she did jump. . . . He was grand with Sibyl when she tried to come it over him. He never let her."

"And she didn't—didn't jump?"

"No," said Maisie, her lip and nostril stretching. "Not that time she didn't."

She tilted her chair back, extended her torso, folded her arms and sank her chin into her collar. At this unbecoming angle, her face looked extraordinarily heavy, masculine, magisterial.

"About eleven," she went on, "Gil carried Sibyl upstairs to her room. Oh, how she did enjoy being carried by him! . . . Then he came down and said good-night to us and went away through the park. Harry went to bed—I suppose. . . . I suppose Harry goes to bed. His room's right at the other end of the house from Sibyl's. Tanya and I sat on on the terrace in the moonlight. Then Tanya said she couldn't go to bed on a night like this, she was going for a walk. I knew I wasn't invited."

"Why not?"

"Because she was going to Gil, of course."

"Oh! . . . they were—they'd fallen in love then?"

"She hadn't told me, but I'd guessed. At least I knew *she* was in love, from the way she couldn't look away from him whenever she looked at him. Also I knew she'd been flitting down to the river at nights fairly frequently—because I'd seen her from my window."

"Did Mrs. Jardine—not mind?"

"She hadn't twigged, believe it or not. So much again for intuitions." Maisie snorted; but after a pause added judicially: "But it's quite true—in some ways she's extraordinarily trusting and like a child—she can't see further than her nose: though in other ways she's such an arch-spider. You see, she thought she'd got it fixed up this time good and proper, all serene, everybody revolving round her like dancers round a maypole, without an eye or a thought to spare for anybody else. . . . Oh, she was so sure of Gil!"

"You mean—sure that he loved her best?"

"Exactly. That what she meant to him was so terrific and—different, so on some superior plane that only she could reach and he could understand, that—well, that there couldn't be room for any other woman in his life, in spite of her age, and everything."

"You talk as if . . . she couldn't have been . . ."

"I mean, of course, that she was in love with him," said Maisie loudly.

"Good Lord! I didn't know it could happen," I said, aghast. "Why, she's old. She might be his mother. Perhaps—surely—that's how she felt about him: as if he was her own son?"

"Perhaps," said Maisie, dry, shrugging. "I haven't any experience of what mothers are like with their sons. I dare say you know best."

"Oh *no*," I said, abashed. "It's only that I got a bit of a shock."

"Sibyl's capable of anything," said Maisie, mollified. "As for Gil—oh, I don't know. I don't understand men."

"How old is he?"

"I don't know. I never remember ages. He's about twenty-eight, I think."

Suddenly moved to confide in her my own experience of man's enigmatic nature, I said:

"He kissed me just now."

"Oh, he did, did he?" She paused. "Where?"

"In the dining-room."

"Where on your *face,* I mean?"

"Oh . . ." I touched my cheek, where the spot still seemed to burn. "There." Her expression was cryptic, her manner clinical; and regretting my impulse, I added: "It was rather a surprise."

"Were you upset?"

"N-no."

"Pleased?"

"Well, not exactly. . . ." My regrets were now wild. "It wasn't anything. He was thinking about the war—or something. I didn't mind. I'd almost forgotten it till you. . . . Do go on about that night."

"I told you," she said rather scoldingly, "he always makes people feel he's fond of them."

"Yes. Do go on."

"Where was I when you interrupted? . . ." She drew a hissing breath; paused, frowned; then went on: "I watched Tanya disappear towards the river. She had a white frock on, so she was very visible. Below the terrace is a paved rose garden with a pool and a fountain in the middle of it. I thought I'd take a walk round and smell the roses. I was feeling worked up and queer, too restless to go to bed. I kept on seeing that person in the bright skirt, and wanting to see her again, and hoping I never should. I strolled around the pool, and then I went to the end and leaned up against the low sort of stone parapet at the farther edge of the terrace and had a good stare at the house. It did look a thundering great pile in the moonlight, so steep and naked, with all its long windows glittering like black ice. I looked to see if there was a light in Sibyl's room. There wasn't. Her room is in the middle of the front, on the first floor. The windows reach from floor to ceiling. They were open. Then," said Maisie, casual, stirring and stretching softly in her chair, "I saw her."

"You saw her?"

"Standing by the edge of the curtain. With a pale-coloured cloak wrapped around her. I could see her plainly."

"What was she doing?"

"She was in ambush. Watching."

The words, the flat way in which she spoke them, made my skin crawl. I saw the apparition.

"It gave me a turn," went on Maisie. "Last I'd seen of her, stretched in white lace and ruffles on her sofa, stitching at her embroidery,—the portrait of a lady; then being carried off, smiling, in Gil's arms. Next view—straight, upright, posted there, towering above us like an avenging Fury. Oh, it seemed as if she'd been there for centuries—that she was the ghost of the wicked old house, and now I understood the secret of its sinister face! I could almost see her eyes glitter."

"What could have happened," I said, "in that short time?"

"She must have spotted Tanya going through the garden,"

said Maisie, "and all of a sudden put two and two together. Or maybe she *had* begun to get suspicious before she went upstairs. The atmosphere was certainly electric. She wouldn't, of course, give a sign; but later on, alone in her room, she'd begin to think, and prowl. She'd have Gil on her mind, and—that strange woman. Then Tanya making off . . ."

"Yes, I see," I said, pacing the room in France with Mrs. Jardine, feeling the thread in the maze vibrate, lead on through her to me, to Tanya and the river. "Did she see you?"

"I don't know. She probably did, but she never stirred. I got the feeling she was looking far far beyond me, down to the river and the mill. She wasn't thinking about me."

"What did you do?"

"I could only think of one thing: to get down as quick as possible to somewhere where I could keep a look-out for Tanya. I thought, if I could join her when she left Gil and come back with her, it wouldn't look so shady. If Sibyl was still watching she'd see us reappear together, and we could say we'd been for a swim by moonlight. And get away with it. *Maybe.*"

"What a good idea."

"So I went in a leisurely way down the steps that lead from the paved garden to the lawn. At the end of the lawn there are railings and you go through into rough meadows where the cattle and horses graze. I strolled down the lawn till I got into the shadow of the big trees at the bottom. Then I was over the railings and I ran for it. I zigzagged from tree to tree in the fields until I got to where it slopes down sharply and I knew I must be out of sight. And then—oh! I fairly pelted down till I came to the river."

Maisie stopped speaking. She stared into the fire and bit her thumb. I heard my own breath loud and fast as if I were running behind her, down through the steep fields to—what destination?

She was silent for some time; then she said:

"It all began to seem like dreaming. I wondered what on earth I could be doing there—the only person left in the world, and the world nothing but water, moon, trees and shadows; and in the middle of it all the mill-house sticking up blank and flat like a great white tombstone with nothing written on it; and the only sound the weir pouring, pouring. I thought: '*Anything might happen; and if it did, who should I be?*' I wasn't inside myself any longer, if you see what I mean."

"Yes, yes," I said, thinking of my own phantasmagoric excursions by moonlight alone, over the lawn, among the garden trees at home.

"I went into the inn garden by a little wicket gate. I went down to the landing stage and looked across. Not a sign of life. It seemed queer to think there were two human beings loving each other there, inside that mausoleum. I thought the only thing to do was to sit and wait where I couldn't miss her when she did come out. I went and sat in the summer-house I told you about. It's a rustic affair with white roses and jasmine climbing up the wooden pillars and tumbling over the roof. The scent was unbelievable. I sat there and began to get my breath back. I wondered which room the woman had, and whether she was asleep."

"Were there any lights in the inn?"

"None. I don't know how long I sat there. What with the moon and the weir I felt absolutely dazed. There wasn't a breath of breeze, it was stifling. All of a sudden I *felt* someone was near me . . . and then I saw a figure steal across the grass, not ten yards from me. It went very rapidly, in a stealthy way, to the edge of the water, then stood still on the landing stage and looked across at the mill. Then it started across the bridge."

"Tanya?"

"Not Tanya. I thought for a moment: Sibyl! But it wasn't." "*Her?*"

"Yes. I thought: 'This is it. What I was waiting for.' "

"What did you do?"

"I got up straight as if I was sleep-walking and went after her across the bridge."

"Did you realise for certain then who—who you were following?"

Maisie paused, drawing her brows together, hesitating.

"I wasn't surprised," she said.

For the first time since the beginning of her narrative she turned her large luminous eyes full on me. A faint bewilderment shot through them. I saw that she confronted not my face of simple goggle-eyed expectancy, but the image that had once stunned her. In that one momentary contraction, I saw memory struggle, brace itself to deal with its too-heavy burden. Once more, and for the last time, and vanishing even as I became aware of it, the lonely face of the child Maisie, umbrageous, vulnerable, lit with the passionate effort to communicate, glowed out of our lost place in the walnut tree.

"I wasn't surprised," she repeated. "It seemed as natural as meeting her in a dream; and I'd had plenty of those dreams. . . . There's a kind of grove of poplar trees on the other bank close by the mill. She stopped under them—I stopped too. Then she moved out into the open, over the blinding white grass and on to the door of Gil's house. I went after her in a hurry . . . and she heard me then. She whirled round on me as if I'd thumped her on the back. She stared at me. She had the moon full on her: I saw her face plain."

"Was she the same?" I breathed.

"No, she wasn't," said Maisie. "She looked frightful."

"In what way frightful?"

"Oh . . . all fallen in round her mouth. An expression—I can't describe it—peevish and—*glaring*. Haughty. What's the word?—autocratic. And petty, feeble as well."

One after another she hammered in the epithets, to my desolation.

"I'm pretty sure," she went on, drawing her brows together, "that's how women in lunatic asylums look. It's not like what you imagine, when people are really bats. They're not vacant, or gibbering and tearing their hair. I see them looking *mincing* —full of airs and graces. Drawing themselves up as if they were empresses, and giving orders in furious, pompous, venomous voices. *Sly* . . . Sidling up. . . . Oh, and so *self-important*. That's how I see them. I should very much like to know what goes on in lunatic asylums. One day I will. It would be fascinating. . . . The worst is, they seem so obscene. I'm sure they have a bad smell. They're not mad all the year round, you know. Part of the time they're as sane as any one else. Then it comes on; and they're *absolutely different* from ordinary people. It's not like managing someone in a raging temper or depression or hysterics. There's no way to reason or argue or scold or sympathise or appeal—or show you love them. You might as well put on a smashed gramophone record and expect it to play the right notes in order. It's this *separateness* which seems so—shocking." She drew a sharp breath. "I told you I would never marry and have children—even in the unlikely event of some ass offering me the chance—and that's the reason. There's madness in my family. Malcolm doesn't know, and I don't propose to tell him. The chances are he'll be killed, anyway, before he can start to become a father."

"You know for certain?" I inquired, impressed by this distinguished fate.

"For dead certain." She uttered a brief laugh.

"What happened next?" I said. "Did she speak? Or you?"

"I said: 'Don't be frightened. It's Maisie.' "

"Just like that?"

"Just like that. It didn't seem possible to say: 'Hallo, Mother,' or anything of that sort."

"And what did she say?"

Maisie paused, then said with a smile:

"She told me to go away."

"Didn't she know you?"

"She said: 'Ah, Maisie. Yes.' Very formal and polite and distant, as if I was a slight surprise and nuisance she'd come on by chance out walking."

"Oh, *Maisie!* . . ."

"Yes, it was peculiar. Though I can't say I was exactly hurt at the time. It was all so like a dream; and then I was too busy trying to make out what she was up to. She told me in a condescending way to run away now, like a good girl. When she said it, I suddenly remembered something."

"What?"

"She'd said the very same thing once before, in that particular voice."

"When?"

"I can't get it back, when it was exactly; but I think it must have been a short time before she went away from us. I remember seeing her from the window one evening, dressed in her best, going up the street towards the town moor. I ran after her . . . and she told me to go back. I remember how her voice came out through her veil—*smooth;* and she gave me a little push. I knew Father didn't like her to go out alone because she wasn't well. I went back, and he was just coming into the house. I told him she'd gone out, and it acted on him like a squib under him. Auntie Mack was just coming downtairs from putting Cherry to bed. He let out a shout at her—she jumped as if she'd been shot—and then he went haring off down the street. I couldn't make head or tail of it . . . but I'd given up trying to understand what went on in our house, it was all so mystifying. Auntie Mack told me to come along upstairs at once; and she brought us up supper later with a flaming red, choked sort of face. But that was always happening. Poor old goose. Poor Father. When I think about his life, I *cannot* bear it."

Maisie leaped violently from her chair, stood rigid for a minute, head lifted, glowering at the copper pots and pans on the shelf above the range; then sat down again.

Unwilling to encourage, at this juncture, any deflection from the main stream, I said hastily:

"What happened next?"

"She was carrying a big fat envelope. I said, if she'd got something for the person who lived here wouldn't she give it to me and I'd see he got it in the morning, I thought he'd be in bed and asleep at this time of night. I spoke in a perfectly ordinary way—I knew I must. 'Certainly not. He's expecting me,' she said, very dignified. She said she'd given him all the facts, and as he wished to take the matter in hand immediately she had promised to deliver the document in person. 'So that he will know, once and for all,' she said in a crisp, efficient sort of way—it reminded me of Sibyl—'what is necessary to be done.' I was stumped. Then I said: 'Couldn't I read it too? I'm very interested.' She looked at me horribly cunningly and stuffed it under her arm. It was that look that made me realise, all in a rush, that she was plumb crazy."

"Oh Maisie! Weren't you terrified?"

"Yes," said Maisie simply. "I nearly yelled for Gil. Then I pulled myself together and thought: 'I *will* manage. Years and years I've spent telling myself I'd find her, wherever she was; and whatever it was like, whatever had happened, I'd—I'd make it come right. Now I've found her, and I've *got to*.' I heard myself say in a very confidential, sincere sort of way: 'I've always been on your side, you know. If you tell me all about it, I give you my word of honour I'll help you.' Her face worked, and she started whimpering and crying and looking all round. I took her hand. I thought: I'll make her know me, or die. I said: 'Look at me. It's Maisie.' She didn't look at me, but she went quiet and —sort of attentive. Then I noticed she'd got on her pearl necklace: I remembered it so well. She always wore it when we were little: her father used to add two pearls a year to it, she'd told us, on every birthday till he died, so you can imagine it was a beauty. She was just the person for pearls. I said: 'Oh, you still wear your lovely pearls. I *am* glad.' She looked at me then, quickly, in a startled way—or puzzled—and fingered them."

Maisie stopped. She threw at me a half defiant, half shy glance and said:

"I used to have a rather idiotic nickname for her."

"What was it?"

"Well . . . I used to call her my Pearly Pet. I reminded her."

"Did she remember?" I said a little awkwardly, concealing a flicker of embarrassment at the soppiness of the epithet.

"I saw her give a smile. Then she said, rather doubtfully: 'They were to go to my eldest daughter.' 'That's me,' I said."

In Maisie's voice rang an echo of the entreaty, questioning, gentleness, passionate assertion with which she had pronounced these two words.

"And then——?" said I eagerly, anticipating the triumph of maternal recognition.

"She began to moan and twist her hands, and said: 'But I have no children.' I said: 'Yes, yes. There's me—and Malcolm. You remember Malcolm.' She said: 'Of course I remember Malcolm. He was such an affectionate little boy,' as if she was talking about somebody else's child she remembered just a little. I said in a joking sort of voice: 'Pearls wouldn't suit Maisie, would they? She's not at all the type for necklaces.' She said consideringly, no, Maisie was a very heavy, unornamental type of little girl, but clever and a strong, good character. You know, the whole time, from the moment she said, rather melodramatically: 'I have no children,' I had the feeling she was pretending to herself and to me—sort of shutting a door, very deep down. I said: 'Cherry would have been the one, she was beautiful like you.' She put her hand up to her mouth and wailed out: *'Oh, Maisie!'* "

I put a finger in my mouth and bit it hard. But Maisie went on, calm:

"She knew me then. I said: 'Yes, darling pet, it is Maisie. And Malcolm's all right too. But Cherry's dead, you know. . . .' I thought it was best to say it at once, quite matter-of-fact and quiet. . . . But it was a mistake." She blew out a great rueful breath. "It set her off again."

"She went—queer again?" I said nervously.

"Queer's not the word. She began to nod and put a finger to her lip and say sssh! she'd tell me something, just a word in my ear, strictly on the q.t.—that sort of thing. I began to get the hang of what madness was like."

"What did she tell you?"

"She whispered that Cherry wasn't dead—he'd got her in there. He was hiding her."

"Oh *God!* . . . I should have died. What did you say?"

"I said yes, yes, I quite understood. Hadn't we better go for a little stroll and talk it over, what was best to do? She seemed to trust me this time, and I walked her off in the opposite direction, along the bank. We walked and walked. . . ."

"Talking to each other?"

"Oh!" said Maisie, groaning at the recollection. "She clutched

270

my arm and gabbled and gabbled, absolute nonsense, about lambs and God and blood and Heaven knows what; and secret rites where babies were taken from their mothers and walled up in cupboards as a sacrifice; oh, and barred windows and plots to get her shut up, and her documents that proved it; and the evil in the world, how she had to suffer it all, the whole damned lot—only she." Maisie paused. "And other startling things . . . I was afraid the people in the inn would wake up and come out to see what was happening; but luckily the weir muffled her. After a bit she began to drag on my arm, and say her head hurt her. I suggested we should go back to her room, and, thank the Lord, she took to the idea. I thought I might get her to bed and she'd sleep it off. Error number two. . . . So back we trundled over the bridge. Needless to say she'd forgotten which was her bedroom, but I guessed which it would be—the best one, looking over the garden, and I took her there. She seemed to be going all weak, she could hardly stand up. I think she'd been on the go for hours and hours, scribbling and walking up and down."

"Was she still talking?"

"No. I'd impressed on her we must be absolutely *dead* quiet, it was a frightfully important piece of stratagem, if we were going to go through all the documents: if someone came and found us it would be fatal. By this time I seemed to be able to will her to do what I wanted."

"You are amazing," I said, low and fervent.

"I told her to lie down till her head was better, I'd stay with her. There were dozens of medicine bottles and pills lying around, and I found some stuff called *Cachets Fèvre* which I knew Sibyl took for headaches, and I gave her two. She swallowed them like a lamb; and then I undressed her and put her to bed. She kept saying: 'Poor Ianthe's so tired,'—like a baby. It seemed queer undressing one's own mother. She was so thin: her hips stuck out and her legs had gone to nothing but bone. It was pathetic. She used to have a perfect figure. I brushed her hair. It used to be thick and dark and glossy and long enough to sit on: she was very vain of it. But now it was thin and grey, and it looked brittle, dead, as if it hadn't had a brush through it for weeks. Also her neck was grubby. I got her into bed. Once or twice she said: 'Maisie,' in a whimpering, petulant sort of voice. Oh yes, and *this* is extraordinary—once she said: 'Tilly.' I could swear she did."

I caught my breath.

"I suppose she imagined she was back to being a little girl, when Tilly looked after her," I said.

"I suppose so. It sounded a bit uncanny." Maisie brooded. "And all the time," she went on, "I had to keep one eye cocked on the garden, in case I missed that Tanya tiptoeing back across the bridge. I went and sat by the window. She never stirred. I thought the headache pill was working and she'd drop off to sleep. It wasn't very long before, to my great relief, I did see Tanya. I was in a stew about having missed her, perhaps, while I was walking mother about. I went and stooped over the bed. She was breathing quite peacefully and evenly. I thought: Thank God, she's off. I'll risk it."

"Risk what?"

"Well, don't you see, I had to do *mutually incompatible things,* my girl. Know what that means? I had to go back to the house with Tanya, in the hope of saving our bacon *there;* and I had to stay with Mother—I'd promised her. Apart from the promise, I'd come to the modest conclusion that I was a Great Healer: that my powers were curing her madness, and if I stuck to it she'd wake up in the morning all serene and unmad again." Maisie suddenly let out a great shout of laughter. "Like Sibyl, isn't it?" She went on laughing and laughing, too much; then checked herself abruptly and said: "God, I was a bloody great green fool!"

"What did you do?"

"My scheme was to see Tanya home as quick as possible, then come straight back. I streaked down like a cat and met Tanya by the bridge. She did get a shock. I never knew before that one could see a person blush by moonlight. I told her to hurry, and as we went along I started explaining everything."

"About your mother too?"

"Yes, I had to. I knew I could trust her. I'd decided anyway that Gil and she and I would have to co-operate. She was simply *horrified*, of course, what with that and the news about Sibyl. We tore back, and then when we got to the garden we started to go quite slowly up towards the house, in case——"

"And was she?"

"She was still there."

"She wasn't!"

"Yes. Sitting now, full in the window. I could just see the outline of her, in a great armchair with a high straight back. Think of her, drawing it up to the window and planting herself in it to keep watch! She must have been there three hours at least. We crept up to Tanya's room, and I was just saying, well, there it was, we must take jolly good care to have our story pat and watch out for traps, when the bell made us jump out of our skins. She had an electric bell connecting with Tanya's room, across the passage, in case she felt ill in the night. There was nothing for it but to go along—and go at once. So we went. There she sat, with a white shawl over her head, and the cloak on. 'Ah,' she said. 'Both of you. Still up?' "

"How did she sound?"

"As mild as milk. You bet! I said we'd been down for a bathe and just got back. 'Ah, delicious,' she said. 'How wise you are to profit by this night.' 'I *thought* I spotted you as I came up the garden,' I said. 'Did you indeed?' she said. 'The moon is so extravagantly brilliant. I rang, Tanya, to ask if you would be so good as to fetch my fan. I left it downstairs. In point of fact I have rung several times within the last hour. But no matter: you were out. I have that unpleasant feeling of suffocation.' Tanya flew for the fan; and I said oughtn't she to go to bed? But she said she'd found her discomfort increased when she lay down, and she preferred to remain where she was. Tanya came back with the fan. She asked Sibyl if she'd like her to stay and fan her. She thanked her politely and said no, it wasn't necessary, she'd like us to go to bed now. Just as we were making off, she said in a gentle way: 'You must have a care how you swim among those water lilies. I should not like you to be under the impression that you could easily extricate yourself, were you to become en-

273

tangled. This applies to you particularly, Maisie. You are a trifle rash and injudicious. The lilies should probably be cut. As soon as I am able, I shall go down to the river and see for myself what needs to be done.' "

"*Oh!*"

"Yes, there was something fishy all right. It was her manners being so extra stately that worried us most. Only we had no time to worry I had to get back, I was in a panic about Mother. I wanted to go alone, in case the bell rang again. It was a ghastly dilemma. However, Tanya refused point-blank to let me go without her, she said there was no knowing, I might need help: she'd just stand below in the garden until I gave her a signal that I was all right, anyway. I couldn't waste precious time arguing." Maisie blew out another great breath. "It's as well she did come."

"Was it?"

"Yes. Because . . . when I got back, everything had blown sky-high."

I dared not speak. All questions died upon my lips. I gazed at her.

"Tanya waited in the garden. If Mother was asleep, I was to wave to her from the window. When I left her to meet Tanya, I'd gone out by the garden door and locked it and put the key in my pocket, so that I could get in again; also, to be certain she was locked in safe. I crept upstairs. I was afraid Monsieur Meunier would wake up and come at me in his nightshirt—but there wasn't a sound. I got to her room and went in. And she wasn't there."

"Not there!"

"Gone. I guessed in a flash what she'd done: jumped for it. There was a little balcony outside her window: she'd jumped from that. My God, my blood did freeze then! The first thought that occurred to me was—she'd gone into the river."

Still I gazed at her, dumb.

"That spurred me on to jump too—and it was no mean jump. Tanya was waiting. We took an attentive squint up and down the river: it seemed remarkably smooth and normal. She said we must go at once to Gil and tell him. So we went, hot-foot. I might have known. . . ."

"She was there?"

"She was there," said Maisie, drawling out each word with a sinister stress. "She was there all right."

"What was she doing?"

"She was smashing up the whole place."

I heard myself faintly groan.

"God knows why I'm telling you all this," said Maisie with sudden fierceness. "I've never told a soul, apart from a garbled version to Auntie Mack. Shall I stop?"

"Please, please go on," I entreated. "If you don't mind too much."

"I must go on," she said, still fierce, "now I've begun." She waited a moment, then went on quietly: "There are two rooms in the mill. First, the enormous studio, and behind it a smaller room where he sleeps—slept. The front door was open. The lights were on in the studio, but it was empty. We heard the sound of glass smashing in his bedroom, and her voice crying and raving. We tried to get in, but the door was locked. We shouted that it was us. We were frightened. He shouted back at us to run round and get in by the bathroom window. So we did. And we went in. He was holding her by the wrists. Her hands were streaming with blood. She'd been smashing the windows. There was broken glass everywhere. I thought he was hurting her. I rushed to her and tried to push him away, to hold her myself. He said: 'Don't be a fool, Maisie.' God, she was strong! He was holding her with all his strength: I didn't realise. All the good I did was to make him lose his balance; and she got loose and made a dive for the jagged window. He caught her again round the knees, and she went down crash on the ground. I dashed and got a towel from the bathroom and tied it round her ankles. But she didn't try to get up. She was pretty well knocked out. She just lay and moaned. I knelt down beside her and put her head in my lap." Maisie stopped abruptly, bit her lip. The difficult blood surged up, made her face dark. In her eyes I saw the glitter of tears. When she spoke again her voice was unsteady. "She looked so terrible. Broken. Like something thrown out for the dustbin. And Gil stood breathing in great gasps, as if he'd run a ten-mile race. The sweat was streaming off him. And wretched Tanya petrified, nearly fainting. I told her to get water and handkerchiefs. I wanted to wash her hands and tie them up. But Gil suddenly came to and took control again. He took Tanya by the shoulders and fairly rapped out orders to her: to run to the village *at once,* as fast as her legs could carry her, and bring the doctor. There wasn't any telephone, you see. He told her what to say: to bring stuff—you know—to shoot into her, a hypodermic. She nodded and flew off. I knew she couldn't be back much under an hour. So there we were. Gil got water in a basin and bathed her forehead and her hands. He was so gentle. He did it much better than I could have. Better than any nurse. He picked out splinters of glass from the cuts and washed them clean with disinfectant and bound them up tight to stop the bleeding. It was a miracle she hadn't cut a vein or an artery; but there was blood everywhere, all over her clothes, and on the floor, and on the curtains."

"Had you stopped—minding blood," I said, "by then?"

Her lips turned down in a grim smile.

"I hadn't stopped at the beginning," she said. "I had by the end. I just *would not.* I . . . He gave me some brandy. Yes, that night cured me. I don't mind blood any more. Considering what a lot of it people have in them and how easily it comes out, it's as well to get used to the look of the stuff. . . . He couldn't help hurting her and she cried bitterly and he talked to her in a soothing, encouraging way. Then we lifted her on to the bed. She was just dazed, not violent or talkative any more. She said thank you to him for bandaging her. She even started to stammer out something—sort of apologising—but he told her to rest and not worry, we'd look after her. I didn't dare speak to him or to her for fear of setting her off again. I sat beside her, and he made her a drink of hot milk and coffee, and I raised her head a little and held the cup to her lips while she sipped it; and he swept up the glass and put the room to rights. There must have been a devilish commotion: the chairs and tables were upside down, and both the lamps smashed. Then he came and looked at her. Her eyes were closed, and she wasn't crying any more. And then he looked at me. And then he gave me a kiss—the first and the last," said Maisie, smiling wryly. "And then he went and sat by the window. It was getting light. The birds were all singing."

She stretched a long, luxurious stretch, arms above her head, and looked at me cloudily, a little shy.

"If you want to know what he looked like," she said, "he looked more handsome than anybody I've ever seen. And if you want to know what I felt like I felt more happy than I'd ever felt in my life, or ever expect to feel again. I dare say that sounds batty to you."

"No," I said truthfully. "Not a bit."

"I thought: I'm not alone with this thing any more. Somehow, it's all going to come out straight. I saw he was thinking about it with all his mind; and nothing else mattered. You may not believe it, but I forgot the whole staggering terribleness of the night; at least, it seemed to melt softly away. I'd got through it; and he was with me. I felt like those birds, opening out all their throats to the light." She paused. "Of course," she added, "it was only one moment in the whole thing. I dare say it was simply reaction. But it seemed real at the time; in fact, it still does. I've never forgotten it. One can't just say feelings are all rot because they don't last—or don't come to anything."

"They didn't come to anything?" I said, mournful; receiving through some sixth sense whose function was to apprehend the intangible sad rejoicing forms of love, a vision of Gil and Maisie in that dawn; and in the same moment, feeling it blown upon by the sterile breath of mortality.

"Of course not," she said, a little sharp and scornful. "Nothing came out straight. Everything got worse." She stopped; then suddenly sat up straight and said with loud emphasis: "But I made a vow then . . . a solemn vow . . . that if ever there was anything I could do for him, ever, in all our lives, to show my gratitude at finding a person like him—equal to everything—I'd do it. And that's true anyway."

Presently I broke in upon her brooding to say timidly:

"Did the doctor come?"

"He came. I don't know how long it was before he did turn up. It seemed ages; but in another way far sooner than I wanted. He came on horseback. He did all his rounds on horseback, which was rather nice. I wonder if he still does. . . . He's a little old freak with gimlet eyes behind very strong steel-rimmed spectacles and a dirty straggly grey beard and a voice like a rasp. He's got an enormous head and tiny little legs and a paunch in between like a pumpkin. He's frightfully clever, and *cynical*—my word! He never seemed to give a damn what happened to human beings, but cure their contemptible bodies he could and would, because that was his job. When we heard him arrive, Gil asked me to go away: he thought the fewer people about the better while he explained what had happened. He wanted to keep me out of it as much as possible, for fear of awkwardness with Sibyl. She was his favourite patient. He was always popping in to see her, and they'd grate and rattle away about literature and philosophy for hours on end, and say afterwards that each was the most remarkable intelligence the other one had ever met. Gil promised me to keep the secret if he could—of who Mother was, I mean. I don't know what he did say. I went and made some coffee in the kitchen and Tanya turned up while I was making it. She'd run all the way back, and she was dead beat. I could hear voices in the bedroom, Gil's and the doctor's, and then *her* voice breaking out; getting worked up again. I heard her shriek out: '*The Heads! The Heads!*' She sounded in the most extreme state of horror; but I forced myself not to go in. Then she started gabbling in French to the doctor, crying out over and over again: '*Attendez, Monsieur, attendez que je vous explique.*' But I couldn't hear what she did *explique,* if anything. After a bit she stopped. Tanya, who'd been sitting hunched up taut in her chair, *not* blocking her ears with all her might, let out a great long breath of relief and said that whatever the doctor had put into her must have started to work. We listened. And there was nothing more. It was nearly seven o'clock before he went away. We stayed in the kitchen, and Gil came in, and we all drank coffee. He told us he'd asked the doctor to call at the inn and make

some story for Madame Meunier: that she was an old patient of
his from Paris who'd had a breakdown and come down here to
be under his care and get the benefit of country air. Unfortunately she'd over-estimated her strength and gone out for an
early morning walk and been taken with faintness just by Gil's
door and called to him for help. Gil had been rather alarmed
and come on his motor-bike—he had one—and knocked him up,
etcetera, etcetera. She was resting now and would stay where she
was until he called again. We had to say something, because they'd
have presumably made a hullabaloo when they found her room
empty; and Rosette, their girl, always came in in the middle of
the morning to clean and sweep for him. I said: 'What about the
window?' He said: 'Don't worry, I'll fix it in no time.' And he did.
When I came back later, I found he'd taken out the broken pane
and found another one in an outhouse somewhere, and fitted it
in. He can do anything with his hands. Then he told us to go
straight back to the house and get some sleep if we could, and
not come again till the afternoon. Then we'd decide what to do.
He said she was heavily drugged and wouldn't stir for hours. I
went in and had one more peep at her. She might have been
dead. . . . And I wish she had been. Her face looked . . . it
looked as if it had ashes and cobwebs on it. I told him I was
awfully sorry I'd pushed him. Then we went back. On the way,
I asked Tanya if she loved Gil very much. She said yes. That
night she'd asked him to marry her."

"*She'd* asked *him?*"

"Yes. Why not?"

"Oh well. . . . What did he say?"

"He'd said no. He'd explained something to her, she said, that
she didn't know."

"What was it, I wonder?"

"She didn't say. Something about Sibyl, I guessed."

"Oh." Nameless vistas opened on me, lurid, obscured with
vapours; closed again. I turned from them. "Was she sad?"

"I didn't ask. She said he'd told her he loved her too. But she
saw she'd been silly, it wouldn't do. That's all she said. She was
quite calm."

279

"It was nice that he said he loved her too."

"Very nice."

"Did you get back without Mrs. Jardine knowing?"

"I couldn't say. There was nobody about on the way to our rooms. I went to bed and I slept till ten. When I woke up, I heard Tanya practising scales. For a moment I thought it was all a dream."

She got up, crossed the room and opened a cupboard.

"What about a cup of chocolate?" she said. "I found some—the real stuff. And there's plenty of milk. Do you want some? Or do you want to go to bed?"

I said yes to the first query, a passionate no to the second.

"I only asked," she said, "because you look somewhat bemused. It's long past your bedtime."

I watched her make a rich mixture in a saucepan and pour it into two breakfast cups.

"Twice the quantities stated on the label is always my motto," she said.

It was inexpressibly delicious. When we had sipped about half, I said:

"Could you go on?"

"Yes," she said, as if in faintly ironic meditation. "We'd better go on to the end, now we're fortified. . . . I hung about the house, and tried to read a book. It was roasting hot. Sibyl didn't emerge from her room, and I didn't go in to see her. I got more and more restless. About five I told Tanya I must go down. She said I must go and see Sibyl before I went; that although she was being quite ordinary on the surface, she seemed—as if she was bubbling up underneath. So I went. She was lying on her long couch, propped up; she looked an icy blue colour, her eyes very bright. I said I was off to the river, and if it got late, I hoped she wouldn't mind if I stayed and got supper off Madame Meunier. I did do that sometimes."

"What did she say?"

"She said: 'Ah yes. Thank you, my child, I like to know your plans. I have your word, have I not, that you will give me no cause for anxiety in the matter of those water lilies?' " Maisie chuckled. "You know the way she talks."

"You do imitate her marvellously," I said.

"I promised; and she said: 'I cannot think why, I have those plants inextricably in my mind these last few days.' Then she gave me a ravishing smile and told me to go along: it would give her pleasure to think of me refreshing my limbs in the cool shady water. Just as I got to the door, she said: 'Should you see Gil, tell him I expect him as we arranged. I shall just stay quietly where I am till he comes to carry me down.' "

"Oh!"

"Yes. I asked her if there wasn't anything I could do for her. I suppose it was guilt that made me feel—sort of affectionate. She said no, just the message to Gil. So I went. I arrived in a bath of sweat to find Gil working as usual in the studio. He said she was very drowsy. The doctor had been again, and shot some more stuff into her, and said it was absolutely essential that she shouldn't be moved till her nervous system had had a complete rest. 'How long?' I said. He shrugged his shoulders. 'What are we to do?' I said. He said he didn't know—yet. He told me to prepare myself and be sensible. It was a hundred to one she would have to go into—a place, to be cured. He said our duty was to try to discover where she'd been, who'd been responsible for her during these years. He asked how much I knew. I said: only that she'd been in a convent somewhere. He said that was all he knew too. I asked him if he thought she'd been in a—place before, and he said undoubtedly she had been. I asked if she'd given him that document with it all written down. He said, oh yes, she'd given it to him all right but he was afraid it wasn't very helpful."

"Why not?"

"Because it was all gibberish. Interesting, he said, rather than informative. Poor Mother, think of her scribbling away at it for *hours*. He said the doctor had taken it away to study. I asked him if she'd mentioned to him a plot to get her shut up. He said yes, he'd had all that; and it meant she *had* been shut up. He said the only person to hand who could presumably give us information was Sibyl. I said Sibyl *must not* be told. He said: 'She may have to be.' I gave him her message, and he said: 'Then she smells a rat already.' I said I thought she certainly did, but I wasn't sure what sort: I rather suspected it was about him and Tanya. His eyebrows went up and he whistled. I really began to be awfully desperate. I saw what a fix we were in. He'd still got the door between the two rooms locked, so I went round and looked at her through the half-closed shutters. She still lay for dead, flat on her back. She had her poor bandaged hands folded on her chest. I forgot to tell you the doctor had had to put stitches in one cut, down the palm. Then I came back and sat on the step with Gil. I asked him why he kept that door locked; and he said to prevent her at all costs from getting into the studio, because . . . because, he said, the statues and heads were more than she could stand."

"You mean . . ." An inspiration flashed upon me: "Did she think they were *alive?*"

"Not exactly. I don't know how to explain to make you understand. She seemed to think—they were *hiding things that were alive.* People, I mean. That he was a terrible—sort of witch doctor who was making stone masks over living people's faces—and setting them up round the room—like cursed things—to work evil. Something like that." She drew a heavy breath, and added slowly: "A circle of evil round the child in the middle. She thought there was a live child cased up in the marble."

"*Cherry?*" I breathed.

She nodded.

"It was when she came the first time, to ask the way to the Post Office, that the—the germ got planted in her."

"I haven't quite understood what made her come at all, the first time. Had she seen the statues through the window?"

"No." Maisie's lip and nostril stretched in a way that made me think of Mrs. Jardine. "She'd seen Gil come into the inn that morning for lunch; and he'd caught her fancy. At least that's what he gave me to understand in a modest way. She came to visit him with the enterprising notion of making advances to him. She suggested coming in at once, *tout de suite,* to live with him, I gathered. She made no bones about it at all."

"How awful!" I exclaimed, deeply shocked.

"Oh, do you think so?" said Maisie, sharp, raising her eyebrows like Mrs. Jardine, as if surprised. "Why?"

Stung this time to defend myself, I said obstinately:

"It doesn't generally happen that way round, that I do know. I'm certain the gentleman usually does the asking."

"Well, I don't know much about it," she said mildly.

"In fact, till you told me about Tanya, I didn't know the—the lady ever did."

It struck me that that made two proposals to Gil in one day: surely a phenomenon. I did not say so.

"Heavens, my good girl, that was absolutely different," she said, still agreeable. "No. I did feel rather upset, as a matter of fact, when he told me. But he explained to me it was just part of her not being normal. I began to piece things together then."

"What sort of things?"

"Things I remembered." Her manner was abrupt, and I knew better than to press her. After a pause she went on: "At first, he said, she was just rather scatter-brained and embarrassing. But he dealt with her all right, and she dropped all that quite suddenly, and began to ask about his work in an intelligent way. She always had very good taste. She'd been brought up to know a lot about art. Then I suppose something went snap for good in her head: probably from the shock when he told her—you know, when he said the name Charity Mary Thomson. He said she looked scared then, and vacant; and then put out her hand like I told you and touched the figure; and then muttered something. He said he was pretty certain, when he got rid of her, that she'd be back again. He thought it was just a nuisance he might have to cope with until it flashed on him, up at Sibyl's, who she probably was; and then he was appalled. He explained to me that after she had left him her mind must have gradually got everything more and more mixed up: him and the statue and Cherry and the heads. She mixed it all with terrible experiences, he said, that she couldn't face remembering and kept deep down in her, corked up. And the cork blew out. Do you understand?"

"Like it does in dreams?"

"I suppose so—yes. Everything *turned into something else;* so she was quite lost. He said . . . you see, in one's mind an object can never be just itself: it connects up with other things that remind you of it for some reason, things you've seen or remembered, sometimes from years and years ago when you were a child. For instance, whenever I come into a dark room at night and see firelight flickering, I think of being ill in bed when I was little."

"Oh yes! Me too."

"Watching the patterns it made on the night nursery ceiling. So that, in a way, I'm in this dark room and back in the night nursery, both at the same time. I'm split. And if I'd been very unhappy or frightened in the night nursery, it would come over me again, although I was standing calmly years and years later in a different room, and had forgotten, perhaps, the reason for my fright or sadness. But because I'm sane it would be only for a minute, and I'd know what was happening and could sort out the links and brush it all aside. But when people go off their rockers, all the links get jumbled up or break altogether. Then they get real, complete delusions. Probably we'd never find out, he said, why that room of his should be the last straw for her. But I can see, can't you, that if you were barmy, a room full of cold, silent, absolutely still stone figures and casts and heads would be *terrifying*? It would be like the Chamber of Horrors. You'd think they were all threatening—or mocking—or keeping some ghastly secret behind their mouths and eyes."

Maisie's eyes dilated, her voice sank low, vibrating. A sympathetic dew broke out on me.

"That's why she screamed out: 'The heads!'" I said faintly.

She nodded.

"And there was Cherry in the middle of it, quite changed and turned to stone, or covered up with stone. But it was Cherry, *because he'd said so,* and she'd got that into her head. When she came back in the middle of the night, it was to get Cherry."

I let out a groaning breath.

"Is that what he said?"

She nodded.

"That document I caught her with was really meant as a sort of blind—an excuse for getting in. And to—sort of *propitiate* this

284

terrifically powerful person she thought he was. Partly a kind of
—counter-magic to him, partly an absolutely water-tight justification, *so she thought,* of what she was going to do. At least that's
how he explained it to me, but it was difficult to follow, and I
can't make it a bit clear. I believe now she was only pretending
to be quiet and go to sleep when I left her in the inn. Mad people are very cunning. Anyway, I felt—simply terrible when he
told me she'd come for Cherry. He said that figure I told you
about in the group, the bowed-down, shrouded, mother or death
one behind the child, seemed to be the chief trouble. She thought
it was—was holding Cherry prisoner, like under a deadly spell;
and the reason why it was so terrible and so powerful was that
*its face was hidden.* She was transfixed by terror of it. As if it
was something too ghastly to show itself. She kept clutching him
and pointing at it and panting out: 'There! There!' And then
she looked wildly over her shoulder—and she saw it again, on the
stand."

"How do you mean?" I cried, aghast.

"That head of Sibyl covered with a cloth that she'd asked him
about. She thought it was the same Horror again, *pretending not
to be there,* stuck up there to watch itself—to watch Cherry . . .
I can't explain. I suppose *two* of it made it doubly bad: if there
were two of it, there might be hundreds of it, popping up wherever she looked. She was gibbering with fear. So he thought the
best thing to do was to go in a very quiet, ordinary way and take
the cloth off, to prove to her it was nothing but a harmless bit of
clay modelling. So he did. He went and lifted the cloth off and
showed her the face."

Silence.

"Did she recognise it?" I said.

"She recognised it."

"What happened then?"

"It was the finish. At the top of her lungs she shrieked out:
*'There she is! There! I knew it! Kill her! Kill her!'* And in a flash
she seized up one of his modelling knives, and rushed at it and
jabbed and jabbed. . . . 'It must have been a good likeness anyway,' said Gil."

Maisie burst into laughter, and I laughed too. We both went on shaking for about half a minute.

"Did she jab it to bits?" I said. "Spoil it absolutely?"

"Pretty well. It wasn't there any more. He said he'd broken it up afterwards: he thought it was best to destroy all trace of it. . . . He let her go on knifing it for a bit, and then he told her that that was about enough, she'd quite killed her off, would she give him the knife now, so that he could clean it? He had a nasty moment, he said, thinking she might start on *his* face; but she was more or less exhausted by her effort with Sibyl, and she gave it back like a lamb. He spoke to her by her name—Ianthe—in a cheerful, friendly way, and persuaded her into the other room and locked the door between. She got quite quiet. The only thing she said was: 'Is she dead?' He wasn't sure if she meant Cherry or Sibyl. He said yes, she was. She said: 'You swear it? You swear she won't ever come back?' So then he knew she meant Sibyl; but of course he had to swear it. They had a chat about this and that—very tricky for him, she was quite off it: he agreed with her how much more satisfactory things would be now. After a bit it began to dawn on her she hadn't got Cherry yet, and she started to boil up again—and went for the door, and then for the window, and him. . . . And then we turned up. The rest you know."

"Yes," I said, sighing. "Though I keep on wondering if I'm dreaming you're telling me such things."

"I said to Gil: 'Well, whatever Sibyl may have to be told, it's obvious she mustn't *see* her.' You see, what with Mother thinking she'd done her in, and having it sworn to by Gil, it would be unfortunate all round, I saw, if Sibyl rose from the dead and appeared before Mother, as fit as ever. I thrashed about with schemes for taking her away myself as soon as she was able to travel. But Gil said he counted on me to be sensible and not turn out one *more* of this family who thought she could bring off what was impossible. I saw the force of that. I said I really must apologise for the frightful nuisance and embarrassment we'd brought on him, and I did want to thank him. He told me to shut up. 'Not that I don't simply detest having your mother in my bedroom,' he said. 'But I guarantee my corpse in the last ditch.' We drank some lovely cold white wine; and then we agreed he'd better go up to the house, to Sibyl, and leave me. He said I needn't be afraid anything would happen while he was away. I wasn't afraid. We decided we must simply concentrate on keeping quiet for to-night, and make up our minds to-morrow what was to be done. He told me to help myself to eggs to make an omelette, and then he went away. I couldn't be bothered to cook, I ate some rolls and butter; and then I went softly into the bedroom, and sat in the armchair. . . . When he got back I don't know, because, though I tried to keep awake, I went bang off to sleep and didn't wake up till seven o'clock next morning. It was queer coming to with a start and seeing her half sitting up in bed, watching me. I said: 'Hallo, Mother,'—I did say it then, I was sleepy; and she said— what do you think she said?"

"What?"

"She said: 'Maisie, you shouldn't sleep with your mouth open, you've been snoring.' "

"She didn't!" I said joyfully. "Just like that?"

"Absolutely. Just having a long cool stare at me, and teasing me, like Malcolm or anybody might. I made some sort of a joke, and she giggled. I don't know *when* I'd last heard her laugh in that cheerful sort of way. It reminded me of that time in the London hotel, when that Tilly came. I heard her giggling in the next room with Tilly, while she was dressing to go out. She said she was hungry, so I got her some breakfast and she enjoyed it and polished off every scrap; and I washed her face and tidied her up a bit, and she smiled and chatted all the time. She complained that her head tickled, so I said would she like me to wash her hair, and she said yes, very much. So I helped her out of bed—she was remarkably spry—and I took her to the bathroom and washed it in the basin with some of Gil's hairwash, and gave her head a jolly good massage. I said: 'That'll clear away the cobwebs,' and she laughed and said it was what Tilly used to say. Then I took her out and sat her in the sun to dry it. I managed to take a peep through the studio window and saw Gil lying fast asleep on the couch. I put her chair round the corner, well out of sight of him.

She looked like a little girl with her hair all loose over her shoulders. And that's how she behaved," added Maisie, looking slightly grim. "She was a little girl of six, and I was her nurse."

I said timidly:

"Did it seem—sort of—all right?"

"Yes—and no. No. She seemed a bit on the silly side. Silly and *placid*. Considering everything, it wasn't exactly natural to be so carefree. But I was so relieved, I didn't worry about that. I decided it was the first step towards recovery."

"Didn't she mention anything? About what had happened?"

"Not a syllable. She looked at her bandaged hands in an interested way, but she didn't refer to them. She didn't ask whose house she was in or where Gil was or anything. It was as if the whole thing had been sponged clean off her mind and she was starting again from scratch."

"Did she treat you as if—as if she knew she was your mother?"

"I can't say she did," said Maisie, sardonic. "Merely as if I was familiar to her, and could be trusted to—to keep things bright and jolly."

"She didn't talk about Cherry?"

"Oh, dear me, no. Never mentioned her. Nor Malcolm. And of course I knew better by this time than to refer to them. No, I just let her rip. She wanted to teach me German words—most peculiar. And she sang a little German song. In between times she sat staring, rather vacant, but not in the least dejected. She carried on as if she was having a nice holiday with somebody she took for granted would look after her. The only thing I didn't like was that now and then I felt her watching me when I wasn't looking at her; and directly I did, she'd look away. She wouldn't meet my eyes."

"Oh yes——"I began eagerly, recalling the eyes of Ianthe, fixed, sliding aside, in Florence, in Bohemia. I checked myself.

"Yes," agreed Maisie, unsuspicious. "It's a symptom. I realised it was queer, but all the same I didn't bother about it. The great thing was to feel so *certain* there was no violence left in her; and that I could keep up *my* part in this new sort of act, as easy as kiss my hand. After about an hour of it she said she wanted her own brush and comb, and wanted to put on a clean frock. So I decided to risk taking her back to the inn. I thought the Meuniers would probably be busy in the back regions; and as it was the middle of the week there weren't likely to be many people coming in. I looked in again through the studio window, and saw Gil still fast asleep. I told her to wait a moment and tiptoed in and scribbled on a big piece of paper to say where we were, and everything was perfectly all right, no need to worry, and left it propped up against a jar on his table. She never asked me what I'd been doing, or gave so much as a twitch of the head as we went by the door. She still had her hair down her back, and she would stop to pick wild flowers in the bank; and on the bridge she stopped for ages to look at the shoals of little fishes. She simply delighted in them. I told her to hurry up and change, and I'd take her on the river. If she couldn't manage to do up her dress by herself, I'd see to it when she came down. I thought I'd better not go up with her in case somebody saw us and thought it peculiar. I went and untied our boat and brought it up to the landing stage. While I was waiting, Pierre Meunier came down and said 'Bonjour,' and told me his wife had gone to the market. I told him I was going to take the English lady for a row. He nodded in what I *thought* rather a meaning way—but all he said was, ah, her health was re-established then; and I said yes, and that I'd made friends with her. And he said it must be agreeable for her to meet some compatriots; and then he said: '*Alors, bon voyage, Mademoiselle,*' and went away. And what if anything the Meuniers saw, or guessed, of what happened before, or what came after, I know no more than the dead. . . . She came down in a blue embroidered muslin frock, and was as pleased as Punch when I admired it. I did her up at the back and she called me clumsy. She brought a blue ribbon for me to tie her hair back. She asked how she looked and I said lovely. She said rather petulantly she was sure I'd made a horrid bow. So I had. But she didn't look too bad. And off we went for a jolly row."

"*Was* it?" I inquired, not optimistic.

"Well, taking it all round, it *was*. Yes, I must say we had a pleasant morning. She was all smiles and smoothness, and she examined every detail of the little houses as we passed, and made remarks about them. She said: 'I do like this place, I'd like to live here. I've always wanted to live by a little river full of cresses and reeds and rushes and little fishes.' She talked about a wonderful farm in Bohemia where she'd stayed once when she was a girl; and a stream where she used to go fishing. I suppose that's where she learnt German—though it's funny she never sang those German songs to us when we were little. . . . The only what you might call realistic moment was when she glanced sideways at me and off again, and said suddenly: 'That man won't come again, will he?' 'Which man?' I said; and she said: 'The bad one with the beard.' "

"The doctor."

" 'Mm.' I said perhaps he would just come to see that her hands were getting better; and she said: 'I don't want him. Keep him away. *You* can do my hands.' I said casually I thought he was really quite kind, it was only his beard that made him look nasty; but much to my relief she changed the subject. She said she was hungry again, so I rowed back, and when we got to the landing stage, there was Gil, looking very forbidding. He said good-morning to her politely, and gave her a hand out; and then on the pretext of helping me get the boat round into the boathouse, he jumped in beside me and muttered in a furious voice: 'Maisie, you must be mad.' I saw he'd been frightfully anxious. I said: 'But she's all right, I promise you. It's all over. You can see for yourself.' He said it was time to stop playing with the situation. 'Well, what do you suggest?' We snapped at each other rather. He said: 'To-day, Sibyl must be told.' 'Who's to tell her?' I said. 'I shall,' he said. But," added Maisie slowly, "he didn't.' "

I waited, silent. She went on:

"We landed from the boathouse—it's a wet boathouse with steps leading into the garden—and joined her. She stood, and looked up at him very, very searchingly. Just as much as she avoided looking at me she looked deep at him with her enormous dark eyes. I wonder what was in her mind. . . . He said in a friendly formal way he hoped she would have no objection to his joining us for lunch. As a regular customer at this inn, he would like to introduce her to the delicious *cuisine*. She said: 'Do you live here?' and he said he was living temporarily near by. She said wistfully: 'I wish I lived here. It's such a gentle place.' It sounded affected, I thought she was showing off to him. He said he'd go in and see Madame Meunier about an extra special lunch, and she and I went and sat in the summer-house. And gradually the change began to come over her."

"What sort of change?"

"She got silent. She didn't smile any more. She stared at the table and looked dejected. When the food came she wouldn't touch it."

"Oh dear!"

"What a meal, my God! Gil and I exchanged some remarks about the weather. My heart began to sink into my boots. Not that she was violent or suspicious or anything. Just miserable. Suddenly she raised her eyes to Gil again, and said like an anxious pleading child: 'I *wish* I could stay here. I *do* want to.' "

"What did he say to that?"

"Oh . . . Poor Gil! He put his head in his hands and ruffled his hair up, thinking hard. Then he began to ask her questions in a very kind way—where she'd come from, what sort of life she'd been living, had she any friends—questions like that."

"Did she answer?"

"She answered quite simply and straightforwardly. She said that she'd had a very unhappy life for a long time; and that in the end she'd tried to kill herself. She said it was three years ago, but she didn't go into it. She'd been very ill," she said, and was nursed by nuns in a convent, somewhere in the south of France; and that when she got better she wanted to stay there, and never come out into the world again. So she stayed. She'd been very happy and peaceful at first, she said, and felt sure she had the vocation to become a nun and end her days there. But after a bit she began to have doubts and to lose her faith, and wanted to get back to the world; and finally they turned her out. When she came out she didn't know what to do. She went to Switzerland—Geneva, I think—where she thought she still had some friends. I've heard about them. The husband was a Cambridge don, and she lived with them for a time before she married, and went out to India with them. She was very fond of them, I think. But she found that the husband had died ages ago, and the wife had left Switzerland and gone away, she didn't know where. Then she decided to go to Paris to find a man who'd once loved her—who she thought would be glad to see her again. She called him Marcel."

"That one!" I exclaimed. "That you took a dislike to in Paris that time."

"What a memory you've got. That one. And if I could hunt him down I'd murder him."

"What did he do?"

"Fled from her like the plague, I suppose. She said: 'He didn't want me. . . .' Well, she had changed. She'd lost her looks. I don't know who he is, or anything about him. I've just got it stuck in my mind, I don't know why, that he was a very prosperous well-known worldly man—a famous actor or something. Of course he'd be annoyed to have a wreck like her hanging round, doing him no credit."

"What did she do then?"

"She lived with men, I think. Ones she picked up, who gave her money." Maisie paused. "She didn't say so in so many words, she was very vague about it—or confused. And we didn't ask her, of course. But out of the blue, staring at Gil, she said suddenly that once, in Paris, she met what she called a terrible sad man: an Indian; and he had a skin disease; and in the whole wide world he had nobody at all. She stayed with him, she said, because he was so much—lower down than she was; and while she was with him she didn't need to pity herself. She was better off than *someone*. But he disappeared one day and never came back again."

"*He* left *her?*"

"Perhaps," said Maisie slowly, "he preferred not to be pitied. Or perhaps he killed himself."

"Was she left absolutely alone after that?"

"I suppose so."

"She must be very brave."

"She was always brave," said Maisie, pleased with me. "Gil said the same. He wanted to give her a bit of conceit of herself." She paused; then added, judicial: "Not that it was really necessary. She sounded rather proud of it all. I think it's only in books that women are ashamed of being prostitutes. Her idea was to make herself interesting to Gil—dramatic, important."

"What did she do next?" I said, matter-of-fact, hoping to conceal shock.

"What she told *him* was that she realised then that it was time to change her life—that she knew that *work* was the only real salvation. She decided to take up teaching again, she said. She told him all about her super qualifications, and how any seat of learning would be more than pleased to have her on their staff. But first she wanted to write a novel about her experiences— that's why she'd come down here: to dash off a stunning novel. Funny how writer's blood will out."

"What? I thought she'd come to——" I saved myself. "But she didn't want to say that, I suppose."

"Oh no. She'd washed all that out. It was only later, as I told you, that I found out she'd written to Auntie Mack for news of us. *And* begged her for a small loan. Which Auntie Mack sent by return. No—I'm perfectly *convinced* the real reason why she came down, poor thing, was to visit Cherry's grave in secret. And then, I expect, she meant to come on to England and see Malcolm and me."

"I'm certain that's what she meant to do," I said earnestly.

"But it turned out she had too much to face when she got there: too many memories, I suppose, too many shocks. It brought on her madness again. And now she'd got a new brainwave: not to go away. To settle down where she was."

"To be near you?" I hazarded.

"Near *me*? Good God, no!" said Maisie, with a coarse bark of laughter. "Presently she leaned over to Gil and whispered confidentially: 'I do wish this girl would go away.'"

"Meaning *you*?"

"Meaning me."

I writhed in my chair.

"And then we saw Tanya. She was starting to cross the bridge, and Gil called out to her. She did look staggered when she saw us. She stayed at the bridge and beckoned to me. I went down to her, and told her the position as quickly as I could. And she said there was trouble brewing up at the house: I must go back immediately. Sibyl had appeared at lunch, on the war-path. The fact that I was down *again* at the river had been ill received. She'd said: 'If that obsessed creature cannot be weaned from her addiction, I must personally inspect the water-weeds this very afternoon. I do not wish a fatality to mar her design of acquiring gills.' "

Once more, I could not refrain from laughter.

"At least, I bet that's what she said. I wasn't present. Tanya also said she'd remarked in a sharp though casual way that she presumed I had returned some time last night to lay my limbs on terra firma. Tanya said, oh yes, of course. She'd ruffled up my bed, she told me, to make it look slept in. I asked if Sibyl had rung her bell in the night. She said yes, twice. And that the second time she'd asked her to open the shutters wide so that she could see the moon; and said in a gentle reflective sort of way: 'This summer moonlight has an intoxicating quality. I expect you find it so.' "

"*Oh!*"

"Yes. Tanya had managed to get away herself by pretending she was going up to the dressmaker in the village for a fitting. I said I couldn't possibly leave Gil to cope, as things were turning out now. We paced despairingly back to them, absolutely stumped. No sooner had we reached the table than——"

Maisie stopped dead, as if suddenly choked.

"What?" I murmured, in fearful trepidation.

She sketched a curious gesture, holding up her hands.

"She did like this—Mother—to Tanya. She held her hands up and said plaintively: 'Oh please, would you see to my hands? They do hurt me.' And she began to pull at the bandages and tear them off. Tanya was awfully good. She said at once in a bright way: 'I expect you'd like them bathed again. We'll go and do that in a few minutes. Just for now, let me do them up again a bit looser. I expect the bandages were too tight, and made you uncomfortable.' And she did them up again very deftly, talking like a kind practical trained nurse.

"Mother fastened vampirish eyes on her and said: 'You'll look after me, won't you? I know you're kind. You've got such a good face.' Then," said Maisie in a light voice, "she looked at me over her shoulder, an awful vindictive look, and she said: 'That girl is very cruel. I've been in such terrible pain and she wouldn't do anything for me. Send her away.'"

I looked down, down at the kitchen floor. The blood-tide of shame, mounting into my head, seemed about to burst me open, or sink me beneath the tiles. Never, I thought, could I look up, meet Maisie's eyes again.

"Perhaps you don't know," said Maisie, "that when people go mental they nearly always turn against their nearest and—their nearest relations. It's one of the first signs."

"Oh yes, of course," I said, with huge relief, raising my head after all. "I've heard that."

"Oh, you have. I hadn't at the time. If I had, I might not have been such a fool. As it was, it rather took the wind out of my sails. Gil put his arm into mine and led me a little way off and said: 'Darling Maisie, you must go. You can't do anything here just now. Go at once; and tell Sibyl as best as you can. She'll come immediately with you, I expect. I'd like to spare you this, but you see that I must stay here.' I said I supposed the shock might kill her, but he said no, it wouldn't. He said he and Tanya would take Mother back to the mill and try to plug some pills into her that the doctor had left. He expected the doctor quite soon anyway. So I left them and started back for the house."

In some inexpressible way, Maisie expressed in her voice the dragging, beaten, yet urgent way she had forced her feet, one step after another, up the long slope, through the gardens, up the terrace steps, up into Mrs. Jardine's house.

"Sibyl was in the hall. Dressed to go out, with her big white straw garden hat on, and a blue veil over it, tied under her chin. Remarkable sight. She said: 'Ah, Maisie. You appear very much *à propos*. I have ordered the pony carriage, and my intention was to ask Blaise to drive me down to the river.' Blaise was a nice groom they had. 'But now you have come you will perhaps do me the great kindness of accompanying me in his stead. I do not feel altogether equal to taking the reins myself. . . .' So there she was, all prepared, with her nose lifted as if she could smell the battle from afar. As I knew she would be."

"And then," I said, putting my head down into my hands and closing my eyes, "you told her."

"No," said Maisie. "I didn't tell her."

After a moment I looked up at her. She was staring fixedly at nothing, her face expressionless.

I repeated:

"You didn't tell her."

"I said: 'All right, I'm ready. Is the trap round?' She'd got this old-fashioned trap with yellow wheels she used to drive round the lanes in, with an adorable pony. It *was* a pretty little comical turn-out. She said Tanya had gone to the village, and I said: 'Oh yes. For her fitting.' And we set off. . . . I loved driving that trap. It's a long winding way down by the road. We scarcely spoke. Once she gave me a piercing look and said: 'You are flushed. Have you a fever?' I said of course I hadn't. She said: 'You are accustomed, I know, to going hatless, but the sun is unusually powerful. To succumb to a heat-stroke, even for a few days, would interfere with your pleasures, so it would be sensible, would it not, to take a few elementary precautions?' I said I was all right. The word 'pleasures' struck me as amusing."

Silence.

"Well, *what could I have said?*" burst out Maisie, savage. "What? *What?* . . . 'Oh, I nearly forgot to mention, Sibyl: you'll find Ianthe down there with Gil and Tanya. And by the way, she's mad.' "

I shook my head despairingly.

"Break it to her gently, I suppose you'd say. 'Sibyl dear, I must prepare you for a great shock. We've been deceiving you, but it was entirely out of consideration for you. Now we're in a proper fix; we need your invaluable assistance. It's a little matter of an

asylum for someone you used to know slightly.' I suppose that's
how *you'd* have put it?"

I was dumb.

"O-o-o-oh!" she cried out—a long exhalation of breath like a
groan of mingled misery and exasperation, loud, then dying away.
Then: "No," she said, in a normal voice, "I should have known
how to do it. I should have said . . . Never mind what I should
have said. I didn't say it. I didn't care any more what happened,
you see. I thought: 'Let them all blow up.' There wasn't any
point any more in trying to keep things going, or bursting myself
to find a way out. . . . Seeing that *she'd* turned against me, I
mean . . ."

"Yes, I do see," I said, sympathetic. "I'd have felt the same.
Even—even though——" Maisie's eyes turned on me, sharpening
ominously, and I began to flounder—"I might have realised she
didn't mean what she said."

"The point is," she said witheringly, "if you'd felt the same
you'd have been a fool, like I was: more than that: a criminal
idiot. I put myself and my wretched hurt feelings first, see?—so
I decided to take it out on *her*—on Sibyl. I deliberately decided
to let it all go to blazes. And as long as I live, I shall never forgive
myself. Because, with a million to one odds against her, she behaved well. I don't like people to behave better than me when
things are ticklish. Especially her." She stopped, sniffed, shrugged;
then added: "But that's a mere trifle. The thing that goes on—
scorching me is—is a different matter altogether." Her voice
dragged. She added with an effort: "If I'd—prepared her, the
final—thing that happened—needn't have happened. Perhaps."

"What was it?" I said, making my voice as flat and impersonal
as possible.

"We drove down, on that glorious sunny afternoon. I drove
into the back yard of the inn and took the pony out of the
shafts and tied him up in the shade of a lovely big chestnut tree.
I asked her if she wouldn't like to go in and rest for a bit, but
she said she preferred to get her business over first, and have a
word with the Meuniers afterwards; and she went marching
through the garden, over the bridge, with me in tow. You know

how she flashes her eyes round, noticing details, awfully brisk and busy—picking out one rose in the hedge and admiring it, spotting a microscopic wild flower, or an almost invisible bird, and naming it—to teach you. Well, that was going on, all as usual. The worst choked-up bits of the stream were just beyond the mill-house. She strolled along, deciding how much must be cut, and demonstrating how she was going to show Pierre the proper way to do it, with a bill-hook bound on to a pole—just *so.* . . . You can imagine it. . . . Well, there isn't much more to tell."

Silence.

"You came to the mill?" I said.

"We came to the mill. I know I began to be very voluble and loud—in case there was any noise going on, to drown it. She looked at me rather surprised. Gil was standing in the open doorway—he'd seen us coming, I suppose. . . . I can see her now, going towards him smiling a great triumphant smile to think how unexpected and how welcome she would be, and how he was standing there all joyful to receive her. She went towards him with her head lifted, feeling extra beautiful in the shadow of her big hat. He stood there and watched her. He looked very grave and intent. When she came near he put out his hands and took hers and drew her in, and said in a low voice: 'Darling, how are you? It was good that you could come at once. The doctor is here, waiting to consult you. He thinks it would be advisable——' And then he stopped short, or she interrupted, I don't know which. Anyway, she might have been mowing him down with that sickle, the way her voice cut, saying: 'What are you talking about?' And her eyes opened, opened on him, icy, like wild crystals. And I said to Gil: 'I haven't told her.' Then there was the sound of voices in the next room, a wailing one and a deep one. She said: 'Whose are those voices?' She listened, her eyes darting round the room as if—— Then she said: 'Ianthe!' "

"Called it out, you mean?" I gasped.

"No. Just announced it. And she drew herself up and shut her lips in a long line and marched to the door. Gil put his hand on her arm to intercept her, but she said, like a knife still: 'Move, please.' And she turned the knob to fling the door open; and it was locked. She said to Gil: 'Kindly unlock this door.' He had the key in his pocket. He said, rapping it out like orders: 'Wait. There have to be explanations. Don't go in.' But she didn't even look at him. She looked . . . oh, as if she was going to charge the door down with her forehead, as if her eyes were boring through it; and she repeated very loud and clear: 'Unlock this door.' Then there was a shriek from the other side: *Who is there?* And she cried out, in *such* a voice!—I can't describe it: 'Do not be afraid, Ianthe! I am coming to you.' There was absolute silence on the other side. And then Gil gave up and put the key in the lock and opened the door."

Maisie's voice had sunk to a thrumming monotone, the pitch and tone, almost, of a person speaking in a trance. Her eyes, too, looked asleep between half-lowered lids, but she went steadily on, without a tremor, through my heavy breathing.

"Everything happened so quickly. It can't have been more than a few minutes from beginning to end. I don't remember what it all looked like. I saw them all, I suppose—but I didn't see them. I've got the impression there was Mother reared up by the bed . . . or on the bed . . . high, high as the ceiling, with her hair like black snakes; and struck to stone. And Tanya and the doctor holding on to her, one on each side; and Sibyl advancing towards her. Then there was God! such a scream, one long scream, and she seemed to swoop through the air and out of the window. And Gil swooped after her. He gave a great spring . . . I'm sure . . . and a roar: 'Stay where you are!'—catching Sibyl by the shoulder and whirling her aside as he sprang past her. I looked out of the window and saw figures running fast along the river bank—and then the willow trees hid them. Sibyl and I were alone. I turned away from the window. We went back into the studio and she shut the door. She said: 'We will just wait quietly together.' We put our arms round each other. The silence seemed enormous."

In the kitchen, too, as Maisie's voice ceased, the silence grew huge wings of pity, grief and terror.

"Sibyl only said one other thing. . . . She said: 'I heard that scream long ago.' I don't know what she could have meant."

I remembered another door, the farmhouse door in Bohemia, set between Mrs. Jardine's listening ear and the unconscious eyes of Ianthe, postponing by years the scream that she would give. But I was dumb.

"She jumped," said Maisie, "where the little islands are, round the bend—into the thick of the water lilies. Of course it's not deep there in summer. It must have been more like jumping into a marsh; but the mud and the tangling stalks and the jungle of that ribbon weed mixed up with them might have pulled her down, I suppose, if she'd struggled to get out. And of course she would have. Nobody, mad or sane, would let themselves sink down and choke by inches in mud and muck. Nothing romantic about it—not like Ophelia."

"Did—did a lot of people come?"

"No. That was luck. It was the hottest hour of that burning afternoon. There was nobody about. All the prudent French inhabitants were taking siestas behind closed shutters. Looking out of the window was like looking into a painted landscape, a back-cloth of meadows, with a river winding through it, and trees in the wings. Then these figures scuttling silently across the empty stage: not real at all. At least, that's how I see it when I think about it. Or rather, I don't *think* about it—I see it. But I'm not even sure if I did look out, or if I saw anything at all. The only other things I remember for certain are . . . oh! such a smell of river mud coming into the place. . . . I could smell it through the very walls—I can smell it now. . . . And low voices. Someone came through the open door and spoke to Sibyl—Gil, I suppose—I didn't look. By that time I was past anything—I just kept my hands over my face. The mud smell suddenly got much stronger. He must have been covered in it. I heard her say in a voice of stone: 'Is she safe?' I suppose he nodded. Then she said, to tell the doctor that if anything was wanted from the house it would be fetched without delay. She said: 'I shall remain where I am. No doubt there are urgent family matters to be settled.' Then she told him, if Tanya was available, to send her in at once. And

Tanya came; and she gave her icy instructions: to go back immediately to the house, and to take me with her; and to say nothing to Harry. So we went away."

"And left Mrs. Jardine there?"

"Yes. Sitting bolt upright on a chair, beside the figure of the child."

"She didn't say anything to you?"

"Yes. She said: 'Have courage, Maisie.' "

After a moment, Maisie got up and riddled the ashes in the grate and put another shovelful of coal on. Then she wandered about the kitchen in an aimless way, shifting things on the table, and with a flick of her finger setting the mistletoe swinging on its string. It seemed that she had finished all she had to tell me.

"And that was how it all ended," I said, in a false tone of satisfied curiosity.

"That was how it all ended." The swing of the bough fanned the drift of pheasant's feathers, and one or two small downy ones floated up into the air. She caught one and let it go again and blew it upwards towards the ceiling. Between puffs at it she brought out jerkily: "Tanya and I left the next afternoon. We crossed over to England by the night boat. It was nine days before war broke out."

"And you didn't see Ianthe—your mother again?"

"No, no. Dear me, no. She was taken straight off to a—most excellent—most comfortable—Mental Home. The last word in up-to-date treatment and equipment. She's still there. Two years. Makes you think, doesn't it?"

She stopped blowing and watched the feather describe a wavering downward arc and sway to the floor. She sighed.

"I'm very sorry," she said, "that I've never been able to go and see her; because in between times she's quite herself and reads and draws and plays the piano and does basket work or something; and I expect she'd be rather pleased to see me and have a chat. It would be a change for her. I shall go after the war—if she's alive. Her health's deteriorating, so they tell me. She wasn't ever strong. I don't expect she'll live much longer."

"I suppose you saw Mrs. Jardine and—and everything was all right before you left?"

"Yes, I saw her. What happened that night, down at the mill, I don't know. Late, long after I'd gone to bed, I heard the pony trap come up the drive and stop; and then someone drove off again towards the stables. It must have been Pierre, I think, bringing her back; because it seems Gil went with the doctor, when Mother was taken off. I'd been a bit worried about the pony. Then presently my door opened; and it was Sibyl. She didn't come in. I pretended to be asleep, I *could not.* . . . She stood and listened for a few minutes, and then she went away. Next morning Tanya was summoned, for a *brief interview.*"

"I wonder what it was about."

"I wonder!" Maisie uttered a bark of laughter. "Tanya's never been quite the same since. She takes things very hard; she doesn't bob up again like I do after a biff on the crumpet. The long and short of it was, Tanya was dismissed for treachery."

"Treachery," I repeated.

"And for not being a lady."

"Why wasn't she a lady?" I said, puzzled.

"My good girl," said Maisie, raising pained eyebrows at me, "must I explain? Tanya had had the *extraordinary* vulgarity to fall in love, on the sly, under a real lady's sacred roof, with a piece of a lady's sacred property."

"Oh, I see," said I dubiously, struggling to resist this attack upon my conviction of Mrs. Jardine's perfect justness and magnanimity.

"Haven't you ever heard of moral taste?" said Maisie, severe. "If you don't see how unseemly it was, what an abuse of hospitality it was, and of confidence, and all that, you also must be lacking in the instincts of a lady. Indeed, I often fear you are."

"Do you think Tanya told her she'd asked Gil to marry her?"

"Of course she did. She spilt the whole bag of beans at the very start. She still hadn't got it into her feeble head, in spite of what Gil had told her, that they were *rivals.*"

"Rivals in love," I said weakly, clutching at a familiar phrase.

302

"Exactly. You've got it. So the subject of marriage didn't go down very well."

"Why not?" I persisted, feeling, not for the first time, in my extremity, that more would be gained than lost if by hammering nails into my coffin, I let in a chink of light. "Mrs. Jardine couldn't possibly have wanted to *marry* him, could she?"

"Why not?"

"Well, because—because, of course, she couldn't. She was married already."

"So she was! And Tanya wasn't."

"And then—what I said before. She'd be much too old."

"Well done, well done! You do stick to your points. And Tanya wasn't too old. She was young, young! She was free to marry him and young enough to marry him. *Now* do you see why it was unforgivable?"

I was near to tears; and after a painful silence Maisie said gently:

"I know how you feel about Sibyl. Tanya felt the same: that she was a person you could always tell the truth to, and she'd understand. That's why she sank down under it so. She could hardly crawl. It was appalling to see a person so horrified—at herself, at everything. You see, Sibyl managed to put it across her that by bringing marriage into it—suggesting to Gil that they should get married—she'd done something really outrageous. Like a housemaid, she said, howling to be made an honest woman of. It was perhaps natural, she said, that Gil should be attracted by her. But *marriage!*—Gil would be simply disgusted by her—if he wasn't simply laughing at her. She told her some things about men, as from a woman of the world, that upset her horribly; she's very innocent. And some things about Gil—his views on women, making it sound as if she knew everything about him, and they were in a kind of plot together, and Tanya outside, an utter fool and object of their mockery and contempt. You've got to take into account," added Maisie judicially again, "how unspeakable the shock had been for Sibyl. She must have been absolutely terror-stricken. The shock about Mother didn't go nearly so deep. Once she grasped it, she could see all round it at once and deal with it on the spot; and she was magnificent. It didn't have a lot of loose ends about, and it didn't humiliate her, like the other thing."

"Gil humiliated her too," I said. "It was just as much his fault, wasn't it? Why wasn't she angry with him? Or was she?"

"Oh, Gil would have to be allowed to do what he wanted. He's too precious to her, she'd never dare risk blaming him, however much he betrayed her and hurt her. She'd know if she made a fuss to him, he'd up and leave her. So Tanya had to be sent packing quickly instead. I was a good excuse: I had to be removed at once from painful associations, and Tanya must go with me to look after me."

I thought it all over, gloomy. It seemed so very awkward, so raw all round. Nobody had been in the slightest degree comfortable.

"She went on being nice to you?" I said finally, snatching at a straw.

"I went down after lunch to say good-bye to the Meuniers," said Maisie. "I wanted to see Gil really, for lots of reasons. But when I got down, I found Sibyl there, sitting in the summerhouse, all by herself. She told me Gil was still away, he'd gone to make some arrangements for her. I think it was true. But she had posted herself there to keep watch. I don't know quite what was in her mind: perhaps to see that Tanya or I didn't try to get in to the mill and leave a note. Perhaps . . . I sometimes think . . . to guard Cherry . . . I don't know . . . to cast out all the wickedness by just concentrating with all her might, willing quietness to come back again, and everything to be as it was before. You know how queer she seems when she's alone. She said: 'We will say our good-byes now, Maisie. I have come away to rest here quietly until the evening. This mysteriously beautiful spot takes away my agitation. Write and inform me of your safe arrival in Devonshire. You will be much in my thoughts. Good-bye, Maisie.' And I said: 'Good-bye, Sibyl'; and I went away and left her there, staring, staring over, like I told you, at the mill. I looked at it too, for the last time. More than ever, I thought, it looked like a house that—that couldn't be lived in. It had put on one of its expressions; but what it was, I was as far as ever from being able to make out. Only, it looked perfectly strange to me—unfamiliar; and I knew it had spat us all out—that Gil's time there was nearly over. . . . When I think of it now, you know, I feel that something was always wrong with the whole place. Why was it so suffocating down there? Something's sucked all the air out. And the *shape* of the landscape just on that bend—the trees, the weir, the islands, the way the mill-house sits and broods in the middle of it. . . . What's wrong? Ninety-nine times you look at it, and you think it's your dream of a riverside resort. The hundredth time it suddenly strikes you there's—a distortion on it; very, very slight: like a smile that you suddenly look at again and realise isn't a smile at all but a leer. It's a *mad* place, that's what it is," declared Maisie, with an air of having solved a mystery. "No wonder everything happened. It was made for it."

I shivered; and as I stared into the barred grate, a square of landscape slipped in a flash before my eyes, and was gone again. Luridly dark and brilliant, unreal, like a slide on a magic lantern, it glared at me. As it vanished, the slide tipped crooked, the landscape gave a shudder, the tiny white block in the middle grimaced at me.

"That was the last of it," said Maisie, with a yawn. "I went back to help Tanya pack her trunk. But Harry had been helping her. There was nothing to do."

My fevered imagination created another vision: Harry bending purple-necked over a trunk, folding and packing Tanya's clothes with shaky hands: a shockingly inappropriate occupation for him.

"At least," said Maisie, "he hadn't been able to help much. He'd just been hanging about. He drove us to the station and gave us each heaps of money for the journey and bought us some chocolate. He never said a word. I thought Tanya was going to faint dead away. She never spoke either. Her heart was broken. I do believe she suffered more, she was more *damaged,* in her spirit, than any one; which was unfair. There was Gil, and there were the skeletons tumbling out on her without any warning

305

from our family cupboard. Between the two she was made mince-meat of."

"Didn't Harry. . . . Do you think Harry had been trying to comfort her?"

"Yes, he had. But he couldn't. You see, nothing could be brought out into the open between them. They had to be dumb to one another. I didn't care for it myself—the thought of leaving him alone with Sibyl again. But it was a mere flea-bite compared with what Tanya felt. She thought she'd let him down so infernally. However, as I told her, Harry's used to disappointments; and he'd never, *never* blame her. . . . No, it was worst for Tanya by far. It wasn't only the torture about Gil: it was losing her *home*. She'd had to grow up from a baby without one, and then at last she'd found one. She loved them both dearly, and got used to feeling secure with them—feeling she'd got a family and a background; and now she was banished. She was an orphan again."

It was very sad, I knew. I sighed; but this time my springs of feeling, overtaxed, refused to flow. I contemplated Tanya's state without one drop of sympathy.

"She got into a very morbid frame of mind," said Maisie, rubbing her eyes. "I had an awful time with her. She got to feel that her loving Gil had somehow caused the whole crash, Mother and all, and she must spend the rest of her life in a condemned cell. She got this job teaching music at my school—that would be expiation enough, I should think, for any crime—and she spent all her holidays with us, wherever we were, and for a year I never saw her smile. She went about like an automaton, looking *grey*. Gil wrote to her, I know, but she wrote back that she could never see him again. I discovered her howling that night, so I wrote to him too. He didn't answer. But one evening next summer, when we were in Devonshire, somebody came to the door of the farm; and it was Gil. He was a Tommy. He was just going abroad. He spent seven days with us. And by the end of that time she had quite a healthy colour and was making jokes. So I knew he'd made a good start anyway, destroying her principles. And by the end of his next leave, they agreed to marry each other. So much

for principles. Ah well . . ." Maisie yawned again with violence.
"The human race must go on, I suppose, in all its wicked wanton-
ness, or where would it be? . . . Now I'm going to break the last
six eggs and make an omelette. And you can go and bear the tidings to those athletes. They'll be getting muscle-bound. Do you
notice it's three a.m.?"

Bemused, I followed her to the table and stood by her side,
watching her smartly crack egg-shells against the lip of a basin
and pour into it their contents.

"Did Mrs. Jardine write to you after you left?" I said.

"Oh yes. She wrote me a long friendly letter about this and
that—the war, you know, and the pony and the farm. Oh yes, she
writes to me regularly—taking an interest in my school activities,
you know, and telling me all about the hospital."

"Not a word about—anything?"

"Once. She wrote me one letter about Mother. A good one.
After that, not a syllable."

"I do wonder how Gil got on with her after you and Tanya
had gone."

"Oh, very well indeed. She was superb—he told me so—about
the whole business of Mother."

"Didn't they have a—a row at all about Tanya?"

"I expect so. But it wouldn't matter. They understood one another all right. Perhaps, but for the war, he'd be there still. Yet,"
said Maisie, holding the fork high and letting the beaten egg
mixture drip from it, "I *wonder.* . . . He'd say it was the war,
he must go, and she mustn't try to keep him—not that she would
try to anyway, she's a smashing patriot—but deep down in him it
would start gnawing at him that he must get away from *her:*
she'd done him out of something he'd wanted. And war or no
war, it would grow to be the one thing he had to have. Yes.
That's how it would be."

My head was whizzing round, hectically active but at the same
time hopelessly confused. I could not begin to follow this. There
was one more point of importance to elucidate before the opportunity irrevocably vanished. Maisie had resumed the character of
preoccupied cook; my chance was slipping. What could it be?

I fixed my eyes on the ceiling. The mistletoe began to whirl round like a Catherine wheel. What, what could it be? Suddenly in the dead centre of the giddy bough I pounced on and pinned it.

"By the way," I said, "what *did* she do when she left you?— before she went into the convent?"

"Oh . . ." said Maisie, examining a frying-pan with a frown. "Let me see. I got it out of Auntie Mack afterwards. But she would put it all so delicately and go off sideways with such wild wing-flaps, I never quite made head or tail of it. Auntie Mack's gone right down to the bottom of the class, of course, with Sibyl. Expelled, in fact. More treachery. It's an awful knock for the poor old goose. You can't play that game for ever: one more line, and you suddenly see you've had to make a noose; another, and you've hung yourself. Let me see. . . . Yes. Mother got queerer and queerer. Father couldn't always be rushing off up and down the town after her to prevent her—talking to strangers. He got so that he'd go tearing out of school in the middle of a class; and they began to think *he* was nuts. The doctors thought if she got right away from us all, and never saw Father again, she might calm down. She couldn't stand married life, you see, and being a mother. These friends I told you about offered to take her in and look after her. So she was removed abroad in charge of some sort of mental nurse; and for about a year she *was* much better. They travelled about in Europe, and she enjoyed that. She loved the sun and the beautiful places and the lack of responsibility. But then she suddenly got much worse. And they had to put her inside. In Germany it was, somewhere in the south."

"That was when the postcards stopped coming, I suppose."

"The postcards. . . . Good Lord, fancy your remembering! Yes, it must have been then that the postcards stopped coming." Maisie yawned again. "She stayed in about a year, and then she seemed to be cured and she came out. I don't know what she did after that, till the religion came on . . ."

At this moment, Jess and Malcolm came smiling, flushed into the kitchen. Maisie cooked the omelette, and we ate it with rapturous acclamations; and Malcolm and Maisie drank more beer, and chaffed each other a lot; and we were all very merry.

Then we all went to bed. Jess told me as we undressed in our double bedroom that she had had a very nice time. They had danced for a good while, and then played halma; and then Malcolm had taught her to play picquet. And then they had danced a little more. She'd been a bit bored now and then, but only a tiny bit: and he had turned out frightfully nice, with a frightfully good sense of humour. He had asked her to write to him; and she had promised to knit him a Balaclava helmet. She asked me if I hadn't been bored sitting the whole of the evening in the kitchen, and I said no, not at all.

We got into our chilly soft beds, side by side, among the rose cretonnes, old mahogany, old prints of Mrs. Jardine's spare room, and I buried my head in the pillow and resisted her watchful questioning presence. It was the first night I had ever stayed away from home without my parents, and I felt unsafe and homesick, as if I were drifting helpless outside with the black night, in the dead hush after a raging storm. One moment I was awake, listening to the silence. When next I became conscious it was ten o'clock in the morning, and Jess was saying in an anxious scolding voice that we must get up immediately, everybody would have finished breakfast long ago.

It was the day before Christmas, and the car was coming for us at eleven-thirty. We had to help our mother to dress the Christmas tree for the village school children in the afternoon. When we got downstairs with our suitcases packed, we found, to our surprise, that Malcolm, fresh and cheerful as ever, was the only person in the dining-room. He rang the bell and Mrs. Gillman's daughter Doris brought in plates of porridge for us. Her expression was reticent. We both felt particularly well and brisk, and ate a large breakfast.

The rain had stopped, and outside shone a luminous greenish humid day of the kind that comes so often in December: a day with blackbirds in it, and silvered lichen on mauve apple boughs, and snowdrops stirring in the mould.

Then it was nearly time to go, and I said would Maisie be down soon. He laughed and said: "Not if I know her," and suggested that I should go and rouse up the old girl.

It seemed impossible to leave without saying good-bye to her; so I went upstairs and knocked on her door. There was no answer. Noiselessly I turned the handle and looked in. She was lying on her back, flushed, deep asleep, her hair on end all over the pillow, both arms in blue striped flannel pyjama sleeves behind her head. I said very low: "Maisie, I'm going now. Good-bye"; but she did not stir. There was nothing for it but to shut the door and go downstairs again.

# I X

MALCOLM must have gone out to the front early in the New Year, for letters from France came to Jess in a regular flow all through the winter and into early spring. She kept them carefully in a drawer, and answered them. He said he was sending her a photograph of himself that he had had taken before he left England. He hoped she didn't mind. Would she please send him one of her? The photograph arrived. He had signed it: *"Yours ever, Malcolm."* She added it to the modest gallery of naval and military cousins and friends' brothers upon the schoolroom mantelpiece. In default of a studio portrait, she sent him a smiling snapshot of herself with the dogs; and she knitted him the Balaclava helmet. He told her it was the greatest treasure he possessed, and that every time he put it on, which was every single day, he thought of her. Things were fairly quiet, he said, where he was —not too bad except for the foul weather. He was very snug in his dug-out, and he was with the most marvellous lot of chaps you could ever hope to find. He was expecting leave soon, and wished awfully, as things had turned out, that he could get over the Channel; but Grannie was expecting him and he couldn't disappoint her. Next leave after this he'd spend at the Priory for dead certain, and we must have another party: lots more parties. His love broke, almost imperceptibly, out of a shy school-boy phrase, the hint of a hope, a wish, here and there; a tiny cross, that seemed like an apology, after his signature.

In the spring he was killed. We read his name in the Casualty Lists. Jess cried a little, strictly in private, and tied his letters all together with a white ribbon. His photograph remained upon the mantelpiece, not very like anybody in particular: mass-produced photograph of a dead English subaltern, blond innocent mask, faintly smiling and staring from beneath the peak of a uniform cap. Since he was, so far, the only one to be killed, it did not seem suitable to leave him without distinction in the gallery; and after a bit she took him away and put him with his letters; and the mantelpiece was eased of an embarrassing burden of awe and pathos.

We wrote to Maisie. Many weeks later she answered; a few lines only, inarticulate, of pity for poor old Malcolm. My mother wrote to Mrs. Jardine; the reply came promptly. There was nothing unusual about it; hundreds of people in Europe were writing and receiving such letters every day. Mrs. Jardine took her place without ostentation among the bereaved, mourning with the same pride and tenderness, the same poignant but not savage questioning, the same resignation as everybody else. She was deeply thankful, she said, to have had that glimpse of him; to have seen for herself the fine character Malcolm had carved out for himself out of the unpromising material handed down to him. He had justified all her belief in him. *"In fact,"* she wrote, *"I may say that he became, within his own range, a perfect character. He was so fond of your girls—particularly, perhaps, of dear Jess. He spoke to me of her with an admiration which could not have failed to touch you. Would that he could have had the profitable happiness of seeing her for longer. Alas! It is these boys cut off before their loves, falling transparent, blank, like abstract figures falling—it is they who break my heart."*

In the autumn of that same year came another letter from Mrs. Jardine, to tell us that Harry was dead. Walking by the river in the November fog, he had contracted a chill. In two days he was dead of penumonia. He had put up no fight at all, said Mrs. Jardine. For thirty-six hours on end she had sat by his bedside. Nothing, not a word, had passed his lips, save of punctilious thanks to the nurse for her attentions. Harry had not wished to resist death. *"He died,"* wrote Mrs. Jardine, *"with his hand in mine."* She was arranging for the eventual sale of the whole of the French property. It had painful associations for her now; and in any case she had been left far less well off than she had expected. Harry had in his will made various legacies and bequests which had come to her as a surprise. The Priory was hers for her lifetime. She hoped to return there as soon as the war was over, and to end her days there. Afterwards it would pass to Maisie, and to Maisie's children.

That night I had a dream of Harry. He sat in an armchair on the lawn of the Priory, lifting a cup of tea to his lips. His hand shook, the tea spurted everywhere. He set down the cup, then lifted it again, patient, concentrating; and the shaking got wilder. A voice, loud, harsh, rang suddenly in my ears: *"Why don't you help him?"* I took the cup and lifted it to his lips. He sipped from it noisily; then stopped and slowly turned his eyes on me. It was the self-same look, ponderable, incurious, that Tilly had fixed on me, on the wall, on the sewing table, on all the lightless clay world before the end: a cemented grief, sealing the excavations of an extinct human territory. He nudged me and, leaning close, said in a ventriloquist's voice: "How does she know? She doesn't know anything—stands to reason. *She can't get in.* She tries it on—but I've got her taped. Lock and bolt—that's the ticket." He nodded, conspiratorial. "Two can play at that game." Extreme malice distorted his dusky, half familiar face. Then someone cried: *"Look!"* and I looked in terror over my shoulder, and saw under the dark trees a figure folded in a blue cape, faceless, motionless, watching me.